Glimpsed

Glimpsed

G.F. MILLER

SIMON & SCHUSTER BFYR

New York   London   Toronto   Sydney   New Delhi

An imprint of Simon & Schuster Children's Publishing Division
1230 Avenue of the Americas, New York, New York 10020

Text © 2021 by G. F. Miller
Jacket illustration © 2021 by Julia Yellow
Book design by Jess LaGreca © 2021 by Simon & Schuster, Inc.

For information about special discounts for bulk purchases, please contact Simon & Schuster Special Sales at 1-866-506-1949 or business@simonandschuster.com.
The Simon & Schuster Speakers Bureau can bring authors to your live event. For more information or to book an event, contact the Simon & Schuster Speakers Bureau at 1-866-248-3049 or visit our website at www.simonspeakers.com.
The text for this book was set in Adobe Garamond Pro.
Manufactured in the United States of America
First Edition
2 4 6 8 10 9 7 5 3 1
Library of Congress Cataloging-in-Publication Data
Names: Miller, G. F., 1977- author. | Title: Glimpsed / by G. F. Miller. |
Description: First Simon & Schuster, BFYR hardcover edition. | New York : Simon & Schuster, BFYR, 2021. |
Summary: As eighteen-year-old high school Fairy Godmother Charity faces an existential crisis and blackmail from Noah, on whom she has a crush, she learns a great deal about her magic and herself.
Identifiers: LCCN 2020016238 (print) | LCCN 2020016239 (ebook) |
ISBN 9781534471351 (hardcover) | ISBN 9781534471375 (ebook)
Subjects: CYAC: Fairy godmothers—Fiction. | Magic—Fiction. | Wishes—Fiction. |
Mothers and daughters—Fiction. | High schools—Fiction. | Schools—Fiction.
Classification: LCC PZ7.1.M5682 Gli 2021 (print) | LCC PZ7.1.M5682 (ebook) |
DDC [Fic]—dc23
LC record available at https://lccn.loc.gov/2020016238

To the flibbertigibbets.

I salute you.

1

Happily Ever After? I Got This.

*P*rince Charming surveyed the sea of hopeful courtiers dispassionately, unaware that, at that very moment, his destiny was speeding toward the castle in the form of a pumpkin carriage. Inside the erstwhile pumpkin, Cinderella marveled at her sudden change of fortune . . . and footwear.

Meanwhile, the fairy godmother, disguised as a parlor maid, was two-handed stress eating French pastries as she watched the minute hand on the clock tower.

But that last part never gets included because *nobody cares.* It's not her story. So nobody gives a magical mouse turd about the fairy godmother's problems.

Except for me.

I know exactly what that chick was going through because, right now, Coach is preparing to start the Poms tryout *without Carmen.* The ball is on, and my Cinderella is nowhere in sight.

Carmen texted fifteen minutes ago that she had a flat tire. But having a legitimate reason for missing the tryout is not going to get Carmen on the squad. Coach is hard-core about starting on time. If we're even thirty seconds late for practice, we have to stay after and do wind sprints. But if you're late for the tryout, you're just out of luck.

What we need is a delay.

With a wink, I launch a mental *nudge* at Coach, magically knocking the location of her clipboard out of her mind. She begins to wander around the gym, looking flustered. My right hand immediately gets pins and needles but, hey, worth it.

Come on, Carmen, I silently plead as I watch Coach flounder. We are *not* flushing six months of work down the toilet because of a flat tire.

The clock ticks to 3:02.

Then 3:03.

The *nudge* wears off. "Aha!" Coach says triumphantly to no one in particular, picking the clipboard up from the bench, where it's been sitting in plain sight the whole time.

I desperately wink another *nudge* at her—a sense that the sound system settings need to be checked. She gives her forehead a little massage, feeling the strain of too many *nudges*. I feel it too. My whole right arm is asleep now, all the way to my shoulder. It's super annoying.

But it buys us a few more minutes. She goes to the control

panel and ponders the knobs and sliders, inputs and outputs.

"Uuuuuugh!" Scarlett Okumura groans from the spot next to me, her knee bouncing a hundred miles an hour. "What is the problem? Coach *never* starts late."

Scarlett's the team captain and obviously feeling the tension in the room. I *nudge* her a little calm, wishing I could do the same for myself.

"It's only 3:05," Gwen Strope replies from her other side. She doesn't look up from her phone screen to deliver this information, and her face is entirely obscured behind a halo of tight black curls.

To my undying relief, the gym doors open, and Carmen comes skidding through them in compression pants and a crop top, a black smudge clearly visible on her forearm. She doesn't stop to catch her breath but takes her place in the second row. She scans the bleachers, and when our eyes meet, she gives me a tiny nod. I nod back—*you got this.*

With a sigh of relief, I let myself relax a little, rubbing my arm to try to realign my chi or whatever.

A few seconds later Coach says, "Okay, sorry for the delay. Let's get started."

The dancers set, the sound system crackles, and I am in knots again. This is it. Carmen's whole Happily Ever After hinges on this two-minute routine. I sit in the bleachers with my Poms squad mates, composing my features into a perfect mask of indifference, while mentally juggling glass slippers at the stroke of midnight.

Next to me Scarlett whispers, "Who do you think is going to make it this year?"

Electro house pumps out of the gym's sound system, saving me from having to answer. The forty or so new Poms squad hopefuls do a quick series of moves: head snap, ball change, flex kick, punch. Carmen hesitates on the kick. I bite the inside of my cheek because the tension has to go somewhere. The triple fouetté turn is coming up. With every neuron in my brain, I will Carmen to stick it.

She does.

That wasn't some kind of *nudge*, by the way. Carmen is an awesome dancer. Her problems were lack of confidence leading to general social awkwardness. Whether it's fair or not, making the Poms squad is about more than dancing. You've got to project that *all eyes on me* vibe. I've spent the past six months teaching Carmen how to walk into every room like she owns it. I clandestinely taught her this tryout routine weeks ago. She's been practicing nights, weekends, every morning at five. . . . She deserves this.

From the other side of Scarlett, Gwen leans in and says over the music, "Second row, third girl from the left. Do I know her?"

I think, *You've gone to the same school for three years, but you've been looking right through her.* Outwardly I shrug. "I think her name is Carmen?"

"Carmen?" Scarlett visibly scans her vast mental catalog of the JLHS who's who. "Wait. Carmen Castillo?"

She looks at me for confirmation. I give her a *that sounds kinda familiar* face.

She grunts, "She's different."

"Yeah." I put a studied measure of surprise into the syllable. Carmen does a stag leap.

I want to cheer for her like one of those superfans who go to football games in full body paint. It's almost a miracle that I can stay reclining on the bleachers. But the fairy godmother thing is strictly black ops. It has to be. People feel cheated when they find out somebody else got an assist. Plus I'd never get a rest. People would be begging me to grant wishes 24/7, and that's really not how it works. That's why all my Cindies are sworn to secrecy.

Carmen lands the toe touch, then pops back up. The recruits all freeze in an asymmetrical second position with their arms crossed on top of their heads. The last beat of the tryout song echoes off the gym walls.

Ultimately, Coach will decide who gets on the squad, but Scarlett is obviously spellbound by Carmen's transformation, and she's already whispering Carmen's name to half the team. Only a hint of a smile betrays the proud-mama thrill that's like fireworks in every nerve of my body. This is the first moment of Carmen's Happily Ever After.

But of course—I *glimpsed* it.

You want to know why a few lucky people get a fairy godmother while everyone else is stuck slogging it out on their own? It's the *glimpse.* Sometimes, out of nowhere, I get a *glimpse* of someone's deepest wish, and I know my job is to help them get there. The picture is always quite clear, and, not to brag, but I can make it come true 100 percent of the time.

Six months ago Carmen brushed past me in the parking lot, watching her feet as she walked, huddled into herself like she was trying to be invisible. And I got a *glimpse*:

She was here in this gym, standing in the exact pose she is now. She was sweating and panting and smiling, and the whole Poms squad was cheering for her. Then Coach put a little star next to Carmen's name on her clipboard.

So I pulled her aside and offered her my assistance. She accepted, obviously. And here we are. Making it real.

Scarlett whips out her phone. She snaps a photo just before the dancers drop their final pose. "I'm posting this," she says to no one in particular, and then mutters her caption. "All the hopefuls for JLHS Poms . . . Carmen Castillo killed it!"

Scarlett loves breaking news. She loves it so hard. Especially if she's the one who's breaking it. I think she has FOMO on behalf of the entire Jack London High School student body.

Meanwhile, Gwen puts her phone in her lap and starts slow clapping. The rest of us join in, and the applause gains momentum. Coach touches her pen to her clipboard before she waves her hand for us to cut it out so she can make her end-of-tryouts speech.

"Thank you, ladies. You've all worked really hard this weekend, and you should be proud of that. Unfortunately, we only have spots for four of you. The roster will be posted on the gym door tomorrow morning."

As soon as Coach stops talking, the bleachers erupt with chatter like a science project volcano. It's all predictable trivialities—love your earrings . . . did you see the *Fresh Prince* reboot . . . so much homework . . . who gives a test on a Monday . . . blah, blah, blah. A few people have a long enough attention span to talk about the tryout, but mostly everybody's already over it.

I spend 3.8 minutes dutifully chatting everybody up before making my way out of the gym. Carmen is waiting for me outside the double doors, amid a few other lingering hopefuls. I want to go in for a full-on hug-and-squeal, but for the sake of propriety, I make it a purposefully awkward "Um, good job in there. I'm sure Coach is going to pick you. Carmen, right?"

She bounces on her toes, sweat still gleaming on her exposed skin, a victorious "whoop" poised on her lips. I need to create a space cushion before she blows our practically strangers cover story.

But impressively, she manages to limit herself to a loaded "Thanks, Charity. For *everything*." She makes a *you know what I mean* face. So not subtle. Then she leans in conspiratorially, which is even worse, and whispers, "How did you stall Coach after I texted you about the flat tire?"

I draw my eyebrows together in feigned confusion. "What are you talking about? You texted me?" I glance at my phone like it's been misbehaving and, when I look back up, give the tiniest shake of my head. *We don't know each other.*

Carmen backs up, searching my face. I assume she's looking for a sign—did we really have a phone fail, or is this more subterfuge? I give away nothing. She'll have to draw her own conclusions about what happened here today.

None of my Cindies know about the *glimpses* or the *nudges.* All they need to know is that they got their wish. No use complicating things by oversharing about the magic.

Let's be real: the wow-factor of my magic is basically zero. My powers seem pretty underwhelming most of the time. But I do appreciate their subtlety. *Nudges* are much easier to hide than, say, turning rats into horses or flying around in a red cape. Ever lost your sunglasses and then it turned out they were on your head? Sent your phone into lockdown because you messed up your password so many times? Tripped over your own feet? Wandered around a parking lot looking for your car? I'm not saying you were fairy godmothered. But I'm not saying you weren't.

Carmen looks like she wants to ask more questions, but I *nudge* the words out of her head. Then, with buzzing fingers, I pretend to check my phone as a few of the other hopefuls pass by in a clump, nervously jabbering to each other about how they think they did. They exchange a few "good jobs" and "see you Mondays" with Carmen as they pass.

And now we're at the part of Carmen's story where I fade into the background. It's bittersweet. In some other reality we could have been good friends—we'll both be on the Poms squad, and she's got a huge heart.

But I'm not her friend. I'm her fairy godmother. My Cindy's transformation is complete, and she no longer needs me. We both have to move on now. With one last farewell finger wiggle and a "See you around," I stride away, careful to project carefree confidence.

I pour my post-wish endorphin rush into making pasta primavera and bruschetta for dinner. My mom comes home from San Diego tonight. I expect her around seven. By 6:58, the table is set, dinner is ready, and there's nothing left to do but wait.

And wait.

We live in the Inland Empire of Southern California—that's all the towns without a coast and no more than the average silicon. It's a two-hour drive from San Diego. Every few minutes, I do a mental calculation: *If she left at seven, she'll be here any minute.* . . .

The pasta gets cold and waxy-looking.

If she left at seven thirty, she'll be here any minute. . . .

The bruschetta begins to shrivel around the edges.

When I get tired of watching the food decompose, I wander to my bathroom and dye my hair mulberry. It's bright enough to celebrate today's triumphs, but with a deep-purple undertone that feels right.

Two years ago, out of boredom, I dyed my blah brown hair for the first time. Peacock blue. It inspired a ninety-second conversation in which my mom was looking up from her computer the entire time. I believe her exact words were "Exploring your inner mermaid, Charity?"

I accepted that for the huge compliment it was. Mom is the executive director of the Marine Conservation Coalition, so she spends every waking moment thinking about ocean life.

When I sent a peacock-blue-haired selfie to my sister, Hope, I got the fastest text back in recent memory: Nice. Bernice loves it.

Bernice is an elephant. Hope is in vet school and has spent the past three summers in Thailand giving trauma care to elephants with PTSD. I'm not kidding. That's a thing.

But who am I to judge? I'm a fairy godmother with a whole closet full of hair dye. And *that's* a thing too.

Fairy godmothering has been passed through the women in my family for generations, but it skips around like freckles or red hair. My grandmother has the magic. I have it. My mom and sister don't. But being a fairy godmother isn't just about magic. It's about a deep need to fix things. It's a calling.

Here's the deal: If somebody's worthy—and if there's something they long for with their whole heart—then the Universe puts me on the case. I get a *glimpse* of the Happily Ever After moment downloaded directly to my brain. And then my job is to make sure all the stars align in their favor, to grant the wish they maybe didn't even know they had.

At least, that's what I pieced together from the family history passed down from my grandmother, a bunch of crusty fairy tales, and my own experience. I grew up on the stories of my ancestresses back in Europe granting wishes, solving problems, kicking butt, and taking names.

I had my first *glimpse* when I was twelve, the day after I got my period for the first time. That was a beast of a week, let me tell you. I mean, Memom had kind of explained about the *glimpses*, and Hope clued me in about the girl stuff. But nothing really prepares you, you know? Mom was on a whale-watching trip with some major donors. By the time she got back, Memom had already helped me deal, and it seemed kinda late to bring it up.

Okay, full disclosure: I *tried* to bring it up, but she kept changing the subject back to the whales and how majestic they are. So I decided, screw it, she doesn't get to know. Ever since, we've been doing this dance where we both skirt around anything bordering on wishes, *glimpses*, *nudges*, or fairy godmothers. Maybe if she *ever* talked to Memom, she'd get the deets from her. As it is, we're stuck in this weird "don't ask, don't tell" loop. Anyway, it's been six years—it doesn't even bother me anymore.

Which brings us back to the fact that I'm hanging out waiting for her to return from her latest ocean rescue mission. After drying my hair, I plant myself on the couch in the great room with a book. From here I have a good view of the door leading in from the garage to the kitchen at the other end of the great room.

Her electric Tesla Model S makes not a sound when she arrives close to ten. I leap from the couch when I hear the garage door open. The moment Mom walks through, dragging a carry-on-sized rolling bag behind her, we have a clear full-body view of each other. Rather, I have that view of her. She would see me, though, if she looked up from her phone.

She's wearing a fitted black suit with a flouncy seafoam blouse to add a touch of femininity. Instead of heels, she's wearing Skechers. A few hours ago she was perfectly made up, but now her choppy dark blond hair is limp, and the skin under her eyes is gray with melting mascara and eyeliner. She is texting furiously with one thumb.

"Hi, Mom. Welcome home."

She doesn't respond immediately, just taps her thumb on her phone a few more times before looking up. Then she smiles, and I think she's really glad to see me. "Hi, sweetheart."

Mom leaves her rolling bag in the kitchen, and we meet in the middle for a hug. After a few seconds she pulls back and fluffs my long mulberry waves with both hands. "This is new."

I shrug like it totally doesn't matter that she noticed. "Time for a change."

She smiles brilliantly and shakes her head the tiniest bit, like, *Silly girl.* She takes a step back.

I say, "How was San Diego?"

Dramatic exhale. "I wouldn't know. I spent the whole week in a conference room, slogging through board reports and budgets." She goes to the cupboard and pulls out the Motrin. "The board liked the new fundraising initiatives and approved my ideas for generating more international, interagency cooperation. It's everybody's ocean, you know?" As she talks, she pops two Motrin and retrieves her luggage. She takes a few mincing backward steps toward the hall, as if maybe I won't notice that she's trying to get away from me.

I feel a childish desperation to keep her talking, to keep her *here*. I wish I could *nudge* her to ask about me, but unfortunately, *nudging* doesn't work on her. Trust me, I've tried. So I resort to words. "Will you be working with that Dutch foundation?"

ICYMI, a guy in the Netherlands invented a way to collect floating trash out of the ocean a few years back, when he was like seventeen. He's kind of a BFD in the world of ocean advocacy. Usually bringing him up buys me at least thirty or forty seconds of Mom face time.

But not tonight. She shoots me an apologetic look. "Hon, I'm sorry. I have a raging headache, and I have a videoconference at six a.m. Can we catch up more later?"

The classic "raging headache." *Nice out, Mom.* I used to worry that she had a brain tumor. Now I just worry that she's trying to avoid me. I swallow a feeling like gulping down sand and smile. "Sure, Mom."

She calls, "Thanks for understanding. Love you. Lock up," as she retreats down the hall.

Okay, so, yeah, my home life isn't perfect. But honestly, I don't have time to wallow.

I'm needed. Elsewhere.

My new Cindy appears in record time. Less than seventy-two hours after Carmen's triumph, I'm walking down the math-and-science hall after Poms practice when I happen to see a girl bent over a textbook, all alone in Chem Lab A. Her hair is in a haphazard ponytail, and she picks at her face absentmindedly while she reads.

And I get hit with a *glimpse*. I stop and put my hand on the lockers to steady myself as the here and now spins away.

The girl is rocking a deep-red sari, standing in line with three other girls in formal dresses on the track that rims the JLHS football field. Vice Principal Martinez says, "Vindhya Chandramouli," into a microphone before placing a silver-and-rhinestone tiara on her silky black hair. The crowd in the bleachers goes wild—cheering, pounding feet, banging cymbals. . . . Vindhya perches carefully in the back of the VW Bug convertible and waves regally as the car makes a lazy path along the track.

The *glimpse* dissolves as quickly as it came. I blink the present back into focus: this hallway, these lockers, Chem Lab A, Tuesday. The girl—Vindhya.

A familiar feeling of purpose and power sends my shoulders back and my chin up, as my personal problems fade into the background. There's a Cindy in need. That's what matters now.

I tap lightly on the open door as I step into the room. She

glances up, sees me, and pinches her eyebrows together like my presence is suspicious. I offer a smile. "Whatcha reading?"

She tilts the book up so I can see the title: *Talking to Humans: Coding for Dynamic User Interface.*

"Looks riveting." No hint of irony creeps into my voice.

She glances around—looking for an exit? Reinforcements? Then she retreats back into her coding book.

Still smiling, I pull up a stool at the lab table, facing her. "I don't think we've really met. I'm Charity." I raise my eyebrows, inviting a response.

She clears her throat. "Vindhya."

The next part is always a bit touch-and-go. How does one broach the subject of secret dreams and deepest wishes—of life as you know it doing a sudden 180—without inducing panic or sounding like a wacko? The rip-off-the-Band-Aid method is my fallback. I'm a cut-to-the-chase kind of girl. "Would you like to be homecoming queen this year?"

She fumbles the book. "What?"

I say it again, word for word. Standard procedure for a first client meeting—lots of repetition. Lots of disbelief.

Vindhya laughs—one strained, unamused *Ha.* "Yeah. Right."

I resist the urge to respond but don't break eye contact. Sometimes an uncomfortably long pause is the thing that really draws people out.

After said pause she says, "Like I would even want to participate in the homecoming court thing. It's objectifying and . . . and shallow."

She hesitated. Even if I hadn't *glimpsed* her true desire, I would know she's fronting. She's in denial now. Unruffled, I nod. "Yeah, it is shallow. But still . . ." I sigh. "Wouldn't it be amazing to see the smart girl wearing the crown for once? Instead of the girls who play to every patriarchal, beauty-over-brains, pretty-princess stereotype?" Okay, that might have been a stretch. Last year's HQ ran track and got into Pepperdine. But sometimes you've gotta sell it.

Vindhya's back straightens and her eyes flash. "How would that ever happen in a million lifetimes?"

"It's in you, Vindhya. I see it. And I'll help you, if you'll let me. Under one condition—no one can ever know I was involved."

Vindhya's eyes go wider and wider as I speak. When I pause for her response, she blinks twice rapidly and glances around the room again—maybe looking for a hidden camera. "Is this a joke?"

"No joke. No strings. Just a legit, onetime offer." I hold out my hand to her. "What do you say, Vindhya? Do you want to be queen?"

She's vibrating a little now. I hope she doesn't pass out. That has happened a couple of times, and it's just so awkward. Thankfully she stays lucid and I . . . I wait with my hand in the space between us.

In case you're wondering, I won't *nudge* her to agree to anything. It would be wrong to *nudge* clients into something that is going to change the course of their entire life. Besides, the effects of *nudging* are short-lived—usually only a couple minutes—so not very useful in swaying major life decisions.

She stares at me for another long moment. Finally releasing her death grip on the textbook, she reaches out in slow motion to seal the deal. As our hands meet, she mutters, "But . . . why are you doing this?"

I give her hand a reassuring squeeze. "Because I'm your fairy godmother."

2

The Art of the Meet-Cute

*I*t's time to see Memom.

There's no time to shower after Poms practice on Wednesday. Not if I'm going to drive forty-five minutes to the retirement home, have dinner with Memom, and do my trig homework before I pass out tonight. So I go for the Euro-shower on the run. I head out of the gym, scrubbing my armpit with a wet wipe. But right as I'm about to push open the door, it swings away from me. My momentum sends me stumbling forward, arms flailing.

My hand holding the stinky-armpit wet wipe connects with someone's face.

He throws his arms out in self-defense and grazes my boob.

"Sorry! Sorry!" he sputters.

"Oh my gosh! I'm so sorry!" I say at the same time.

I right myself and hide the wet wipe behind my back. Like maybe he won't notice he just tasted it.

"Wow. Okay," the guy says, avoiding eye contact. He takes off rectangular glasses, cleans the smears off on the hem of his T-shirt (which says A RESCUE ATTEMPT WOULD BE ILLOGICAL, by the way), and puts them back on. He rubs at the pink spot by his nose where I accidentally clobbered him. Then he pushes his hand through his mass of brown curls, as if to smooth them down. But it has the opposite effect. They spring back even more chaotic, which is kind of . . . cute. In fact, his whole look screams "adorkable." I'm a fan.

Finally he looks at me and pulls a face that's a cocktail of confusion, recognition, and suspicion.

Confusion I get. I'm feeling it too. And recognition makes sense. Even though JLHS is too big to know everyone, he's probably seen me perform with the Poms at basketball and football games. But suspicion seems a little uncalled for. Does he think I smashed a dirty wipe in his face on purpose? I smile apologetically, hoping to demonstrate that I'm a non-jerk. "Sorry about that," I say one more time. I duck my head to make my wink less obvious as I *nudge* a little positivity his way—just a faint *Charity's cool* to make this less awkward. My fingertips barely tingle.

He blinks at me, looking even more confused. As if the positive thought about me is creating a *does not compute* error in his brain.

So that backfired.

I give up and point toward the hallway. "Excuse me."

He steps to the side with a sweeping arm gesture that is so gallant it's dorky. I maneuver past him and continue my advance down the hall. Two seconds later I register his voice behind me say, "Uh, Carmen? Can I ask you something?"

Aw. Our newly minted princess has an admirer. Sweet boy was probably waiting outside Poms practice so he can ask her to homecoming. I hope she says yes. That would be adorable.

I'm alternately grinning about Carmen and cringing about the collision when I get outside. I drop my wipe in the trash can, dig a deodorant out of my gym bag, and swipe it under my arms. Then I climb into my Honda Fit and drive.

Memom is shrinking. Every time I see her, she's just a bit smaller. It makes me feel guilty for not making time to come more often. But with the fairy godmother gig on top of school and Poms—it's exhausting. Somehow two months have slipped past without a visit.

But when I get a new client, I have to see Memom right away. I mean, she's the only other fairy godmother I know, as well as my actual grandmother. She's my mentor.

Today she's leaning into some classic old-lady stereotypes. She's wearing a polyester floral-print shirt-and-pants set, and she has on ridiculously large octagonal sunglasses. We're sipping tea on the balcony of her assisted-living one-bedroom apartment.

She waves her hands impatiently. "So? What happened after the tryout?"

"She's living the dream, of course. She's doing what she loves, dancing till she drops. Goofy guys are throwing themselves at her."

"Ah." Memom sighs contentedly. Then she brightens again. "And? Someone else *flashed* you already?"

"That means something else, Memom."

She blows her lips out, like, *Don't bother me with trifles.*

So I say, "I've got nine days with this one. She's going to be homecoming queen."

"Nine days?!" Memom spills tea on her polyester blouse. "You can't be serious!"

"I know, right? Six weeks is my old record."

Memom looks exasperated. "Even six weeks is too fast. We've talked about this. We're working with real people, not paper dolls. People need *time* to change. You can't rush transformations."

I throw my hands up, maybe a little too dramatically. "What am I supposed to do? I *glimpsed* it."

"Maybe it's supposed to be for homecoming next year."

"No way. That's forever from now." It comes out a little whiny.

"You young people are always in too much of a hurry."

"Whatever. Don't act like you know any other young people."

She giggles. Then she sobers up and looks at me pointedly. "In 1979, one guy *flashed* me, and I spent eighteen months working him over."

I yell-laugh-choke, "OMG, Memom! Don't say 'flash.'"

She waves me off again. "The point is, it's best to take your time. Baby steps—that's all people can really handle. One small change. Let it sink in. Then another change."

I shrug, unmoved. "I hear you, Memom. But this one's a quickie."

She smacks my hand. "Don't say quickie." Then, with a grin and a twinkle in her eye, she winks at me pointedly.

I feel a little *ping* in my subconscious and roll my eyes. Whatever gene mutation enables us to send *nudges* also makes us impervious to them. "Memom, seriously? You know it's not going to work."

She shrugs, unabashed. "One of these days I might get you."

"Aren't you the one who told me to never, ever use the *nudges* except to help a Cindy?"

She scrunches her wrinkled face with a petulant humph.

"You need a hobby."

"I need a *Cindy*." She pouts a little, not unlike a three-year-old.

Is this what I'm going to be like in fifty years? Just me and my quirks, swathed in polyester, living for the next *glimpse*? I love her, but the idea is pretty demoralizing. I drop my head into my hand with a sigh.

She rises creakily from the table. "I have Little Darlings. I'll get some."

I don't have the heart to tell her how nasty Little Darlings are. Mix together one part sawdust, two parts lard, and a boatload of sugar, wrap the whole thing in cellophane and let it cure for ten years, and you've got Little Darlings. Memom thinks I love them because I used to scarf them when I was like four.

I take the first one my fingers make contact with and begin to pick the plasticky faux-chocolate coating off. Memom says, "You're being careful, right?"

"Of course. I'm always careful."

She scoffs, "You're a teenager. You don't even know what 'careful' means."

"Well, you're an old lady. If you ever knew, you've forgotten." I nibble a corner of the peeled Little Darling.

She snorts. "Secrets are hard to keep. Even back in my day. Now with the TikTok and the Instant-Grams—"

"Instagram."

"You can't give anything away. That's all I'm saying. You can't put yourself out there like other girls."

Like I don't know that. As if my whole life isn't about making sure people don't get too close. I say, "Memom, I'm so black ops it's ridonculous."

"For Pete's sakes. Use real words." This from the woman who just said "Instant-Grams." I roll my eyes.

And now I can't put it off any longer. I take a big, squishy bite of the Little Darling while Memom beams at me.

While I gag the Little Darling down, Memom and I talk about Hope. Only a couple more months until we're all together for Thanksgiving and she's home from Thailand for good. Memom points out that Hope will be off doing her final semester of vet school after that, but I choose to focus on the fact that she'll be 7,900 miles closer than she is now.

Finally, I tell Memom I have to leave. Trig is calling my name. As she shuffle-walks me to the door, she suddenly tugs my elbow. "How's my Katie?"

That would be my mom. Memom's daughter. She prefers Kate, actually. No one but Memom calls her Katie. I try to sound bright and happy, but it comes out a tiny bit forced. "She's great. Super busy. You know."

Memom grunts. "Always saving the world, that one. Tell her that I'd like to see her before I'm dead."

I kiss her cheek. "You can't die. Not ever. But I'll tell her."

Later that night, when my brain needs a break from equations, I text Sean Slater: In the market for a badass campaign manager for homecoming court. Will you do it?

While I wait for him to respond, I check to see if my dad is online. He's not. But it's after midnight in DC, so he's probably sleeping. You might be wondering what the deal is with my dad. Here it is in a nutshell: He's an environmental lawyer. He worked a bajillion hours a week when I was a kid, so I have almost no memories of actually doing actual things with him. Two weeks after Hope left for college, he and Mom realized they wanted to save the world more than they wanted to be married. He lives in DC now, lobbying Congress for better environmental laws on behalf of the Sustainable Policy Institute. I see him on holidays. Sometimes.

h emotional distance as possible. But with Sean, for

n—maybe because I gave him a whole year of my

t quite cut all ties. Don't get me wrong . . . we're not

s. Let's call him a colleague.

ow he does what he loves without dealing with haters

le I silently cheer him on. And, incidentally, he's far

most popular guy in school now. Which makes him

mpaign manager for Vindhya's run for queen.

⸻

next day, I have to *nudge* two chess clubbers and a

to give up the seats next to Sean. He's exhaustingly

hout a word, I slide a paper bag onto his tray. It's

Empire Bakery—we went there together at least a

es sophomore year. He snags the bag like a famine

ns his face into the top, and takes a dramatic deep

savior. I almost had to eat this compost they serve to

He pushes his tray away, lifts a cream cheese croissant

, and takes a decadent bite. "Mmmmm. Mm-hmm,

m really scared right now, Charity." He glances at my

ression as he takes another bite. "Because I already

vhat can this bribery be for? She's a troll, isn't she?"

s not. I'm allowed to pay homage to the Great Sean

particular reason whatsoever."

ts delicately.

Since Dad's not online, I check in on my sister. It's a thirteen-hour time difference to Thailand, so she should be starting her day about now. I message her: How's Bernice?

She doesn't respond. Maybe she's traipsing around the jungle already.

Finally, my phone *shwoops* Sean's incoming text: Seriously? Are you running for HQ?

I text: Nope. Cindy. Say yes.

Sean: I'm busy. SMU audition coming up.

Me: Come on, it's in nine days.

Sean: That's not enough time! Prom maybe. Homecoming no.

Me: Impossible for lesser men. I need the Sean magic.

Sean: What part of *SMU audition* are you not getting?

I want to shoot back: *What part of *nine days to transform a Cindy* are* you *not getting?* Instead, I press my finger between my eyebrows and take a Zen breath, trying to decide the best way to persuade him. I can't *nudge* him. Remember, decisions based on a minute's worth of thoughts or feelings don't stick. Besides, I have to have a direct line of sight to *nudge.* But no worries. There's always good old-fashioned guilt-tripping.

I text: You owe me.

Twelve interminable seconds later, Sean writes: Fine.

I lean back with a sigh of relief. Playing that card was a crappy thing to do, and I feel genuinely bad about it. But I can handle a little cognitive dissonance if it helps Vindhya. Sean knows better than anyone how far I'll go for a Cindy.

Once upon a time, Sean Slater was miserable, lonely, angry, and adrift. For good reasons. In eighth grade it leaked that he was in a ballet class. Riverside East Middle School turned into *Lord of the Flies*. Those of us who weren't part of the tormenting could only keep our heads down and try to stay out of the way. I did try to *nudge* the bullies, but I couldn't be everywhere. And besides, the more emotional I am, the worse my aim is. *Nudging* requires a calm, cool psyche. At thirteen, with exactly one Cindy on my résumé, my parents' divorce in full bloom, my sister away at college for the first time, and facing a gang of rabid pubescent trolls . . . let's just say I wasn't the picture of fairy godmother levelheadedness that I am today.

Anyway, where was I? Right—the cannibal island that was eighth grade. Sean ended up quitting ballet. Then he quit school. He finished junior high online.

When high school started, Sean was back. But he was a silent, skittish version of his former self. Then one day that spring, I got a *glimpse*. I saw him wearing tights and dancing onstage in front of the whole school—leaping and twirling with grace and power and passion. Loving it. Owning it.

So I offered him my services. And he accepted. After what felt like a hundred hours of heart-to-hearts, Sean decided to go back to ballet. I didn't pressure him or *nudge* him or anything, just listened

to him talk about everyt
he had talked himself ou
people define him. His r
that she drove him an ho
which was still sad. But h
He started to be himself a

It was magical.

Meanwhile, I went on
the tide of public opinion i
things into conversations
played Spider-Man was t
blowing up social media
jetés and pas de deux. I co
Bolle and kissed it twenty-
ballet and bragged for weeks
And, of course, I sent all kin
who would hold still long e
sophomore year with my arr

By the time I was fini
classmates forgotten they ha
but classical ballet had becon

Midway through that
announced he was signing u
did. And he crushed it, exac
instant sensation. After that l

created as muc
whatever reaso
life—I couldn'
actually friend

Anyway, n
every day, whi
and away the
the perfect ca

At lunch the
soccer player
popular. Wit
from Inland
hundred tim
survivor, cra
breath.

"Ah. My
the masses."
from the bag
mm-hmm. I
innocent exp
said yes. So
"No she
Slater for no

He snor

I take a pull of orange juice. "So. Homecoming."

Some sophomore girls stop by at that moment and pull Sean into an intense discussion about the latest post from some YouTuber they're all following. One of them has lime-green highlights that don't work at all with her strawberry blond hair. It's an ill-advised imitation of my Grinchy look from mid-December. It used to make me all kinds of nuts the way people always copied me, until Memom sagely said, "Charity, imitation is the fondest form of flattery."

She was probably quoting a Hallmark card or something. I don't know.

Regardless, I *nudge* the idea into lime-green girl's head that maybe it's time for a change. Why not? I've got the time.

Sean says, "So. Homecoming."

Aaaand we're back. The girls have moved on.

"Okay, it's Vindhya Chandramouli. Know her?"

He scrunches his face like he's concentrating. "Girls Who Code? Or . . . maybe . . . Robotics Club."

"That's her."

"So?" Sean is impressively blasé.

"So, I think she'll have a solid voter base within the Accelerated Learning Program and the STEMers. So all you have to do is get her nominated and swing the other influencers her way."

Sean ponders that for a moment. Then he says, "I'm thinking she and I need a meet-cute ASAP. I'll take it from there."

"I'm on it." I jump up, suddenly alight with creative energy. Planning meet-cutes is one of my specialties. "You're the best."

He waves me away with a dispassionate "You owe me now."

"Nope. Now we're even." I slide my phone into my back pocket and gather my trash. As I walk away, I toss over my shoulder, "*If you pull it off.*"

The student body president takes my seat before I'm even out of earshot, and Sean is on to the next thing.

Before I head out, I whip off a quick text to Vindhya informing her of tomorrow's meet-cute. She texts back immediately: No! I'm not ready!

Me: Why not?

Vindhya: It's SEAN SLATER!!? I don't know what to say. I don't know what to wear.

Two seconds later she sends another text: I thought there'd be a makeover or something first.

Part of me cringes. But if a makeover will give her the confidence to embrace her destiny, well, she wouldn't be the first Cindy that needed one. (True story: Memom gave Celine Dion a total makeover in 1982. At least that's what she claims.) So I text back: No problem. Meet me at Angelic Hair and Nails at 5.

She replies: I have robotics until 6.

Me: They close at 6.

Vindhya: . . . . Okay. Never mind. I'll be there.

I slide the phone into my pocket with a satisfied smile and

amble toward the courtyard doors, thinking, *I really do love my job.*

Halfway there, my butt vibrates. I pull my phone out of my back pocket and glance at it. There's a new text notification. It's from a blocked number.

The message reads: I know who you are.

3

It's Nothing the
Fairy Godmother Can't Handle

I almost drop the phone. That has got to be the creepiest text ever. Right?

I swipe the message off the screen, glancing around for stalker types. The courtyard—an enclosed brick box with no ceiling and about forty circular tables with attached benches—is a beehive of activity. Almost everyone is on their phone, at least tacitly. My eye is drawn to a knot of cheerleaders huddled around one phone, whispering what I can only imagine to be jealous rumors about yours truly. Then I notice Carmen's homecoming suitor sitting with a couple of AV Club guys. He's wearing a T-shirt that says LIVE LONG AND PROSPER, and he repeatedly opens and closes what could be—I'm not kidding you—a *flip phone*. Not too far from him there's a highly suspicious Goth girl with black lipstick who looks away too quickly. Then my gaze lands on a fishy group of probable hackers who look like they haven't showered in weeks. They're snickering secretively.

It might be any of them. Or none of these people. I consider *nudging* them one at a time with a strong urge to fess up. I do some quick mental math and decide I would look like I was having a stroke if I tried to do that many *nudges*. So that's not going to work. I decide I have no choice but to keep walking and blow this off.

Five steps, and the phone vibrates again. I look down almost against my will.

It says: Bibbidi bobbidi boo.

My first instinct is to make a run for it. My skin is crawling, and my leg muscles itch to engage evasive maneuvers. But that's pointless. I can't run away from my own phone. The creeper could be here, or a thousand miles away, or waiting on the other side of the door. I shiver.

But, you know, if I did panic-run out of the courtyard, I'd probably become a meme in ninety seconds flat. Plus I'd be faced with the JLHS version of the Spanish Inquisition. Who can afford that kind of bad PR?

So I do what I have to. I pocket the phone and walk—nay, strut—from the courtyard, as if all's right with the world. I travel through the double doors, down the hall, past my next class, out another set of doors, and across the parking lot . . . all with perfectly measured strides and swaying hips to project carefree confidence.

When I get to my car, I lock the doors and cave in on myself, panting. My armpits are sticky with nervous sweat. I close my eyes and give in to the freak-out for a minute. Then I dig my phone out of my pocket. The message is still there on the home screen: Bibbidi bobbidi boo.

I swipe it away, wishing I could make the whole situation disappear that easily, and dial Memom.

"EH?" Memom yells into the phone. There is loud music playing on her end.

I yell, "Memom, it's Charity."

"Charity? You sound strange, honey. What's wrong?"

"I've been made."

"You made *it*?"

"No! Jeez, Memom. I mean my cover's blown. Somebody knows about me."

There's a pause. I wonder if she didn't hear me and I'm going to have to say all that again. Suddenly the music clicks off, and she says quite seriously, "Oh. Mercy."

There's a long pause. I hear her talking to someone else in the room. After about four seconds, I huff, "Uh. Hello? Could use some sage advice right about now."

"Charity, sweetie." Memom has never sounded this serious. Ever. Her voice is low and secretive. "In 1998, a nosy little gossip found out about my *side job*. I was working at a diner in the cutest little town outside Chattanooga."

Uh-oh, she's detouring into Irrelevant Land. I steer her back on track. "What did you do?"

"The whole town turned on me and my clients. They called me

Since Dad's not online, I check in on my sister. It's a thirteen-hour time difference to Thailand, so she should be starting her day about now. I message her: How's Bernice?

She doesn't respond. Maybe she's traipsing around the jungle already.

Finally, my phone *shwoops* Sean's incoming text: Seriously? Are you running for HQ?

I text: Nope. Cindy. Say yes.

Sean: I'm busy. SMU audition coming up.

Me: Come on, it's in nine days.

Sean: That's not enough time! Prom maybe. Homecoming no.

Me: Impossible for lesser men. I need the Sean magic.

Sean: What part of *SMU audition* are you not getting?

I want to shoot back: *What part of *nine days to transform a Cindy* are you not getting?* Instead, I press my finger between my eyebrows and take a Zen breath, trying to decide the best way to persuade him. I can't *nudge* him. Remember, decisions based on a minute's worth of thoughts or feelings don't stick. Besides, I have to have a direct line of sight to *nudge*. But no worries. There's always good old-fashioned guilt-tripping.

I text: You owe me.

Twelve interminable seconds later, Sean writes: Fine.

I lean back with a sigh of relief. Playing that card was a crappy thing to do, and I feel genuinely bad about it. But I can handle a little cognitive dissonance if it helps Vindhya. Sean knows better than anyone how far I'll go for a Cindy.

Once upon a time, Sean Slater was miserable, lonely, angry, and adrift. For good reasons. In eighth grade it leaked that he was in a ballet class. Riverside East Middle School turned into *Lord of the Flies*. Those of us who weren't part of the tormenting could only keep our heads down and try to stay out of the way. I did try to *nudge* the bullies, but I couldn't be everywhere. And besides, the more emotional I am, the worse my aim is. *Nudging* requires a calm, cool psyche. At thirteen, with exactly one Cindy on my résumé, my parents' divorce in full bloom, my sister away at college for the first time, and facing a gang of rabid pubescent trolls . . . let's just say I wasn't the picture of fairy godmother levelheadedness that I am today.

Anyway, where was I? Right—the cannibal island that was eighth grade. Sean ended up quitting ballet. Then he quit school. He finished junior high online.

When high school started, Sean was back. But he was a silent, skittish version of his former self. Then one day that spring, I got a *glimpse.* I saw him wearing tights and dancing onstage in front of the whole school—leaping and twirling with grace and power and passion. Loving it. Owning it.

So I offered him my services. And he accepted. After what felt like a hundred hours of heart-to-hearts, Sean decided to go back to ballet. I didn't pressure him or *nudge* him or anything, just listened to him talk about everything he had walled up inside. And when he had talked himself out, he decided he wasn't going to let other people define him. His mom ugly cried, she was so happy. After that she drove him an hour three times a week to dance in secret, which was still sad. But he started to stand taller and laugh more. He started to be himself again.

It was magical.

Meanwhile, I went on a no-holds-barred campaign to change the tide of public opinion in Sean's favor. I started subtle—slipping things into conversations like, "Did you know that the guy who played Spider-Man was trained in ballet?" Pretty soon I was blowing up social media with video clips of ripped men doing jetés and pas de deux. I covered my locker in a poster of Roberto Bolle and kissed it twenty-six times a day. I bought tickets to a ballet and bragged for weeks about how lucky I was to get the seats. And, of course, I sent all kinds of little pro-ballet *nudges* to anyone who would hold still long enough to receive one. I spent most of sophomore year with my arms and legs tingling.

By the time I was finished with JLHS, not only had my classmates forgotten they had ever tormented a boy for dancing, but classical ballet had become The Thing.

Midway through that year, Sean came up to me and announced he was signing up for the spring talent show. And he did. And he crushed it, exactly like I had *glimpsed*. He was an instant sensation. After that I did a standard-protocol fade-out. I created as much emotional distance as possible. But with Sean, for whatever reason—maybe because I gave him a whole year of my life—I couldn't quite cut all ties. Don't get me wrong . . . we're not actually friends. Let's call him a colleague.

Anyway, now he does what he loves without dealing with haters every day, while I silently cheer him on. And, incidentally, he's far and away the most popular guy in school now. Which makes him the perfect campaign manager for Vindhya's run for queen.

At lunch the next day, I have to *nudge* two chess clubbers and a soccer player to give up the seats next to Sean. He's exhaustingly popular. Without a word, I slide a paper bag onto his tray. It's from Inland Empire Bakery—we went there together at least a hundred times sophomore year. He snags the bag like a famine survivor, crams his face into the top, and takes a dramatic deep breath.

"Ah. My savior. I almost had to eat this compost they serve to the masses." He pushes his tray away, lifts a cream cheese croissant from the bag, and takes a decadent bite. "Mmmmm. Mm-hmm, mm-hmm. I'm really scared right now, Charity." He glances at my innocent expression as he takes another bite. "Because I already said yes. So what can this bribery be for? She's a troll, isn't she?"

"No she's not. I'm allowed to pay homage to the Great Sean Slater for no particular reason whatsoever."

He snorts delicately.

I take a pull of orange juice. "So. Homecoming."

Some sophomore girls stop by at that moment and pull Sean into an intense discussion about the latest post from some YouTuber they're all following. One of them has lime-green highlights that don't work at all with her strawberry blond hair. It's an ill-advised imitation of my Grinchy look from mid-December. It used to make me all kinds of nuts the way people always copied me, until Memom sagely said, "Charity, imitation is the fondest form of flattery."

She was probably quoting a Hallmark card or something. I don't know.

Regardless, I *nudge* the idea into lime-green girl's head that maybe it's time for a change. Why not? I've got the time.

Sean says, "So. Homecoming."

Aaaand we're back. The girls have moved on.

"Okay, it's Vindhya Chandramouli. Know her?"

He scrunches his face like he's concentrating. "Girls Who Code? Or . . . maybe . . . Robotics Club."

"That's her."

"So?" Sean is impressively blasé.

"So, I think she'll have a solid voter base within the Accelerated Learning Program and the STEMers. So all you have to do is get her nominated and swing the other influencers her way."

Sean ponders that for a moment. Then he says, "I'm thinking she and I need a meet-cute ASAP. I'll take it from there."

"I'm on it." I jump up, suddenly alight with creative energy. Planning meet-cutes is one of my specialties. "You're the best."

He waves me away with a dispassionate "You owe me now."

"Nope. Now we're even." I slide my phone into my back pocket and gather my trash. As I walk away, I toss over my shoulder, "*If you pull it off.*"

The student body president takes my seat before I'm even out of earshot, and Sean is on to the next thing.

Before I head out, I whip off a quick text to Vindhya informing her of tomorrow's meet-cute. She texts back immediately: No! I'm not ready!

Me: Why not?

Vindhya: It's SEAN SLATER!!? I don't know what to say. I don't know what to wear.

Two seconds later she sends another text: I thought there'd be a makeover or something first.

Part of me cringes. But if a makeover will give her the confidence to embrace her destiny, well, she wouldn't be the first Cindy that needed one. (True story: Memom gave Celine Dion a total makeover in 1982. At least that's what she claims.) So I text back: No problem. Meet me at Angelic Hair and Nails at 5.

She replies: I have robotics until 6.

Me: They close at 6.

Vindhya: . . . . Okay. Never mind. I'll be there.

I slide the phone into my pocket with a satisfied smile and

amble toward the courtyard doors, thinking, *I really do love my job.*

Halfway there, my butt vibrates. I pull my phone out of my back pocket and glance at it. There's a new text notification. It's from a blocked number.

The message reads: I know who you are.

3

It's Nothing the
Fairy Godmother Can't Handle

J almost drop the phone. That has got to be the creepiest text ever. Right?

I swipe the message off the screen, glancing around for stalker types. The courtyard—an enclosed brick box with no ceiling and about forty circular tables with attached benches—is a beehive of activity. Almost everyone is on their phone, at least tacitly. My eye is drawn to a knot of cheerleaders huddled around one phone, whispering what I can only imagine to be jealous rumors about yours truly. Then I notice Carmen's homecoming suitor sitting with a couple of AV Club guys. He's wearing a T-shirt that says LIVE LONG AND PROSPER, and he repeatedly opens and closes what could be—I'm not kidding you—a *flip phone*. Not too far from him there's a highly suspicious Goth girl with black lipstick who looks away too quickly. Then my gaze lands on a fishy group of probable hackers who look like they haven't showered in weeks. They're snickering secretively.

It might be any of them. Or none of these people. I consider *nudging* them one at a time with a strong urge to fess up. I do some quick mental math and decide I would look like I was having a stroke if I tried to do that many *nudges*. So that's not going to work. I decide I have no choice but to keep walking and blow this off.

Five steps, and the phone vibrates again. I look down almost against my will.

It says: Bibbidi bobbidi boo.

My first instinct is to make a run for it. My skin is crawling, and my leg muscles itch to engage evasive maneuvers. But that's pointless. I can't run away from my own phone. The creeper could be here, or a thousand miles away, or waiting on the other side of the door. I shiver.

But, you know, if I did panic-run out of the courtyard, I'd probably become a meme in ninety seconds flat. Plus I'd be faced with the JLHS version of the Spanish Inquisition. Who can afford that kind of bad PR?

So I do what I have to. I pocket the phone and walk—nay, strut—from the courtyard, as if all's right with the world. I travel through the double doors, down the hall, past my next class, out another set of doors, and across the parking lot . . . all with perfectly measured strides and swaying hips to project carefree confidence.

When I get to my car, I lock the doors and cave in on myself, panting. My armpits are sticky with nervous sweat. I close my eyes and give in to the freak-out for a minute. Then I dig my phone out of my pocket. The message is still there on the home screen: Bibbidi bobbidi boo.

I swipe it away, wishing I could make the whole situation disappear that easily, and dial Memom.

"EH?" Memom yells into the phone. There is loud music playing on her end.

I yell, "Memom, it's Charity."

"Charity? You sound strange, honey. What's wrong?"

"I've been made."

"You made *it*?"

"No! Jeez, Memom. I mean my cover's blown. Somebody knows about me."

There's a pause. I wonder if she didn't hear me and I'm going to have to say all that again. Suddenly the music clicks off, and she says quite seriously, "Oh. Mercy."

There's a long pause. I hear her talking to someone else in the room. After about four seconds, I huff, "Uh. Hello? Could use some sage advice right about now."

"Charity, sweetie." Memom has never sounded this serious. Ever. Her voice is low and secretive. "In 1998, a nosy little gossip found out about my *side job.* I was working at a diner in the cutest little town outside Chattanooga."

Uh-oh, she's detouring into Irrelevant Land. I steer her back on track. "What did you do?"

"The whole town turned on me and my clients. They called me

34

a con artist in the town newspaper. Can you believe that? It got so bad, one of my Cindies lost his job. Another one's wife left him, and he never saw his kids again." There is panic in Memom's voice now.

My throat is closing up. "So *what did you DO?*"

"I pulled your mom out of school midyear and hightailed it out of town. What else could I do?" She goes a little Granny Delta Force. "You've *got* to seal the leak. *Now.* Before it blows up."

"How?"

She doesn't respond. She's talking to someone else again.

I yell, "Memom! You need to concentrate. I'm in crisis!"

"All right, all right. I'm here." There's a little pause. Then she offers, "Dig up some dirt on her—mutually assured destruction. Real old-school Cold War stuff."

"Seriously?" I bite my lip. I can hear someone talking in the background again. "Memom? What the heck is going on over there?"

"Oh, Lonnie Stevens next door *flashed* me this morning— shows me her wedding to John Tramond in 14C." There's a dramatic pause, then Memom says, "She's eighty-six, Charity. And I have to get her hitched before she croaks. That's *my* crisis."

I groan in self-pity. Selfish Lonnie Stevens. "But, Memom! I need you!"

"I have complete faith in you. I know you'll handle it. Like I said, get ahold of her dirt. Or do her a favor so she owes you. Or move to Toledo and change your name."

"Very funny."

"You're right. Move to Portland. Take me with you."

"I'm not moving."

"Okay. I'm giving Lonnie a dance lesson. I gotta go, sweetie. Call me with an update tomorrow." Just before she ends the call, I hear the opening riff to Bon Jovi's "Bad Medicine."

A momentary smile sneaks past my agitation. Even though Memom was less than helpful, the mental picture of eighty-six-year-olds finding their OTP is exactly what I needed to calm my hysterical reaction to the skeezy texts.

Anyway. Problem number one with following Memom's advice is that I don't know who I need to dig dirt on. Problem number two is that I seriously don't have time for this right now. I have trig this afternoon, Poms practice after school, Vindhya's salon appointment, and a meet-cute to plan. I heave a sigh.

First things first. I stare at my phone for a long time, composing the text. I really—like so bad—want to say, *I will have you arrested, you creepy POS.* But no, I've got to play it cool. Reel them in. Finally I tap in: You know who I am, but who are you?

I send it, then drum on the steering wheel impatiently, waiting for the reply. When it hasn't arrived twelve seconds later, I pull up a list of the top-ten high schools in Portland. I'm scrolling through the photo tour of Oceanview Academy when the incoming text pops up: I'm Captain America. I don't like bullies.

What in the Marvel Universe is that supposed to mean? Stalker is delusional. I send back: What do you want?

The answer comes more quickly this time: No more wand waving. Further instructions to come.

I chuck the phone onto the passenger seat and crank up some electro house on my stereo until the car windows rattle. I close my eyes and try to lose myself in the beat. It doesn't work. There are too many questions swirling around my brain. How much does this piece of human flotsam know about me? Where are they getting their intel? Why do they have it out for me anyway? I grab the phone again and type: And if I don't feel like playing your game?

Three and a half agonizing minutes later, I read: This goes public: Carmen Castillo, Holly Butterman, Sean Slater, Teresa Saint Clair, Olivia Chang, Sara O'Rourke.

It's everybody. Every single Cindy since freshman year. This deluded cyberstalker would out six people—submarine six lives . . . seven, if you count mine. At the very least I'd get major side-eye. But it's the Cindies who would really suffer. They'd be rejected as fakes and poseurs. I tell myself I'm overreacting. I run through the list with best-case scenarios. Carmen has no chance, obviously. Her transformation is too fresh and fragile. Holly is dating JLHS's star cornerback. He'll for sure drop her like she's hot. Sean *might* be popular enough to withstand the backlash, but what if he's not? I *cannot* watch him be tormented and bullied all over again. Teresa, Olivia, Sara . . . They'll lose everything.

How could anyone be so horrible? Why attack innocent

Cindies? I can't, *I cannot*, let this psycho destroy their Happily Ever Afters. Blinking back tears, I write: Why are you doing this?

My finger hovers over send. But as I stare at the words I've written, indignation rises inside me and ferments into resolve. Fairy godmothers don't whine. We don't beg for mercy like little wusses. Fairy godmothers take charge. We take the steaming crap other people don't know what to do with and turn it into freaking flower gardens. And above all, we take care of our Cindies.

I delete the wuss-out message and send: I think we should meet.

The incoming buzz is instant: Soon.

⸻

Despite Stalker's injunction against "wand waving," I keep my appointment with Vindhya at Angelic Hair and Nails. The show must go on. Besides, they didn't mention Vindhya in the list, so they must not know about her. Finally, this salon is two towns over from ours. Chances of being spotted are negligible. Nevertheless, paranoia that someone might be following me has me checking the rearview mirror every few seconds as I drive.

There's a prickly feeling on my forehead as I navigate into a parking spot, completely unrelated to my stalker anxiety. It's just an annoying sensation, like too much static electricity in the air. "Argh," I complain to the empty car. "Not again."

Some Cindies give me a headache. It's so random. I had a headache client last year—Holly. Every time we worked on her wish, it was like *Drumline Live* on my forehead. But it's been a while, and I was hoping I grew out of it or something.

I get out of the car and walk toward the salon, telling myself maybe it's allergies. Just gotta push through.

Angelic Hair and Nails is where so much magic happens. It's a tiny storefront with two massage-chair pedicure stations, a manicure table, and one hairstyling station. A brother and sister, Tuan and Phong (whom I genuinely believe to be wizards) run the shop. Phong seems to do everything from answering phones to mopping floors to creating intricate nail art. Tuan does hair. The real mystery is that they're rarely busy. They seem to prefer to not have customers, actually.

Vindhya pounces on me the moment I walk in the door. "Where do we start? What should I get done? Is there some way to fix my face?"

I kind of want to *nudge* her some self-love. But it wouldn't last anyway. Besides, I guess it's good to have such an eager Cindy. So I gesture toward Tuan's station. "How about a little hair therapy?"

Vindhya shrugs and takes a slouching step in that direction.

"Wait!" I say. She freezes, turning her head slowly like she may have stepped on a land mine. I put my hands on both her shoulders. "You need to walk like a queen. Head back, chin up, pretend you're squeezing a pencil between your shoulder blades."

She pulls her shoulder blades together with a grimace. "This is *not* comfortable."

"Yeah. From now on, if you're comfortable, you're probably doing something wrong." I give her a little prod to start walking.

Pulling her shoulders back even harder, she moves forward, each step meticulous, her face set in determination. Eventually she's going to need to learn to look relaxed while she holds this pose, but we've got a little time.

Tuan, who has watched the whole scene dispassionately, welcomes me to his station with a double handclasp and a "Hey, girl, hey."

"Tuan, this is Vindhya. She's here for a shape and trim."

Tuan waves her into the chair and begins finger combing her long, messy curls. "What are we thinking today?"

Vindhya says matter-of-factly, "Can you just basically make me completely different?"

Behind her back, Tuan and I exchange a silent: *Seriously?* But he's a killer stylist and I'm a fairy godmother, so, I mean, *yeah.* We can.

He signals Phong over, and they have a conversation with Vindhya that feels uncomfortably like she's buying a phone or something—*Do you want to spring for extra storage? Better camera? Rose-gold shell? Hair extensions? Highlights? French tips?* In the end she decides to have them cut her hair, wax her eyebrows, manicure her nails, and do a deep pore cleanse.

While Phong and Tuan get to work, I cook up the meet-cute.

"Vindhya. Focus. You with me?"

She's watching Tuan's scissors while Phong files away at the nails on her right hand.

I wave my hand between her and the mirror to get her attention. "You've got to be early for physics tomorrow. Sean has that teacher the hour before you do, so you can run into him on his way out."

"What do I say to him?"

"Nothing. You literally *crash* into him. Knock his ass over if you can. He'll take it from there. But the whole thing hinges on you getting there right when the bell rings."

"That's impossible. I have to go all the way from the foreign language hall—"

"Leave early. Tell her you started your period."

"*Him.* And I'm not saying that." She grimaces. Tuan gets out the hair dryer and the round brush.

"WHATEVER IT TAKES!" I yell over the roar of the hair dryer. Normally I would be more cautious, but there's no one else in the shop and, seriously, who are Phong and Tuan going to tell? "JUST GET THERE."

Vindhya nods, newly sculpted eyebrows still pinched together. It's too much trouble to keep yelling, so we lapse into silence until Tuan finishes the blowout and pronounces, "Now you are a woman."

Vindhya's black waves cascade past her shoulders, framing her face. Her skin is so detoxed it looks polished. Every remaining eyebrow hair is perfectly tamed. But her eyes are the main event—large and dark, made dramatic by her naturally thick lashes, and open extra wide as she takes herself in. I move to prep the Transformation Tears Protocol (to-go pack of tissues, a piece of dark chocolate, and a speech about inner beauty). But then her lips part into a smile, revealing straight white teeth.

I smile back at her reflection in the mirror, even though the prickling on my forehead has turned into a full-on tap dance.

4

Just One Sucker Punch After Another

My sister and I have dinner together every Thursday night. Well, I'm eating dinner. She's eating breakfast. And we aren't really together. I have the tablet propped up next to me so we can vidchat while we eat. But it's better than nothing—at least until she finishes her internship and comes home in a couple months. We usually spend half the call talking about our current events, then the other half making plans. We're going to backpack around South America over Christmas break. And we're going to room together while she works at a pet clinic and I take classes at Cal State next year.

I love Thursday nights.

It's pouring rain in Thailand, and Hope's windows don't have any glass. She's eating granola and yogurt out of a Hello Kitty teacup. I'm eating take-out pad Thai, which Hope declares to be totally Americanized, but it still makes me feel a little closer to her.

I just finished telling her about Vindhya.

She says, "I still don't know why you do it. Like, what's in it for *you*?"

I tell her for the millionth time, "It brings me joy to see people's wishes come true. I'm putting positive things into the Universe."

"Whatever." Hope's eye roll looks choppy over our long-distance connection. "Mom working late?"

"Of course." I twirl a forkful of noodles in the peanut sauce.

"How's Memom?"

"She's awesome. Planning a wedding for one of the ladies at her retirement complex."

Hope laughs.

"Guess what?" I ask with my mouth full.

"What?"

"I figured out that I can create my own Personal Image Consulting major at Cal State by combining fashion, sociology, and marketing classes. How perfect is that?"

"Cool." She sounds less interested than I'd hoped she'd be.

I venture, "How's Hope World?"

"Good." There's something heavy in that word. And in the way she looks out her window at the rain.

"Hope? What's up?" I prod.

Eight thousand miles away, she turns to face me again. "Chay, I decided to stay here. I'm not coming back."

"Oh."

For a moment that feels stretched into slow motion, I see myself, looking stunned, in the little selfie-feed in the corner of the screen. I can't swallow my noodles.

Hope rushes on like she's been rehearsing. "They've offered me a two-year contract. My school's going to count it for my last few credits so I can graduate in absentia. And Bernice needs me. She really does. And . . . I met someone."

"Oh?" It's my new go-to syllable. Barely holding it together.

"Yeah." She bites her lip. "He's . . . I don't know if it'll be anything, but it's worth sticking around to find out, you know?"

"Yeah. Um. Yeah." I open my eyes wide and lift my eyebrows, checking the selfie to make sure I look excited for her. "That's great."

"Aw, I *miss* you, sis." She pretends to hug me through the tablet, but it's just pixels. Not real. "And we'll still have breakfast-dinner, okay? And maybe you can come visit on spring break. You'd love it here!"

I pull it together to tell her I love her back and that it would be awesome to visit. Then I end the call. I stare at the home screen for a while. It's a picture of Hope and me with our arms around each other at the airport. The picture blurs in front of me as the truth settles in: my sister threw me over for an elephant and a guy she barely knows.

I dump the rest of my pad Thai in the trash, walk calmly to the bathroom, and dye my hair deep lavender. Like loneliness. Like a Thai rainstorm.

I get a text at 6:08 a.m., which is a really craptastic time for a text. I push the tangle of lavender hair out of my face with one hand and feel around for my phone with the other. When I find it, the screen seems blindingly bright to my barely open eyes.

I squint and read: Unknown. So it's from Stalker. The text says: Tonight. Then there's a pin dropped at the playground at Rotary Park.

I rub my sleep-crusted eyes and hammer off a response: There's a football game tonight.

Stalker: After.

Me: I'm not meeting you at a park at night. Kidnap people much?

Stalker: I thought you wouldn't want to be seen. But okay. Inland Empire Bakery.

That place will be packed. Every decent place within ten miles will be packed on a Friday night after a football game. Stalker is right. I don't want to be seen with them. And I most definitely don't want to be overheard. I sigh heavily.

Me: Fine. The park. But I'll have pepper spray with me.

Stalker: Me too.

Me: I'll have a Taser.

Stalker: I'll have a photon torpedo.

A surprised laugh—more of a blat, really—escapes my lips. Did Stalker just make a joke? Or is Stalker a permanent resident of Imagination Land? I send back: You know only one of those is a real thing, right?

I catch myself half smiling as I wait for the reply, and rearrange my features on principle, even though no one is around.

Stalker: **10:00. Don't be late.**

Vindhya's physics class is the last hour of the day. Even though there's a chance Stalker is watching me—now and, well, always—I can't resist sprinting there after trig to catch the meet-cute in progress. As I round the corner into the science hall, I slow to a socially acceptable pace and then stop when I have a clear view of the doorway. Vindhya and Sean are both on their hands and knees, surrounded by books and the contents of Vindhya's purse. Judging by the blast radius, she must have hit him like a linebacker. Dang, I'm proud of her.

They're both reaching for books and sorting out his things from hers. They're also creating a total roadblock in the process. No one can go in or out of the classroom. Which is brilliant, because all those people are now witnessing the meet-cute.

Sean says something that Vindhya smiles at. Their audience grows as more people arrive for class. Sean hands Vindhya a book, still talking. I really ought to learn how to read lips. I inch closer.

Gwen and Scarlett appear in front of me, totally blocking my view. Scarlett exclaims, "Hey, Charity! I don't usually see you here!"

I shift slightly to see past her shoulder. Sean gallantly helps Vindhya up. I mutter, "Yeah, I think I forgot something at chem this morning, so . . ."

Scarlett notices me looking past them, turns to see what's going on, and gets an eyeful of the Sean-Vindhya meet-cute playing to a packed house. She says, "Guys, check it out."

All three of us move in closer, just in time to hear Tim Smith, baseball player and resident jagoff, say, "HEY, PRETTY BOY! Get out of the way so the rest of us can get to class."

I clamp a hand over my mouth to hold back a horrified gasp. No, no, no. Tim's spewing hate speech all over my meet-cute! I try to make Tim back off with a *nudge*, but I can't get a clear shot. There are too many people milling around—not to mention Scarlett, who will not keep still.

"I said MOVE, Twinkle Toes." Tim shoulders into Sean, who backs away looking miffed.

Vindhya steps in. *"Excuse me?"*

Tim says, "I was talking to Ballerina Barbie here, not you, Kama Sutra."

Without missing a beat, Vindhya winds up and punches Tim in the temple. The hallway erupts in applause. Tim grabs his head, swearing, looking both shocked and in pain. The bell rings.

The rent-a-cop security guys appear on Segways to break up the crowd, calling, "GET TO CLASS! EVERYBODY GET TO CLASS. YOU'RE LATE!"

The audience begins to disperse, the security guys following the slowest group in the direction of the cafeteria. Tim Smith stalks toward physics looking acidic. Even though it serves no purpose, I *nudge* his depth perception just enough to make him run into the doorframe. He smacks his face and reels back, erupting in another round of not-school-appropriate words.

Not sorry.

Scarlett and Gwen both turn to me openmouthed. Gwen goes, "OMG. Was that real life?"

Scarlett responds, "That girl is so freaking badass. How do I not know her?"

I shake my head, like, *I have no idea what's going on.* But inside I'm weeping for Vindhya and Sean, seething at Tim, blaming the Universe for giving me such pathetic powers, and feeling vaguely guilty for putting anyone in Tim's line of fire.

The girls announce that they've got to go to class. As they walk away, Scarlett says, "Didn't you used to have a crush on that Tim guy?"

Gwen makes a gagging noise. "Don't remind me."

They disappear into a classroom. I approach Sean cautiously, not sure how deep his wounds are. He gives me a half smile that might be conspiratorial . . . but could just as easily be his brave face.

I stop him with a hand on his arm and a whispered "Are you okay?"

He gives me a nod and a *haters gonna hate* eye roll.

"I'm so sorry you had to deal with that."

Sean brushes off my sympathy. "That guy is his own worst enemy. Besides, our plan was good, but that drama—you can't *buy* that kind of press."

Hmmm, when he puts it that way . . . maybe we can make this work in our favor. But first I have to check on my Cindy. I text her: **Tim sucks. Nice right hook, though. You okay?**

As I hit send, an incoming notification pops up that Scarlett just posted a video. I click through.

"—*not you, Kama Sutra.*"

Vindhya's eyes blaze. Her arm blurs.

Tim staggers and grabs his head.

A squee escapes me. My Cindy is now the knight in shining armor to JLHS's It Boy. And Scarlett caught it on camera. This is going to blow up. I turn the phone to Sean. "OMG. You were spot-on."

"You doubted me?"

I whisper, "Wait twenty or thirty minutes for this to build up some steam. Then comment, okay? Make sure you mention Vindhya by name."

Sean quirks an eyebrow at me.

"Please."

He nods, lips pursed.

One of the rent-a-cops returns and barks, "You two! CLASS!"

Sean and I go our separate ways. Sure enough, the video is looping on all of Scarlett's feeds before I even make it to lit. By the end of class it has fourteen shares and thirty-eight comments. Comment thirty-eight says *Vindhya Chandramouli for homecoming queen!*

5

It's Not Illegal If It's Self-Defense

*E*ight hours post-meet-cute, with our social media campaign going strong, I turn my attention back to the Stalker problem. I arrive at the swing set at 10:02. My heart is pounding, and I can practically hear Memom yelling, *"Contain the breach!"*

I'm here mostly to protect my Cindies. But I can't help worrying about myself a little. What if Stalker knows about the magic? I might literally have to drop out of high school and become a wandering fortune-teller in Baghdad or something. I tell myself there is *no way* Stalker could know. It's not even in the realm of possibility. Here's what's going to happen:

I'm going to meet Stalker, put the smack down, and be done with this detour.

I rock in the swing while I wait. I came straight from the game, so I'm still wearing my Poms uniform under JLHS-branded warm-up pants and team jacket. My hair (still lavender) is up in the standard high ponytail.

The night is cool, dark, and still. There's a half-moon, a nearby streetlight, and crickets to keep me company. Fourteen seconds of that reverie is enough for me. I pull out my phone and check on the meet-cute video. It's up to ninety-six shares.

There's a crunch nearby, and my head pops up. Stalker is backlit by the streetlight—a lanky guy, about six feet tall. I can't see his face. Without taking my eyes off him, I put the phone away and clutch the pepper spray in my pocket, finger on the trigger.

He takes another step, and I launch out of the swing, facing him, pepper spray out at arm's length. Just as fast, he whips out his own spray can, aimed at my face.

I growl, "This is law-enforcement strength."

"Mine is for grizzly bears."

He takes the step that brings him into the light. Disheveled curls. Glasses. A T-shirt that says DAMN IT, JIM, I'M A DOCTOR, NOT A MIRACLE WORKER. It's Carmen's goofy admirer—the one I actually thought was cute—the kid sporting the flip phone in the courtyard when I got that ridiculous *bibbidi bobbidi boo* text.

"YOU!" I shout the accusation. *"You . . ."* Words fail me.

"Noah." He looks cocky in a way unique to dorks—like he just leveled up in Dungeons & Dragons.

Neither of us has lowered our pepper spray. My arm muscles start to burn a little, mostly because Coach had us do a hundred push-ups yesterday. But the lactic acid in my arms is nothing compared to the fury coursing through my veins. I'm so freaking mad. All my plans for levelheaded diplomacy go out the window. I mean, I've never done anything to this guy. I was rooting for him. I feel betrayed. I launch a vicious *nudge* at him: *Hit yourself in the face.* But I'm way too upset, and it shoots off into space or somewhere. I'm left with both hands tingling and nothing to show for it.

I hiss, "What the hell is your problem?!"

"*My problem?* You are unbelievable. I can't even—" He ends with a single *Ha.*

I finish the sentence for him: "Can't stop being a creepy little turd goblin for no reason?"

He laughs—something between surprise, mirth, and anger. "That is the first time I've been called that." He edges to the side, possibly preparing for a left-flank assault.

"Seriously? Because you seem like the kind of guy that would get that a lot." I swivel just enough to keep him directly in my sights. My arm is really burning now.

He runs his free hand through his mangy hair. "This is getting us nowhere. I'll lower my weapon if you lower yours."

I hesitate. "Fine."

"Okay. On three?"

I shrug, like, *I don't care either way.* My arm feels like Jell-O flambé.

He says, "One, two, three," and we both slowly lower our pepper spray. Sweet relief. But I don't take my finger off the trigger. I try another *nudge*: *Drop the weapon.* It does nothing but spread the pins and needles all the way up my arms. I'm still too mad.

I smack my thighs to wake my hands up. "Okay. Let's get this over with. What the fffff—"

"Just shut up and listen. Here's my list of demands." He pulls a piece of notebook paper out of his pocket, unfolds it, and reads, "Number one, stop messing with people's lives."

"Okay," I snap, "I don't know where you're getting your intel. But let's get something straight. I don't *mess* with people's lives. I grant wishes. I make people happy."

"You manipulate people for fun. You're criminally insane."

"*I'm* criminally insane? Only one of us has blackmailing, cyberbullying, and stalking on their rap sheet. You're a freaking wacko."

He jerks his arm up, but not faster than me. So we're back to square one, staring down each other's pepper spray dispensers.

He grinds out, "It's not called 'stalking' if you're the good guy. It's called 'staking out a perp.'"

I laugh incredulously. "Oh my gosh. You actually think you're Captain America."

"And you actually think you're a magical, wish-granting fairy."

'Cuz I *am*. We glare at each other in silence for a long moment. He blinks first.

He takes a deep breath, looks toward his outstretched hand, and says more calmly, "Can we de-escalate this, please?"

I tilt my head to the side in tacit compliance, and our arms hover down to neutral again.

I match his calm tone. "Okay, Captain Stalker. Seriously. What's this about? The people on your list are happy. Why would you want to mess with them?"

He is inexplicably angered by that totally reasonable question. "The people on that list are brainwashed sheep. They were happy *before*, and they were *real*. You assimilate people like the Borg Queen."

I don't know what that means, and I don't actually care. What I'm really wondering is how much he knows about my magic. How do I defend myself without giving anything away? I hesitate. "That's not true. I only help people get what they tell me they want."

"LIAR!" He jabs his notebook paper in my face. "Holly never would have told you she wanted to be arm candy for that mouth breather."

Aaaaah. Holly Butterman. One of my headache clients. She spent all her time blending into the background and trying not to cast a shadow. Then last year I *glimpsed* her at prom with Kade Kassab—JLHS star cornerback—dancing in the center of a human sea of deep-green envy. A few well-timed encounters, a little *nudge* at the opportune time . . . They've been a couple ever since.

Now we're getting somewhere.

"You have a crush on Holly Butterman. That's what this is about."

"Not a *crush*. We were friends. Maybe more than friends. I was taking Holly to junior prom. It took me months to work up the courage to ask her. Then I see the two of you talking in the

55

auditorium, and the next day she tells me it's off." His shoulders slump a fraction.

Argh, sympathy. Remorse. It sucks that helping one person broke someone else's heart. I feel genuinely bad about it. But current events require a stiff upper lip. I tap into my "I'm not a therapist but I play one on TV" voice. "What makes you think those events are connected?"

He goes rigid again and sneers, "Come on. People like you don't hang out with people like Holly . . . like she was before." He continues, sounding rather self-satisfied in a bad-guy-monologue type of way. "I've spent five months looking for patterns. Other people this has happened to. It's amazing that I'm the first one to notice, actually. It's so obvious once you know what you're looking for. The sudden change of fortunes. A moment in the spotlight. The meteoric rise to popularity. You, always one or two degrees separated from it all."

Popularity? That's all he thinks this is about? Reconciliations, romance, dreams come true. I do it all. I'm transforming lives up in here, punk.

There's a cutting remark about how off base he is ready on my lips, but I bite it back. I need to be strategic. He's showing his cards, giving me a chance to find out exactly how much he knows. I give his ego a little prod. "Smart. But why did you say, 'no wand waving'? That's kind of out-there."

"When Carmen made the Poms squad, I figured she was the most recent victim. So I went to her and told her you had offered to help me, and I wasn't sure if I should accept. She gave me all the deets—how you approached her out of the blue, how she was sworn to secrecy and is never allowed to talk to you in public, how you called yourself her fairy godmother, and how you somehow managed to stall the tryout when she got a flat tire."

Oh, Carmen, you sweet, gullible child. I want to smack you upside the head right now.

I huff out my irritation and keep my head in the game. No denying he's holding some disturbingly good cards. But now I know I've got a few too:

He has no proof, really. It's possible that I could get people to dismiss him as a conspiracy-theory fanatic.

He doesn't know about the *glimpses* or the *nudges.*

He's in love with Holly.

I pocket my pepper spray and hold out both my hands, palms up, speaking with the most contrite voice I can muster. "I'm so sorry about junior prom. But think about it. If you publish that list, Holly will suffer too. Kade will dump her. She'll have no friends."

"She'll have me." There he goes sounding heartbroken and sincere again. It tugs my heartstrings in the most annoying way. He shoves his hands in his pockets. "I'll only publish the list if you force me to. Which brings me to demand number two: undo whatever you did to Holly."

Irritation overrides my momentary lapse into sympathy. I snap, "I can't undo it. It doesn't work that way."

"You could if you wanted to. Undo the brainwashing."

I shout in frustration, "*I don't brainwash people!* I *glimpse* their wishes, and I help them get to their Happily Ever After."

As soon as the words are out of my mouth, I realize I just let Captain Stalker into the People Who Know About the Magic Club. He officially knows me better than my own mother now. On one hand, it was a major tactical error. Memom is going to read me the riot act for an hour. But it feels kind of good to tell him. Now he knows I'm the real deal, not the narcissistic puppet master he's made me out to be. Maybe he'll ease off me a little.

Stalker registers the information I've given him with slack-jawed incredulity. "You *what?*"

I repeat it, clear and steady, because I might as well own it now. "I *glimpse* their wishes."

"What does that even mean?"

"I see something that is meant to happen in their future."

"HA!" It's not a laugh, exactly. It's the sound of a mind being blown. He shakes his head, making his clown curls jiggle. "You . . . you *glimpse* . . . their *future.*"

"One specific moment in their future. The moment their deepest wish comes true."

Disbelief gives way to anger again. I can tell because he turns hot pink from his neck to the tips of his ears. "You're telling me Holly's *deepest wish* was to date a meathead football player?"

"I only—"

"Do you know one single thing about her? She's ar

draws her own comic books. She makes these cookies

beautiful to eat. If you get her laughing hard enough,

so loud. She . . . she . . ." He trails off, scrubbing one

his forehead.

I'm speechless for the first time I can remember. I did

know those things about Holly. The truth is, it never

me there was anything I needed to know that the *gli*

show me. I clear my throat, about to confess. Then I

done nothing wrong, and he's neither a priest nor a judg

chin and declare, "I'm only interested in people's future

is not relevant."

He coughs into his fist. It sounds like "Hag."

I roll my eyes.

He stuffs the notebook paper back in his pocket,

a moment, then says, "Okay, so you had this little fo

moment, and then, based totally on that, you just *conv*

and Holly to date each other?"

"That is super cynical. But . . . okay. Sure. Whateve

"Then just *convince* them to stop dating."

"I won't. But even if I wanted to, I *can't*."

"Give me one good reason." He crosses his arms an

fists into his armpits.

Where do I start?

1. No *glimpse*, no wish. It's as simple as that.

2. I don't negotiate with terrorists.

3. If granting a wish gets people to Happily Ever After, then ungranting one derails destiny.

I could think of like fifty more. But I pick, "Ruining someone's happiness goes against my code of conduct."

"You ruined mine."

"That was inadvertent," I huff, because he really needs to let that go. "I *grant* wishes. I don't destroy them."

"Fine. You grant wishes. Then grant mine. I wish for Holly Butterman to fall in love with me."

"Aaargh." I throw my hands up. "You are impossible. I'm *really sorry* that you lost your girl. But it's time to move on. She chose someone else. It happens. I'm not fixing you up with her. Get a life. The end."

He sighs, like *I'm* the one who doesn't get it. "I thought maybe the ditzy Poms thing was just a stereotype."

"Hey!"

"Try to get this through your glitter-filled head." He starts talking really slowly, like I'm four. "You grant my wish, or I destroy your popular little life along with the fake lives of every person you've conned into ditching their real friends for a spot at the cool table."

Now he's really pissing me off. I grit back, equally slowly, "You give it your best shot, *Captain*. You've got no proof. It's your word against mine. You will be the butt of every joke for the rest of the year—the gullible, paranoid, conspiracy-theory-touting *loser*."

I just played my last card. And, yeah, it was mean. But worth it to win.

He sighs and reaches into his pocket. I whip out my pepper spray, assuming we're having another quick-draw competition. He slowly pulls his phone out and holds it up. "I don't think that's how it's going to go, though. Because I recorded this whole conversation."

The words are a gut punch. I gasp, "That's a felony."

He pulls a *whatcha gonna do* face. That smug expression puts me completely over the edge. With a primal roar, I squeeze the trigger on the little can in my hand. It takes only a second to empty its contents. Then everything happens at once. The pepper spray has the desired effect—the look on his face morphs to pain and panic. He fumbles the phone, then clutches it to his chest as he drops, facedown in the fetal position, to the wood chips.

I try again to *nudge*: *Drop it. Drop IT.* But my *nudger* is way too overheated to get the signal through. My arms and legs go buzzy, and he's still got a death grip on his phone. Looks like we're doing this the old-fashioned way. Coughing on secondhand fumes, I dive at him with only one thought in my head—*get the phone.*

I wedge both hands between his body and the ground, find his hand wrapped around the phone, and claw at his fingers. He wheezes every possible profanity at me, angling his body away. My arms are pinned. I wiggle my fingers and dig my knee into his back. I pant, "Give me the phone. Give it to me."

61

He suddenly rolls away and onto his back. His face is red and splotchy and drenched. Fluid pours from every orifice. His eyes are clamped shut. He's panting.

Okay, I feel a smidge guilty for doing that to another human. But I have to get the phone. I launch myself onto him again, desperately prying at his fingers.

His other arm flashes up. I hear a hiss. And I am on fire.

I scream, my hands instinctively covering my face. Instantly I'm a mess of snot and tears and saliva—streaming into my hands, running down my arms, pouring off my chin and soaking my jacket. I am blind. My conflagrated eyes refuse to open. My throat constricts. Between coughing fits, I rasp, "You're . . . Satan."

"You . . . drew . . . first . . . blood."

We don't talk again for a long time. For five or twenty minutes, the only sound is coughing, gasping, groaning, and nose blowing. Finally, the feeling of being incinerated alive begins to abate. I contemplate my situation while I wipe smears of watery eye makeup onto my sleeves.

This bottom-feeder is basically trying to force me to quit my job—my *calling*, my very purpose on earth—the same week my sister hit me with the news that she's ditching me for good. And in case that doesn't burn enough, he's deployed a chemical weapon on me. I don't even know if what he wants is possible. And even if it is, I'd rather break both his legs than help him. But the brutal reality is, he has me in a corner. I take off my jacket and mop my face with it.

I hear Stalker mess with his phone, but I'm too spent to restart the fight. There's a *shwoop*, and he croaks, "I just emailed the audio file to myself."

Game point, Captain Stalker. I concede the win with "I hate you."

"I despise you."

I want to cry. I want to throw myself into the wood chips and bawl like a baby. Instead I take my first deep breath since getting Maced in the face. The night air feels like Icy Hot on my scorched throat and lungs, and it reinflates me with cool resolve. I'm the fairy godmother. The fairy *freaking* godmother. My defeat is transitory. My revenge will be swift and sweet.

Feigning dignity not truly possible in the aftermath of pepper spray, I pull my lips into a tight, saccharine smile and lilt, "Fine. You win. I'll grant your crappy wish." I lean into his personal space. "But that means you do exactly what I say and *only* what I say. From here on out, you don't put on your tighty-whities without my permission. Got it?" I jab my finger into his collarbone for effect, and he rewards me with an uneasy look. His eyes are pink and puffy and bloodshot. I must look the same.

I stand up, still holding my soggy jacket and empty pepper spray can. I pivot to make my grand exit, but all the swagger has been burned out of me. Instead of a strut, all I manage is a dead-limbed plod. At the edge of the circle of light, I turn back for the mic drop. "Congratulations, Noah. You've got yourself a fairy godmother."

6

This Is How I Go to War

Eight hours. That's how long I get to recover from the disaster with Noah. At 7:05 on Saturday morning, he texts: Can I put on my underwear now?

This is sleep-deprivation torture. It's sick and twisted and inhumane. As I lie in bed contemplating ways to murder him and make it look like an accident, I hear clanging in the kitchen. Without responding to the text, I roll out of bed and pad toward the source of the noise.

Mom is there—dressed in a suit, hair done, and makeup applied. She looks like she's been up for hours. When I appear from the hallway, she gives me her deal-making, check-collecting, world-saving smile. "Good morning, sweetheart. Coffee?"

"I'm trying to quit." I don't drink coffee. Maybe she's being cute, but I suspect she doesn't know this about me.

"I'm making eggs and toast. You want some?"

"Sure." While Mom cracks eggs into the frying pan, I pour myself a glass of orange juice and flop onto one of the high bar chairs at the counter. Once my morning throat has a protective coating of OJ, I say, "So, you look nice. You going into work today?"

The question is so casual, like it's just trivia.

I hear my phone chime in my room. It might not be Captain Ambush. It might be . . . someone else who gets up way too early on Saturday. Who am I kidding? No one who doesn't hate me would be texting right now.

"I have breakfast with a major donor at nine, and I don't want to be too hungry."

"Oh."

My phone chimes again. It could be Hope forgetting what time zone I'm in.

Mom puts a plate of eggs and toast in front of me and sits down with her own. While we eat, my phone keeps cheeping from my bedroom, and I keep ignoring it. I wait hopefully for Mom to ask me something—anything—about my life. I fill the space by prepping responses, just in case.

Imaginary Mom: Your eyes look puffy. Are you okay?

Me: *It's kind of a funny story, actually. This nerd vigilante attacked me.* . . .

Imaginary Mom: How did the halftime routine go last night?

Me: *It was fine. I'm not really that into Poms, though. I only do it to keep up appearances.* . . .

Imaginary Mom: How are you doing in trig?

Me: *I'm working really hard, but . . . this is the first time in my life I've felt like I might fail at something. I'm scared, Mom.*

Daydreams. She chews placidly. I realize she's not really here. She's rehearsing what she's going to say to her major donor, and what they might say back, and how she'll respond. Resentment churns the eggs in my stomach, followed quickly by shame. She's literally trying to save the ocean from floating garbage and oil slicks. What kind of an attention-starved whiner would resent that?

I finish my breakfast, slam the last few ounces of OJ, and take my dishes to the sink. I make my voice as cheerful as it should be. "Well, have a great meeting. I hope they give you a million dollars."

Her eyes come back into focus. "I'm going to ask them to let us use their yacht for a fundraising dinner."

"Oh. Cool." The wish bubbles up again: *Ask about me.* It's petty. I release it with a sigh. "I might go see Memom later. Or maybe tomorrow . . . She's been asking when you're coming to visit."

Mom stabs her egg like it's earned a quick execution. "Really? She's guilt-tripping me through *you* now?"

"I think she just—"

"I'm sorry, Charity. You shouldn't have to be our go-between. I'll try to call her . . . sometime."

This is officially awkward now. They've been this way since I was like five. I have a vague memory of a shouting match where Mom accused Memom of filling our heads with fairy tales and Memom called Mom a disappointment. They've barely been on speaking terms ever since. I try not to get involved.

My phone chimes again in the distance, and I back toward the hallway. "I'd better go see who's texting me. Thanks for breakfast."

Mom waves her fork. "Okay, hon. Have a good day."

⸺

7:14, Noah: My underwear. The final frontier.

7:16, Noah: All right, it's between blue with the Starfleet insignia or the ones with the schematic of the starship Enterprise across the crotch.

7:19, Noah: I went with the Enterprise. Hope that's okay. Now is it okay to pick out my socks?

7:23, Noah: My mom wants to know why my eyes look like raw meat. Should I tell her I was attacked by a PMS-raging pompon girl? Or should I lie?

I glare at the phone, trying to strategize, caught in the purgatory between laughing and screaming. If Noah's play is to annoy me until I come completely unglued, it's working. On the other hand, maybe he's simply a loser with nothing but time on his hands and no filter. Either way, I have to set some boundaries *now*.

While I consider what it would take to get under Noah's skin, he texts me a picture of his feet. One sock has lime-green, royal-blue, and fluorescent-yellow stripes. The other is orange with purple polka dots. If I look at them long enough I'm pretty sure I'll have a seizure.

The next incoming text reads: Which ones?

Then there's a GIF of a guy with pointy ears and a bad Caesar haircut raising one weird eyebrow.

Curse the day this kid got my number.

It's time to take the war to his front door. I write: Text me your address. We start today.

I punch send with unnecessary roughness and toss the phone on the bed. Dealing with this is the last thing I need right now. I should be focused on Vindhya's wish—now made even trickier by the fact that I'm going to have to accomplish it without Noah figuring out what's going on. I seriously have zero time for teaching sketchy exes of former Cindies basic phone etiquette.

But you know what? The fairy godmother can handle any challenge. I head to the bathroom for a shower.

When I return to the phone—clean, dry, dressed, and primped—forty-five minutes later, Noah has sent his address, along with twenty-three more texts. Six are about choosing breakfast cereal, eleven are unintelligible sci-fi references, two are pictures of a "weird spot" on his knee, and four are video clips of Wiggles songs. I want to claw my own eyes out.

This is definitely weaponized geekery. No one on earth could be accidentally this obnoxious.

I check myself in the mirror to make sure I'm battle ready.

Every curve is accentuated in my short shorts and pink tank top. I adjust to reveal a peek of red lace at my cleavage. My lavender waves are in a devil-may-care tousle. Carefully applied concealer has erased last night's trauma. Satisfied with my look, I douse myself with satsuma body spray and slip into sandals.

My plan of attack is simple:

Set off every hormonal trip wire in his feeble boy brain.

Once he's mentally incapacitated, demonstrate how easily I could crush him.

Leave him terrified to cross me again.

⸺

Noah's house is unnervingly close to my house, it turns out. He lives six blocks away from me. The houses on his street come in the same three floor plans as the houses on my street. Mom and I have the one-story Spanish Revival the color of sand. They have the two-story Spanish Revival the color of slightly darker sand.

I park on the street and march to the front door for Operation Stalker Smackdown. I jab the doorbell. Eight seconds pass with no answer. While I wait, I scroll through the texts Noah has sent in the past hour. Thirty-six messages, and they're all pointless. It infuriates me all over again just when I should be finding that Zen place where I could *nudge* something truly debilitating into his head.

Maybe I could make him forget his own name for a minute. Or eat paste. Or humiliate himself online . . .

Noah opens the door. Despite the fact that he has obviously been up since 7:05, he looks like he recently rolled out of bed. His hair is in a wilder mop than usual, if that's even possible. His T-shirt has a hole near the collar and a faded drawing of the dude with pointy ears. He's wearing lounge pants.

Lounge pants.

He's sporting an *I just beat you in a chess tournament* smirk, but it morphs into openmouthed stupefaction as he registers my appearance.

Phase one complete. My adversary is weakened. Time to go for the throat.

I jam the phone toward his face. "You think this is *funny*, grunt? Because, so help me, I will strangle you with my bare hands and leave your worthless corpse in the desert to—"

"Noah?"

The door opens a little more to reveal a middle-aged woman. She has the same untamed brown hair and prominent nose as Noah. The expression on her face is the look one would give to a hooker yelling death threats at a toddler.

It honestly didn't occur to me that some people's parents are actually home on Saturday mornings. I cringe, now hyperaware of how low-cut my tank top is and that I sound homicidal. I would very much like to crawl into a hole and stay there for the next twenty or thirty years. But there are no Charity-size holes in sight, so I put my game face on.

With a big, apologetic smile, I stick my right hand out. "You must be Noah's mom. I'm Charity."

She purses her lips and gingerly shakes my hand. "Lisa."

"Nice to meet you," I say, all politeness. I wonder if I could inconspicuously tug my top higher. No chance—all eyes are on the ta-tas. Actually, Noah manages to wrench his eyes upward enough to shoot me an evil glare. There's nothing to do but hold my head high and will my hands to remain at my sides.

Noah's cheeks turn pink in an *I'm caught between my mom and a red lace bra* kind of way. He slouches against the doorjamb, avoiding all eye contact. "Uh. Charity and I are working on a project together. For school. The death threats are just her thing."

Mom's eyebrows go up, but her look softens. "Oh."

Noah backs away from the door, waving at me to follow him. "So we'll be up in my room."

The eyebrows go higher. "Oh?"

I trail after Noah into the house and down the hall, taking the opportunity to adjust my shirt to a mom-appropriate area of my chest.

When we're halfway up the stairs, his mom calls, "Keep the door open."

Noah goes, *"Mom."*

I wonder what it would feel like to have a mom who cares about what you're doing and who you're with. I slap the thought away.

Noah gestures me into his room, enters behind me, and shuts the door. I look back pointedly at the sound of the click.

Noah says, "So . . . what's with the outfit? Is that for my benefit, or do you dress like Shahna of Triskelion every Saturday?"

"That is a nerdy-ass comment that I'm not going to dignify with a response." My hands go to my hips. Unfortunately he seems to have successfully rebooted his brain cells, and Lisa stole all my thunder. So much for my attack plan. I'm forced to at least pretend to negotiate. "Now, before we get started, let's go over some ground rules."

He crosses his arms over his chest, casting a peeved look my way.

I recite, quickly and formally, "You shall not, during or anytime following the expiration of our wish-granting agreement, directly or indirectly disclose the nature of our relationship to any living person. No part of our dealings may be posted on any public forum, including but not limited to social media, online platforms, or school-based communications."

Noah's eyebrows drift upward during this speech.

I continue. "Furthermore, you shall not approach me in public places or seek me out for purposes outside the scope of your wish. At the time of the fulfillment of your wish, all contact between us will immediately and irrevocably be terminated."

Normally that last part is a tiny bit sad, but I relish it now. And then I add a clause especially for him. "At which time you will also destroy your list of previous clients, the illicit recording of any conversations between us, and any other evidence of past, present, or future dealings that you hold with or without my knowledge. Do you agree?"

He shifts his weight from one leg to the other, holding the back of his neck. I'm pretty sure I detect an undercurrent of scoffing as he says quite seriously, "So basically, we pretend we don't know each other, I never tell anyone about this, and once I get Holly back, we never talk again."

"Correct."

He smile-grimaces like you would if your detention got shortened by fifteen minutes, like, *This sucks 25 percent less than before.* "Fine by me. I literally cannot wait to never speak to you again."

"It's so mutual." I'm about to get to work on his room when he jams his fist into the space between us. His pinkie pops up. I narrow my eyes at it. "What's with the finger?"

"Pinkie swear." His voice modulates into a lawyerly formality. He's mocking me. "The pinkie swear is the only universally acknowledged method of making a verbal contract such as this one legally and morally binding to both parties."

I roll my eyes. He jiggles his pinkie. With an exhale of contempt, I hook my finger around his for a brief second. It's not nearly as repellent as expected. His skin isn't clammy or sweaty or oily or scaly. In fact, if this digit were attached to someone else's hand, I might even admit that my little finger seems to fit perfectly into the crook of his larger one. As it is, I snap my hand back the instant we make contact and huff, "Now shut up. I'm working."

I stare at him hard, willing myself to *glimpse* . . . something. If I knew his destiny, this whole thing would be much less onerous. I visually bore into his forehead, trying to drag a *glimpse* out of him. Absolutely nothing happens.

"This is really awkward." Noah clears his throat. "What are you—"

"Nothing." I look away. "It's a fairy godmother thing. You wouldn't understand."

Giving up on the *glimpse*, I take in his bedroom. *Star Trek* posters cover most of the wall space. On his dresser is a detailed model of a spaceship inside a Plexiglas box—its placard reads "NCC-1701 USS *Enterprise*." Next to it are vintage action figures in aging boxes.

A photo stuck to the mirror draws my eye. It's of Noah and Holly in a kitchen. She's holding a plate of intricately frosted cookies and smiling bigger than I've ever seen her smile in real life. He's pretending he's about to steal a cookie. They both have frosting in their hair and on their faces. Remorse for meddling with their relationship tries to creep in on me, but I tamp it down. No mercy for blackmailers.

I turn away from the desk.

There's a bookcase stuffed with paperbacks. The flip phone I saw him with the day he first texted me lies on top of a Nintendo Switch on top of a laptop next to an Xbox.

The whole room seems like it has been cleaned for my benefit. There is a thin line of dust around the edges of things, like they were wiped down in a hurry. And there are vacuum lines in the carpet.

I turn ninety degrees. His bed is against one wall—a twin with a dark blue bedspread and a stuffed bear wearing a *Star Trek* uniform. There's a pair of well-loved hiking boots on the floor next to the bed.

I take a deep breath and blow my lips out. "Obviously I'm the first girl who's been up here."

Noah stands near the door with his arms crossed. "Do you have a point, or are you just always mean for no reason?"

I shrug. "I figured, since you and Holly were *so close*, you two would have spent some quality time in here, but . . . obviously not."

He lifts and recrosses his arms. "Or maybe she likes me for who I am and we *did*."

"But you didn't." I turn to look him straight in the eye.

He holds my gaze for two and a half seconds. Then he shifts his weight and looks away. "No. We didn't."

Ha. I knew it. I move toward the dresser with a satisfied smirk and open the first drawer I come to. "Okay. Let's get started."

The drawer is full of socks and underwear. Nasty, I know. But a surgeon doesn't flinch when he cuts you open. I pull them out one by one and throw them on the floor with only the most cursory of glances. Mostly I'm doing it to be mean. None of my other Cindies have been subjected to such humiliation, but none of my other Cindies blackmailed and pepper sprayed me either.

Noah goes, "Hey . . . uh . . . wha? . . . *come on* . . ."

That's right. Feel my wrath, Evil Cindy. In thirty-six seconds, there are two pairs of boxer-briefs and one pair of socks left in the drawer. I move on to the next—T-shirts.

I hold them up one at a time and add them to the reject pile behind me. "No. No. No." I survey a shirt with cartoon versions of the *Star Trek* characters. I wrinkle my nose.

From behind me Noah says, "That's vintage."

"Ugh. Hell no." I chuck it.

Next comes one that says . . . TO BOLDLY GO WHERE NO MAN HAS GONE BEFORE. I shake my head. "Nooooo." I toss it over my shoulder.

Noah says, "Hey!"

I open the next drawer—shorts and pants. I throw out everything except one pair of jeans. "Dude, so many drawstrings. Are you in some kind of button-hating cult?"

Instead of responding, Noah demands, "Could you just *hang on* a minute?"

I whirl around. "What?"

"What the heck do you think you're doing to my stuff?"

"This is phase one of a desperately needed wardrobe fix. As per our contract."

Noah scoops some of his T-shirts off the floor and haphazardly shoves them back into the drawer. "No thanks."

I snatch them back out. "What did you *think* a fairy godmother would do for you? You said you want Holly to fall in love with you. You blackmailed me into helping you. So this is it. This is me helping you."

He wrenches the T-shirts from my arms and says through clenched teeth, "Let's get this straight right now. I want Holly to fall in love with *the real me*. I'm not going to let you screw with me like you did with the others. I'm not changing my clothes or my interests or the way I talk. Got it?"

For a moment I am too stunned to formulate a response. Only because of years of practice do I manage a pseudocalm "Yeah. I get it. Cool. I mean, you do you. *But . . .*" I can't keep the irritation out of my voice as I slowly explain. "At some point you're going to have to choose between *this guy*"—I thrust my arm out to point at the action figure box on the dresser—"and Holly."

His eyes flick toward the action figure. Then he looks down at himself and shrugs like he doesn't see the problem. "She liked me before."

"Yeah. BEFORE. Before she was dating KADE freaking KASSAB. Okay? He's your competition now."

"He's an idiot."

I throw my arms out, exasperated. "I'm not saying he's a brain trust. But he looks like Mena Massoud. And he has boy-band hair.

And he can run an interception back thirty yards for a touchdown. So if you want Holly, you're going to have to let me do my job."

I punctuate the speech by grabbing the T-shirts back out of his arms. We glare at each other over the pile of cotton, both of us angry breathing. Without breaking eye contact, I pointedly drop the shirts on the floor at my feet. Noah flinches but doesn't look down.

We hold the stare-off for a few more silent beats. He blinks first.

"Fine." His jaw works. "Fine. You can give me *advice* on clothes and stuff. But I'm still going to be me. And if I don't see results by homecoming, I'm outing you."

"A week?! Not happening. Granting wishes takes time." My inner fact-checker brings up Vindhya, but I tell her not to interrupt me while I'm ranting. "I can guarantee results by Christmas."

"End of September."

"Thanksgiving."

"Fall break."

I hesitate, making quick calculations in my head. Fall break is about four weeks out. It'll be tight, especially for the likes of Noah, and I've got nothing to go on—I've never tried to grant a wish without a *glimpse* before. Plus I have to get a crown on Vindhya's head six days from now. On the other hand, it would be nice to get this on the "done" pile. And hey, I believe in me.

I give a curt nod. "Fine. You cooperate. I guarantee results by fall break." I jab my hand toward him to shake on it. He holds out his pinkie with an audible sigh. Either he's really committed to the pinkie swear, or this is the maximum skin-to-skin contact he can stomach. Like I care. I lock my finger with his. For reasons unfathomable to me, Noah looks profoundly sad the moment our fingers touch. Like he's lost a piece of his soul in the deal.

7

Families Are the Worst

*N*o sooner do we break the sad pinkie-link than my phone cheeps and the door opens in the same moment.

Noah's mom says, "I told you to leave this open, Noah. You've earned yourself poop duty."

A girl's voice calls, "Are you guys making out?"

Noah slaps his hand over his face and groans. "NO! Leave us alone."

Instead, they both walk in. His mom surveys the pile of clothes on the floor. "What is going on in here?"

This is not the first time I've run interference with parents. I volunteer, "We're doing a donation drive. It's part of the project Noah mentioned."

His mom picks up the WHERE NO MAN HAS GONE BEFORE shirt. "You aren't getting rid of your *Star Trek* T-shirts, are you? You love these."

"No. I'm not." He plucks the shirt from his mother's hand and stuffs it into his open dresser drawer. He bends down to pick up the rest, while she takes the shirt back out and folds it.

A girl I'm assuming is his little sister comes to stand between us. She looks to be in middle school, with braces and the family's signature curls. She chimes in, "Are you giving him, like, a *Queer Eye* makeover? He totes needs one."

Noah shoves her. "Get out of my room, plebe."

She sticks her tongue out at him. His mom tsks, continuing to fold and replace T-shirts. I smile at Kid Sister. "I don't think we've been introduced—"

Noah says, "Oh yeah. This is Charity. Charity, this is my sister, Nat the Brat." The way he says our names, he might as well have been introducing Loki to Thanos.

"Natalie," she corrects. "You seem way too hot to be hanging out with my brother."

I smile to make the next thing I say seem like a joke. "Well, he blackmailed me to get me here."

Natalie snorts.

Noah growls, "Seriously, *get out of my room*."

His mom says, "Okay, okay. We're going." She propels Natalie out the door, leaving it open a few inches.

Eight seconds of uncomfortable silence ensue. He breaks it with "Sorry about my family."

I cross my arms. "It's fine. They actually make you seem a tiny bit less like a budding domestic terrorist." I rock on my toes. "So. What's 'poop duty'?"

"When we piss off my mom, she makes us clean the cat's litter box." He crosses his arms.

I pull a face. "Ick."

Then I drop my arms, because his are crossed.

This is plain awkward—the two of us standing in the middle of his room, talking about cat poop, trying not to mirror each other. Besides, I have more work to do. I brush past Noah, sit on his toddler bed, and pull my phone out. There's a message from Sean: Call me.

Obviously, I can't call him right now with Noah and his whole family dogging my every step. It'll have to wait. I swipe away the text and open my browser. I glance up at Noah. "Wi-Fi?"

"The network is TrekkieFam. The password's, uh, 'stardate-2-2-8-5.' All one word."

Oh swell. The whole family is obsessed. I shake my head as I tap it in. Once it connects, I navigate to one of my favorite online shopping outlets.

Apparently to fill the silence, Noah asks, "So . . . what's the punishment of choice at your house?"

I'm caught off guard. I wasn't expecting him to ask about my life. To be honest, pretty much all my human interactions are based on what I can do for other people. My stuff never really comes up. I keep my eyes on the selection of trendy shirts on my phone. "There is none."

"You literally never get punished for anything?"

I shrug and add a button-down shirt to the cart.

He mutters, "That explains a lot."

I look up, eyes narrowed. "Don't do that. You don't know anything about my life."

"Then enlighten me."

"Nope. Backstory is not included in our arrangement." I return to picking out clothes. I'm on to jeans now.

The bed dips as he plants himself next to me. "Then you leave me no choice but to make assumptions."

I pry my eyes off the task at hand and level them at Noah. How is it possible for anyone to be *this* exasperating? "If you *must* know, my dad lives in DC and my mom's too busy for things like rules and consequences."

He grins. "That sounds awesome."

I train my eyes back on my phone and swipe away a pair of guy jeggings. "Well, it's not. It's not awesome."

He makes a *hmm* noise. For a few blessed seconds he says nothing. Then, "So what are we doing now?"

I don't bother looking up. "Buying you better clothes, of course."

The bed shifts as he settles back further. "Oh goodie. Are we going to do the shopping montage, where I try on all the outfits for you while a One Direction song plays?"

I roll my eyes. "No. I already picked out what you need. You're going to give me some form of payment, and, poof, it will arrive at your door in a few days. Magic." I hold out my hand and wiggle my fingers expectantly.

His brow knits. "How much is it?"

"Less than a vintage *Star Trek* action figure, I bet. Pony up."

Instead of handing me a piece of plastic, he takes my phone, looks through the items in the cart, and deletes two things, muttering, "Like you'd even know . . . I'm not wearing that . . . ridiculous . . ." He checks out with PayPal, making every finger motion an act of silent protest.

As soon as he gives the phone back, I get up and head for the door. He says, "That's it? I thought we would strategize or something."

I pause to pick up my purse at the doorway. "There's no 'we.' *I* strategize. *You* do what I tell you. Tomorrow starts phase two."

"What's phase two? What time tomorrow?"

"The fairy godmother isn't taking any questions." I take my sunglasses from my purse and slide them on. "Have fun with the litter box."

I'm out the door before he can irritate me further. All I want is to get to my car without any more family interactions. Instead I have to step over Natalie, who is sprawled on her stomach across the hallway, flipping through a magazine. She looks up with a metallic grin. "See you later, Noah's hot girlfriend."

"Just girl. Not friend." I don't stop to register her reaction.

His mom stands sentry at the bottom of the stairs. As I approach, she nods curtly. "Charity."

I tilt my chin. "Lisa."

I figure I'm in the clear outside the front door. But no. A middle-aged man is pushing a mower around the front lawn. He's tall and skinny like Noah—wearing a floppy fishing hat, Ray-Bans, plaid shorts, and a T-shirt that says MAKE IT SO. Now I know where Noah gets his fashion sense. When the man sees me, he shuts off the mower and approaches. I exhale in resignation.

"Well, hello there. I'm Paul, Noah's father." He takes off his hat, revealing a glistening bald head. He wipes a handkerchief across it and stuffs it in his pocket.

"Charity."

Awkward pause. I seriously consider *nudging* him to just walk away and let me leave. But before I've made up my mind, he says, "Nice to meet a friend of Noah's. Hey." He does the finger gun at me, pointing with his thumb up. "Take it easy on my boy, okay?"

I'm not sure what he means—probably "don't break his heart" or "wear a little more clothing"? At any rate, I fully intend to make Noah's life as miserable as possible for the next four weeks.

I smile and return the finger-gun point. Then I hightail it to my car, making sure not to look like I'm in a hurry. As I pull away, I can't help but think how *full* Noah's house seems . . . how interconnected his family's lives are. My heart aches inexplicably. I'm guessing it's annoyance-induced heartburn. That's probably a thing.

As I merge onto the freeway that leads to Memom's retirement community, I tell my phone to call Sean.

Four rings, and Sean's irritated voice fills my little car. "Ninety minutes later. Seriously, Charity?"

I should suck up, but the past thirty-six hours have been a real grind, and I'm crabby. I grunt, "I was busy."

"Whatever. You practically ghost me for two years, then turn around and ask me for a favor, and now I feel like you've dumped the whole thing on me and checked out."

"No, I haven't. I'm totally in it to win it." That possibly sounded sarcastic.

"Yeah? Because if you think I'm babysitting Vindhya for—"

"Of course not. I'm sorry. I'm here. I'm listening."

Sean sighs, makes me wait six more seconds just because he can, then says, "I was *going* to offer to do Dynamic Duos Day with our girl."

Damn it, I forgot about spirit week. I mentally string together six or seven of the worst words I know. How is it possible to forget something so all-encompassing, so vital to the entire JLHS social fabric? Noah has completely derailed me with his stalking and his blackmail and his tacky T-shirts and his pepper spray. . . .

"Hello?" Sean snaps when I don't immediately respond. "Please don't tell me you forgot about spirit week."

"What?! Pfft. Of course not."

"Because she needs to be fabulous."

"I know! Okay? I've got it handled!" It comes out accidentally snippy. I'm simultaneously lying and taking out my frustration on Sean.

He matches my nasty vibe and ups it by 10 percent. "Fine. So I guess you don't need my help."

Instant 180 time.

"Nononono. No. Sean. I'm sorry. PLEASE do Dynamic Duos with Vindhya." I can't afford to fall out of Sean's good graces. With everything else going on, I need his help to keep the Vindhya thing from going completely off the rails. I've never failed to make a *glimpse* come true before, and I'm not going to fail a Cindy now.

He clears his throat pointedly. I haven't groveled enough.

I try harder. "I can't do this without you. You're the magic man. And I'm just . . . just a hack of a fairy godmother." I pause to see if I've debased myself enough. There's no response, so I add, "And I'm sorry for snapping at you. And for not calling you right away. And for being so distant since . . . a while." He's still silent. I moan, "What? *Please?*"

"Yes, the SMU audition went super well. Thanks for asking."

I punch the air a dozen times, silently swearing some more. I totally forgot about his audition. This is why, traditionally, Cindies are cut loose after the destiny moment. Relationships are too messy. There are too many obligations. Too many opportunities to screw up.

I moan, "Oh my gosh. Sean! I want to hear all about it.

Sometime. Really soon. I know you're going to get in. They'd be fools not to accept you." I pause and add a tentative, "About Vindhya?"

"Fine. You don't deserve it. But I'll do it because I'm a giver."

"Thank you." I exhale with relief.

Sean declines to tell me about his specific plans for Dynamic Duos Day but assures me he will handle everything. We end the call, and I drive another three miles toward Memom. I really need to verbally vomit this whole Noah situation on her. I need her to reassure me that we really are the good guys and that all of Noah's wild accusations are just the rantings of a seriously unbalanced individual. I want her to tell me senile stories about how she faced some vaguely similar thing and kicked it to the curb.

But . . .

I have four spirit days to plan for, and I can't even remember what they are. Sean is right—Vindhya's participation in spirit week has to blow JLHS's collective hair back. On top of that, I have to keep my involvement under Noah's freakishly accurate radar or he'll publicly roast me. And, if that's not enough, I have a paper on serfdom and a crap ton of trig to slog through this weekend.

I take the next exit and get back on the freeway heading toward home. Seeing Memom will just have to wait.

JACK LONDON HIGH SCHOOL SPIRIT WEEK
GO WHITE WOLVES!

Monday: Literary Character Day
Dress to impress with the fictional best! Nominees for homecoming court will be announced at the spirit assembly.

Tuesday: We Are the World Day
Celebrate your cultural heritage! And don't forget to stop by the bake sale table hosted by the band boosters.

Wednesday: Sci-Fi Day
Use the Force or join the dark side! This is the last day to buy tickets to the homecoming formal. $50 each or $90 per couple.

Thursday: Dynamic Duos Day
Flaunt your fabulous with your bestie! Be sure to vote for homecoming court, and don't miss Cheer v. Poms powder-puff football at 5 p.m.! Tickets are $10.

Friday: JLHS Spirit Day
Bust out the purple and gray, White Wolves! Show us your school spirit! Varsity football against Corona High starts at 7 p.m. (JV at 4:30 p.m.). We'll crown the court at halftime, so come prepared to pay homage to this year's royalty!

Saturday
Hey, early birds, come cheer on the runners at our home cross-country meet at 6 a.m. Girls volleyball faces off with Jurupa Valley Prep at 11 a.m. Homecoming formal is 8–11 p.m. at the Mission.

8

Spirit Week Is the Actual Worst

Monday morning, I retrieve the crumpled flyer from the bottom of my locker, tearing it almost in half as I yank it out from under the textbooks. This would have been good to have over the weekend. But it's fine. I cobbled together outfits for today with intel gleaned from Scarlett.

My hair is cherry-Kool-Aid red, the ends dip-dyed Tang orange. I teased the waves into a wild mane of fire. I'm in black from my fingertips to my toes. Somewhere in this school, Vindhya is wearing a full-length lavender traveling cloak and a wispy crown Hope made from craft wire a few years go. I dug the ensemble out of Hope's closet on Saturday and took them to Vindhya's house. Not to brag, but she looks exactly like Arwen from *The Lord of the Rings*.

This is a BFD. I need to make sure Vindhya gets noticed this week if she's going to be a queen by Saturday. Sean is taking care of

Thursday, and she can rock cultural heritage day without any help from me. When I dropped off the Arwen costume, she showed me the rainbow of kurtas hanging in her closet. Friday is a no-brainer. So that just leaves Wednesday.

Sci-Fi Day. The Universe hates me. I smash the flyer into a ball to punish it for crossing me. But I can't afford any more screwups, so I smooth it out again and slide it into my backpack.

"What's your deal, Charity?" Scarlett's voice behind me is accusatory.

Well, crap, what else did I do wrong?

I wipe the scowl off my face and turn toward her with spirit-week-worthy enthusiasm, hoping to smooth over the problem, whatever it is. She and Gwen are rocking an Amazons of Paradise Island look. My stomach sinks. I must have missed the memo that the Poms were coordinating our costumes today. That's a huge infraction, because group identification is the heart and soul of spirit week.

Her hands go to her mini-skirt-armor-clad hips. "Why did you blow us off?"

"I, uh—"

Barely sparing me a glance before returning to her phone screen, Gwen mutters, "Who even are you? Lava Girl?"

"She's Katniss Everdeen. The girl on fire," Sean announces as he arrives. He's wearing a ruffled shirt, a cape, and a delicate black eye mask. He has a small red flower pinned to his collar.

"The Scarlet Pimpernel. You sexy beast." We trade European air-kisses, just like in the movie.

Scarlett looks ready to go to war.

Sean glances between us, registers my predicament, and—God bless him—comes to my rescue. He turns his most charming smile on Scarlett with a sweeping gesture toward both her and Gwen. "Ladies, you're gorgeous. And fierce. Please don't hurt me."

Gwen's eyes flick up and back to her phone, the corner of her mouth ticking upward. Scarlett breaks into a full-on smile, though.

Leveraging the better vibes, Sean deftly changes the subject. "Speaking of fierce, have you *seen* Vindhya Chandramouli yet?"

"What? No. Tell me." Scarlett's FOMO kicks in instantly.

"Words cannot describe it. You need to experience it." He leans in conspiratorially. "She was last seen in the courtyard."

"Let's check it out." Scarlett takes Gwen's arm and guides her away.

I breathe a sigh of relief as I watch them leave. "That was almost bad."

He arches an eyebrow. "*Now* you owe me."

"I mean, I could take them," I hedge, because fairy godmothers don't need help and we definitely don't owe anyone anything. "They aren't actual Amazon warriors."

"Yeah, but Scarlett could still end you—socially speaking."

"Anyway . . ." I reach back into my locker, fishing around for nothing in particular.

"Anyway," Sean parrots, blessedly dropping the "you owe me" issue. "Vindhya's Arwen costume is killing. Did you come up with it together?"

Honestly, it never even occurred to me to ask her. I'm used to doing things for people, not with people. All I say is "Ah, no. Just me."

I close my locker. As I twist the face of the lock to secure it, a male form lands against the locker next to mine. I register a white T-shirt and jeans and glance up to the face of Surya Agrawal. He's one of the three-sport jocks and the captain of the swim team—top of the food chain for the male population at JLHS. His hair is slicked back. I'm guessing he's repping *The Outsiders*.

He croons, "Charity?" The word weighs three hundred pounds.

I sigh.

From behind me, Sean quips, "This is turning a little too *Riverdale* for me. See you later, Charity." Before he's taken six steps, he's surrounded by half the volleyball team—all dressed as characters from *Alice in Wonderland*.

"Charity," Surya says again. "Will you go with me to the homecoming dance?"

He's all puppy eyes and pleading eyebrows. I would feel sorry for him if I thought this were real. Instead I say remorselessly, "Aw, Surya. I can't. Because you asked me all wrong. I mean, no flowers, no giant poster made of candy bars, no bad poetry . . . You didn't even get on one knee or hold a stereo over your head outside my window."

"But will you, though?"

"Really, no."

He grimaces. "Man. You're cold."

I grin. "What's the pool this year?"

The past three years, the jocks have egged each other on to ask me to the milestone events—homecoming, prom, spring sports banquet . . . that sort of thing. It started when I was a freshman because I was a new addition to the Poms squad, friendly, decently good-looking, and upheld an "always say no" policy about dating (or really any relationships). You know how it is—everyone wants what they can't have. So now they always ask, and I always make up some random reason to turn them all down. And the colder I am, the higher the stakes have gotten for the betting pool. I could spend all my time pissed about objectification and overinflated male egos, but really, what's the point? I choose to take it as a compliment.

Surya groans. "Come on. I'm asking for real."

"Sure you are." *No he's not.* "And I'm saying no for real." Because even if he was, the fairy godmother can't date. I'm here to lend a helping hand, not to get dragged into the drama. I smile to soften the blow. "But let's just imagine for a moment that I *had* said yes. What's the take this year?"

"The football team put in ten bucks each. I would have gotten the whole pot."

I pat his cheek. "Sorry, dude. It's *not* happening. But I'm very flattered that you asked." The one-minute warning tone sounds. I back into the flow of students heading to class and blow Surya a kiss before turning to join the current of humanity.

Every third person is wearing Hogwarts robes. There are also a good number of superheroes, so I guess comic books count as literature. Holly—Noah's crush—walks toward me, solidly pinned against Kade Kassab's side. Like Surya, Kade is dressed as a greaser from *The Outsiders*. Holly has on a circle skirt and a cute fifties neck scarf. My forehead immediately starts to thrum like it does whenever Holly's nearby.

Kade holds out his fist, and I bump it on the way past. Holly and I exchange a noncommittal smile. I keep moving with the crowd, only to notice Noah standing off to the side with his eyes trained on Holly's back. He's wearing his standard *Star Trek* T-shirt—no effort whatsoever to show solidarity with the rest of JLHS.

There's no way I'm going to talk to him at school. But I pull out my phone and shoot him a quick text: **Stop staring. You'll creep her out.**

He glances down at his phone, looks around, and finds me. I flick my hair. He pushes up his glasses, looking embarrassed that he got caught being pathetic. One point to the fairy godmother.

At 3:06 I get a text from Noah: **That was some twit skit. Brain cells withered and died every second it dragged on.**

Apparently, this is his way of paying me back for calling him out earlier. Well, he picked the wrong time to egg me on. We just finished the spirit assembly. It was not my favorite. The low point—to which Noah is clearly referring—was a staged dance-off between the Poms and cheerleaders to get people to buy tickets for the inherently sexist powder-puff football game. Jameela took the big fake trophy home for the cheerleaders with an obligatory tumbling run. We, the Poms, responded by chanting "We want a rematch!" Then we all danced together to the school fight song. It managed to be both trite and humiliating.

On the upside, Vindhya did get nominated to the homecoming court, and her posture was 90 percent great the whole time she stood up there. Everything's going according to plan.

Now I'm sitting on the bleachers in the mostly empty gym in the few minutes I have before Poms practice, desperately online shopping for something sci-fi fabulous. Vindhya has been no help. She's even more sci-fi averse than me, as implausible as that seems. She claims she's never even seen a sci-fi movie. I've scoured the web for *Star Wars*, *Guardians of the Galaxy*, and even *Star Trek*. But it's too last-minute. Nothing can get here by tomorrow night. I've got zilch. Nada. Nothing.

So tonight I have to go to the only year-round costume shop in a hundred-mile radius, after I spend the next hour practicing our routine for the homecoming halftime show. Then, by some miracle, I need to wrap my brain around freaking Euclidean vectors so that I don't fail Wednesday's trig test.

Noah texts me again: **Man, I just don't know who to cheer** for on Thursday—the bimbos or the airheads.

If pyrokinesis were my thing, my phone would be incinerated in my hand right now. I'm formulating a scathing response when the gym door opens and Noah walks in. He hunches his shoulders a little when he walks, ducking his head the way guys do when they're fresh off a massive growth spurt—like he's afraid he'll scrape his head on the ceiling. The fairy godmother in me immediately starts to plan walking lessons, while I simultaneously concoct scalding remarks and physical torments worthy of my archenemy. I give pyrokinesis one more try as I watch him approach. Disappointingly, he does not burst into flames.

He approaches with impunity and plants himself right next to me, but one row down. I growl low in my throat.

Without looking at me, he says, "So you got my texts, then."

I respond without moving my lips, ventriloquist-style. "What the effing crap? I told you to stop texting me and to never, *ever* talk to me at school."

"You didn't actually come right out and say—"

"It was heavily implied. I'm serious. Get away from me. You're going to blow our cover."

As per usual, he ignores my totally reasonable request. Instead of leaving, he rests his elbows on the bench next to me and leans back so that his mop of curls brushes my arm. He says, "When do we make our first move with Holly?"

I release a breath through clenched teeth. "You aren't remotely ready. Maybe in a couple weeks. Also, every ignorant text I get from you sends your reunion meeting floating farther downstream."

Actually, the real reason is that I'm too busy with Vindhya to deal with his wish right now. But as soon as my schedule clears, I plan to devise an assortment of torments for Noah before granting his wish. It's important he regret messing with me enough to never try a stunt like this again.

He runs one hand through his hair, clearly frustrated. "She should be going to the dance with *me*. Not that . . . Ken doll."

"That ship has sailed, *Cap*. Concentrate on the big picture."

"Which is what? Letting you turn me into a fake hipster for the next four weeks?"

Oh yes. And more.

Scarlett and Gwen enter the gym through the locker room door, ready for practice in compression pants and athletic tanks. Gwen starts warm-up stretches, casting curious glances at Noah while she lunges. I sigh. The only thing Gwen loves almost as much as her phone is boys. All boys. She's so obsessed that she'll check out any male—even Noah, of all people.

Scarlett scans the room, sees us, and marches toward us like she wants an exclusive. With only seconds till contact, my desperation to contain the destructive force that is Noah spikes. I hiss, "I don't know you. We weren't talking. Say nothing, and leave casually."

I see him straighten in my peripherals. "Just slink away? No way. I'd look like a noob."

"Don't say 'noob.' Now go."

I work up a *nudge* for him.

Too late. Scarlett stands in front of us, hands on hips. "Ummm, Charity? Practice? And . . . who's the . . . guy?"

"Guy?" I look around like I didn't notice anyone was sitting near me. "Oh! Him? No idea."

He stands and holds his hand out to Scarlett. "Noah."

She doesn't shake his hand. "O-*kay*, Noah. We're going to have practice in here now, and we don't really let people watch. So you're going to have to . . . you know . . ."

"Close my eyes?"

"Leave."

He points at her. "That was my next guess."

I am on the brink of both dying of mortification and combusting with anger when Scarlett actually, inexplicably, laughs. It's a quick chuckle, but I'd swear it's genuine. The corners of her eyes crinkle, and she says, "You're kinda funny."

What was that head tilt for?

He says, "Thanks?"

"Scarlett." She gives him her name like a gift. Noah's eyes flit toward me, his cheeks pinking up like the day I met his mom.

Dude, it's a name. Get a grip.

Scarlett blinks more times than strictly necessary. "Sorry to make you clear out." She smiles again, bigger this time. "Thanks for being cool about it."

Un-freaking-believable! My eyes dart from Scarlett to Noah as I try desperately to make sense of this. He pushes up his glasses with a self-conscious grin, and it's dorky. But, like, sweet dorky. I guess he isn't completely vile. His face is symmetrical at least.

Fine. He's adorable. He looks like Ross Lynch. But it can't make up for his evil, blackmailing soul.

Coach shouts for us to bring it in, and Scarlett jogs away. Noah hoists his backpack over his shoulder. The moment is gone as suddenly as it struck.

I follow quickly behind Scarlett, not willing to risk the wind sprints that dawdling would earn me.

But all through practice, my mind whirls with previously unimaginable possibilities. Maybe Noah wasn't totally wrong. Perhaps there's a slight possibility—and we're talking fractions of a percent here—that a girl who could be with anyone would choose him. As is.

9

Fairy Godmothers Do *Not* Need Help. Except Maybe Just This One Time.

Two hours later, I'm staring down the guy with a shaggy hipster beard and black eyeliner who works at Comics 'n Costumes. And I'm thinking, *I probably should have seen this coming.*

He gestures noncommittally at the cleared-out shelves and mumbles, "Sorry. The last week has been like a bantha stampede. I could get something here for you by . . ." He taps a few keys on his computer. "Friday."

"Thanks anyway," I growl. Even though this isn't his fault, I barely hold back my inner tigress as I jam my sunglasses back on my face. He hopes I have a nice day.

I take my frustration out on my gas pedal. When I get home, I text every girl on the Poms and cheer squads, Sean, and several jocks the same message: **Any chance you have an extra costume for sci-fi day?** It's humiliating to ask for help. And, as it turns out, pointless. No one can help me. I'm not surprised. I mean, who keeps spare sci-fi costumes lying around?

Your friendly neighborhood Stalker Trekkie. That's who.

I refuse to stoop that low.

Instead I follow the scent of Vietnamese takeout to the kitchen. Mom and I have a "working dinner." (That means she responds to texts and emails the whole time we're eating and dismisses me with "Sorry, hon. Lots of fires to put out tonight.") Then, before bed, I wrestle down my homework.

Sci-Fi Day haunts me in my dreams. My phone's chirp interrupts dream Vindhya wailing, "My wish is dead. Everything's ruined. You *failed me*."

The phone chirps again, and I automatically reach for it. The screen says 6:08 a.m. and displays a text from Noah: **Are you wearing a tooth fairy costume for cultural heritage day?**

I throw my phone across the room with a primal roar. It lands in a pile of dirty laundry. But it doesn't stay there long.

By six forty-five I'm getting texts from Vindhya. She tries on a dozen kurtas trying to decide what to wear. Then she moves on to sending pictures of her hair because she can't get it to look exactly like Tuan did.

To avoid a complete meltdown, I offer to meet her in the locker room before school for a strategy session. So even though I want to crawl back under the covers and sleep for the rest of the day, and even though my head is pounding, I pull myself together in time to get to school twenty minutes early.

Vindhya is alone in the locker room when I get there, following a makeup tutorial video with a shaking hand. She's lighting it up in a gorgeous orange kurta and pink leggings. When she sees me, she sets her phone and makeup brush aside. "Charity, I don't know if I can do this. I think I'm going to throw up."

"You did 'this' yesterday. Nothing has changed." I take a seat on the bench across from her. I don't get it—she stuck the landing yesterday, and she can't know that Sci-Fi Day is an impending disaster. So why the freak-out?

"Everything has changed! Everyone is judging me now. Everyone is comparing me to Jameela and Shannon and What's Her Name. I don't know what I'm doing. I can't—"

"Hey. You're *fine*." I take her hand. She looks like she's going to cry.

I *nudge* some confidence her way.

She says, "Did you just wink at me?" But she immediately sits a little straighter.

"What? Oh. It's allergies." I pretend to sniff. "You've got this."

"Yeah. I can do this."

"Just remember: squeeze your pencil, do not touch your face, and do whatever Sean says."

"It's weird. I can code like a boss and play a symphony, but this being-in-the-spotlight thing—" She picks up her makeup brush and evens out her blush. "This is way more pressure than I thought it would be."

She starts to sag. The magical confidence boost is wearing off fast. I *nudge* her again, smacking my hands against my legs to drum out the pins and needles. "You're doing great. How do you feel?"

"Kind of—" She raises her eyebrows like the answer is unexpected. "Better, actually."

"Then let's go."

Walking out of the bathroom is an event. All the people I usually say hi to notice that I'm with someone new. And I take the opportunity to *nudge* lots of pro-Vindhya feelings their way, even though all my limbs are numb from the effort.

Vindhya sees their smiles and curious looks and smiles back in a forced way.

Ah well, it's the best we can do for now. At least her hands are at her sides.

After second hour, Sean posts a selfie with Vindhya.

I check my phone while I'm standing in the lunch line and smile to myself. The Sean-Vindhya selfie has twenty-eight likes. Not too shabby.

My smile drops when an all-too-familiar voice behind me says, "Let me guess, your cultural heritage is 'white trash'?"

I glance down at myself. I'm wearing the same outfit as all the Poms today—cutoffs so short that the pockets hang out the bottom and an American-flag tank top.

The lunch line inches forward.

"All-American girl, actually." I turn around, ready for a fight, and give him a once-over. "And I see you went with 'alien species'?"

He looks affronted. I tally one point in my column. He smooths a hand over his T-shirt, which says I'M GIVING HER ALL SHE'S GOT, CAPTAIN. "You have no idea how much *Star Trek* has influenced our culture. Cell phones were based on the communicators. The first NASA orbiter was named after the USS *Enterprise*. Public interest in the space program was—"

I feign nodding off, complete with snoring, then jerk awake. I know I'm being rude, but he brings it out in me, you know? The line moves forward. I grab an orange juice. "Sorry. That's fascinating. No. Really."

Surya and Gwen show up then, saving me from having to hear more *Star Trek* trivia. Surya is in the middle of saying, "... Wolverine. It's going to be awesome!"

Gwen gushes, "Wow! How long did that take you?" Surya asked her to homecoming, so she's fawning. It's the only thing that could make her tear her eyes from her phone for this long.

He says, "Like two weeks." He holds out his fist and I bump it with mine. "Hey, Charity!"

"Hey, Surya. Hi, Gwen."

Gwen says, "Hey. We were just planning our Sci-Fi Day looks. Do you know how few freaking black girls are actually in sci-fi? And most of the time, if they're there at all, they're painted green or something. Like, I could count on one hand the black female characters who aren't Wakandan."

"Really?" I did not know that and am genuinely disgusted. "That's total crap."

"Uhura," Noah says. We all look at him like, *If you're going to butt in, at least speak English.*

"*U-hur-a,*" he repeats more slowly, which helps not at all. He looks at us like he's waiting for our brains to come online. Then gives up with a disappointed tsk. "Starfleet officer, fluent in *all three* Romulan dialects, first interracial kiss on television." He pauses to gauge our reactions. I stare at him blankly. He gives me stink eye. "She's one of a hundred reasons why TOS is awesome."

I don't know what TOS is, but I don't want to ask and send him on another geek tangent. Plus, does it matter?

Gwen tilts her head, like she's not sure what to make of Noah. "That's . . . cool." Then she turns back to me and Surya. "Anyway, we're doing an X-Men theme. I'm going as Storm. Do you think I can pull off a white wig?"

"Totally."

"What about you?" she asks.

"Me?"

"Yeah, are you ready for Sci-Fi Day?"

I casually turn back toward the buffet. "Yup. All set." I hope that didn't sound as fake as it felt. The truth is, I have zero plan.

"Okay." Gwen hesitates. "'Cuz after your text last night—"

"No. Yeah. I got it squared away." I grab a soft pretzel.

"Okay." She shrugs. "So I'll see you at practice."

"See ya."

As Gwen and Surya walk away, Noah scoffs, "Sci-Fi Day. Ridiculous."

"Right?" I agree. We both reach for the same apple. I jerk my hand away just in time to avoid brushing against his fingers. My heart thumps as if cooties are a real biohazard. I grab a different apple, then finally register the anomaly in our conversation. "Wait. *You* think Sci-Fi Day is ridiculous?"

"Pfft. Yeah. X-Men? *Star Wars?* Please."

"What's your problem with *Star Wars?*"

"Only that it's not sci-fi. It's a soap opera set in space. For something to be sci-fi, there has to be actual science involved. I mean, come on, a lightsaber defies the laws of physics. And the entire fandom has spent forty years backfilling story lines because George Lucas didn't know a parsec is a unit of distance, not time."

I make a face like, *You're redlining the geek-o-meter again*, but really I never thought about that before. It's a tiny bit interesting.

Then my mouth goes dry with the now undeniable knowledge that he's my last best hope to salvage Sci-Fi Day for Vindhya. Not only is asking for his help humiliating and degrading, but there's a 99 percent chance that it will alert him to my secret wish-granting activities. The last time he got mad at me for granting wishes, I ended up writhing in a puddle of my own snot and tears.

Okay . . . there has to be something else I can do. Vindhya could stay home sick tomorrow. We could let Sci-Fi Day flop, and then I could . . . I could straight-up cheat. I could stuff the ballot boxes. But it's mobile voting. I could hire a hacker to rig the system.

Ugh. What have I become?

Not this.

We've reached the cashier. She scans my ID and waves me on.

Instead of escaping to the table where Sean and Vindhya are waiting for me, I grit my teeth, turn back to Noah, and say, "So . . . speaking of Sci-Fi Day . . . Ineedyerelp."

"What?"

"I need . . . yer*elp*."

A slow, obnoxious smile of understanding spreads across his face. He cups his hand around his ear. "I couldn't quite hear that. You need my *what?*"

I wrench the words from my parched throat. "Your. Help."

Grinning like the Cheshire cat, he pops a tater tot into his mouth and chews pensively. I squirm. Finally he starts walking toward an empty table, forcing me to follow like a pathetic puppy. He says way too loud, "What could the fairy godmother—"

"Sshh!"

"—need my help with?"

"I was hoping maybe I could borrow a costume from you? For tomorrow? Please?"

For a moment he looks like, *You've got to be kidding me,* but then his eyes glint with humor. He's enjoying my humiliation way too much—not that I can really blame him. He lifts his chin. "I guess I could loan you something."

I release the breath I've been holding. That was easier than I thought it would be. "Okay, I'll come over after practice."

"I'll be at work. I get off at eight."

I didn't even know he had a job. Not that it matters, because I couldn't care less about the details of his existence. Ten to one he works at a comic book store. But I say, "Sounds good. See you then."

I move to walk away, but he stops me with a "Hey!"

"Huh?"

"What about Holly?"

"What about her?" I ventriloquist whisper, really, really wishing he wouldn't keep bringing this up at school. But I make an extra effort to overlook the offense, since I need his help with the costume.

"When do we make a move?"

"Just chill. I'm working on it." By which I mean, I *will* work on it. Eventually. I just have to get through homecoming first.

10

It's Not Stealing.
It's High-Stakes Borrowing.

The lights are on at Noah's. As I approach the door, I can hear laughter from inside—happy family noises that never occur at my house. Especially not now that the one person I might have laughed with is never coming home. The sound makes me want to turn around and go back to my car, maybe call Hope and see what she's having for breakfast. But I need this costume. We're at DEFCON 1.

I ring the bell and wait. Noah opens it before I have time to even pull my phone out and mess with it. He's wearing black pants and a partially untucked white undershirt, and he's slouching more than usual.

From within the house, his sister's voice wails, "BETRAYAL! How could you do this to your only daughter?!"

I don't try to mask my attempt to see what's happening—like rubbernecking at a car crash. Noah glances over his shoulder, then back at me. "Uh. They're playing Settlers of Catan. It can get pretty brutal."

I pull a face that says, *Like I care.* He steps aside to let me enter. As we head up the stairs, Noah calls, "Charity's here. We'll be in my room."

His mom's voice responds, "Not too late, okay? It's a school night."

What are we, eight?

Anyway, I'm not staying long. This is a precision strike—get in, get the goods, and get out. I just texted Vindhya that I would drop her costume off before ten.

When we get to Noah's room, I'm immediately sidetracked by an enormous orange-striped cat. It weaves in and out of my legs, pushing against my shins with the side of its face on each pass. I squat to scratch behind its ears, and it rumbles its approval.

"Wow. Dr. McCoy likes you." He sounds surprised that anyone would feel that way about me.

"Well, animals have a sixth sense about people's character." That's the gospel according to Hope.

Noah doesn't miss a beat. "Yeah, that's dogs. This cat gravitates toward sewer rats and Nazi sympathizers."

I stand, fists clenched. Dr. McCoy looks slighted and sidles out the door. With great effort I keep my voice calm. "Costume?"

His lips curl into a disturbingly mischievous smile. "Right. I've got just the thing." He disappears into the closet for a moment, emerges with a green vinyl monstrosity, and holds it out to me. "Okay, here we go."

I clamp my hands behind my back and grit out, "That's a Godzilla costume."

"Wrong. It's Gorn. I wore this to Comic-Con last year. It was a huge hit."

"What else do you have?"

"This is it. Sorry." He doesn't sound sorry. At all.

Wrong answer. I wink a *nudge* his way—a mental SOS.

"Do you have something in your eye?"

It's not working—I'm too overwrought. I haven't really slept in days. I've come to my mortal enemy for mercy. I cannot send Vindhya to school in a Godzilla costume. And the countdown to total social self-destruct is at T-minus ten hours. Frustration and mortification press hard at the backs of my eyes. I will myself not to cry, but my next words sound a little too much like pleading. "I'm sorry for being snarky before. Okay? But *please.* You must have something else."

Noah thrusts the Godzilla costume toward me. "Come on. You hate it now, but wait till you try it on."

I squeeze my eyes closed and slowly shake my head. In a second I'll start moaning and rocking. He can defeat me now with one cutting remark, one well-aimed accusation.

But then there's a hand on my shoulder. "Hey." Noah's voice pierces my run-up to a nervous breakdown, softer than I've ever heard it. When I open my eyes, he's looking at me thoughtfully. "Look who turned out to be human."

From behind his glasses, he studies me like a puzzle. Then he says, "I don't get it. Why do you care so much? It's just a spirit day."

I press my lips together and shrug, still channeling all my energy into maintaining composure. If I speak, I'll crack.

Because for me it's *not* just a spirit day. My whole life is crumbling around me. All I have left is my Cindy. I need her. I mean, I need to do this for her. She needs me. And I've got *nothing left*.

His hand is still on my shoulder, and that touch is unexpectedly helpful in holding me together.

"Okay. Come on." He turns away, dropping his hand, and takes a few steps. I don't move. He stops at the door and gestures for me to follow him. "Let's go, Tinker Bell."

I follow stiffly—a cardboard cutout of myself. Noah pauses in front of a hall closet and opens the bifold doors. He shoots me a smile that's more good humor than malice and says, "Maybe one of these will work."

I close the gap between us and look into the closet. There are at least two dozen *Star Trek* costumes hanging inside. I gasp and clap both hands to my chest. Joy and triumph revive me in an instant. I round on Noah and punch him in the arm at 75 percent of full force. "You jerk!"

He rubs his arm. "Sorry I messed with you. I really wanted to see you in the Gorn costume, though."

I laugh—pure relief. "Never in a million years."

"And you know I'm only helping you to grease the gears on the Holly thing, right?"

"Fair enough."

"Truce?" He holds out his hand, and I shake it gratefully. The touch is warm and firm and feels like the beginning of better things.

"Behold, the lord of all Catan!" Noah's mom loudly announces herself with a grand sweep up the stairs. Noah and I drop our handshake, probably more hastily than the situation calls for.

"Gloaters aren't *real* winners!" Nat's voice calls up after her.

His mom—Lisa—laughs maniacally, *mwah, ha, ha.* Then she switches it off and turns her attention to us. "What are we doing in the cosplay closet?"

It's ridiculous that "cosplay closet" is a thing here. But I love it just a little.

Noah says, "Can Charity borrow one of your costumes for Sci-Fi Day at school tomorrow?"

Lisa gives him a look like, *Is that girl our friend now?* Noah grins reassuringly, and her look changes to surprised acceptance. "Okay. Let me in here."

She elbows her way between us and starts forcing apart tightly packed hangers.

My internal family-entanglements alarm goes off. The thing is on a hair trigger. I mean, with relationships as short-lived as mine are, involving family makes endings way too messy. So many questions and hurt feelings. No thanks.

As Lisa clucks over costumes and how big around I probably am, I tell myself to chill. I'm just here for a costume. It's strictly business. No bonds are forming.

One by one, she drapes minidresses in mustard, blue, and red over her arm. "Let's see," she says, holding the blue one up to me. "I think these will fit you. But what color?" She calls down the stairs, "NAT! PAUL! What color uniform should Charity wear?"

Without missing a beat, two voices from downstairs call back, "RED!"

Lisa glances at Noah as if this is a controversial answer. But Noah says with a little smirk, "Definitely red."

"If you say so." Lisa hands me the dress.

I like the red. So why do I feel like I'm missing the joke? I decide voicing the question could create a Pandora's box situation, so I just shut up and take the dress. I remind myself it's for Vindhya and my problems don't matter.

But Noah and company still think they're outfitting me.

"You'll need black boots and tights to go with that." Lisa sizes me up. "What size shoe do you wear?" Without waiting for my answer, she gets down on her knees in the closet and crawls halfway in.

"I have boots, actually," I say to Lisa's backside. "Thank you so much for the dress, though. This is gr—"

"MOM!" Nat comes thundering up the stairs in pajamas, headgear, and glasses. "What about Deanna Troi?"

Lisa's head emerges from the uniforms. "You think?"

"Yeah. Charity would look amazeballs in that."

Lisa stands up and takes down a peacock-blue dress. It's long-sleeved, full-length, daringly low cut, has a thigh-high slit, and comes complete with matching leggings. "What do you think?"

I think it's majestic. Perfect for a future homecoming queen. I smile broadly as I take it from her and drape it over me. Vindhya will look amazing in this. I look down and go, "Wow!"

"Wow," Noah echoes softly.

Nat rolls her eyes. "Need a drool bib, Noah?"

"Shut it, Bratalie."

"You two, stop it," Lisa commands. She sizes me up and concedes, "Yeah. You should wear it. But be *really* careful with it, okay? I had this custom made. This dress is my baby."

"I thought I was your baby." Natalie pouts.

Lisa squeezes her face and coos, "You *are* my baby. But *you* don't have to be dry-cleaned for fifty bucks a pop. Speaking of which . . ." She sniffs Natalie's hair. "When's the last time you took a shower?"

I feel sick to my stomach, and I try not to look into anyone's eyes—90 percent because the family stuff is so awkward. But 10 percent because I feel guilty for taking this dress under false pretenses. Okay, FINE! It's mostly the guilt thing. But I have no choice. My Cindy is in need. I'm only doing what has to be done.

Mercifully, Lisa shoos Natalie off to bed (or shower or whatever), tells me to take home both dresses to try on, and disappears down the hall. Noah walks me to the front door and says, "So, good night. See you tomorrow, I guess."

I accidentally make eye contact, and, you know, it's not that bad. Noah's looking at me like maybe we don't have to be archenemies.

I should tell him I'm borrowing the dress for Vindhya. I should seize the moment and come clean. But he's such an anti-wish-granting zealot. I can't risk it. Besides, why complicate the cease-fire?

So I say brightly, "Okay. Thanks again. Good night."

Then I get in my car and drive straight to Vindhya's.

11

I'm Not Crying. Who's Crying?

The house smells like coffee when I wake up for school the next morning, and I'm so tired that I decide to drink some. There's a note on the kitchen counter: *Left early for work. Have a great day. Love you.* —*Mom*

Leaving the note untouched, I pour a cup of coffee and take one tiny, bitter sip. Bluch. It's not worth it. I dump the rest out and resign myself to feeling like crap.

After a long shower and primping routine—complete with stripping the red out of my hair and recoloring it bubble-gum pink—I do feel a smidge better. I don the red *Star Trek* minidress, put my pink hair in a French twist, and slip on black knee-high boots. Mirror-me reflects back a tired but satisfied smile. Objectively speaking, I'm crushing the *Star Trek* thing.

There are several messages from Noah waiting when I retrieve my phone.

7:03: Not to be creepy, but how does the dress look?

7:04: My mom wants to know.

7:06: Forget it. Nat said that was totally creepy.

7:07: I mean, I realize what's creepy. My sister doesn't have to tell me.

It's ridiculous how much these texts mess me up. Guilt about taking the Deanna Troi dress under false pretenses floods me all over again, accompanied by the bleak certainty that Noah's and my fragile truce can't survive the day. At some point in the next few hours he'll realize how I used him, and I can't expect him to forgive me for it. He might even publish the Cindy list when he realizes I'm still granting wishes.

Unless he loves Holly enough to keep our bargain anyway. Strangely, this thought doesn't make me feel much better. It mostly makes me realize that she's the one who's supposed to be getting his random dorky texts in the morning. Not me.

At the same time, I'm imagining what must have been happening at Noah's house while these texts were written—everyone eating breakfast while his mom and sister offer less-than-useful advice. It's hilarious and adorable. And so completely the opposite of my silent, empty house. I stare at my phone, feeling nervous and happy and guilty and lonely and . . . damn it, I'm crying.

The perfectly flippant reply is obviously: Don't worry about it. You've been way creepier. 😉

A tear drips onto the phone screen as I hit send—almost 100 percent because I didn't get enough sleep. Anyway, I end up having to totally redo my makeup before school.

⸻

By third period, social media blows up with Vindhya as Deanna Troi. The chances of Noah not noticing what became of his mother's dress get slimmer with every new repost. But there's nothing I can do about that now. The fairy godmother has to put her Cindy above everyone and everything else.

At lunch a jock named Pablo asks me to the dance, complete with flowers and a candy poster. It goes like this:

Me: This is so sweet. But you're just not my type.

Pablo: Come on, Charity. You're the Ice Princess. Who *is* your type?

Me: Well, ballet dancers, *of course.* Also Italian soccer players and, um, John Cho.

Pablo: Who's John Cho?

Me: He was in . . . never mind.

Star Trek. He was in *Star Trek.* And I'm dressed like a freaking starship *Enterprise* go-go dancer. How did I get here?

I manage to shake it off and proceed with my day. I actually catch myself scanning the halls and the lunchroom for Noah. At first I want to punch myself in the head, but then I realize that if I can talk to him *before* he flips out about the Deanna Troi thing, I can make sure he doesn't out my Cindies by reminding him that he still needs my help to get back with Holly. So that is the one and only reason I look for him everywhere all day.

I wonder if he's wearing one of the other costumes from the cosplay closet. Maybe he's in science-officer blue. Or (God forbid) the Gorn costume. Anyway, I don't see him.

Not that I care.

Then, at 1:58, I get a text from Noah. It's a photo of Vindhya as Deanna Troi. The message says: You are in breach of contract.

Busted.

Another text swoops in a second later: I can't believe I helped you.

My cheeks burn, and my stomach twists. What is this feeling?

Remorse

Regret

Shame

All of the above

You know what? I don't even have time for a pop quiz on human psychology right now. I silence my phone and go to class.

12

Revenge Is Revoltingly Sweet

Somehow, I get through the rest of Wednesday and a whole night of anxiety-induced insomnia, cover it all with makeup, and present myself at school on Thursday morning wearing a mask of total confidence. The internet hasn't blown up with a JLHS Cinderella Tell-All, so I'm still waiting to see what Noah's next play is.

Sean and Vindhya show up at my locker about five seconds after I get there looking like they stepped right out of the Great Depression. Sean's wearing a three-piece suit and a fedora. Vindhya has on a red dress and a beret, her dark hair wound into a tight twist. She looks less enthusiastic than I would like but manages to wave and smile when Scarlett and Gwen pass by dressed as a very girlie Batman and Robin.

I wave too, and then turn back to Sean and Vindhya. "You're Bonnie and Clyde." They are perfection.

Sean takes a bow and then surveys me. I've cut apart white and black tank tops and sewn them back together in the yin-yang. Yes, I am a duo unto myself. The fairy godmother stands alone. Sean gives the ensemble an approving nod.

Meanwhile, Vindhya is gesturing behind his back: *you—me—bathroom—now*. I respond with an eyebrow quirk. She tacks on a little prayer-hands *please* and a pleading look.

Sean says, "Okay, Bonnie, we have two more hallways to hit before the bell."

"Okay. I just need to use the bathroom first." Vindhya shoots me one more meaningful look. I excuse myself and join her.

Two girls dressed as Salt-N-Pepa are touching up their makeup. I wash my hands slowly and wait for them to leave. Vindhya paces in front of the stall doors.

After the girls finish their lipstick and adjust their funky eighties hats, they walk out. I dry my hands. As the door closes behind them, Vindhya thrusts her phone at me. "Did you see this?"

I scroll through the comments on the photos of Vindhya's various looks from the past three days. It's mostly good, but the standard negativity has crept in. Some people are calling her a poseur, pointing out every little flaw . . . that sort of thing.

I hand the phone back. "It's just trolls. Ignore them."

"No! This isn't what it's supposed to be like."

"What is 'it'?"

"Everyone is supposed to love me."

I bite my lip, unsure how to handle this. Should I tell her that there's no way to make *everyone* love anybody or anything? That there are always going to be people who get off on criticizing and cutting down anyone who stands out in any way—whether it's because of her brains or her beauty?

I'm too tired and my head is buzzing. I put a Band-Aid on it with a quick *nudge* of positivity and hustle her back out to Sean. He can talk her down when the *nudge* wears off. She just needs to keep it together for one more day. Tomorrow night she gets the crown and starts her Happily Ever After.

I go out for lunch to make sure I don't run into Noah in the cafeteria. Then I hide in the locker room before Poms practice until I hear the warm-up music start. I'm not scared to face him. I just want to make it happen on my terms. My plan is to avoid him until after the game tomorrow night. Then, once I can honestly say I'm done working with Vindhya, I'll return the *Star Trek* costumes, complete with a huge apology and a whole bag of cream cheese croissants from Inland Empire Bakery.

I barely have time to recover from Poms practice before the powder-puff game. I'm not half-bad, although I couldn't tell you what position I'm supposedly playing. I actually catch the ball a couple of times. Even though it's technically flag football, we end up hitting each other and the ground kind of a lot. The Poms beat the cheerleaders 17–13, and the crowd goes wild.

Afterward, both teams go out for ice cream to celebrate together. Thirty-five dirty, sweaty girls in JLHS T-shirts pile into the Arctic Marble Creamery, ready to stuff ourselves with hot-fudge sundaes and concrete mixers. Which is how I find out where Noah works.

He works here. Right now.

He's wearing a pink-and-spring-green button-up shirt, an ice-cream-smeared apron, and latex gloves. He's wielding an ice cream spade, and he has a pink-and-green ball cap crammed over his hair with unruly curls fanning out along the bottom. He's currently asking Jameela what she wants mixed in with her ice cream. After she orders, he chops up a candy bar on the frozen slab of marble behind the glass, like a ninja chef. He throws a scoop of ice cream on top and proceeds to cut and scrape the concoction together. Then he shovels it into a plastic cup and adds a pink spoon with an überdorky flourish that makes her giggle.

He catches sight of me as he hands Jameela her order, and his eyes hold none of the friendliness of Tuesday night. In fact, I would put the look somewhere in the realm of *prepare to die*. Then he turns his attention to the next customer.

As the line moves forward, I become increasingly uncomfortable. I don't know how Noah plans to punish me for not telling him about Vindhya. But I do know that he currently has an audience with the entirety of the Poms and cheer squads, if he chooses this moment to out me.

There's a whisper in my ear. "Is everything okay with you and Noah?"

I jerk my head around. It's Carmen. She's looking at me like, *Why are Mommy and Daddy fighting?*

Instead of responding, I loudly change the subject. "Hey, you QB'd like a boss tonight, Carmen."

She looks sheepish. "I play in the backyard with my brothers a lot."

Gwen has been staring at her phone since the moment the game ended. She looks up long enough to say, "And Angie with the interception! What?!"

Pretty soon everyone is talking about the game. Awkward question officially dodged.

But Noah is glaring at me hard enough to melt all the ice cream in this room. I shoot him a quick *not now* look and then avert my eyes. I'm three people from the front of the line and getting more uneasy by the minute. Any hope I had for talking this out in private evaporates. Noah's about to turn state's witness in front of JLHS's collective social jury.

This would be the perfect time for a quick exit. As the girl in front of me orders, I consider my options for escape:

1. Fake emergency text. Estimated time required to pull out phone, make a big deal, arrange alternate rides for the girls I brought here, and walk out the door: 125 seconds. Pros:

Relatively easy to fake. Cons: Slow and clunky. High drama. Way too big a window for Noah to call me out.

2. Phantom nausea. Time required to double over and run out the door: 12 seconds. Pros: Quick and easy to pull off. Cons: Potential pregnancy rumors.

3. *Nudge* somebody to pull the fire alarm. Time required to wink the temptation into someone's head: 2 seconds. Pros: Extremely effective and untraceable. Cons: Pins and needles for a couple minutes and a lifetime of guilt feelings for getting someone in a crap ton of trouble.

"Charity?" Carmen prods me from behind. "Your turn."

I snap out of it and face off with Noah over the cash register. Intriguingly, his eyes aren't just one color—they're a starburst of bright green, clear blue, and light brown. *Like stirred-up mud puddles,* I tell myself resolutely.

Said muddy eyes have a dangerous glint in them. Under different circumstances, I'm fairly certain he would take me down with pepper spray right now. My eye twitches, but I don't look away.

Scarlett squeezes in next to me. "We know this guy, Charity. Remember? He was creeping on our practice a few days ago." She says it with a smile in her voice. She leans toward him over the counter. "So you work here?"

Noah is forced to break the stare-off to look at Scarlett.

Without missing a beat, he says, "No. I work at Tastee Freez."

Scarlett laughs. "Really?"

Noah raises his eyebrows. I rub the spot between mine.

Scarlett looks from me to him, still oblivious of the number of stereotypes she's perpetuating. Then she makes an *I figured it out* face. "You two *do* know each other, don't you?"

Noah motions toward me with his ice cream spade. "Yeah. Actually, she comes in here all the time. You'd be amazed at the secrets I know about Charity."

Scarlett looks hungry—like she's on the brink of a Pulitzer. I press my lips together. Noah and I lock eyes again.

Mine say, *Have mercy.*

His say, *Payback time.*

He moves to the stone slab and dips his spade into one of the tubs. "For instance, I know that Charity secretly loves cotton candy ice cream."

I really wanted a hot-fudge sundae. But if me eating cotton candy ice cream makes Noah feel like justice has been done, so be it. I remain perfectly still.

He says, "And I know all her favorite toppings." He ladles some blueberries into the dish. Fine, I'll eat blueberries on my cotton candy ice cream.

He picks up a squeeze bottle of caramel sauce. Blueberries and caramel? Who does that? My tongue feels violated just thinking about it. I *nudge* him to stop. He pauses for a long moment before shaking his head and proceeding to squirt on an obnoxious amount of caramel.

Scarlett and Carmen are enthralled. Gwen pokes her head into the huddle, scrunches her nose, and goes, "Eew. You're going to *eat* that?"

I can't even.

Noah answers for me. "Oh yeah. She's going to eat every . . . last . . . bite."

I lift my chin slightly. I hear the threat in his voice—if I don't consume this miscreation, he'll out Vindhya. And me.

I try another *nudge*, both arms buzzing now: *Be kind.*

His hand stills again, his jaw works, and he visibly crushes the invading thought. My wimpy magic can't overpower his legit anger.

With renewed determination, he heaps on rainbow sprinkles, like a mountain of tiny unicorn turds. Then his hand hovers over the toppings bar as he considers what else to add.

He meets my gaze. His fingers rest on the lid of the gummy worm jar. Only slightly more appealing than actual worms.

Going for genuine sympathy over magic, I silently plead for him to stop. *Haven't I been punished enough?*

He smirks. The worms go into the cup, followed by mini-marshmallows—the kind that were born stale. Then peanut butter. Chunky peanut butter—the ugly stepsister of nut butters.

Finally, he holds the cup of retribution out to me. I take it with a smile, but my eyes say, *You're a monster.*

Scarlett pulls out her phone to record and post this moment. "Seriously, Charity? That's so gross."

I smile plastically for the camera. "I . . . uh . . ."

Noah cuts in. "You know, we even named this treat after someone *very special* to Charity."

Scarlett, Carmen, and a handful of girls within earshot all lean in.

Please don't do this, I silently plead.

"It's called Vind—"

"Spoon please," I squeak.

Noah says, "Vin Diesel's Just Desserts. That's what it's called. She's such a fangirl." He hands me a spoon. "That'll be eighteen fifty."

———

Thirty minutes later, I don't have to feign nausea. After gagging down Noah's version of humble pie, I am so sick to my stomach that I tell Scarlett and Gwen I have to leave, and Angie offers to give them rides home.

As I reach my car, Noah's voice crosses the dark parking lot. "Why did you do it?"

The thing is, he sounds so hurt. Apparently he poured all of his anger into the sugar bomb I just ate, and now what's left is the pain of betrayal. A new wave of shame washes over me. I pause, my hand on the door handle. "I'm a fairy godmother." It comes out hollow.

"You've been messing with Vindhya this whole time, haven't you?" He makes a noise of sheer contempt. "I can't believe I didn't realize what you were up to."

I can't make myself face him, even though staring at my car door has become officially awkward at this point. I compromise by turning halfway around and fixating on a crack in the blacktop. "We still have a deal, though. Right? I help you with Holly; you keep the Cindies' secret."

"You're unbelievable."

I finally force my eyes upward. Noah's pink-and-green shirt is untucked and unbuttoned, revealing the white undershirt beneath. The apron is gone. The Arctic Marble ball cap is now being crushed in his fist.

I cross my arms defensively. "I don't know what you want from me."

"Really? Because I feel like I've been *super* clear about this." He takes a commanding step toward me. "Stop what you're doing to Vindhya."

I press my back against the car. "*I can't. I glimpsed it.* I have to finish this."

"So these *glimpses* give you the right to use people? Con anyone and everyone into doing whatever you want? Lie, cheat, steal?"

Okay, can we get some perspective here? It was just a dress. He's making it sound like I smuggle guns to warlords or something. "Look, I'm sorry. I'm *really* sorry, okay? But I had to—"

"No, you didn't. You don't *have to*. You could just let people live their lives."

I take a calming breath and try again to explain who and what I am. Maybe he can hear me better now that neither of us has a biological weapon. "The Universe wants me to make these wishes come true. My Cindies *need me*."

He laughs, breathy and humorless. "Or do *you* need *them* to make you feel important?"

"Stop it!" My voice chokes from the tension, but I'm not on the verge of crying. I'm not. I press a finger between my eyes to calm down. "Once I get a *glimpse*, I *have* to make it happen."

"Why?" he demands again. "What if you don't? Do you melt into a puddle? Assume your true, hideous form? Does somebody turn into a pumpkin?"

His questions hang in the air unanswered for a beat. Then two. Finally, I admit, "I don't know. I've never failed."

"So, are we talking about magical enslavement here? Are you like a genie in a lamp? Or are you just afraid of failure?"

I've never asked myself this question. When I was twelve, I *glimpsed* Kelly Bodworth cuddling a slobbery, shaggy, black-and-tan puppy. And I just *knew* I had to bring them together. She and I spent the whole summer scouring alleys and animal shelters for that dog. I *nudged* the Humane Society guy to waive the adoption fee. She named him Juggernaut. Every *glimpse* I've ever gotten since that first one comes with the conviction that

I'm supposed to make it happen. But why? What's driving me?

All my air catches near my sternum, and I have to force out the truth. "I don't know."

He sets his jaw. "Then stop. And see what happens."

I can't do that. That's what I'm trying to tell him. Either he's not listening or he's being purposely obtuse. I mean, seriously, what is his deal? I apologized about the dress. I agreed to help him get his girl back. I ate every bite of his Frankenfrosty. I've basically been a slave to his every whim. Now he wants me to drop my Cindy like a bad habit less than twenty-four hours before the ball? And *I'm* the one with a problem?

My hands clench into fists at my sides. I snap, "You know what? You're such a hypocrite. You're perfectly happy to have me do my thing when it benefits *you*. But if I help Vindhya, suddenly I'm a villain."

He throws his hands up. "Don't you see the difference? I *asked* for your help. She didn't. You just decided for her what turn her life should take. It's sick, and it's wrong."

"Vindhya had a choice."

"Or did you coerce her into it?"

"NO! It's her deepest wish. I *glimpsed*—"

"How do you even know what you're glimpsing? What if you're glimpsing pure evil—literally the worst thing that could happen to that person? Or whatever random thing is crossing their mind in that moment? Or a figment of your own imagination?"

Another question I've never asked myself. Ever since Kelly and Juggernaut, I've felt that the *glimpses* were unimpeachable. It's a gut thing. And Memom—she always trusts the *glimpses*. Plus, how could popularity and true love and puppies be evil? Come on, they're *puppies*.

I blurt, "I just know."

We study each other in the dark. There's a breeze playing with his curls. His hands are in his pockets, and his glasses reflect the distant streetlight. Behind the frames, his eyes look deeply disappointed. Finally he says again, "You need to stop." Then he turns to walk away.

And suddenly I don't want him to go. Maybe I can't handle anyone not thinking I'm God's gift to JLHS. Maybe I'm that much of a people pleaser. To keep him here I say, "Why are you so sure that I'm the bad guy?"

He doesn't stop moving away from me but calls over his shoulder, "Why are you so sure you're not?"

13
Okay, Not How I Pictured This Going

The obnoxiously loud and long buzzer sounds the end of the second quarter, officially ringing in halftime at the homecoming game. We're down by two. My hair has been White Wolves Purple all day. I'm so over it already. But, you know, gotta represent for school spirit day. The Poms mill around the track waiting to do our routine, while the football team jogs off the field for their halftime pep talk, and the homecoming court nominees are led onto the field for the big reveal.

It's all background noise. Inside my head, a movie called *My Fight with Noah at the Arctic Marble* is playing on repeat. I spent the whole first half looking for Noah in the bleachers, because, I don't know, maybe he's cooled off. Maybe he's sorry he called me a bad guy. But he's not here. Which is good, and I'm glad.

I mentally smack myself to pay attention. This is Vindhya's destiny moment, her metaphorical dance with Prince Charming.

The fairy godmother does not phone it in at zero hour. I train my gaze on Vindhya, lined up with the rest of the court about twenty feet from me. She is stunning in the red sari that I *glimpsed* ten days ago. Thick black eyeliner makes her eyes look enormous—like cartoon-princess big.

My forehead feels like tiny carnies are setting off fireworks on it.

Ms. Martinez, the vice principal, signals the pep band, and the school fight song overpowers the noise in the bleachers. As soon as they hit the last note, Ms. Martinez lifts the microphone to her mouth and yells, "Happy homecoming, White Wolves!"

The crowd cheers. She proceeds to announce the homecoming court, one at a time, starting with the freshman duke and duchess. She works her way up to the king and queen. There's no doubt in my mind that Vindhya is going to be crowned.

"White Wolves, I present this year's homecoming king: Kade Kassab!"

Holly's football-star boyfriend. How predictable. The crowd goes wild. Kade, in his football uniform, dripping sweat and undoubtedly stinking, jogs forward to accept the crown.

"And now the moment you've all been waiting for. I give you this year's queen of the White Wolves . . ." Dramatic pause; the pep band amps the theatrics with a drum roll. "Vindhya Chandramouli!"

I cheer along with everyone else, flooded with proud

endorphins despite my malaise beforehand. Vindhya's smile is seismic. I can feel the shock waves of elation even when she covers her mouth with both hands, and it makes me shout and clap that much louder. Another wish officially granted. All the drama from the last few days—it was all worth it to give Vindhya her Happily Ever After.

Ms. Martinez places the silver-and-rhinestone tiara on her silky black hair. The noise from the bleachers is bananas—pounding feet, whooping, woofing, the band blasting random notes and banging cymbals.

Vindhya and Kade are guided to the back seat of a convertible and driven slowly around the track. She sits straight and tall, waving gracefully like a true queen—radiant, confident, owning it. Exactly as I *glimpsed* her.

Her adoring subjects cheer and cheer. The foot stomping turns rhythmic. The band plays the fight song again. As the car completes its circuit around the track, the noise finally subsides, but it's almost instantly replaced by chanting. It starts kind of jumbled and indecipherable but gains volume and clarity with each round.

"SELLOUT," they shout.

"SELLOUT!"

"SELLOUT!"

I look toward the source of the chorus. My first thought is, *Did Noah do this?* There's a whole section of STEMers—I recognize them because they're sporting Coding Club T-shirts and MATHMAGICIAN T-shirts and shirts that say, GOT ROBOTS? They wave banners and signs with Sharpie messages like POSEUR and QUEEN OF GARBAGE. They chant "SELLOUT! SELLOUT! SELLOUT!" Loud. Angry. Extremely well organized.

I look to Vindhya. Her smile is frozen on her face. Her eyes are huge with horror. Imagine it's the zombie apocalypse, and a horde of zombies is marching toward you, and smiling is the only way to keep your brain from being eaten. That look is on Vindhya's face right now.

Her gaze cuts to me, and it's like, *Why did you release all these hungry zombies? And is that brain matter running down your chin?*

I'm numb with shock and horror. This isn't how it's supposed to turn out. The seconds tick down on the halftime clock.

Kade, of all people, comes to the rescue. He offers Vindhya his sweaty arm. When she takes it with a shaking hand, he guides her out of the car and off the field. Meanwhile the chant continues. "SELLOUT! SELLOUT!"

The adults scramble to salvage what's left of homecoming. Ms. Martinez herds the rest of the court off the field in a hurry. Coach waves us frantically onto the field. The moment we're set, the thumping bass of our routine mix blasts through the sound system louder than it has ever played before. Loud enough to drown out the chanting.

Two minutes and forty-two seconds later, I strut off the field, holding my poms at my lower back just like the rest of the squad, so they bounce in time with every step. We march across the track and through the entrance to the players' area. Several minutes of mandatory post-performance chitchat and commentary on the Vindhya scandal must be endured. But as soon as propriety allows, I melt away from my teammates.

I find Vindhya in the girls' bathroom. She's sobbing into one of those scratchy brown paper towels. The door swings closed behind me. "Vindhya—" What makes this better? *Ignore those haters? I'm sorry this happened? You looked magnificent out there?*

I don't need to figure out what to say, because Vindhya looks up, black eyeliner streaming down her face, and yells, "Get out of here! Leave me alone!"

I hesitate for a moment, all the things I should say still poised on my lips. But none of them would make this suck less. And the moment I *glimpsed* has come and gone. There's no road map, no precedent, for further intervention. I'm not a hugger. I'm a fixer. And I can't fix this.

Vindhya screams, "I SAID GET OUT!"

So I do. I walk away and leave her there.

———

The next morning I fall through Memom's front door and belly flop onto her couch. The chanting still rings in my ears. *SELLOUT! SELLOUT!* A tousle of White Wolves Purple falls over my face, blocking out the world.

Memom's voice comes from the other side of the hair shield. "I haven't seen an entrance that dramatic since *Beaches*. Hello."

I mumble, "Hello."

"I'll make some tea. Nice hair, by the way."

"Thanks." I listen to Memom putz around with the teakettle and cups. Even though I've come running here for a shoulder to cry on, I'm not sure how to confess to her that I let a wish go so far off the rails. Maybe I actually want to get yelled at. Maybe she'll fire me. How would that even work?

When I get tired of hairs tickling my nose every time I inhale, I push the mop away from my face. A tower of wedding magazines has taken over the coffee table. So I guess Memom's current Cindy is progressing nicely.

Memom returns, rolling her vintage tea cart. It's from that era when mirrors made absolutely everything classy. There's a plate of unwrapped Little Darlings right in the middle of the upper-level mirror—the chocolate cake kind with cream filling. And I'm using "cream" in the loosest sense. It tastes like corn syrup whipped together with Silly Putty.

She parks the cart by me, lowers herself into the recliner, then waves her hand toward the spread. "You pour. I'm an old lady."

Even though I don't feel like drinking it, I pour orange pekoe into two cups. Then I flop backward onto the cushions again, trying to decide how to broach the subject of my total fail.

She does it for me. "This is your Cindy's weekend, isn't it? Don't you have work to do?"

I rub my forehead. "It's done. She's queen. But . . ." Suddenly I realize maybe it's not me who failed. I did my job. I made the *glimpse* happen. Maybe it's the Universe that failed *me*. I sit up and face Memom. "How do we know the *glimpses* are telling the truth?"

Memom doesn't miss a beat. "People lie, Charity. Even to themselves. When people *flash* us, that's their most honest moment. Their deepest wish. That's why it's so powerful."

I'm too distraught to remind her *again* that "flash" is off-limits. "But how do you know? I mean, what if we're wrong? What if the *glimpses* are . . . I don't know . . ."

She waves me off. "An eighty-six-year-old woman was doing the Electric Slide with the man of her dreams last night at the Friday social at an old folks' home. If that's not good magic, I don't know what is."

I clutch the couch cushions, like I can squeeze coherency out of them. "But has there ever been a Cindy that you think . . . that they would have been better off if—"

"Did something happen with your Cindy?" Memom leans toward me with a concerned look.

I blow a long breath onto my tea, watching the surface ripple like a tiny, stormy sea. Then I look up. "When they crowned her queen, a whole section of the bleachers—all her old friends— they booed her off the stage. I left her bawling her eyes out in the bathroom."

Memom settles back into the recliner, closes her eyes, and rocks herself pensively. It takes her a while to answer, and I think maybe she fell asleep. Finally she says, "The Original Fairy Godmother had a sister, you know. There was a girl she tried to help—pretty girl, sweet as could be, but . . . well, she was determined to run away with this loser she thought was a prince. Our great-auntie could see what a phony he was, but the girl was completely hoodwinked."

She pauses dramatically. I prompt, "And?"

"And she locked the girl in the attic and *nudged* the guy away every time he came around. Eventually the girl used her own hair to lower herself out the window and ran away with the King of Sleaze anyway. But—"

"Is this RAPUNZEL?!" I slam my cup down, not caring that hot tea sloshes out. "Our great-aunt was the witch in 'Rapunzel'?"

"A fairy godmother makes *one* mistake and suddenly she's a 'witch.'" Memom dismisses that with a wave of her hand.

"Are you telling me that all the witches in all the stories—they were all fairy godmothers gone bad?"

"Maybe not *all*."

"MEMOM!"

She shrugs. "Every family has a few black sheep."

"Black sheep?! Are you kidding me?" My whole life, all Memom has told me are stories about how good fairy godmothers are—how we fix everything and make people happy. That's the legacy I thought I was part of. Why choose now to drop a truth bomb?

"Oh, keep your panties on. Any woman with an ounce of self-determination was called a witch back then."

"She held her Cindy hostage. That's pretty dang witchy."

Memom sips her tea. How can she be so cavalier about this? I'm devastated by my part in the events of last night. I mean, forget Happily Ever After—Vindhya didn't even get five full minutes of happiness. I pretty much just completely trashed somebody's life. What if I'm one of those fairy godmothers that my great-grandnieces never talk about because I just suck? What makes me not a wicked witch?

I mutter, "I might be a witch." Then with more conviction, "I might be a wicked witch."

"Stop it. You are not."

"How do you know?"

"Because you have a good heart—the heart of a fairy godmother. You want to help people."

I give her a look that says she needs to try harder.

"Just do what I always told you—the *flash* is the road map. Stick to the map, and you'll be fine."

"I stuck to the map for Vindhya, and it. Was. Horrible." I push the words through gritted teeth, my hands clenched in my lap.

"Well, if you had let me finish my story . . . I was going to say that Rapunzel's fairy godmother—"

"Witch."

"—went on to grant lots of other wishes. She did a lot of good. So, you win some, you lose some."

My stomach threatens to empty itself. I cover my mouth. "I can't do this."

"Can't do what?"

"I can't follow the *glimpses* if they don't always create Happily Ever Afters."

"Don't be silly," she snaps. She seems rattled, but immediately recomposes her face into a deeply etched smile. "You *can* trust the *flashes*. And you've always loved granting wishes. You've made so many people happy. It was just *one* setback. Have a cake." She scoots the plate closer to me. I pretend not to notice.

"What would happen if I ignored the *glimpses*? Maybe—"

"No, no. Don't talk nonsense!" She looks more shaken than I've ever seen her before.

"Have you ever tried to control it? Can we turn it off and on?"

"Enough, Charity!" Memom stands on creaky knees, trembling with emotion, her smile long gone. "We don't control the *flashes*! We don't second-guess the Universe! We grant the wishes as they're revealed to us—no more and no less. Now stop this!"

Memom has never yelled at me before. I think I broke her. I swallow the rest of my arguments.

She stares me down for a few seconds and, when it's clear I have nothing more to say, she returns to her chair. She pats my knee affectionately. "Have a cake."

I give in and pick at a Little Darling while disturbing questions pinball around inside my head. If *glimpses* aren't always HEAs, and we can't control them, and we can't ignore them, well . . . things could get real, and fast. What if someone's wish is to die? Or what if the person is evil? What if their deepest desire is to murder someone? Would I *have* to help them? Or what if it's someone like Vindhya, whose innocent reach for a little happiness ends in disaster?

Maybe Noah's right about me. Maybe I *am* the bad guy.

I toss the Little Darling onto my saucer. I can't make myself eat it today. Not even for Memom.

———

I had hoped that visiting Memom would make me feel better, but it actually has the opposite effect. I leave her apartment more conflicted than I've ever been in my life. *Every family has a few black sheep. . . .*

A few, she said. Who else don't we talk about?

When I get home, I find Mom—dressed for work from the waist up, her lower half sporting yoga pants and bare feet—staring at her computer screen. I'm about to say hi and maybe "Help! I want my mom!" But she waves me off, pointing to the Bluetooth in her ear.

She says, "That's a good point, Steve. Thanks for bringing that up. We *do* need to consider the cost-benefit here. . . ."

I recognize a conference call when I see one. I give her a silent thumbs-up and proceed down the hall, realizing more than ever how completely on my own I am. Mom isn't going to help me pull myself together. Memom gave me zero useful guidance. Hope is a million miles away. Sean? Scarlett? No. They couldn't possibly understand what I'm going through, even if we were close enough to talk about it. Which I've made sure we aren't. So I shut myself in my room with my tablet and do the only thing I can do—comb through the entire collected knowledge of the planet looking for the truth about who I am.

Can I trust my magic? Are the *glimpses* really for the best? Do fairy godmothers always dole out success, happiness, and true love, like I thought? How many went to the dark side?

Trying to sort out truth from fiction is tricky. Most of my family history—where it has survived at all—is in the annals of fairy-tale lore. And fairy-tale writers had a tendency to embellish whenever they thought that fiction would sell more books than facts. Memom raised me on these things, reinterpreting along the way. So there's nothing new here. I reread a dozen or so stories anyway, this time paying way more attention to the witches.

In these tales, my relatives appear as mysterious women handing out magic beans and berries, making cryptic predictions, assigning seemingly impossible tasks. Or—possibly—feeding people poisoned apples, cursing babies, and threatening to eat little kids. Their morals are, at best, ambiguous.

Determined to dig deeper, I type "fairy mythology" into the search bar. Now we're getting into the realm of "tiny winged mischief babies." They're not remotely real or relevant. They fly around, disappear at will, turn into animals, emerge from flowers . . . Just. No.

About the time I want to beat my head against my tablet if I have to read one more word about insipid little pixies, an overly academic sentence buried in some fairy zealot's blog catches my attention: "The Latin verb *fari* means 'to speak,' implying the faeries' ability to make predictions or to prophesy someone's destiny."

Holy crap. I found the Grail.

Maybe the *glimpses* are predictions about destiny—not wishes at all. My heart pounds as I plow forward. In another of his posts, the blogger writes, "Folkloric references to faeries seem to preserve within children's bedtime stories a veiled remnant of a conquered people group." It makes perfect sense—all this "hide who you are and what you can do" stuff started as a way to survive some kind of premedieval genocide.

Two hours and dozens of blog posts later, I've read about Celtic, German, Italian, English, and Scottish fairy stories and made a list of what I know:

> *Real fairies look human (I would say are human)—no wings or green skin, not weirdly small or anything like that.*
>
> *All fairies are women. Not a big revelation. Memom already told me the magic only manifests in females and only once we hit the big P.*

Fairies are sometimes helpful and sometimes kinda horrible.

Fairies manipulate people for their own purposes kind of a lot. (Sigh.)

<u>*Humans who fall in love with fairies are royally screwed.*</u> *Seriously, it always ends very badly for the hapless human. Which explains so much about my family tree.*

Several blog posts talk about a woman called the Queen of the Fairies, Morgan le Fay. She was the last queen of the conquered people group in the Irish, Scottish, and Welsh myths. I keep reading and reading about her, clicking every link, comparing every story to find the threads of truth.

And I want to love her *so bad*—my great-grandmother a zillion times removed. But here's the truth: She was a train wreck. A manipulative, self-absorbed, relationship-sabotaging control freak. Which is eerily, depressingly similar to Noah's assessment of yours truly.

I shove my tablet under the comforter and bury my face in my pillow. I can't take any more. For a few minutes my thoughts spiral out of control. Then I sit up, drag my hair out of my face, and take a bracing breath. I've come to a very important conclusion.

I need an intervention.

14

Humble Pie Basically Tastes Like Chicken

I drive to Noah's but can't make myself actually stop the car, so I end up driving around aimlessly for an hour. There is so much raw emotion swirling inside me that I feel like a human blender of angst. I still have a guilt hangover from the Vindhya debacle. I just found out I might be evil. And there's the whole "asking for help instead of giving it" role reversal that is obviously way out of my comfort zone.

On top of all that, I'm about to try to get a friend back (or, more accurately, a frenemy). That's not something I've ever done before. Goodbyes are always on my terms, and they're for keeps. Trying to figure out how to reverse that scenario is terrifying. Maybe it's not even possible.

And how did I even get to the place where *Noah* is the one person I think can help me out of this tailspin?

I think about this a lot as I circle his block ten or fifteen times.

The thing is, he's the only person outside of my family who knows two things about me: that I'm magical and that I'm screwed up. Actually, I may be giving my family too much credit. Noah saw way before I did that I was in trouble, and if I'd listened to him earlier, maybe I wouldn't be in this mess.

Eventually I swallow my dread and my pride (easier than expected, as there is so little of it left) long enough to park the car and march myself to the front door. Because if it's between baring my soul to my nemesis or spiraling into a legit evil fairy, I've just got to be brave.

I trudge along the walkway and up the front-porch steps, glancing around to make sure there are no potential eavesdroppers. What I have to say is scary enough without extra ears listening in. The street is empty.

As soon as I ring the doorbell, I can hear muffled activity inside. Noah's mom's voice calling from deep within. Scuffling and arguing. The doorknob jiggles from the inside, goes still, jiggles again. Right inside the door, Noah's little sister sings part of the "k-i-s-s-i-n-g" song, some of the words muted like her mouth is being covered. Noah yells, "OUCH! Mom, Nat bit me!"

Lisa shouts, "You two, STOP IT! Natalie, come *here*." And Natalie's voice recedes in a whine about life not being fair, she's bored, and what is there to eat. Nat the Brat indeed.

Noah opens the door a second later, his face a mask of disdain. It's so incongruous with what I just heard through the door that a surprised laugh catches in my misery-clogged throat and chokes me. As soon as I get the coughing under control, though, I shove a dry-cleaning bag at him. "Here are the costumes. I had them cleaned."

Noah takes them without a word or a look of acknowledgment and moves to close the door.

Before he can totally shut me out, I stop the door with my hand and blurt, "The *glimpses* can't be trusted like I thought. I should have listened to you. You were right about everything. I really screwed up, and I shouldn't have borrowed the costume for Vindhya without telling you. I'm sorry. I'm so, *so* sorry about everything with Vindhya and Holly and . . . everyone. I want to make it right, but I don't know how."

He crosses his arms. "Maybe my idea, where you just *stop*. Let's start there."

As if I haven't humiliated myself enough, now I have to admit how little I actually know about my own magic. I stumble over it. "The problem is, I can't control the *glimpses*. They just sort of . . . happen. But maybe I can ignore them? Memom says we can't. But I'll try."

For an instant Noah looks puzzled. Then he gives me the *look who turned out to be human* face from Tuesday. I'm ridiculously relieved. He drops his defensive pose. "You've had this thing your whole life?"

"Since I was twelve."

"So five, six years. And you have *no* idea how it works?"

I shake my head. It seems so pathetic when he says it like that. "And, um." *Out with it, Charity. You've come this far.* "There's something else I can do."

"Okay?"

"Remember at Arctic Marble when you were making me that . . . thing. And you kept feeling like maybe you should stop?"

"Stinking conscience," he mutters. Then his eyes go wide. "How did you know I— Wait, that was *you*? You were messing with my head?"

I press my lips together and look at the ground.

"That's so evil!"

My head pops up. "It was self-defense!"

He drags his hand down his face, back up again, and through his curls. "Why are you telling me this? Why now?"

I hug myself but force my eyes to meet his. "You were right all along. Homecoming proved that. I don't want to be the bad guy, and I don't know who else could help me."

"You want my help?" He's still holding the dry-cleaning bag. It rustles in his arm. "The last time you asked for my help—"

"I know! I said I'm sorry!"

He narrows his eyes at me for an uncomfortable beat. Then, without a word, he turns around and goes into the house. I let my head fall back against the porch pillar in defeat. I wonder how much a ticket to Baghdad costs.

But a minute later he returns, free of the dry-cleaning bag. He doesn't look upset anymore. Actually, the mixture of curiosity and concentration on his face makes him look like a very young college professor or maybe a mad scientist. He clears his throat. "Okay. I'll help you figure out how to control your psychic abilities."

I've never thought of my magic like that. It sounds completely off. I shift uncomfortably.

"But no more lying, and definitely no—" He pokes at his forehead.

"Nudges," I offer.

"Seriously. No *nudges.*" His eyebrows pop up behind his glasses. "Unless you think we could send telepathic messages back and forth? Because that would be awesome."

"It really doesn't work like that."

"Yeah. Forget it." His eyes roam the yard for three or four seconds. Then he focuses back on me. "I would say the first step is to try to *glimpse* something."

"Wait, what?" I seem to have stumbled into Opposite Land.

He pushes his glasses up his nose. "Yeah. If you want to teach a dog *not* to bark, first you teach it to bark on command. So it—"

"I'm not a dog!"

He looks appropriately flustered. "No. Yeah. I just mean, doing a thing is easier than not doing a thing. If you can choose to do it, then you've found the switch, as it were, and you should be able to turn it off, too. See?"

It scares me so freaking much that what he just said makes sense. I realize my eyebrows are pinched together and press my finger to the spot between them. I lick my dry lips. Then I nod. "Okay. I'll, um. I'll do that."

"Okay, go for it."

"What?"

"Try it on me."

"I don't know—"

"Come on. No time like the present." He shakes his arms out, like he's prepping for a dead lift.

I wasn't prepared for this. I thought the next step would be to stare at my ceiling and contemplate the cosmos or something. Besides, I already tried it on him a few days ago and got nothing. I shake my head in protest.

He's not paying attention. He closes his eyes and touches his middle fingers to his temples, around the frame of his glasses. I roll my eyes. "What are you doing?"

He doesn't open his eyes. "I'm concentrating on my wish."

"So . . . Holly?"

"You won't know for sure until you *glimpse* it."

"This is ridiculous."

"We don't know. Maybe this is how it works. Come on. Just do the thing."

What thing? I sigh and, not knowing what else to do, stare at him hard. I think, *Go!* . . . Glimpse! . . . *Activate mind powers. . . .*

I wish I could see the wish. . . . Noah's brain, I command thee to open to me. . . .

"This isn't working."

Noah finally opens his eyes. He makes a face like, *This Rubik's Cube is tricky.* "What are you trying?"

I don't want to tell him how silly it was. I mutter, "I just . . . tried to . . . concentrate on your brain."

"Hhhmm." He nods. "Okay. Wishes are more of a gut thing though, right?"

"You want me to concentrate on your guts?"

"Well, I mean, no."

"Technically it all happens in your brain."

"Yeah, but maybe you need to focus more on emotion. The heart. The eyes. Yeah. The eyes are the window to the soul. Who said that?"

"How would I know?"

"Okay, let's do it." He opens his eyes wide and points his face at me. This is getting more and more awkward. And what if someone I know drives past? I glance at the empty street. He huffs, "Come on. Look into my eyes."

Reluctantly I focus on his eyes. But I'm not sure which one to look at, and it's pretty much impossible to stare into both eyes at once. I lick my lips again. "Take your glasses off."

He takes them off with a little flourish. "Should I tear my shirt open too? Like Clark Kent?"

"Eew. No. Plus you're wearing a T-shirt, weirdo."

I roll the tension out of my neck, take a deep breath, and look into his eyes again. And the truth is, they aren't muddy at all. They're viridian, with gingerbread near the pupil and cobalt around the rim of the iris. Striking eyes, really, when you look.

I inch a little closer. But all I see are his eyes, no *glimpse* at all. I think, *Noah, tell me your deepest desire. . . . I command you to make a wish. . . . Abracadabra. . . . Bibbidi bobbidi boo.*

I shake my head. "Still nothing. Are you focusing on your wish?"

He looks flustered. "Yeah. Uh. Yeah."

"Maybe . . ." I can't believe I'm doing this. "Maybe if I . . ." I reach out and gingerly place my hand over his heart. He flinches a little when I touch him. Come on! Am I really that repellant?

I give him a (hopefully) reassuring nod before I close my eyes. I focus all my remaining senses on the spot where my hand makes contact with his chest. He's warm through the soft cotton of his T-shirt. I suddenly realize I haven't read it. I don't know what it says. It feels like a secret of the Universe. Should I open my eyes and read the shirt?

No. I've got to concentrate. I force them to stay closed as I focus on our point of physical connection. His heart seems like it's beating kind of fast, but I'm not a nurse or anything. Maybe that's how fast hearts always beat. Maybe he's scared that I'll do black magic on him.

My hands feel a little buzzy—like they get when I'm *nudging*—and I realize that my own heart seems to be matching pace with his. Maybe this is it! Maybe this is what conjuring a *glimpse* feels like! I reach out with my mind, through my fingers, into Noah's soul.

It's like diving into a pool of blackstrap molasses. I feel around in the dark, not sure what I'm looking for, every inch of progress a struggle.

I place my other hand on his chest. Feel his heartbeat. Breathe. Reach.

I close the distance between us and touch my forehead to his collarbone. Now I can smell him. Me thinkest I detect a hint of Old Spice. But it's not offensive. It's kind of nice, actually. I inhale. Reach. Exhale. Get lost. Try to remember what reaching feels like.

And then his arms come tentatively around me. I'm inside a Noah cocoon. I can feel his breath, a warm rhythm along my temple. And I'm only kind of trying to find the *glimpse* switch. My brain feels like melting chocolate. Slow and thick and sweet and gooey.

"Get a room! Gross!"

I jump away from Noah like he's high voltage. The world feels blindingly bright and chafing. Nat the Brat's voice screeches in my ear. "You guys are, like, totally making out in front of God and everybody."

Noah's cheeks are hot pink. His eyes flit from me to his sister. He grabs Natalie by the arm and drags her through the door, while she screams, "Ow! This is child abuse! MOM!"

I stand blinking in the sunlight for a few seconds, trying to reboot. What. Was. That?

Noah reappears, scrubbing a hand through his hair. His eyes are trained on my knees. I fixate on the doorknob. He mutters, "Um. So. Did you get anything?"

I clear my throat. "No. I thought maybe. But . . . no."

He puts his glasses back on, still looking anywhere but at my face. "Okay. Maybe we'll figure it out another time. Another day, I mean. Whenever."

"Yeah," I say to the doorknob. "'Cuz I should probably. Go." Ugh. There has got to be a way to turn this thing around. I'm the fairy godmother. When did I get this awkward? I set my jaw and look at Noah's face—his completely nonstriking, not-melting-my-brain face.

He has freckles. That should be noted. I want to study their constellation. What? No, I don't. I want to punch myself in the head.

I say crisply, "I'm going to get to work on the Holly thing."

"What?" His green-blue-brown eyes flicker to mine. For a second he looks confused, like, *Holly who?* And my heart beats faster again. Then he snaps out of it. "Oh. Right. Good." He shoves his hands in his pockets. "See ya."

"Yeah. See ya."

I remember to check his shirt for the secrets of the Universe before I turn to walk away. It says SET PHASERS TO STUN.

15

A Tiny Bit of Fraternizing with the Enemy. NBD.

efore I open my eyes on Sunday morning, I smell French toast. I roll over and check my phone. It's 8:52. There's a text from Noah from 7:02: Glimpse anything lately?

I should take this moment to say that the strangeness yesterday was 75 percent stress-induced hysteria, 15 percent relief that the War of the Dress was over, and 10 percent overactive hormones. Noah's probably just as weirded out by it as I am. We should definitely never talk about it so we can pretend it never happened.

I smile at his text. There are worse ways to wake up. I reply: Glimpse free. Cuz I was ASLEEP.

I take the phone with me to the bathroom. While I'm brushing my teeth, Noah says: Took you long enough to answer.

I spit, rinse, and send: Do Not Disturb mode, suckaaaaaaaa.

I watch the writing bubbles blink, then: Bacon, eggs, and biscuits is happening over here.

It's kind of nice that he's telling me pointless stuff about his day. It reminds me of how it used to be with Hope, before she moved eight thousand miles away. And with Sean before his wish was granted.

Maybe it's too nice, actually.

I set the phone facedown on the counter without responding.

It chirps.

I eye it, sitting there so innocuously. But I don't pick it up.

It chirps again.

After a moment of indecision, I snatch it off the counter. Only because I'm curious. I'll see what he sent, but I won't respond.

Noah: Hello?

Noah: Oh jeez, you're a vegetarian aren't you? And an emoji swallowing his own foot.

If I just go silent now, I realize, Noah will think he offended me, and that's not good for the quid pro quo thing we've got going. I need him to help me figure out my stuff, and he needs me to fix his girl problems. So I send: I'm not a vegetarian.

Noah: Phew. So what's for breakfast, carnivore? Piles of greasy meat?

This is fine. I can definitely text with Noah about breakfast or whatever just until his wish is granted without getting attached or anything. I write: Smells like French toast.

Noah: With sprinkles?

Me: Too soon.

I drop a rainbow poop emoji that might be an Arctic Marble creation.

Watching the screen for his text back, I meander out of the bathroom and flop onto my bed. None arrives. I wonder if I should make an appearance at any of the homecoming stuff today, or if Vindhya will. On a completely unrelated note, I wonder if Noah will be there. I can't ask, though, because I don't want to give him the wrong idea. And it might make him think about Holly being there with Kade, which he doesn't need to think about because it can't be helped.

When I can't wait anymore, I send: Let me guess . . . Star Trek Convention today?

Noah: Alas, no. Hiking with the family.

Me: Wow, your family actually does stuff together. What's that like?

As soon as I hit send, I want to snatch it back. It's too real. Noah and I might not be mortal enemies anymore, but we are *definitely* not friends. He is still blackmailing me. Anyway, it's too late, because his response pops up.

Noah: It's like having friends, but way less cool and more annoying.

I laugh out loud, a conflicted little "ha-ha." But all I write back is: Have fun hiking.

Noah: Talk later?

Me: Yeah, can't seem to avoid you.

Considering that my life has taken a decisive turn toward teen angst—what with the whole "who am I and what is my purpose in life" thing I've got going—I enter the kitchen on surprisingly light feet.

Mom greets me with her signature smile. "Morning, sleepyhead. You woke up happy."

"Morning, Mom." I retrieve orange juice from the fridge and pour a glassful, smiling at nothing in particular.

Once I'm planted at the breakfast bar, Mom puts a plate of French toast in front of me. Then she sits next to me with her plate. She holds out her coffee cup. "Happy Sunday!"

I clink the cup with my OJ glass, and we tuck in, eating in silence for a few minutes. The image of Noah's family eating their breakfast flits through my mind. They're probably laughing and fighting and trading *Star Trek* quotes. Lisa might be holding Nat's face and saying, *You* are *my baby.* And after breakfast they'll spend the day doing all the same stuff while hiking. Why does being together seem so easy for them? How could I get a little of that? Finally I risk, "Want a mother-daughter shopping date today?"

The corners of her mouth pull down. It looks like genuine regret. "I wish I could, hon. But I have to get ready for my trip to Belize."

"Belize?" That last bite of French toast won't go down. It's stuck right above my heart.

"Yeah, I told you about it. I'm going to a Marine Life Summit—remember? International cooperation?"

"Oh." I don't remember ever hearing about this before. "I guess I forgot." I try again to swallow the toast. It remains lodged, unrelenting. "When do you leave?"

"Tomorrow morning, early, early."

It's hard to sound chipper with a food traffic jam near your heart. I give it my best effort, though. "Sounds . . . important. How long will you be gone?"

"Only seven days. And I'll miss you every minute." She wraps both arms around me, still holding her fork, and squeezes.

I want to say, *Don't go. I totally messed up somebody's life. I got the fairy godmother gene, but I might be evil or just totally incompetent, and I need my mom. I don't know what to do.*

But I don't say anything. I give her a limp hug back. She holds me at arm's length, concern in her eyes. "Charity? You're okay, right?"

I turn out of her touch under the guise of reaching for my glass. I remind myself not to be selfish. What are my problems compared to floating landfills, melting polar ice caps, and endangered whales? I take a swig of juice to force the French toast down. "Yeah. I'm fine. Just . . . have a great trip."

It doesn't take me too long to realize that it's actually a good thing my mom's out of the country. It gives me plenty of time to figure out how to undo the Vindhya train wreck. Plus I need to strategize Operation Win Back Holly. Because Memom was right about one thing—I *do* want to help people, and that means I'm still a good fairy godmother as long as I don't keep making mistakes. Besides, now that Noah and I aren't enemies, all my plans to torment him are out the window, and I'm determined to help him for real.

By the time Noah texts me at 6:58 Monday morning, I'm already pulling into the parking lot at JLHS. The text says: These clothes make me look like one of the Jonas Brothers.

Ah, the new clothes came. I respond: You wish. Wear them or face my wrath.

Noah: She wakes! What happened to DND?

Me: Already hard at work for you. Going to radio silent.

I put my phone on vibrate, just in case he doesn't take the hint. Then I head to the football field. The football team does three-a-days this time of year: they run drills at 6:45 a.m., lift weights for PE credit during school, and scrimmage in the afternoon.

Holly, being the ultimate dedicated girlfriend, is the lone occupant of the bleachers. The air has the misty coolness of early morning and is filled with the sounds of guys in mortal combat against blocking dummies.

I make my approach with a nonchalant wave, my head already starting to throb. "Hey, Holly. I was hoping to find you here."

She looks justifiably confused by that statement. She mumbles, "Really? I kinda thought you tried to avoid me because . . . you know."

She's not wrong. I do avoid her—mostly because every time

I'm around her I get a headache. I smile. "Actually, I *do* like to do a follow-up survey with my clients—like a 'satisfaction guaranteed' thing. Would you be up for answering a few questions?"

This isn't wholly untrue. On one hand, this will be the first follow-up I've ever done. On the other hand, however, since I'm turning over a new leaf, follow-ups *could* be my thing now. But partly—let's say *mostly*—it's recon for the forthcoming Noah-Holly reunion tour.

Without waiting for her to agree, I sit down next to her, my headache blooming into a classic rock drum solo between my eyebrows. I rub at the spot for a moment, resigning myself to the sensation. Then I take out a notepad and pen to look official. Holly sits up a little straighter, like she understands the solemnity of the survey, and looks at me expectantly.

I begin, "Okay, on a scale from one to ten—one being 'every step is like walking on broken glass' and ten being 'and they lived happily ever after'—how would you rate your quality of life, post-wish-granting?"

Holly chews her lip. "Um. Eight, I guess?"

I'd call anything above seven a win. Good on me. But she did leave room at the top. Which is good for Noah. I jot it down, mostly for show. "Great. Next question: Can you name three things or people that you miss from your pre-wish life?"

Her eyebrows draw together in concentration for a few seconds. "My art, I suppose. I don't have much time for that anymore.

And . . . buh, buh, buh . . . Yeah. That's all I can think of."

I jot down: *art*. Not a good sign that she doesn't miss Noah. But she does have a boyfriend, so maybe she feels like it wouldn't be kosher to say she misses another guy. I try a different angle. "Right. If you could change one thing about your current life, what would it be?"

Holly scrunches her whole face like a raisin. I write: *makes funny faces.* She says, "I'd run less, and I'd eat more ice cream." Her scrunch face morphs into a smile. "I used to eat it by the pint."

"Why'd you stop?"

She shrugs. "I can't get fat, can I?"

"Why not?"

She tosses her hair in that way that makes other girls want to rip it out. Not *me personally*, of course. "I'm in the spotlight now."

Now that we're talking about it, I realize that Holly has gotten skinnier. Last year she was kind of soft-looking in a nice way. Now she has noticeable cheekbones, toned arms, and sharp elbows.

Something like guilt twists deep in my stomach. Without thinking, I murmur, "Noah liked the ice-cream-eating you."

Her voice goes sharp. "Is this part of the survey?"

My pen snaps to attention, and I start scribbling notes. "Right. Sorry. Last question. Tell me your three favorite things about Prince Charming—Kade."

This time she doesn't make any faces or noises. She doesn't stop to think at all. "He's nice, cute, and fun."

If that were any more canned, we'd slap a Campbell's label on it and eat it with a spoon. For half a sec I'm thrown. Then I smile and say, "And three things you like to talk about or do together?"

One eyebrow goes down. "I thought you said the last one was the last one?"

"Yeah. This is 'last one' part B."

She rolls her eyes. "Uhhhhh-kay. Making out."

"Doesn't count."

"Netflix and chill."

Same thing. But I let it slide.

She bounces her knee. "We go to all the parties."

Didn't say she liked it, though. I prompt her to keep going with a little chin bob action.

"And just, like, talking."

"About what? What would you say you have in common?"

She pulls an exasperated face. "You said 'last one' two questions ago."

"This is part—"

"C. Yeah. Got it. Listen, practice is almost over, and I've gotta run to SmoothieQue to get a protein shake for Kade. He needs it by the time he's done showering. But, um, I'm doing good and thanks for granting my wish. Okay?"

"Okay. Good catch-up."

She pulls her purse strap over her shoulder and waves once. "See ya."

She climbs down the bleachers, each step reverberating through the aluminum seats. I feel her descent rumbling through my body.

I hate that I granted her wish.

———

I spend the rest of the day in a constant state of jittery anxiety. The double failure of Vindhya's and Holly's wishes drags on me like trying to drive with the parking brake on. I dread running into any other Cindies who might be less than perfectly happy. At one point I straight-up duck into the bathroom to avoid Carmen. Besides that, the inevitable next *glimpse* looms over me like the blade of a guillotine. Every friendly wave and innocent shoulder bump during passing periods could trigger it. Every tick of the clock over the classroom door brings it closer.

You'll just ignore it, I remind myself. It'll be fine.

Through it all, I wear a flawless mask of confident poise. Because that's what the fairy godmother does.

I don't see Noah at lunch. Which is good, actually. It's important for me to mingle, to keep up appearances, even though socializing is a special kind of torture today. Scarlett must, of course, give me the news roundup from the weekend, including a recap of Vindhya's tumble from grace, the fact that she was a no-show at the dance, and the subsequent social media fallout.

Gwen shows me Surya's latest social media post—it's the two of them decked out as Wolverine and Storm for the homecoming dance, and the caption says *That was fun, and now we're done.* She assures me it was mutual. I leave her to spend quality time with her phone, relieved that she isn't in a relationship crisis that might bring on a *glimpse.*

Carmen waves me toward her table. *It'll be fine,* I tell myself. *She's living the dream.* But a sophomore with crispy, toxic-waste-yellow hair approaches with a tearful plea for advice. I dismiss Carmen with a *sorry* look and a tiny sigh of relief before giving the sophomore a gentle lecture on overprocessing along with Tuan's business card.

I look up to see Sean incoming, pausing every few seconds to acknowledge a wave or a shout-out but moving inexorably toward me. I have a moment of preschool-level indecision—should I run away, hide, or get a hug? A small part of me wants to ask him if he's truly happy, but I can't handle even the possibility of another truth bomb today.

And then he's right in front of me, and it's too late to make a run for it. He leads with "Charity, I'm freaking out about your hair right now. Thank God you got rid of the school-spirit purple. You looked like you were possessed by the minions of JLHS hell."

I snort. "But how do you really feel?"

He gestures broadly, and my eyes follow the sweep of his arm. Six different girls have White Wolves Purple hair today. Sean slips into his priestly advice tone. "Your sins affect the masses. With great power comes great responsibility."

"Thank you for that ancient wisdom from the Marvel vaults, Father Sean."

He threads his arm through mine. "Don't be petty. Especially when I'm right. It *is* gorgeous today, though. Viridian."

When I chose this color from my collection at eleven last night (because Sean's not wrong about White Wolves Purple), I was too tired to analyze why I was drawn to it. Turns out I accidentally dyed my hair to match a certain Trekkie's eyes. I add self-disgust to the emotional baggage of the day, laugh a "thanks," and move on to the JV athletes' table.

By the time I shut myself into the blessed solitude of my car after Poms practice, I feel like one of those Easter eggs with the insides blown out—completely hollow and like the slightest tap could shatter me. And now I have to go home to an empty house, which at least means a respite from worrying about *glimpsing* something but, on the other hand, really sucks. I miss having a Cindy. Nothing takes my mind off my own problems like working on someone else's.

So this is what withdrawal feels like. I pull out of the parking lot feeling directionless.

There's no one for me to take care of. And no one to take care of me. No one to help unwind the tangle of regrets and anxieties I've gotten myself into. No one to distract me or make me laugh or feed me comfort food. I miss my mom. I miss my sister. Or, rather, I miss the idea of them.

My phone buzzes an incoming text. I check it at the next red light. It's Noah: **SOS. The Brat is on a hormonal rampage.**

I'm barricaded in the closet. Shields at 40%. Warp core breach imminent.

I breathe a silent chuckle and text back: What is this warp core you speak of?

Noah: REQUIRE IMMEDIATE EXTRACTION. Condition Green.

Me: Hold tight. I'm coming.

16

I Win. But Not Really.

I can hear Nat screaming through the door. How awkward is it to ring the bell mid–domestic altercation? I hesitate on the front step, not sure of the proper protocol for this situation. Suddenly, unbidden, the door opens.

In the space of time it takes Noah to slip out and close the door behind him, I hear Nat wail, "NO ONE WANTS ME TO BE HAPPY! YOU ALL HATE ME!"

Noah grabs my hand and whisper-yells, "Go, go, go!" He runs toward the car, doubled over like we're taking fire, pulling me along. Then he stage-shoves me through the passenger door, so that I have to climb across the seats with him right behind. He urges, "Hurry. She's been speedballing strawberry milk and Pop Rocks. This place could blow any second."

It takes a good amount of contortionism to get my knees out from under me and my butt in the seat—my Fit is pretty tiny, and

I'm silently laughing. No sooner have I accomplished it than Noah commands, "Warp eight, Mr. Sulu."

The left side of my mouth ticks up, but I flick his ear anyway. "Cindy foul. Holly does not want to be called 'Mr. Sulu.'"

He rubs the flick away with his palm. "FYI, you're not Holly."

It takes me half a second too long to find the right amount of snark for my reply.

"I'm aware. But I'm a girl, and I'm here." I click my seat belt and put the car in motion, not sure where we're going. "This is your big chance to practice not being a goober."

Noah grumbles like that's a tough request while he fastens his seat belt.

The truth is, I feel 1,000 percent better. It's amazing how much being needed brightens my day. I guess it's a fairy godmother thing. I suddenly realize that I barely ate all day, and I'm starving. I make a right turn out of the neighborhood.

"I'm hungry. Are you hungry?"

Noah blows his lips out. "I'm a seventeen-year-old guy. I spend every waking moment eating and thinking about sex."

"And they say guys can't multitask."

"Yeah. That's a myth."

I take the on-ramp for the freeway. Noah shifts in his seat like he just realized I'm a kidnapper. I shoot him side-eye. "What?"

"Where are we going?"

"There's a really cute diner in Highgrove with good burgers."

"There's like twenty places in town with good burgers."

"Yeah. But I can't be seen with you."

He slumps in his seat. "Do you have any idea how demoralizing that is?"

I shrug. "It's nothing personal. We *did* pinkie swear on it. Remember?"

"Whatever."

Seriously? He's going to *whatever* me over a totally logical confidentiality clause in our business relationship? Well, *what-freaking-ever.* I purse my lips and crank up my techno jams. We drive without talking for several miles while Noah presumably thinks about food and sex and how much he hates me, and I stubbornly refuse to admit culpability.

But as the standoff stretches on, the hollowness creeps back in, until I feel too empty to hold on to my irritation. Eventually I turn down the stereo and try to break the ice with "I don't want to fight with you. But if we're seen together, it could mess up things with Holly."

He turns his viridian-and-gingerbread eyes on me. "Why do you do that? Why do you push people away?"

"I don't! Like I said, I just—" I glance at him, and he looks like what I say next matters. Kind of a lot. I stop midsentence. Inexplicably, I find myself admitting, "I don't really do friendships."

"Yeah, right. You have more friends than anybody. You're the top of the JLHS food chain."

"No one at school actually knows me." Why are these things coming out of my mouth? To *Noah* of all people?

"What about me?"

I shake my head, eyes on the road.

"Okay. Then *let* me know you. Tell me something true."

I don't answer right away. My stomach growls. My knee shakes with nervous energy. The thing is, I *want* to tell him things. The self-disclosure train is hard to stop once you get it rolling. The words insist on spilling out of my mouth. "My sister went to Thailand, and a couple weeks ago she told me she's not coming back."

"Why?"

I find myself telling him all about Hope and her elephants. I wrap it up with "So, anyway, I guess I should have said I don't do *relationships*. Even the sister thing isn't working out for me."

"I wish *my* sister would ship herself to Thailand for a while." He's trying to keep it light. But when I don't laugh, he says, "Come on. You're not why she left."

Eyes firmly forward, I counter, "I wasn't enough to make her come back."

He's quiet for a bit, and when he speaks again, his voice is softer. "I'm sorry about your sister. You must miss her a lot."

Someone caring makes it worse. I feel the emotions I thought I'd exorcised rising back up. Which is why I don't want to keep talking about this. Time for a conversational lane change. I say firmly, "Anyway, now we need to talk about Operation Win Back Holly."

"Okay?"

I take the Highgrove exit and end up stuck behind a truck full of onions. One of the joys of living in California—stinky produce abounds. The fumes slowly waft through the air vents. I stick to business. "Okay. I did some recon this morning."

He sits up a little straighter.

"Her HEA is all messed up, but she's not quite ready to admit it yet."

"HEA?"

"Happily Ever After, of course."

"Right."

"The most straightforward scenario is that Kade ends things, and you swoop in to pick up the pieces of her broken heart."

"Why would Kade end things?"

"You don't have to worry about that part. I'll take care of it." I feel dirty just saying it.

"So you would do your brainwashing thing on Kade and get him to dump Holly."

So. Hurtful. I grit my teeth and wrinkle my nose. Because of the onion fumes. "You want the girl or not?"

He clenches his fists on his knees. "I don't want Holly to suffer. And I don't want to be the rebound."

Would it be so onerous to do one single thing the easy way? I press a finger to the spot between my eyebrows. "I was afraid you'd say that. You realize Kade is one of JLHS's most eligible guys, right? He's the freaking homecoming king now on top of everything else. And he *didn't* get booed offstage. How am I supposed to make Holly want—"

"I believe in you." He shoots me a grin.

"You suck."

I run scenarios for a few blocks. Everything that ends with Holly picking Noah over Kade is so far-fetched it can be classified as science fiction. Or possibly space soap opera. I wish I had a *glimpse* to show me what to swing for. No. No, I don't. I'm off *glimpses*. They can't be trusted. I sigh. "I guess a meet-cute can't hurt."

"A what?"

"It's where two people meet in a really cute way. Exactly what it sounds like."

"Except Holly and I already know each other."

"And it's time to get reacquainted."

Noah makes a disgruntled noise in his throat. "Sounds manipulative."

Do his repeated accusations grate at my already shredded self-esteem? Yes. Am I so frustrated that I want to pull over and beat him senseless? Of course. Does some part of me detest the whole idea of a Noah-Holly meet-cute? Maybe. What? *No.*

Fine. There is a tiny part of me that might actually miss the obscure *Star Trek* references and awkward encounters with Noah's goofy family once I grant his wish and cut ties. But I can handle it. Just like with all the others. It's what I do.

Anyway, none of that is why my left eye leaks one drop of moisture. It's the stinking onion truck. The tiny fact-checker in my brain points out that unpeeled onions don't irritate tear ducts. *Tiny Fact-Checker, you're a killjoy and a liar. It's 100 percent the onion truck.*

I *finally* pull around it and hit the gas like Danica Patrick.

I dash the eye sweat away. "Do you want my help or not?"

"Isn't there a way for me to get Holly back without being an a-hole?" It's a plea for help. The kind that melts me every time.

I capitulate with a sigh. "Noah. It's not assholic to put yourself out there. She spends pretty much every waking moment with Kade. If she's going to choose you, she needs some material for comparison. She needs to know there's a choice to be made."

"Man, I don't know if you're making sense or if I'm just caught in your tractor beam."

I raise my flicking fingers in warning, and he holds his hands up in silent surrender. I say, "I'm making sense. Trust me. Tomorrow morning at seven fifteen, you need to be at SmoothieQue. Holly goes there every morning to get Kade a protein shake." I pull into the parking lot at Big Doug's Diner. "And you need to be wearing your new clothes. And please, I'm begging you, use conditioner in your hair."

"And what am I supposed to do there?" He sounds defeated.

"Buy her smoothie."

"Kade's smoothie. You want me to buy Kade *Goldenboy* Kassab a *smoothie?*"

I ignore him. "And talk to her. Smile. Make her laugh. Be chivalrous. Hold the door."

"I'm gonna spit in the smoothie."

I kill the engine and turn to look at Noah. Really look at him for the first time in this conversation. His face is a cocktail of irritation, incredulity, and consternation. But behind his glasses, I see flecks of hope in his viridian-blue-brown eyes. I almost reach toward him but catch myself in time to turn it into tapping off the music. "You're about to take the poor sap's girlfriend away, Noah. Let him have the smoothie."

Big Doug's is a classic diner—one row of booths against a wall of windows, one checkered-floor aisle, and one long bar with bolted-down stools. Everything is black and white and teal and red. On the back wall there's just enough room for a vintage jukebox. Given that it's Monday, the place is pretty much deserted.

It takes our waiter way too long to show up, and when he does, he sloshes our waters as he's trying to set them on the table. His name tag says GREG. He has dirty-blond hair and a ketchup stain across his shirt. He sniffles repeatedly, which makes me feel not great about him touching my food.

179

Greg grabs a towel off his shoulder and mops at the spilled water on the table. He pauses halfway through, looking hard at Noah. "Do I know you?"

I roll my eyes and huff out a serenity-prayer exhale. I'm too hungry for the waiter to waste time on cliché pickup lines.

Noah goes, "Huh?"

Greg sniffles and gestures toward Noah with the dripping towel. "I do know you! You were the guy with the Gorn costume at Comic-Con!"

Noah's face splits into a huge, self-satisfied grin. "You were there?"

"Oh yeah. That was epic, man. I was William Adama."

"Ah, you're a *Battlestar Galactica* man." Noah holds out his hand. Greg wipes his palm on his apron and shakes Noah's hand heartily.

I clear my throat, hoping to remind them that (a) I'm here, and (b) I want food.

Greg's eyes flicker to me momentarily. He sniffles and then leans in toward Noah conspiratorially, whispering, "Are you sure this one's not a skinjob? She's a little *too* hot."

I don't know what that means, but if he were my Cindy, I'd for sure flick ol' Greg in the ear right now. Noah laughs, all dorky good humor. I'm working up a *nudge* to get Greg moving, when Noah says, "Hey, man, can we get some menus?"

Greg straightens up. "Oh yeah. I'll be right back."

As soon as he walks away, I grumble hangrily, "What was that, some kind of brotherhood-of-dorks bonding moment? I thought you were strictly a *Star Trek* guy."

Noah folds his straw wrapper into careful tiny triangles. "*Star Trek*'s in the marrow. But *Battlestar Galactica* has some really first-rate world-building as well."

The only reasonable response to a comment like that is a dead-eyed stare. "This Magic Moment" comes on the jukebox.

Noah finishes folding his straw paper into a tiny five-point star and taps along on the Formica tabletop. My stomach growls. How long does it take to pick up two menus and return with them?

I drop my head against the back of the red vinyl booth. "I'm famished."

Noah looks unconvinced. "You say that. And then you're probably going to order, like, a side salad and a cup of ice or something."

"Or *something*. I just danced my ass off for ninety minutes. I could eat you under the table."

He raises his eyebrows in challenge. "I could eat a double cheeseburger and large fries right now."

I straighten up. "I see your burger and fries and raise you a hot wings."

He leans in. "Chocolate. Milk. Shake."

"It's on."

The eating contest ends with both of us groaning in regret. There are two french fries left on Noah's plate and an inch of melted sludge at the bottom of his glass.

"I concede the contest," he moans. "*W* to the girl with the green hair."

I clutch my stomach with one hand and raise V-for-victory fingers with the other.

Noah wipes his forehead. "Man, I've got the food sweats. How did you do that?"

"Look, kid. You've got skills. I just wanted it more."

He smiles until his cheeks dimple. "Good game." He holds his palm out, and I high-five him. A clutcher. With a fist bump. He blows it up. And for some reason, probably the copious amounts of sugar in the milkshake I just downed, I laugh out loud. Which makes him start to chuckle.

"Ow!" He laughs. "Oh. No. No room for jocularity in there."

"I should high-five you again for that five-star word. But I'm too full to bother."

A sniffle. We both look up and over at the same time. And there's Greg. He contorts his mouth into what I assume is supposed to be a smile and holds out our check. I'm thinking how awkward it's about to get if one of us thinks we're going Dutch, and somebody else tries to pay for everything, and who's going to make the first move, and this definitely wasn't a date so I'm sure Noah will want to go Dutch—

Dizziness washes over me, and the diner dissolves into a driveway and a front lawn with a hedge of blooming purple sage bushes.

Greg runs his hand along the hood of an electric-blue 1967 Camaro. He pauses to buff out a smudge with his sleeve. The look in his eyes is like True Love's Kiss. His connection with this car transforms him altogether—he stands taller; he is complete.

The *glimpse* recedes, and I blink the diner back into focus.

Since neither of us has reached for the check, Greg sniffles and sets it on the table. "Can I get you guys anything else?"

Noah is looking at me kinda hard. Without taking his eyes off me, he dismisses Greg with a "We're good, thanks." As soon as Greg is gone, Noah leans forward. "You okay, Charity?"

"Huh? Yeah . . . I mean . . ." I bite my lip. I feel like I'm pretty good at playing it cool during *glimpses.* It's not like my eyes roll back and my head spins around or anything. Noah noticing means I'm way off my game. I've been telling myself I could ignore the next *glimpse*—that I can quit them cold turkey—but now that it's happened, it feels like a gut punch. I need to grant this wish.

I can try to play it off, or I can tell the truth.

"Charity?"

"I had a *glimpse.*"

"Of *Greg?*" He sounds incredulous, almost jealous. It's kind of cute.

I nod. "He wants a car. A 1967 Camaro."

"Wow, you really know your classic cars." He sounds a little impressed.

I shake my head vaguely. "Lane and Monique made out on top of the exact same car in *Better Off Dead*. That's how I recognized it."

"That's way more random."

I shrug.

"So what are you going to do?"

I'm a pro at this. Five years of wish-granting experience plus my impeccable instincts do not fail me now. "First he needs grooming. Then I'll give him some lessons on how to wait tables and schmooze. We could double his tips by Saturday. If he's a quick study, he could get a job at a *much* nicer restaurant. I could *nudge* the guy selling the Camaro to drop the price at least twenty percent." I do some quick calculations in my head. "He'll have the car by June, sooner if he's already been saving."

Noah is placid. "But you're not going to do any of that, right?"

"But—"

"You promised."

I close my eyes. I can feel my eyebrows pinching together, and I press my finger between them to stop it. I whimper, "But you didn't see what I saw. There is a Camaro-shaped hole in that guy's heart. He needs me. It won't hurt anyone."

Noah's fingers wrap around my wrist and tug my hand away from my face. Not punishing or angry. Kind. I don't open my eyes. The *glimpse* replays on the inside of my eyelids.

"Charity, you've got to get free. Right? Don't do this one. Prove to yourself that you have a choice."

I turn my head away, still allowing Noah to keep my hand prisoner. Greg is wiping off the bar, casting surreptitious looks our way. I should go to him. I'd hold out my hand for a handshake and say, *Hello, Greg. I'm here to help you get a Camaro. I'm your fairy godmother.* To Noah I say, "This one's harmless."

"You don't know that. Every action creates a reaction. What if he would have been a brilliant scientist or something, but because you rocket boost his career as a waiter, he settles for that and the world never gets, I don't know, a transporter? What if he gets the car way sooner than he would have on his own, and because of that he gets killed in a crash or something?"

"What if I don't help him and his destiny is never fulfilled?"

Noah squeezes my hand so slightly that it could be my imagination. "You've got to let it go."

I look down at our two hands and swallow. I know he's right. I said I would do this—try to control the *glimpses.* I've got to get a grip on my life and my powers, or I'm going to end up witching out. Or worse . . . turn into Morgan le Fay. Even if I can't control when I have the *glimpses,* I can at least control what I do with them. So even though my heart feels like it's cramping up with the effort, I nod.

Greg is on his own.

I slide my hand away from Noah's and tuck it under the table.

17

This Is How You Tick Off the Universe

We go Dutch. It only hits a 7.2 on the awkward scale.

But it barely matters. Greg and the *glimpse* are the main event now. When I walk out of the diner without so much as a knowing smile in Greg's direction, my head begins to ache. The pressure starts right between my eyes, but with every mile I put between him and me, the pain blossoms to new regions of my skull. By the time I drop off Noah, I feel like an electro-house concert is playing inside my head and the subwoofer in my brain is about to blow.

"Are you okay?" Noah hesitates to get out of the vehicle.

My eyes are closed. "Yeah. Headache. No big."

Silence. I can feel him looking at me. *Just go,* I think. *Please just go so I can collapse.*

"Okay. See you at school tomorrow."

I manage a feeble "Good luck on the meet-cute."

"Yeah. Thanks."

He gets out, and I don't wait for him to get inside before I go. Driving hurts. Every streetlight is like a burning poker in my eyes. Thankfully it's only a few blocks. At home I drag myself to my bed, hoping for oblivion.

No such luck. I sleep in twenty- to thirty-minute fits throughout the night, interrupted by long and excruciating interludes of sweating, nausea, migraine, dry mouth, and muscle cramps. Sleep is no reprieve, because I dream of Vindhya sobbing, zombies attacking, Holly chained up and blindfolded, Noah as a judge in an enormous courtroom pronouncing me guilty, guilty, guilty. And Greg pleading, writhing, gasping for breath, and slowly dying at my feet.

While the rest of JLHS does the first-hour meet-and-greet, I'm at home, throwing up everything I consumed at Big Doug's Diner. By lunchtime every muscle in my body aches. About the time I should be in trig, I finally fall asleep for real—the kind that's too deep for dreams.

I wake up to pounding, and it takes me a second to realize it's not only inside my head. I stumble to the front door and check the peephole. Noah.

Supporting myself against the doorjamb, I undo the lock and crack the door. All I'm wearing is a T-shirt and underwear. That should be embarrassing. I should ask him how he knows where I live or why he's here. Or say hi. But it's all too much work. I turn around and shuffle back to my room, leaving the door ajar. As I'm climbing into bed, Noah appears in my bedroom doorway.

"Charity?"

"I'm sick."

"I'm getting that." He crams his hands into his pockets. He's wearing the new jeans I picked out. A perfect fit. "Is this because you ignored the *glimpse*?"

I pull my comforter up a little and grunt.

"Does that mean yes or no?"

"I'm *sick*." Like, *Leave*. Like, *I don't want to talk right now*. Like, *Don't make me think*. What part of this is he not comprehending?

Actually, the message must not be completely lost, because he says, "I'm sorry. Okay. What do you need?"

I grunt into my blanket.

"Who's taking care of you?" That's a weird question. I stare blankly. He says, "Where's your mom?"

"Belize."

He makes a sympathetic "aw" sound and says, "Okay, I'll be back."

I hear the front door click. I lie on my back, staring into space, the *glimpse* and the dreams infringing on my semiconsciousness. My head throbs, but it's as if the headache is wearing itself out—the rhythm is unvaried, but each strike doesn't have the same urgency as before. Long monotonous minutes tick by. My throat is dry and tight, and I have barf breath. But I'm too lethargic to get up and get myself a drink. I wish I could call for my mom.

And then Noah is back. Just his head appears first. "You're awake," he announces. Then the rest of him enters, laden with grocery bags. He sets them down on my desk and pulls out a cup of microwaveable chicken soup, a box of honey-lemon tea bags, a bottle of orange juice, a box of tissues, and—who is this guy?—a thermometer. I blink twice. The thermometer is still there, and it's coming closer.

"Open," he commands. I part my lips, and he sticks the thermometer under my tongue. While I'm thus incapacitated, he rambles, "I'm sorry about before. That was insensitive, to nag you when you don't feel good. I'm an idiot sometimes. When you didn't respond to any texts and you weren't at school—don't make fun of me—I guess I got worried, especially because you seemed really off last night after the Greg thing."

Worried?

"So anyway, I tracked you down online, like a stalker—"

Irony.

"—and I had all this stuff in my head I wanted to say all day, so—" The thermometer beeps, and he pulls it out of my mouth. "No fever. Can I get you something? Orange juice or soup or . . . ?"

My lips turn up a little. I mumble, "Tea would be nice."

He leaves the thermometer on my nightstand and heads out of the room with the tea box, like my wish is his command. It's unsettling. I'm always the one granting wishes, never the other way around.

I hear him opening cupboards and drawers in the kitchen, dispensing water, putting a pot on the stove. A few minutes later he returns, walking carefully with his eyes on the cup in his hand. He sets it on my nightstand. "Careful, it's hot."

"Thanks." I pull myself to sitting, and Noah jumps in to arrange the pillows behind me. I lean back, trying to play it cool, like this is totally normal.

He drags my desk chair up to the side of the bed and drops himself into it, knees wide apart as if his legs are just too long to be confined. He leans forward on his elbows like he's ready for a heart-to-heart. I clear my throat and go into fairy godmother mode. "So, how did it go with Holly this morning?"

For a split second I think he doesn't know what I'm talking about. Then his expression changes and he says, "It was . . ." He blows his lips out. It could mean *great* or *horrible*. Who knows? "I did everything you said, and I held myself back on the loogie front. She was friendly and everything. But, I don't know, I thought maybe we'd have this instant reconnection. Like magnets . . . like—" His eyes flit to mine, and he goes hot pink in the cheeks. He fixes his eyes on his knees and finishes with a mumbled "Never mind."

"No, I get it." I stare at my cup—as a professional courtesy because of his embarrassment and not because I'm feeling any kind of way about all this. "Everybody wants that. But maybe it's just gonna take some time." My throat is burning. I take a tiny, experimental sip of the tea.

He huffs out a breath. "Yeah. Well. Anyway. Ten minutes later, I pull up at school and she and Kade are trying to eat each other's faces off in the parking lot." He throws his hands up.

I think, *Poor guy.* Then I think, *His fault we didn't do this the easy way.* Then a little light bulb dings in my head, and I say, "Wait a second. You have a car?"

He shrugs. "Kinda. My mom lets me drive hers."

"Then why the heck did you make me come pick you up yesterday?" I find a throw pillow next to me and cause it to fulfill its destiny.

He deflects it, grinning. "I was being hilarious. I didn't know you were going to swoop in to rescue me like *Star Trek: Bridge Crew*. Plus, it was fun. Right?"

I roll my eyes. "Yeah, until I defied the Universe and my whole body went Fukushima."

He sighs. "Man. I'm sorry. I—"

I shrug. "On one hand, I blame you a hundred percent. But for real, I made the decision. I want to control this." I drink the tea. And it's good. The warm liquid soothes my throat and cleanses the rancid taste out of my mouth. "Don't worry about Holly. She'll come around. I mean, come on, you've got the new jeans and everything."

He looks down at his legs. "Yeah, I can't believe I paid money to look like I'm wearing somebody's Goodwill donation. What's the point?"

I wave him out of his chair. "Get up. Turn around." He obediently pivots, with an audible sigh. His old drawstring sweatpants gave one the distinct impression that he had no butt at all. These jeans hug his backside, with worn spots perfectly placed to draw the eye. Now I can tell he's not one of those chicken-leg guys. I wonder what exact type of gluteal muscles I'm looking at. He definitely doesn't sit on the couch playing video games 24/7, but it's not an "I do two-hundred-pound squats at the gym" butt either. Copping a feel might be the best way to ascertain—

"Are you checking out my butt?" He looks at me over his shoulder.

I jerk my eyes upward. "What? I mean . . . only in a strictly professional, analytical capacity." My cheeks betray me. I can feel the color rising—something between Wildfire Red and Fuchsia Inferno.

He sways his hips ridiculously. "You're totally checking out my butt."

I flop backward onto my pillows and consider pulling the covers over my head. Noah sits back down, still grinning. "So, now that you're done ogling me, what's next?"

I look at him slack-jawed for a second before I realize he means *What's next with Holly.* I snap my mouth closed. What did I *think* he meant, for crap's sake? I rub my cheeks, irritated with them for being hot for no reason. I muster my strictly business brain cells and say, "Do you know where she lives?"

"Well, yeah. I've been there a few times."

"As of now, you love jogging. At five thirty a.m. and after dark. In her neighborhood. Capisce?"

"Huh?"

"Holly looks angular lately. She mentioned something about running. A lot. But it's gotta be either really early or really late, because she spends all her daylight hours watching football practice."

"So I'm going to jog around her house until I accidentally-on-purpose run into her?" His eyebrows are up.

I nod feebly. "Pretty much."

"I think I hate this. When will I sleep?"

I think of all the mornings I was torn from sleep by meaningless texts, and I smile real pretty. "Karma's a bitch."

18

Seriously, What Are Friends For?

K arma's a bitch? Seriously?" Noah looks wounded. "Come on, I made you tea and everything."

He did. He came over and took care of me while I was sick. No one has ever done anything like that for me before. Not even Memom. And I had to go and be snarky. I've gone full Morgan le Fay.

I press my finger to the epicenter of pain in my forehead. "You're right. That was uncalled for. I don't know why stuff like that comes out of my mouth when you're around."

"Probably because you hate me?"

"I don't, though!" That was too eager. I dial back the enthusiasm. "At least not lately. As much. Also, you hated me first."

Noah suddenly stands. He walks to the desk, turns around, and comes halfway back. He stands at the foot of my bed with his arms spread. "I'm sorry." Big breath. "I'm sorry I called you the bad guy. This whole 'not granting wishes' thing is obviously not as black-and-white as I thought."

I blink a few times. That was an IRL uncoerced apology. But instead of accepting it, I counter, "You said I'm manipulative and criminally insane."

"I was wrong. I'm sorry." He looks at his feet.

My turn to say something. I clear my throat. "I'm sorry I called you a stalker."

His head pops up, and his eyes lock on me. "And loser, creeper, dork. And Captain America, but you were being ironic."

I drop my eyes. "All those too."

"Then I'm sorry I called you the Borg Queen."

"I shouldn't have threatened to murder you in front of your mom."

"I implied you were a Nazi sympathizer. That was out of line."

I stick my lip out, eyes up. "You tried to kill me with chunky peanut butter and rainbow sprinkles. That was inhumane."

"I'm sorry." His eyebrows draw together. "But the Deanna Troi costume, Charity?"

"How many times do I have to apologize about the dress? I'm really sorry!"

We both go silent. The only sound is the bass drum in my head and the soft hum of the air conditioner. Then, simultaneously, we both confess, "I'm sorry I pepper sprayed you."

Noah hangs his head and kind of chuckles. He makes his way back to the chair and sits in it. "So, is this an official armistice?"

"You recorded all my secrets on your phone and threatened to put them on the internet."

He sighs, takes his phone out of his pocket, finds the file, and drags it into the trash. Then he goes to his email account and does the same thing. He holds the screen out to me. "Deleted."

I bite my lip. "I'm sorry about everything . . . with Holly."

He drops his arm. "I forgive you."

"I forgive you too." And the miraculous thing is, it's true. My heart feels lighter. My headache is 15 percent less intense.

"Can we be friends?"

I twist the tea bag string around my finger, then slowly unwind it, not sure what to say. The fairy godmother doesn't have friends. Friendship is messy and murky. I need to stay above it all. But the thing is, I could really use a friend right now. Somebody who actually knows what's going on with me and makes me tea and asks me about my life.

I smile. "Friends sounds good."

We go silent again, probably because we don't know how to interact if we're not at war. After six seconds of that, Noah says, "All right, I think standard operating procedure here is a totally platonic 'now we're friends' hug."

I wrinkle my nose. "Ooh . . . I don't think that's a good idea, because I threw up before, and I haven't showered in two days, and I think I stink, and I'm not really much of a hugger, and—"

Ignoring my protests, Noah leans forward with his arms out, gesturing for me to meet him in the middle. "Come on. Bring it in."

"Oh. Um. Okay." Also, I didn't say this one, but I'm not

wearing a bra. Because why would I be? So I give him the most awkward forty-five-degree-angle, only-shoulders-touching hug. There's the Old Spice smell again. And something like cheap strawberry candy. I turn my nose into his hair and sniff. "Did you use your sister's conditioner or something?"

He pulls away and straightens his glasses. "Well, you said I needed to condition."

I give him a noogie, which frizzes out the hair I've been working so hard to convince him to tame. "Looks great. But—and I'm saying this as a friend—you smell like the love child of the Old Spice sea captain and a Strawberry Shortcake doll."

He grimaces.

I smile encouragingly. "I've got you covered. Go in my closet."

Noah obediently rises and crosses the room. He opens the bifold closet doors. His head cocks to the side in slow motion. I count to eight Mississippi.

He slowly turns to look at me, gesturing to the floor-to-ceiling shelves of hair dye arranged by shade of ROY G BIV. "You are a freak." I raise my eyebrows. He seems to realize he violated our truce and adds, "—ishly well-prepared person. It looks like Rainbow Brite is stockpiling an arsenal in your closet."

I let it go. I mean, what's there to talk about? "Conditioner is top left. I recommend Curl Commando."

He retrieves the bottle. "Uh? Thanks."

"What are friends for?"

The next day is more sleepless, lethargic, headachy monotony. Noah texts me sporadically throughout the day.

7:09: Running sucked. I think my left lung just collapsed. No Holly.

7:26: Feeling any better?

8:23: A bird somehow got inside the school and everybody lost their minds. I almost got crushed in the stampede in the humanities hallway.

9:16: Guess where I am? He drops a GIF of Neil deGrasse Tyson doing jazz hands.

I hadn't responded to any of his other messages, even though I read them with huge smiles. But this time I text back: Practicing your sweet dance duet with Neil?

Me: On the moon?

Me: Again?

Noah: You just about got me kicked out of physics for laughing out loud.

Me: You know there's an acronym for that, right?

Noah: YJAGMKOOPFLOL

I was referring to the last three words, of course. LOLing for real, I reply: Nailed it.

By midmorning, I turn on my tablet and find myself watching a crusty old episode of *Star Trek*. It is so hokey and sexist that I almost turn it off after five minutes. But I really want to know what

Noah sees in this cringe-fest, so I leave it on. I quickly realize that the guys in the red shirts get killed on every mission. If someone in a red uniform leaves the *Enterprise*, that chump is *not* coming back. So now I know why Noah's whole family picked red for me to wear. It hurts that they hoped I'd get offed by an alien. But I guess I deserved it.

Six episodes in, it starts to kind of grow on me. I like how Bones and Spock can't stand each other, but actually they're space besties. Captain Kirk has these unexpectedly deep moments. And Spock is a genuine badass.

Sean texts me after school: Where ARE you? I'm adrift in a sea of purple hair and yin-yang tank tops.

Technically, now that Sean's and my Cindy collaboration is done, I should go back to not answering texts and keeping conversations on the level of sports and weather. But using the f-word with Noah seems to have given me a taste for it. I can't quite make myself push Sean away again.

I text back: Sorry. Home sick. I drop an exploding head and a green nausea emoji. Then I really cross the line and send: I miss you, though.

He texts back immediately: Miss you too. Feel better.

My heart races like I just proposed and he accepted. I tell myself not to make it a big deal and go back to watching *Star Trek*.

Wednesday night, my headache finally breaks, and I sleep for fourteen straight hours. I wake up, eat everything in the kitchen, binge ten more episodes of *Star Trek*, and go back to sleep. I also decide something: it's not enough just to do better from here on; I need to fix anyone I've broken. I'm going to talk to every single Cindy, find out if their HEAs are on track, and do whatever I can to clean up any messes I've caused. I just hope I haven't scarred anybody for life.

While I get ready for school on Friday morning, I review the list:

Vindhya Chandramouli—Voted homecoming queen.

Carmen Castillo—Made the Poms squad.

Holly Butterman—Went to junior prom with Kade Kassab.

Sean Slater—Let his inner ballerina out.

Teresa Saint Clair—Reunited with best friend, Tammy Trent.

Olivia Chang—Cast as Adelaide in Guys and Dolls.

Sara O'Rourke—Divorcing parents got back together.

And then there are the ones Noah doesn't know about because they were pre–high school. . . .

Bryce Sayers—One kiss from his secret crush before she moved away.

Kelly Bodworth—Adopted Juggernaut, the slobbery puppy.

I put on extra makeup—armor for today. I'm a knot of

emotions. Reviewing what the Cindies and I accomplished together still gives me the warm fuzzies. But it's mixed with anxiety over what fallout I may have caused. And determination to start making amends by doing whatever I can to help Vindhya get back on her feet, which is really diving headfirst into the cesspool of collateral damage.

A text *swoops* in, and I pause with the eyeliner to check it. It's from Noah: **The jogging paid off.**

He ran into Holly. I should feel like The Boss for making it happen. But it's too soon. We just agreed to be friends, and the end is already barreling toward me. I overcompensate with a perky text back: **You won the presidential fitness award already?!**

Noah: **Yuk it up, Tinker Bell.**

I smile, because I guess I'm glad that we still get to call each other names now that we're friends. I text: **Want a ride to school? You can tell me all about it?**

Noah: **You can be seen with me now?**

Me: **We'll park far, far away.**

Noah: 😳 **ok.**

━━━

Noah slides into my car thirty-five minutes later and greets me with a huge, dorky smile. My heart does some kind of gymnastics, which I had no idea could happen from a friend smile. I still have a lot to learn about friendship, I guess. I smile back, but it comes out way more eager than I meant for it to be, so I recompose my features to my standard placid professionalism. "Okay, you have nine minutes, and I want details."

He makes his voice deep. "Captain's log, stardate 76173.8: I saw her across the park by her house, so I set a course for intercept."

I don't flick him, but I give him a platonic punch in the arm. "Tell me like a normal person, please. What did she say? What did you say?"

He sighs. "She said something like, 'I didn't know you were a runner.' And I said, 'I just started torturing myself every morning and night hoping I'd run into you.'"

There's a stop sign ahead, and I hit the brake too hard. "You came right out and told her that?"

He shrugs. "Well, yeah. I mean, I might as well be honest now instead of having to cover it up forever or fess up later and creep her out."

I go, "Huh," because who's that honest? Then I concentrate on driving better. "Okay. Keep going."

"We just talked, which was fine, and ran, which still sucks, and then at the end I asked if we could jog together again tomorrow, and she said yes."

My reaction is delayed by that same twinge of sadness I felt when I got his first text this morning. I actually like being Noah's friend, and the closer we get to fulfilling his wish, the sooner that friendship will end. This is the problem with getting attached to a Cindy—the nature of the relationship is short-term.

"Charity? It's good, right?"

I throw my whole heart into my smile. "It's awesome. You absolutely nailed it." Then, to prove to myself that I want this HEA, I add, "We'll need to think about exactly the right time for some strategic *nudges*."

Noah grimaces. "No way. Neither one of us even knows what that does. What if you're permanently messing up people's brains or something?"

"Friends don't accuse friends of giving people brain damage." I try to make it sound like I'm joking, and I tell myself that my heart doesn't hurt at all.

He adjusts his glasses even though they're perfectly straight. "Sorry. I didn't mean anything. I'd just rather know that whatever happens is real."

"Yeah. Sure. Whatever." I pull into the school parking lot and park in the farthest space from the building, behind the dumpsters and a huge magnolia tree.

He rubs his hands together. "So, speaking of real . . . I feel like maybe I should kiss her. You know? Break out of the friend zone. Get the spark back."

"What?" I turn to him, appalled. "Absolutely *not*."

"Why?"

I sputter, "Because . . . she's still with Kade! That makes you the 'other guy.' Bluch. Besides, there should be no kissing until after the Grand Gesture."

"Am I supposed to know what that is?"

I inhale bracingly and recite with absolute authority, "In the Grand Gesture, one person declares themselves in a dramatic way to the other. Common elements are (1) finally putting to words previously unspoken feelings, and (2) seeking forgiveness for sins of both omission and commission. The Grand Gesture must be directly proportionate to any wrongs committed in terms of personal risk, public self-effacement, and strength of language."

"Hold up. Are you planning to make me do something I have to grandly apologize for later?"

"Not necessarily. In the rare event that there is nothing to apologize for, the Grand Gesture is a dramatic and creative way to profess your undying love."

Noah looks at me like he's waiting for me to say, *Just kidding.* I look back, expressionless and unyielding. He scoffs, "You're serious."

I continue to stare him down.

"As your friend, let me just tell you that is the cheesiest and most far-fetched thing I've ever heard. And I watch 1960s-era sci-fi."

I crinkle my nose, like, *Your opinion's not valid.* Then I revert to strict professionalism. "Regardless of how you feel about the Grand Gesture as a concept, kissing the girl is strictly prohibited."

He's going to ask me why. He never simply accepts my advice for the sagacity it is. I mentally scramble for a good enough reason

urya Agrawal is having a party over fall break, and
irl on the squad who hasn't been invited."

the warm-up music. We're officially late for practice,
we'll be running sprints afterward. Carmen clearly
fact too, because she darts a mournful look at the
eed to finish this. I say, "Is there anything I can do? I
be happy."

tates. She opens her mouth and closes it. Bites her lip.
murmurs, "They all follow you, Charity."

a little, because *ouch*. She didn't come right out and
my fault the Poms haven't embraced her, but that's
ht? I've been keeping my distance, so everyone else has
my finger between my eyes to ease the tension there.
starting right now, we're friends. Okay? Real friends.
mise you'll get an invite to that party. I'm on it."

iles, but her eyes are puzzled. I put my arm around her
through the locker room door so that everyone gets an
ow tight we are. Coach doesn't pause practice, just waves
e formation.

———

and forty minutes later, I drag myself to my car, still sweating
ping off an hour of dancing with ten minutes of wind sprints.
arms are buzzing from *nudging* Coach to let us leave halfway
our punishment. Noah is leaning against the Fit playing with
phone he had the day he sent me that first creepy text.

to convince both of us. After a moment's hesitation, I say sensibly, "Wait for her to kiss you. Be elusive and hard to get."

"But I already told her I was literally running around the neighborhood looking for her. *Now* I'm going to be hard to get?" He opens his door.

"It adds to your mysterious appeal. You're Spock, not Kirk."

He freezes halfway out of the car and turns back to me with a look like, *Have we met before?* He opens his mouth, but it takes a few seconds for words to come out. "You watch *Star Trek*."

My eyebrow twitches without my consent. "Well, I mean, I've *seen Star Trek*. It's really not the same thing."

He swallows, pushes up his glasses, and looks at me for four more seconds. Then he climbs out of the car.

When I get out, he's waiting for me. I wave him on with a resigned sigh. "Go ahead. I'll hang out here a minute so it doesn't look like we came together."

He shakes his head, like I'm a big disappointment, hefts his backpack, and walks toward the school.

19

So, About Those Happily Ever Afters . . .

I find Vindhya after school in the same room where we first met nearly three weeks ago. She's reading a magazine. Her hair is in a devil-may-care braid—the kind a girl studies hair tutorials to master. I step into the room and close the door behind me.

"Hey, Vindhya, can we talk?"

She shrugs without looking up from the magazine.

I clear my throat. "I just want to say I'm sorry. I had no idea something like that would happen, and I . . . I never would have—"

She meets my gaze finally. She is stone-cold. "What is this? Do you need closure so you can feel better?"

I shift my purse strap on my shoulder. "No. I want to help. Is there anything I can . . . ?"

Her mouth drops open, and she laughs one silent, mirthless *ha*. "I think I've had enough of your 'help.'"

"I'm just trying to—

"Stay away from me.

It stings like a slap, bu

Well, if you change your n

She determinedly look

I walk out the door, hea

So. That could have gon

Ten minutes after leaving
Carmen aside in the girls' loc
others file out to the gym for
closed, I dive right in. "Carmen

"Huh?" She looks like I jus
that may or may not explode in

I try again: "Is your life bet
made it onto the squad?"

"Oh." She looks down at her s
like, *There's no place like home,* and

"That lacked conviction."

Her eyes crinkle. "Well, I mean,
great. But." She shrugs.

"What?"

"I guess I thought I would autom
whole squad, you know? But I feel like
mean or anything. I just . . ." Her head

like, I know S
I'm the only g
I can hear
which means
registers that
door. But I
want you to

She hes
Finally she
I cring
say that it's
the gist, ri
too. I pres
"Carmen,
And I pro

She s
and push
eyeful of
us into t

An hour
from top
Plus my
through
the flip

He glances up. "'Bout time."

I pop the hatch and throw my dance bag and backpack in. "What are you doing here, and why the flip do you have a phone from 2005?"

"You're kinda my ride, genius. And it's a communicator."

I raise an eyebrow. He holds the "communicator" out. I slam the hatch closed. He says, "Actually, it's a Bluetooth. Check it out." He flicks his wrist, and the thing unfolds with a chirp. He says into it, "Scotty, call Charity."

It chirps again, and a second later my phone rings. I answer it, even though Noah is standing three feet away from me. "Hello?"

He grins at me, still talking into his communicator, "Hey, is this the Fairy Godmother Hotline?"

I snicker and cobble together a quick slogan. "We *glimpse* it, we grant it. For girl troubles, press or say 'one.' For all other wishes, press or say 'two.'"

He says, loud and overemphasized, "One."

I can't seem to look away from him. His eyes are mostly green in the late-afternoon sun. They sparkle with teasing humor. I keep talking to him on the phone, possibly leaning in a tiny bit to get a better view of his pretty, pretty eyes. "Go ahead."

"Well, there's this one girl. I've loved her as long as I can remember, and I thought I—" His eyes change. More blue. More longing.

Suddenly I don't want to play anymore.

Listening to Noah gush about Holly is like running my knuckles across a cheese grater. I lower my phone. "Sorry. The hotline's closed. Let's go."

I open the car door and slide into the driver's seat. Noah gets in. To the glove compartment he says, "You okay, Charity?"

"I'm fine. I just . . ." What *is* wrong with me? I *love* love. I *want* Noah and Holly to get their fairy-tale ending. It's gotta be this whole crappy day that's making me irrational. I say, "Carmen isn't happy. Vindhya is miserable, and she won't even talk to me. I mean, what if *none* of them are happy? I'm trying to fix my mistakes, but—" I back the car out and head toward the exit. "Anyway, it'll be fine. I'm sorry for whining."

Noah pushes his glasses up. "What can I do?"

"Nothing. I'll handle it."

He sounds a little exasperated. "Charity, we're friends now. Remember? All you have to do is ask for help."

I stiffen my spine. Leaning on someone who will be out of my life so soon is like setting fire to the garbage pile I'm already in. "Don't worry about it. I'm fine."

"Say 'Help me, Noah.'"

"I'm not saying that."

"*Ayúdame*, Noah," he says in a near-perfect Dora the Explorer impersonation.

I roll my eyes.

"HIQaH," he barks.

"I feel like I should flick you right now. Is that a real language?"

"It's Klingon for 'help me.'"

I reach out to flick him, but he grabs my hand. I tug it until he lets me go. Eyes on the road, I say, "There's nothing you can do. It's my problem."

"Oh." He heaves a dejected sigh. "I guess I shouldn't have gotten the DL about Vindhya from my friends in Robotics Club, then."

I practically yell, "You have friends in Robotics Club?!"

"I just spoke Klingon. How would I *not* have friends in Robotics Club?" He crosses his arms smugly.

"Yeah, come to think of it, why aren't you *in* Robotics Club?"

"I'm more of a theoretical physics man."

I have to think hard for a response to that, and eventually come up with "Cool."

"But don't try to change the subject. Do you want my help?"

"Well." I glance his way. I won't get used to it, I tell myself. I won't depend on him. But it would also be ignorant not to tap into this underutilized resource. I clear my throat. "Okay."

He gives me an *I'm waiting for the magic word* face.

"Please."

"Vindhya missed some Robotics Club meetings the past couple of weeks. When some people called her on it a few days before homecoming, she quit. Without her they have zero shots at medaling at the regional robotics meet."

I groan.

"Basically, you took a future NASA programmer, turned her into a walking Barbie doll, and submarined the entire robotics program in the process, more or less destroying the scholarship hopes of a couple dozen kids."

"Give me a freaking break. I already feel bad enough."

"Come on." He chucks me in the arm. "You're the fairy godmother. I'm Spock. We'll figure it out."

"Yeah." It lacks conviction.

There's an awkwardly long silence. Eventually Noah breaks it with "Hey, isn't there a football game tonight?"

"It's away. Poms don't do away games. We have a competition in the morning, though." We stop at a red light.

"Seriously? Like, who can shake their pompons the—"

"Don't. Make me hurt you." I stick my pointer finger in front of his face. One little inch more, and I could play connect-the-dots on his freckles. Totally platonic friends probably do that. The light turns green. I put both hands firmly at ten and two.

Noah motions zipping his mouth shut.

A couple minutes later we pull into his driveway, and he climbs out, shouldering his backpack. Before he closes the door, he leans back in and says, "Good luck in the morning."

"You too."

He looks confused, like he completely forgot about his wish or something. So I clarify, "Good luck with Holly."

"Right." He straightens up. "Holly." He closes the door and gives me a wave. "See ya."

By the time I'm smelling stale sweat on the school bus after the competition on Saturday, I have a text from Noah: Who shook their pompons the bestest?

I bite down on a laugh. I mean, he's a sarcastic pain in the ass. But on the other hand, he's kind of checking in on me, which is really . . . kind of . . . nice.

I'm tapping a reply when Scarlett's voice accosts me: "Wow! *Who* has got our Ice Princess making goo-goo eyes?" She leans over the seat in front of me, trying to get a peek of the phone.

I lock the screen faster than you'd drop a hot pan. "Nobody. Sean, actually. I'm just texting Sean. And also, my eyes don't goo-goo." To make it legit, I unlock my screen and fire off an invite to Sean for breakfast tomorrow.

Scarlett looks like I have *liar* written on my forehead. "I know you're up to something. Or *someone*."

I don't flinch. I stare her down. Eventually she turns back around.

Carmen gets on the bus, and I wave her over with a "Carmen! I saved a seat for you!" She shoots me a grateful smile and scoots in across the aisle.

I finish my text to Noah: Meh. We got third in our category. How was running? Please tell me the damsel twisted her ankle and you carried her home like Prince Charming.

Or don't. Maybe don't.

Noah: Her ankles are intact. But she laughed so hard

she got a cramp in her side. At the end she gave me a hug. It was . . . sweaty.

For just a second, I think, *Holly, you cheating little skeezer!* I tamp it down, appalled at myself. This is how the fairy tale is supposed to go. Noah gets the girl, and they live happily ever after. I reply: Love is in the air. Won't be long now.

The next morning Sean and I sit side by side at the counter at Inland Empire Bakery.

My bagel sits untouched, while I twist the paper sleeve around and around my cup of orange juice. I already, for once, remembered to ask him about dance stuff. Now we've lapsed into silence. I clear my throat and dive in. "Sean? Is your life better since . . . you know, since you met me?"

He pauses with his cream cheese croissant halfway to his mouth. "Charity? Are we soul-searching?"

I pick at my bagel. "I guess you can call it that."

"Because of what happened with Vindhya?"

"Kind of."

He sets the croissant down and drags his fingers across the napkin in his lap.

I press him. "Are you happy?"

He takes a pensive sip of his latte. "Happiness is complicated, Charity."

I lean in. "You have a million admirers, you set every trend, you're JLHS's It Boy. You *must* be happy."

He swirls his cup and watches the foam churn. "My father has also never been to a single one of my performances. Every person I meet assumes I'm gay, and—you know, not that it matters, but the majority of male ballet dancers are hetero. And even though what I do is just as intense as any other sport, not a single person—apart from maybe my mother—considers me an athlete. Since I don't handle a ball, what I do doesn't count. I don't count. So . . . yeah."

As he talks, my throat gets tighter and tighter. It takes all my willpower to keep it together. I've put a wedge between Sean and his father. I subjected him to stereotypes and prejudice after he worked so hard to get away from them. And I've acted like his details don't matter, just like everybody else.

I eke out, "I'm so sorry. You deserve to be a hundred percent happy."

Sean takes my hand. "It's okay, Charity. I wouldn't change it. I have to be me and let other people deal with their stuff. My father will come around. Or he won't. But it's still better than him loving somebody that doesn't really exist."

I lean into him, and we wrap each other in a hug. He smells woody and minty—it's the cologne we picked out together before the talent show. I tighten my grip on him now, my head on his shoulder. After a long moment, I muster the courage to whisper, "I never told you this, but . . . you're my real friend."

"I know, sweetie. You're my real friend too. And I don't have many of those."

20

Rock Bottom Is Way Farther Down Than I Thought

Mom gets home Sunday evening. In honor of the occasion, I add indigo streaks to my viridian hair. I think it looks like the ocean in a storm. She walks in with her roly bag, her suit-and-sneakers outfit, her airplane-limp hair, and flaking mascara. She gives me a long, tight hug, crooning, "Oh, honey, I *missed* you *so much.*"

"I missed you too, Mom. So much."

She pulls back to arm's length, taking me in with a smile. I brace myself for her exit speech, but she says, "I'm starving, and I want *American* food."

Thirty-five minutes later, we're unboxing a freshly delivered pizza. We scarf it together while she tells me funny stories of cultural confusion and language faux pas between the delegates at the convention. Turns out, getting people from four continents together in one room is a recipe for zany comedy. Maybe UN meetings are secretly hilarious.

This is the most time we've spent together in recent memory. I let myself be happy. I let myself hope that, whatever my mom has been chasing, she found it in Belize.

Rookie mistake.

"Charity, the exciting thing is that the T. C. Barrister Foundation invited us to submit a proposal for a three-*million*-dollar grant! It would be the largest private grant we've ever received." She takes my hand and squeezes. "It's going to mean a lot of late nights and weekends for the next few weeks to pull it together. But it's worth it if we get this grant."

I nod. I mean, I get it. It's a three with *six* zeros. I just can't seem to find my words right now.

She yawns and pats my knee. "Okay. I'd better hit the sack. I've got to start bright and early tomorrow."

She retrieves her roly bag, kisses the top of my head, and makes a beeline toward her bedroom. Right before she disappears, she calls back, "Lock up."

She never did notice my hair.

⸺

At 7:04 a.m. Noah texts: You know what's better than running? Literally everything.

I'm already pulling into the parking lot at school, getting ready to stake out marching-band practice so I can talk to Teresa (Cindy #5). I don't know what comes over me, but after I park, I text back: You know what's worse than running? When your mom leaves for work at 6:30 a.m. after being in Belize all week.

Ugh. Could I be any whinier? I start to type: Please disregard—

But before I can recant, Noah's response appears: Yeah, that's worse. I'm sorry ☹ Want to borrow my mom for a few days?

I look at my phone for too long, unable to come up with a witty reply. After a minute Noah texts again: If you act now, we'll throw in a fat, antisocial cat at no extra charge.

Now I have to smile. Not only does he know exactly when to inject a cat joke, but he also didn't call me out for whining. I had no idea how good it would feel to just let someone see the messy parts and be my friend anyway.

Don't get used to it, I tell myself firmly. *Only friends till the wish ends.* Hmmm, that's pretty good. Maybe I'll DIY that onto a piece of driftwood or something.

All this touchy-feely stuff is costing me precious minutes. I straighten up and text back: Gotta go. I'm on a fact-finding mission, investigating an HEA.

Noah sends a GIF of a very wrinkly, gray-haired Spock doing the Vulcan salute and saying *Good luck.*

I put the phone away and head to the band room. Last year I helped Teresa and her best friend, Tammy, reunite after a wicked fight. My plan is simple: find Teresa and ask her how things are going. Ultimately I don't need to even do that much. I can hear her and Tammy screaming at each other before I even get inside the band room. It's like:

"Why do you always do this to me?"

"Like it's *my* fault! You started it."

"I want my friendship necklace back."

"Take it, you backstabbing piece of—"

"You're such a hypocrite!"

"Screw you!"

Et cetera.

One more fairy tale demystified. Four to go.

I head to English lit, where I cross-examine Olivia Chang while we're supposed to be discussing *Crime and Punishment*. She's Cindy #4, a wisp of a girl with a singing voice twice her size. She's been the star of every school play since I helped her get her big break freshman year. Whatever pleasantry I ever possessed is a distant memory at this point. I just want to tear off the Band-Aid and get it over with. I hiss, "Does your life suck?"

"What the—"

"Since I granted your wish, have you been in, like, a spiraling depression or something?"

"No?"

"Do you wish you never got Adelaide?"

Her eyes shift left, then right. "I mean, I love the shows, but . . . It's complicated."

"How?"

"I don't know. My parents think I'm not focused on school, and sometimes it's just a lot of pressure. Plus I still feel guilty about what you did to Clara."

Clara was the senior shoo-in for the role of Miss Adelaide in *Guys and Dolls* when Olivia was the freshman upstart. And I'm deeply offended by Olivia's accusation. I whisper-yell, "I didn't do anything to Clara!"

"You took her to that party the night before auditions, got her trashed, and then plastered it on Facebook, so the director saw it and banned her from the show."

Ouch. I'd kind of buried that memory. But also I'm not as evil as she makes me sound. I cross my arms defensively. "I acquired an invitation for her, but I didn't make her go. And nobody held her down and poured alcohol down her throat. She did that to herself. Also, I'm not the one that posted the Facebook pictures. Logan What's-His-Face was."

She makes a face like she's got soap in her mouth. "Why are we having this conversation, again?"

"We're not."

We both go back to Dostoyevsky.

⌒

I spot Surya during passing period and chase him down, grabbing his arm to get his attention. "Dude, the hell? Why didn't you invite my friend Carmen to your party?"

"Carmen who?"

"Carmen Castillo. She's on Poms."

"Oh, uh, I don't really know her, I guess."

I *nudge* him a mental image of her, along with some positive vibes.

His face registers recognition. "Oh, right! *Carmen!* Yeah, sure. I'll invite her."

"Today?"

"Yeah."

"You're the best." I grace him with a winning smile.

"I am?" He waves his finger between us. "So maybe you could be my date to the party?"

"Still no." I extricate myself with a wave and a smile.

At lunch I locate Noah with a quick scan of the courtyard. He looks like he's in one of those rom-com movie scenes where the heartbroken guy gets surprisingly deep advice from the bartender while simultaneously getting blitzed. Only he's sitting at a round plastic table instead of a bar. And instead of whiskey, he's drinking Rockstar. And the part of the bartender is being played by his two AV Club friends.

I don't have time to find out what has Noah looking so dejected. I can't afford to slack off on meet and greets. I speed through them so I can go back to tracking down Cindies. I haven't seen Bryce (Cindy #2) since he graduated last year, but I still have his number in my phone. I sit in my car and make the call, then bounce my knees furiously while it rings.

"Hello?"

"Hi, Bryce. This is Charity Keller. Do you remember me?"

"Yeah, hey, Charity." He sounds hesitant, possibly suspicious. Is it because we spent an intense summer before his freshman year chasing around a girl together? Or because I never spoke to him again after that? Probably a little of both. But it's not my fault. It's the way of the fairy godmothers.

I clear my throat. "So, um, I'll make this quick. Do you remember that girl . . . what's her name? Eun-Ae?"

He laughs. "Oh my Lord, that was, like, forever ago. I was ride or die for her."

I laugh along. "Yeah. Remember how she kissed you behind the moving van right before she had to leave forever? That was . . . so romantic, right?"

He laughs again, but this time with an edge of bitterness. "Yeah. But you know what wasn't romantic? That kiss totally gave me mono. I was sick for a month. My spleen ruptured. That was literally the worst year of my life."

Are you freaking kidding me, Universe? Is this *what you've been using me for? This is sadistic.*

I can't force air into my lungs. I manage to rasp, "Sorry. I . . . I've gotta go."

I tap end, chuck the phone onto the passenger seat, drop my forehead onto the steering wheel, and scream. High and piercing and long, until I run out of air. Then I suck in a ragged breath and scream again. Hopefully my car is soundproof. Otherwise, people are going to think someone is performing Civil War–style battlefield amputations in the parking lot.

When I've screamed myself out, I turn back to my phone. I have to finish this. I have to find out if *anybody* had a happy ending. I need to know the depth of my sins.

The problem is, I can't find Kelly Bodworth. Not on Insta, not on Insta . . . not anywhere. If someone doesn't exist online, do they exist at all? I start to imagine the dog I foisted on her ripping her throat out in her sleep . . . mauling her whole family to death. . . . Finally I find a Facebook account for K. A. Bod Worth that looks like it might be hers. (Seriously? Is she forty?) The profile picture is of a big black-and-tan dog. But it's so locked down that I can't see anything else. I take a chance and send a PM:

Kelly, Is this you? This is Charity Keller. Do you remember me? I was just wondering how you and Juggernaut are doing. Is he being a good dog? Are you still glad you got him? Write me back, okay?

I hit send and check the time on my phone. Lunch hour is over. I have to face trig and the final Cindy.

———

Sara O'Rourke (Cindy #3) is in my trig class. Unfortunately, she gets to class right at the bell, and then the teacher promptly announces a pop quiz. So interrogating Sara will have to wait until after I find the freaking area of a quadrilateral using Heron's formula.

After the quiz, I frantically scribble notes for forty minutes. Finally the bell rings, and we all file out of the classroom looking shell-shocked. I maneuver my way through the trig zombies until I'm walking next to Sara.

She notices me and glances my way with both eyebrows up. "Oh. Hi, Charity. Long time, no . . . anything. How are you?"

I give her my fresh, disarming smile, although inside I feel like I've been running wind sprints all day. "I'm good. How are you? How are your parents? How are things at home?"

She hesitates.

"Everything good?"

She takes a deep breath and releases it in a long Zen exhale.

"So, not good?"

She shifts her books. "No. It's good, I guess. I mean, my parents are remarried to each other. They're in love again. It's like a fairy tale." She gives me a conspiratorial look. "It's kind of funny, actually. Exactly ten months after we Parent Trapped them, my mom popped out a baby."

"Whoa."

"Yeah, so he's almost two now. My parents never have time for me because they chase him around twenty-four hours a day. And he's a monster. This morning before I left for school, he colored all over my Kate Spade bag with a blue Sharpie. While me and Mom were dealing with that, he took his own diaper off and peed in my bed."

"Ick."

"Yeah. So, the moral of this story is 'Be careful what you wish for!'" She barks a laugh.

I almost say, *If there's anything I can do* . . . But you know what? There is nothing.

I tell myself that maybe she'll like him better in a few years. Then I think of Noah and Natalie's relationship, and I'm not so sure.

⸺

By the final bell, I've checked off all the Cindies and come to an important conclusion: The Universe is a sadist. And I've been its unwitting pawn. I feel used and duped and utterly horrified. Memom always taught me that the *glimpses* were a smile from the Universe . . . that we had a special gift to make people happy.

But it's the opposite. Destiny is a monster.

I'm a monster.

I will *never* blindly follow a *glimpse* again. I don't even want to be a fairy godmother anymore.

But before I can quit altogether, I need to make amends where possible, starting with Vindhya, Noah, and Carmen. The Carmen thing seems to be making forward progress. But I still don't know why Noah was looking lovelorn at lunch or how I'm going to get Vindhya's life back on track.

I speed change for Poms practice and use my spare six minutes to text Noah from the bathroom stall: You okay?

Noah doesn't immediately respond. I picture him lifting his

hungover head from the bar and fumbling his phone into his whiskey. Eventually, after two dragging minutes of waiting, the phone rings.

It's Noah. I answer, "Hey."

"Hey." He sounds completely sober. Of course.

"I have, like, three minutes before Poms and just wanted to—I don't know. You looked not great at lunch. Did something happen with Holly?"

"Well, she told me we can't run together anymore and that I shouldn't try to see her. She said she doesn't want to jeopardize anything with Kade. Blah, blah, blah. But that's not—"

"It's a setback. That's all." Nope. It's the kill shot. And I've got zero clues how to resuscitate his wish now. Until I figure something out, all I can do is keep it peppy. "It's a good sign, actually. She's afraid of her feelings."

"The thing is—Charity, I . . . I need to talk to you."

"We are talking."

"In person. For more than three minutes."

My heart flutters. Why should that be? Trekkie weirdo + another girl + bathroom stall ≠ romantic arrhythmia. I revert to strict professionalism. "I have an opening after Poms. We could meet."

He sighs. "I work till eight. Can you come over after that?"

"I can make that happen."

I hang up with Noah and make it to the gym with twenty-six

seconds to spare. I'm pulling my hair into a ponytail when Scarlett marches over, a phone in her hand and self-congratulations on her face. Loud enough for anyone who cares to hear, she says, "I *knew* there was something up with you."

I twitch my eyebrow at her.

She holds the phone up, screen toward me. "This is you, right?"

It's a picture of me and Noah holding hands across the table at Big Doug's Diner.

21

The Truth Has a Coming-Out Party
and Everyone's Invited

The photo is on Instagram. And it's as bad as it can get. It was obviously taken right after I *glimpsed* Greg and his Camaro. I was having an existential crisis, and Noah was trying to talk me down from the ledge. But it 100 percent looks like we are planning our elopement. Leaning in, holding hands, earnest expressions . . . Damn. It. The caption reads *Beauty and the Geek IRL #nerdlife #itcouldhappentoyou.* It has fifty-four likes. Nope, fifty-seven. And climbing.

I have just enough time to glance at the username on the post: Camaro_dreamin_67.

I smile at Scarlett while I mentally smack Greg the Waiter upside the head. *I was sick for three days over you! I wanted to help you get your precious Camaro. And the whole time, you were creeping on me. Bush-league, Greg.*

Coach calls, "Let's do this."

Scarlett shoves the phone into her pocket, beaming, and falls into formation. The warm-up music pours out of the gymnasium sound system, and we all start the routine. My body automatically follows the series of stretches I've done at least a thousand times, while my thoughts spin.

Actually, I spend the entire warm-up thinking up new names to call Greg. Wouldn't you? Then I play Six Degrees of Separation: Scarlett-Greg Edition for a while. I fail to figure out how this happened. But I do decide that I'm not mad at Scarlett. She's not mean-spirited. She just has a nose for news.

Stage three is basically outlining the suckage of the situation via a series of questions I can't answer:

Why does this picture make it look like Noah and I were staring into each other's eyes like we'd found the meaning of life?

How am I going to convince another girl that Noah is her OTP, with photographic evidence to the contrary making its way around cyberspace?

How am I going to maintain Ice Princess status without explaining the real reason we were there together, holding hands and looking soulful?

If I'm not the Ice Princess, how am I going to keep everyone at a distance?

Why does my heart hurt when I look at that picture? Is this regret? Longing? Acid reflux? Should I take a Rolaid?

G.F. MILLER

Finally, while Coach has us do the entire competition routine in slo-mo to her counts, I kick myself into strategy mode. It doesn't really matter how we got here or how I feel about it. I have to work the Problem.

Option One: Deny everything. Claim it wasn't even me in the photo. Pros: Straightforward. Cons: Not that many people have viridian hair, and it's a pretty clear shot. I'd have to make the case that Greg actually photoshopped me into the picture and come up with a motive.

Option Two: Throw Noah under the bus. Say he has a massive crush on me, and I was there to let him down easy. Pros: Fairly plausible. Cons: It's a crappy thing to do, he'll never forgive me, and it materially harms his chances with Holly because it makes him look like a creepy loser.

Option Three: Let Scarlett into the People Who Know About the *Glimpses* Club and swear her to secrecy. Pros: Honest. Cons: The internet honors no such oaths. Even if by some miracle Scarlett is the only person at JLHS who has seen this so far, it's only a matter of time before the leak becomes a full-fledged containment breach. Also, Scarlett is the very last person anyone would want for a secret keeper.

There really aren't any good options.

We move from a bent-knee straddle to a lunge. My back leg is a little out of alignment, so I shift to correct it. Out of the corner of my eye, I see Gwen, posed next to me, shift her leg a fraction

230

of an inch too. Then two more girls. Behind Gwen, Carmen's already straight leg gets a little more taut. She glances at me for approval.

They all follow you, Charity.

Suddenly, things click together in my mind, like the combination on a bike lock: Holly soaking in the spotlight with the wrong guy at prom . . . the jocks' Ice Princess betting pool . . . Noah getting rejected this morning . . . Scarlett finding Greg's photo. *Click . . . click . . . click . . .* When I put all the problems together in the right order, they turn into the solution.

I know how to grant Noah's wish.

⟵⟶

I duck out of the building the instant Coach dismisses us. I don't even change, just grab my stuff and bolt.

Waiting until eight to go to Noah's house is a special kind of torture. It gives me way too much time to rehash every detail of the Problem and the Plan, despite having to get through thirty trig equations and two chapters of *Crime and Punishment.*

By seven forty-five I've got full-blown jitters. To kill time, I call Hope.

The screen on my tablet does a pixelated sweep of the rustic room my sister sleeps in, and then I'm looking at Hope's face. She's lying in bed with her brown hair tangled across her pillow. She rubs her eyes. "Hey, little sis. It's not Friday, is it?"

"No. I just wanted to talk."

She yawns. "Hmm-kay. About what?"

I hear an elephant trumpeting in the distance. It reminds me how different our lives are now. How far away she is. What do we really have to talk about? I cop out with "How's the boy?"

Hope looks genuinely clueless. "Who?"

"The boy you stayed in Thailand for. Remember?"

"Oh! Kiet. Yeah. He's a great guy, but I . . . I don't know." Hope looks away, but not before I catch the sadness in her eyes. Her voice is light and airy. "He was getting too serious. I just wanted to keep it light."

Even though I've never met Kiet, and I'm predisposed to hate him because he's part of the reason my sister is eight thousand miles away, my heart sinks at Hope's confession. She was willing to leave her family for him but still couldn't commit to a real relationship? It's profoundly sad.

"Hope?"

"Yeah?" She sits up, adjusting her camera to follow her, and finger combs her hair out of her face.

"Are we broken?"

If I had thought about it for three seconds, I could have come up with a better question. Like, *Are we emotionally distant because our mother is a workaholic?* Or even, *Do you think our parents' divorce made us incapable of accepting love and making commitments?* Or maybe, *Ever heard of Morgan le Fay?*

But it doesn't matter. Sisters don't need all the words.

She takes a deep breath and looks toward her open window. Watching the elephants, maybe. After a few seconds she says, "I don't think relationships work for us, Chay. We're . . . you know we're fixers. . . . We fix things. But we don't *keep* things."

"What do you mean?"

She's still looking out her window. "It'd be like me trying to make Bernice my pet. Or Mom saying the ocean is her private pool. We're catch-and-release people, you know?"

"Yeah." I think I know exactly what she means, actually. And it makes me want to barf all over my tablet.

I press my finger between my eyebrows. Hope chews her bottom lip.

After a sad silence I say, "I hope you work it out with Kiet." And it's true. I really do. I want to know that it's possible.

She smiles like, *Who knows?* Then she says, "Sorry to do this, but I gotta pee."

"Okay. Talk to you Thursday night slash Friday morning."

We end the call. And I realize that I'm late for Noah.

———

I ring the doorbell with more than a little trepidation. Pretty much every time I've been at this door, life has taken a sharp left turn toward Crazy Town. Plus this is the first time I've had to face Noah's family since the Deanna Troi thing blew up, and I don't know if they all hate me or what. This time Noah's dad answers, his bald head shining in the porch light.

He waves me in. "Good to see you, Charity. Noah's in the living room. Straight back there."

That felt too easy. Is it possible they don't know what I did? I step across the threshold, ready for an ambush.

It's an open floor plan like ours, so there are no walls between the front room, the kitchen, and the living room. It's really all one big cavern with a few pillars and furniture defining spaces. However, the alleged living room is tucked behind the stairs. I walk toward it. Dr. McCoy watches me suspiciously from the top of a bookcase. Noah's mom is in the kitchen. She looks up when I'm in range, and her smile seems genuine tonight. I really don't think Noah told them what I did.

Speaking of Noah, I can hear him and Natalie fighting before I see them.

"Move it or lose it!"

"Don't you dare! . . . NO YOU DIDN'T!"

"Ha! You want some bananas, Monkey Boy?"

I round the corner and find them sitting on the floor playing Mario Kart. Noah is still wearing his pink-and-green Arctic Marble uniform, the shirt unbuttoned and untucked and the hat discarded on the couch behind him.

Noah looks my way with a self-conscious grin. "Hey, Charity."

"Hey."

It takes him a second too long to turn back to the TV. His kart hits a bunch of banana peels and goes into a tailspin. Natalie laughs maniacally. A few seconds later she crosses the finish line a kart-length before him. He tosses his controller down in mock disgust while she does a victory dance worthy of an NFL touchdown.

Noah demands, "Rematch. Tomorrow night."

She tosses her curls. "Loser brings the snacks."

"Did someone say 'snacks'?" His mom comes in with a bowl of snack mix—the kind that's, like, all the best worst-for-you chips in the world mixed together. As soon as she sets it on the coffee table, Noah and Natalie pounce on it.

His dad reappears. "Snacks?" He drops onto the couch and commandeers the bowl for his lap. Commence family wrestling match over the junk food, punctuated by protests about access and equality of distribution and loud laughter.

I stand on the sidelines, a voyeur to their chaotic happiness. It strikes me that Noah and Natalie don't hate each other at all. And that love is messy and beautiful.

Natalie launches a Dorito at me. An invitation to join in? Before I can analyze my options for recourse, Noah extricates himself from the tangle of people, grabs my hand, and hisses, "Quick! While they're distracted!"

He runs up the stairs with me in tow. When we get to his room, he carefully positions the door so that it's an inch shy of closed. He still hasn't let go of my hand. I still haven't pulled away. He says, "Sorry about my family."

"They're . . . perfect, actually."

He looks at me like I must be joking. Then his eyes soften. He releases my hand but reaches toward my hair. He's so close I can see every freckle and the gingerbread-colored ring around his pupils.

I don't move. I don't breathe.

He pulls back, holding a chip. "You had a Dorito in your hair."

I inhale, and the air feels unnaturally heavy. There's too much gravity in this room. I say, "Thanks," and the word falls to the floor like a lump of wet cement.

Noah's eyes seem to be locked on mine. "Charity. Listen. I don't think I can—"

At the same moment, I blurt, "I know how to get you together with Holly."

"What?"

"Sorry?"

"You first."

I take another heavy breath, enough to push the thousand-pound words out of my mouth. "I'm going to grant your wish next Friday night."

He turns away from me, flicking the Dorito into the trash can by his dresser. "I need to talk to you about my wish."

"It's okay. I've got a plan, and it's going to work. I'm sorry it's taken so long, but I—"

"Charity, wait. I—"

"I know what you're going to say. You don't want to manipulate her. You want the real thing." He opens his mouth, but I hold out my hand to shush him. I have to rush through everything I have planned to say; otherwise, I don't know if I'll be able to get through it. "But here's the thing about Holly. Why do you think she wanted to be with Kade?"

He shrugs. "He's good at football?"

"But she never cared about football." I pace like a private investigator in an old detective movie. "Holly wants to be envied. She loves having the guy everyone else drools over."

"Really? That sounds so shallow."

"Why else would she be with Kade instead of you? And I didn't *glimpse* her and Kade on a quiet date by themselves. I *glimpsed* them at prom." Noah looks disgusted and vaguely disinterested. Of course, he doesn't want to hear anything negative about his true love. I plow forward with the part about how this works in his favor. "All we have to do is make you the It Boy. Holly will be yours. And I promise you won't have to change a thing."

He laughs raggedly and gestures toward his ice-cream-stained Arctic Marble uniform. "That hasn't gone my way so far. Does this plan of yours involve some sort of rift in the space-time continuum?"

"No." It's almost a whisper. I clear my throat and try again. "No."

"Would I have to make a deal with the devil?"

"No." I concentrate hard on making the word breezy, with limited success.

"What then?"

"You have to date *me*."

As soon as the words are out of my mouth, I know they're all wrong. I analyzed this plan down to the quark. I thought it was perfect. It is perfect. It's just that my heart is screaming, *Not this! Anything but this!*

Noah goes in and out of focus as I try to hold myself together. I press my lips into a thin line and grip my own arms tight, tighter. The truth is suddenly so obvious. And so devastating. I've let myself fall in love with Noah.

22

Yes, I'm Aware This Was All My Idea

Noah stares at me. Stunned. I hold his gaze, my face a mask of tight-lipped professionalism. He blinks like the light is too bright. "Date? You?"

I shouldn't be surprised. I'm not surprised. I'm just in pain. Some tiny part of me was harboring a dream scenario where Noah's reaction to this proposition was to declare his undying love for me.

I make my voice cool. "That's right. For whatever reason, JLHS decided at some point that I'm an influencer. People imitate my hair, my clothes. . . . The jocks have a standing virtual *and literal* prize for whoever can get me to date him. They call me—"

"Ice Princess."

I twitch my eyebrow.

He shrugs. "I'm a dork. I'm not deaf."

"Right."

"Which is why no one will believe—"

"Greg the Waiter took our picture at Big Doug's and posted it. And then Scarlett got ahold of it. We look . . . well, just trust me. Everyone will believe it."

"What about . . . ? What about . . . ?" He stammers, gesturing at nothing in particular. "What about 'I can't be seen with you'? What about the confidentiality clause?"

"It no longer applies. The photo's out there. All we can do is lean into it." I sound impressively matter-of-fact. There's no point in mentioning that my personal aftermath is going to suck in the worst way. Beyond the unavoidable broken heart, it's going to be humiliating to go from "untouchable" status to "lovesick and dumped."

"This is crazy."

"Once we break up, there'll be a queue of girls that want you. And Holly will be the first one in line."

He looks too stunned to speak for a moment. Then he silently shakes his head.

"Noah, this is all I've got. My last idea." I'm pleading. Pleading for the thing that will wreck me. I hug myself. "Either we do this now, or we're done."

"Done?"

"We stick to the contract. You go your way. I go mine." It's all I can do to stay standing as I voice the inevitable. Still, I don't flinch.

"I thought we were friends."

"That only lasts as long as the wish," I lie. I'll never stop wanting to be near him. But there's nothing else I can do for him. It would be wrong to hang on, especially knowing what I know now—that I've left a trail of destruction on every life I've touched.

"Forget the wish, okay? How about, instead of faking things, we just keep hanging out for real. Maybe we could not park behind the dumpsters or—"

"I'm the fairy godmother. I don't hang out. I grant wishes and that's all."

"I thought you were done granting wishes."

I shrug. "It doesn't matter. I don't hang out."

He looks like I punched him. Turning away, he stares at his dresser for a long moment. When he finally speaks again, he seems to be addressing his vintage Spock action figure. His voice sounds gravelly. "So, just to make sure I've got it straight. We have two choices: fake date for a couple weeks—"

"Ten days."

"Or ignore each other completely. And that's because our friendship was never real to begin with."

I swallow. *Be strong for him,* I tell myself. *Don't le Fay this up.* "It's real, Noah. It's just not . . . permanent."

For a long moment the words hang in the air, silencing both of us.

"I see." His shoulders square up. Now it's his turn to pace. "So, if I go along with this, what happens next Friday?"

"You'd break up with me at Surya's party."

He shakes his head again.

My mouth feels like it's full of chalk. "Yes. It's the only way to keep all the mojo you'll get from dating me."

He stops pacing and stands right in front of me, so close that I have to hold my breath to keep from huffing Old Spice and Curl Commando. So close I have to tilt my head back to see his face. His forehead is pinched. He looks like he's begging me for something. Which, in fact, he is. The same thing he's been begging me for since his first stalker text—to fix what I broke, to give him back his true love.

He says, "You really want to do this?"

No! my heart screams. *Don't make me fake it when I want the real thing. Don't make me pretend to have this just so I can give it to someone else.* With my mouth, I say firmly, "Absolutely."

"You want me to be with Holly?"

My heart is having a tantrum. It beats wildly in my chest, trying to break free and expose me as a liar. But my thoughts are more disciplined. I will *not* be one of those fairies who goes around getting it on with guys and trashing their lives. I want him to be happy. Holly makes him happy. And I owe it to him. I promised him. He's my Cindy. And he's my friend. So I set my jaw and say, "I do. One hundred percent."

Noah picks me up for school on Tuesday, our first official day of faux dating. When I open my front door, my heart pounds at the sight of him. He's wearing The Jeans and one of the button-down shirts I picked out way back when. It's unbuttoned, and I can see a sliver of words on the T-shirt beneath. His fingers are tapping a hundred miles an hour against his leg. His curls are wild. The early-morning sun glints off his glasses, so that I can't get a good look at his eyes.

"Hey." I'm poetical like that.

"Hey."

He seems keyed up and verging on cheerful. The total opposite of how I left him last night. I guess he just needed time to let the plan sink in.

Just like I needed time to realize that I can't possibly be in love. What I feel for Noah is 90 percent friendship and 10 percent silly crush. Maybe 80/20. It took me most of the night to convince myself of this, and my insides are goo. I compensated with extra makeup and by adding sky-blue streaks to my stormy-ocean hair.

He bows, sweeping his arm toward his car, and says, "My lady?" He must be nervous. He's always extra dorky when he's nervous.

And him being dorky makes my heart squeeze. I remind it firmly that we're just pretending. I grab my backpack, lock the door, and head for his car.

Did I say "car"? It's actually a white minivan. It has a window decal across the back that says MY CHILD IS AN HONOR STUDENT AT STARFLEET ACADEMY.

We mutter and stutter our way through some small talk on the drive.

At school he parks the van and then runs around to the passenger side to open the door for me. It's so chivalrous. Who does that?

As I climb out, he says, "So. How do we do this? Should we hold hands, or . . . ?"

Holding hands sounds super nice, but I snark, "Are we pretending to be eighty years old? Brother and sister?"

He looks stumped. Ugh. Somehow we have to get 110 percent less awkward in the next sixty seconds, or no one is going to believe we're actually into each other, and the whole plan falls apart.

I take his arm and drape it over my shoulders. My whole body instantly tries to claim this spot as mine forever. The weight, the warmth, the smell . . . It's nirvana.

His arm tightens around me tentatively. I silently remind myself: *None of it is real. Get ahold of yourself.* To complete the ruse, I slide my left arm around him and shove my hand into his back pocket.

He jumps forward. "Hey! Wow."

A couple of people glance our way. Through a big flirty smile, I ventriloquist whisper, "You gonna be okay?"

"Yup. Yeah. I'm good." He straightens up. "Just, maybe warn me next time you're going to . . ." He gestures nondescriptly, blushing all the way down his neck. "You know."

"Grab your ass?" I can't help it. It's so fun to make him squirm. Which he does. People are pointing and gawking now. I hold my smile in place for them. "Get a grip on yourself. It's go time."

We walk toward the double doors, which is a fun little party for my left hand. Noah whispers, "Sorry. I've never been anyone's fake boyfriend before."

The people who were previously looking are positively rubbernecking now. He pulls out of the side-cuddle to open the door for me. I whisper back, "You've never been anyone's *real* boyfriend before either."

As I slide past him into the building, he mutters, "Said the Ice Princess."

I look at him instead of where I'm going, snagging his hand and wrapping it back around me, like I can't bear to have an inch of air separating us. The grand entrance is not lost on the JLHS student body. Conversations falter before stopping midsentence. People literally pull out their phones and take pictures as we pass by. From somewhere in the crowd, I hear, "No way!"

Noah's arm is tense. He leans in and says in my ear, "This is the weirdest thing I've ever done."

I rise to my tiptoes and turn my lips to Noah's ear. "False. I've seen the Gorn costume."

I feel a shiver go through him. *Involuntary breath-on-the-ear reaction. Nothing to do with me.*

We pause at my locker, and Noah untangles us. While I dial in my combination, he surveys the hallway uneasily. "Now do I go to class?"

"Yeah. Um. I guess I'll see you at lunch." I notice Scarlett and Gwen waiting in the wings and give them a little finger waggle.

Noah's eyes flit toward them and then lock back on me. He swallows. He looks stumped again, his hand hovering. "See you at lunch."

The Awkward Walk Away isn't going to impress anyone. So before he can get away, I wrap him up in a quick, tight hug. His arms come around me and he takes a deep breath. Then he lets me go and leaves.

In my head I chant, *It's not real, it's not real.* My heart thunders anyway. They do not call this a *crush* for nothing.

23

Just When You Think Everything Is Finally Going According to Plan

Noah isn't six feet away when Scarlett and Gwen scurry to my side. They squee and jump around so that there is no way Noah can't hear it. Scarlett whisper-squeals, "Ohmigod, ohmigod. I was the first one that knew!"

"Yeah, how did you get that photo, by the way?" It doesn't even matter at this point. I simply hate unsolved mysteries.

Scarlett says, "My cousin Terryn's boyfriend is super into cars. He follows that Camaro Dreaming guy. So I guess Terryn saw it on her boyfriend's feed and reposted it because she thought you guys were cute. And then I saw it on her feed and was like, 'Hello. I know those guys.' So were you two, like, secretly, tragically dating all year?"

Gwen sighs like that's the best thing she's ever heard.

"No. Not all year. We actually just made it official. We weren't keeping it secret. It's more like we were trying to figure us out first.

You know?" I so rarely give Scarlett inside scoops that she looks like she's going to swoon with joy.

Gwen says, "But, Charity . . ." She pauses, twisting her phone in both hands like it pains her not to be looking at it. "Isn't he kind of . . . um . . . a total dork? I mean, you could go out with *anybody*."

"I guess I like dorks." I shut my locker and wave my way off stage left.

Noah is waiting for me right inside the doors when I walk into lunch. He gives me my favorite eye-crinkling smile, and I respond by wrapping both arms around him for some extra-public PDA. He obligingly reciprocates, resting his chin on top of my head. It's been an exhausting morning, so—even though it's only for show—I secretly draw strength from that hug. I smash my face into his T-shirt and breathe him in, just for a second.

Then I turn my face so everyone can see my flushed cheeks and lovesick eyes. When everyone who cares to has had ample time to take pictures, I pull back. Next we go through the lunch line, and even the lunch lady looks at us like we're adorable while she scans our IDs. We find a table in the courtyard and sit.

I should create a point of contact, but what would be best? Subtle yet possessive? I decide to wrap my foot around his ankle. He looks startled and then gives me a half smile. I unscrew the cap on my orange juice. "How's your day so far?"

He leans in conspiratorially. "Are you kidding me? Surreal!

Random dudes—guys that have literally never spoken to me before—keep fist-bumping me. That Poms girl, Gwen, stared at me in Spanish—*the entire hour.* And Surya Agrawal walked up to me out of the blue and handed me a ten-dollar bill."

I can't help laughing.

He says, "Seriously, what am I supposed to say to stuff like that?"

I slide my hand across the table and thread my fingers through Noah's, mostly for show. But not really. "Don't worry. In a day or two everyone will be over it."

Except for me. I'm pretty sure I'll never be over it.

Noah tightens his grip on my fingers. "This is the best part of my surreal day."

I force myself not to react. He's in character. That's all. I quip, "The taco bites or the fruit cup?"

"Being with you."

A wistful little voice in my head says, *This is real. Say something true.* And I want to. But I'm scared. But maybe we could really be together. But fairy godmothers don't keep their Cindies. Only awful fairies try to steal Prince Charming. Besides, he loves Holly.

I jump up like there's a bee on my seat, ripping my hand away from Noah's. "Taco sauce! I need some of those, uh, little packets of taco sauce."

And I run away. All the way to the condiment station. I press my finger between my eyes and breathe.

In the two minutes it takes me to get a grip on myself and then grab a fistful of hot sauce that I don't even want, Noah's two AV club friends have commandeered my spot at the table. They don't see me approach because they're busy bowing to Noah and chanting, "We're not worthy!"

Noah is Rocket Fuel Red. The two proceed to shamelessly man-crush on Noah loudly enough for me to hear it from ten feet away. Loud enough that half the cafeteria is watching.

"Dude, you are the playa of all playas!"

"Henceforth and forever you shall be known as Playa One!"

Noah rubs his forehead. "Jeez, guys. Just be cool." He glances around and seems to realize the full extent of the audience, including me. He tacks on a groaning, "Please?"

AV 1 sits, uninvited and undeterred. "Freaking *A*, man!"

AV 2 says, "Check this out." He holds out his phone, displaying a photo. I close the distance so I can get a clear look. It's Gwen sitting at a desk. The picture was snapped from behind her. Past her mass of black curls and over her shoulder, you can see that she has doodled on her math notes *Dorky is the new sexy.* Noah and I exchange a glance over AV dudes' heads.

AV 1 grabs Noah by the shoulders. "Do you realize what this means?! Our dating pool just turned into a freaking *ocean*! This is—"

"Look, guys, it's *my girlfriend*, Charity!" Noah extricates himself from AV 1's grip, tripping backward over the bench in the process. He manages to stay upright with three hops and a half rotation. Once he's stable, he gestures broadly at the table. "Charity, this is Carlos and the Mouth."

I give them a single wave hello.

Carlos laughs nervously while the Mouth, apparently oblivious, keeps talking. "It's crazy that just yesterday you were sitting here whimpering about—"

Noah cuts him off. "Awesome, guys. That's great." He grabs my hand and tugs. "So Charity and I are going to go . . . make out. Now. For a while."

Carlos's response is a double thumbs-up.

The Mouth attempts a high five but misses, primarily because Noah's not participating.

We back away slowly. Carlos calls after us, "Never forget where you came from!"

Noah whispers, "I'm really, really sorry about that."

We wheel around to escape and more or less collide with Kade and Holly on their way in. Kade, who is typically chill, seems kind of stressed out. Holly seems stressed that he's stressed.

Holly's hand is in Kade's back pocket. I shoot Noah a look that says *I told you so times infinity.* But then I feel bad, because he looks like he accidentally got toothpaste and orange juice in his mouth at the same time. Still so in love with her, obviously.

I reach for his hand and give it an *I'm here with you* squeeze. He clears his throat. "Hey, Holly. Kade."

Kade says, "Hey, man."

Yeah, he for sure doesn't know Noah's name.

Holly says, "So you two are, like, a *thing* now?"

"Yup." I don't hesitate. I wrap my other arm around Noah possessively.

Kade says, "Cool. So I guess you'll be at the par . . ."

The room spins, and I tighten my grip on Noah as a new scene replaces this one.

Kade is in the football coach's office. He hands the coach a thin stack of papers, stapled in the corner. On the front it says "The Social and Cultural Impact of Gutenberg's Printing Press." The date in the header is two days from now, and there's a red, circled "84%" in the upper-right corner.

Coach looks down at the paper, then shakes Kade's hand. "You squeaked in, champ." Coach crosses his arms over his chest. "You've been on academic probation all week. This makes you eligible, but are you ready to face Loma Linda tonight?"

Kade says, "Put me in, Coach. I wanna play."

"Right, Charity?" Noah nudges me.

"Huh? Yeah. Good." I have no idea what I'm agreeing to. Or where I am. I blink. Holly and Kade. Cafeteria. Tuesday.

Holly shrugs. "Okay. Well, see ya."

They walk on past. I silently tell the Universe to get a new Hunky, because I'm not touching this. The Universe responds by lighting a flare right between my eyes. I press my palm against it with a sharp inhale. Noah guides me out the door, ducking his face close to my ear. "What did you *glimpse?*"

He's the only person who has ever noticed me *glimpsing.*

I mumble, "Kade needs help with his World History paper. I guess he's on academic probation from football. He has to get an eighty-four percent to be eligible to play in the game on Friday."

Noah throws his head back and groans. "Come *on.* Did it have to be Kade?"

"Not my fault."

"Are you going to help him?"

"Not a chance." An invisible ninja sword stabs me through the forehead. I gasp. I lean into Noah and let him hold me up. It's that or hit the floor.

"Charity? What's wrong? What do I do?" There's panic in his voice. I have to pull it together.

I straighten up as best I can, as the hallway swirls in a fog of vision-blurring pain. "Just a headache. I'll be fine."

24

An Unexpected Tag Out

I try to take a step but feel like I hit an invisible concrete wall. I stagger backward. Noah steadies me.

He says, "You're not fine. I'm taking you home."

I'm in too much pain to argue. But high school is kind of like prison. You don't just leave. The next however long is a haze of Noah walking me to the office and presenting the case for me leaving, the school nurse asking me questions, me mumbling responses, my mom getting a call at work, Noah's mom getting a call at work, and Noah finally being handed a green slip of paper indicating that we're free to go.

He is silent for a few minutes during the drive home. I keep my eyes closed and concentrate on breathing. On my twenty-third exhale, Noah blurts, "This is like the Kobayashi Maru!"

"Uh?"

"It's a test in Starfleet Academy that no one can pass. You're ambushed on a rescue mission. It's a no-win scenario. I feel like it's the same for you. If you obey the *glimpses*, people get hurt. But if you ignore them, *you* suffer."

I mutter, "Sucks to be me."

The next thing I know, Noah is half dragging me to my front door. I don't know if it's the migraine, the motion, or only the next phase of the Universe's retribution, but by the time we get to the house, my stomach is churning. He opens the door, and I throw myself into the hall half bath just in time to retch my guts out.

While I sit panting, Noah kneels next to me and gathers my hair away from my face. He presses a damp cloth against the back of my neck and says, "Well, I'm never going to feel the same way about taco bites."

I laugh and then throw up again. He holds my hair, and that makes me cry. When it's over, Noah helps me stand and walks me to the closest comfortable place, which happens to be the couch in the front room. He arranges the cushions behind me and gets me a drink of water.

He says, "This is worse than last time."

"Just coming on faster," I croak.

"Why do you think that is?"

I don't want to talk or think. I grumble, "I don't know. Maybe it gets worse every time until my head finally explodes."

"Maybe we should just help Kade."

"No way. The Universe is a sadistic bully. I'm not going to let it use me to screw with people's lives."

The Universe responds with a sledgehammer to my forehead. I cry in pain.

Noah's hands hover over me. "Do you want some Tylenol? An ice pack? What should I do?"

I can't handle him being sweet and taking care of me. Not when I'm trying not to get attached to him. I don't want him to watch me cry. And I don't want to talk with my head pounding like it's pierced with a thousand daggers. I command weakly, "You should go back to school."

"No. You're a mess. You need me."

"I DON'T NEED YOU!" I bury my face in the throw pillow, not caring that I'm ruining it with mascara. "I don't want you here. So leave."

"Ouch." There's a pause and a heavy exhale. "I'll check in later."

I don't lift my face, but I hear the door click behind him.

At 3:22, my headache disappears instantly and completely. It's like magic. As soon as the pain fades, guilt sets in. Noah was nothing but sweet to me, and I threw it back in his face. I text him: I'm sorry.

There's no response.

I turn on *Star Trek II: The Wrath of Khan* and watch it while I do my homework.

At 8:01 p.m. Noah texts me: **How are you feeling?**

I am ridiculously relieved. I was starting to imagine he'd decided I wasn't worth the effort. My first impulse is to send him a gushing text about how grateful I am that he took care of me, then repent for being horrible . . . and, oh, by the way, I love you. But I don't. I write back: **Totally fine now. Sorry for freaking out.**

Noah: **It's okay. What time did you start feeling better?**

Me: **3:20ish. Why?**

Noah: **Just testing a hypothesis.**

What is *that* supposed to mean?

Noah again: **Want to ride to school together?**

Me: **Of course. I'll pick you up. You ARE my boyfriend.** 😊

There is no word in the English language strong enough to describe the obsessive behavior of a "theoretical physics man" trying to figure out magic.

This fact becomes clear to me before we even get to school on Wednesday. First he pumps me for information about how the *nudges* work, and how do I *know* when they work, and how does it feel, and are there side effects.

"Yeah," I admit for the first time out loud. "Actually I get pins and needles. And the more *nudges* I do in a row, the worse it gets."

He nods like he's cataloging that in some scientific chart in his brain. "Fascinating. *Nudging* must be really taxing for your nervous system."

"And you know that because?"

"We get that tingling sensation when our nerves start misfiring. It usually happens because the blood flow is restricted. But in your case, using your telepathic—"

"*Magic,*" I insist.

"'Magic' is just a word for something science doesn't *yet* have an explanation for."

That statement is so gloriously nerdy that I have to hold myself back from diving across the car and kissing him on the mouth. Right now I love his giant brain. I love that he sees life as one big logic puzzle. I love . . . him.

Eventually he moves on from "telepathy" to "precognition." These terms still make me squirm. I've never thought of myself as having paranormal abilities. It's always been *magic* to me. Anyway, semantics. I let it go.

He asks me one thousand and one questions about yesterday's *glimpse,* how I felt before and after 3:22, and was it *exactly* 3:22, and how did it differ from the Greg *glimpse*—

"I don't know." I sound like one of those guys in a movie who's about to crack under intense interrogation. Because that's how I feel. "With Greg it faded slowly over a few days. This time it just, *poof,* vanished. Maybe it's random."

"Nothing is random. There are only patterns we haven't found yet."

I park at school and cut the engine. "Okay, Spock. And the pattern is?"

"Well, uh." He pushes up his glasses and scratches his head. "I . . . offered to help Kade with his paper."

"You *did*?"

"Yeah."

"YOU did?"

"Ironic, I know."

"Why?"

Noah turns his viridian-and-gingerbread eyes full on me. Which is pretty unfair. He stammers, "I just, you seemed so . . . sick. And I thought, 'Maybe this is how it works. Maybe if destiny is on track, the FG's off the hook.' So I tried it."

Oh. Okay. I get it now. "You were *testing a hypothesis.*"

"Well . . . yeah."

I am so pathetic. Here I am acting like all those desperate alien ladies who were always trying to get it on with Captain Kirk. But the whole time Noah's been studying me for *science*. Honestly, he'd probably chop me up in a lab if he thought that was an option.

"Okay. Thanks for that." I paste on a smile and practically throw myself out of the car. I would like to march defiantly away. Or possibly run, weeping, to an emotionally safe space. But there are people all around and appearances to keep up, so I stride—

purposeful yet peppy. I'm about a third of the way to the entrance when Noah catches up to me. He captures my hand, threading our fingers together.

I dart him a look. His cheeks are so pink. He smiles sheepishly and says, "I figured, since we're 'dating,' right?"

"Right," I say brightly.

⸻

The morning unfolds pretty much like yesterday, but with 50 percent fewer paparazzi flybys. Noah and I are *literally* yesterday's news. I try not to feel any kind of way about that. Not happy about additional privacy with my darling research scientist. Not sad that our ten days are slipping away. I don't think about anything except that we'll need to do something soon to grab the spotlight again if we're going to make Holly see what she's missing.

At lunch, while I'm sitting with Noah, Sean graces us with his presence. He doesn't sit, but looks pointedly at Noah and says, "Excuse me, can I borrow your *girlfriend* for a bit?"

Noah is wide-eyed, either because Sean has never spoken to him before or because he sounds like he's accusing Noah of something. I stand with a sigh.

Sean holds his hand out to me. "Charity, walk with me."

As we take a slow stroll around the courtyard, Sean says, "Tell me the truth. Is he a Cindy?"

I bite my lip. "More or less."

"It's a yes-or-no question."

"Then *yes*. He is. *Happy?*" I smile and wave at a group of JV cheer girls.

He gives them a nod. "*NO*. It's an absolute train wreck. Charity, what are you thinking?"

"I've had loads of Cindies. It's never bothered you before."

"You've never crucified yourself for any of your other Cindies."

"I don't know what you're—" I pull away slightly, enough for Sean to notice but not so much that anyone else can tell we're fighting.

"How does this end, Charity? You're too close to this."

His aim is too good. I deflect in an "I'm rubber, you're glue" kind of way. "Maybe you're just jealous. Maybe you're scared that JLHS has a new It Boy."

He looks mortally offended. "Pettiness is so tacky on you."

We give each other the silent treatment for a full ninety seconds before Sean touches my elbow. "Are you in love with him?"

As much as I've been lying to myself, I can't lie to Sean. In nine days, he'll be the only real friend I have left. So I murmur, "More of an infatuation. Strictly one-way."

His hand tightens on my elbow, a reassuring pressure. "I don't want you to get hurt, Charity. Please guard your heart. That's all I'm going to say."

I nod again. We walk on, my hand in the crook of his arm, stopping to chat with a few groups on the way back. I get the feeling Sean is purposely stretching out the lunchroom tour as long as possible. By the time he deposits me back at my table, Noah is gone.

I spend the afternoon tallying up all the messes I've made and trying to figure out how on earth I'm going to clean it all up. Let's see, there's:

Vindhya. Still counter-snubbing all the people who are snubbing her. Still won't talk to me.

Holly. Still acting like Kade's human football trophy. Still no closer to realizing that one of the most amazing people on the planet would sell his spleen for her. Not sure she even deserves him.

All the other Cindies.

Me.

I have depressingly few ideas for fixing the HEAs. What if I try to help and just make everything worse? I'm still deep in this headspace as I drive Noah home after Poms.

"You're quiet."

I grunt.

"Anything you want to talk about?"

"No."

"Did you have another *glimpse?*"

"No."

He shrugs and looks out the window. But after a minute or so, he starts up again. "I've been meaning to ask you about your progress on finding the switch."

"Huh?"

"You've been trying to learn to turn the *glimpses* on and off, right?"

"Riiiiight." Kind of. Got busy.

"So, how's it going?"

"You know." Eyes firmly on the road. I admit nothing. "Good. Slow."

He takes off his glasses and goes to work cleaning them with the hem of his T-shirt. "I wish we had access to one of those electroencephalography devices that can measure the electrical impulses in your brain. We could hook you up to that and figure out which areas are active when you're *nudging* or *glimpsing*. I have a hunch that it's somehow related. . . ."

SERIOUSLY? Why not just jump straight to vivisection? I growl.

He leans forward like he's trying to make sure I can see his encouraging smile. He taps my arm with his knuckles. "Yeah, it's frustrating. But don't give up. I believe in you."

My heart squeezes. I still don't want to disappoint him. I'm like a lab rat that's in love with the guy who's experimenting on me.

So after I drop Noah off, I take myself to the mall, determined to find the switch by trying to *glimpse* the wishes of random strangers. What's the worst that can happen? Migraine from hell, public puking, some Abercrombie worker calls 911, and I die of fairy godmother withdrawal in the ambulance. No big.

Two hours later—exhausted, discouraged, and 100 percent *glimpse*-free—I head home to do trig and watch *Star Trek*.

The next morning Noah shows up at my door looking as tired as I feel. His eyes are bloodshot, and his shoulders are slumped. He's wearing a shirt that says NO INTELLIGENT LIFE REMAINS ON THIS PLANET.

I actually recognize the quote. It's from an episode of *Star Trek* where they get zapped back in time, Spock goes primeval, and the sun is about to explode. I watched it a couple of nights ago. I decide to throw Noah a bone. "Did you come in through the time portal?"

Noah looks startled and then confused.

I point at his chest. He glances down at his shirt and then back up at me, a huge grin taking over his face, which almost immediately turns into a yawn. He covers his mouth with his elbow, then scrubs his hands through his hair. "Come on, Zarabeth."

I smile to myself as I lock the door. *Star Trek* references—it's like a secret language that we both know. Sharing that with Noah gives me a rush of pleasure. Then I remember that Zarabeth totally did it with Spock and then turned out to be evil. So that's awkward.

We trudge side by side to the van, climb in, and buckle. He yawns again. "I don't know how you keep this up. I went from being on public display for two days to trying to get Kade to formulate complete sentences on paper for a few *hours*. Then I had to get my own homework done. When do you sleep?"

I dig at him a little for fun. "Welcome to my life. Now imagine how crappy it would be if someone woke you up at shits-turdy every morning with a bunch of pointless texts."

"Man, what kind of jagoff would do something like that?"

"Right?" I lean my head back and let my eyes close for a second. "Speaking of jagoffs, how'd it go with Kade?"

I shouldn't care. I washed my hands of it. But my inner fairy godmother just can't help but root for Cindy, whoever he may be.

Noah pulls a *here's hoping* face. "I'm not gonna lie. I had to give him all the big words. And he types at a mind-numbing eight words per minute. Anyway, he turns it in today. Ms. Adams is going to grade it overnight because, you know, the world will end if Kade doesn't play in the football game tomorrow."

I feel Noah's pain. How many times have I been in the same thankless situation? I put my hand on his knee. "The whole school owes you one. You know that? You did a good thing."

Noah looks down at his knee and blushes. "I didn't do it for the whole school."

Right. He did it to test a hypothesis. Whatever.

At school, hardly anyone takes our picture or watches our every move. I do catch a weird look from Holly, though, which makes me think we've got her attention at least. So that's great. I guess.

After Poms and homework, I have my regular Thursday-night call with Hope. She spends most of the time talking about how pathetic Kiet is being. He's been writing her poetry, sending gifts, texting her way too much. When she told him she wanted space, he literally got on his knees and begged her not to shut him out.

"Wow," I breathe. "It sounds like he really loves you."

"Yeah. That's the problem. He's *such* a great guy. And he does love me. But I can't get tied down here."

Or anywhere. To anyone. I stir my plastic fork pensively around my Thai green-mango salad. "Sis, you know, you are coldhearted."

She laughs.

it could have been an accident if I hadn't done it on purpose.

Noah exhales.

The inch of air between us feels effervescent. It's like magic.

"Here he comes!" Noah shoves me away from the door. "Run, run, run!"

We trip over each other for a few feet and tumble into the weight room in a giggling tangle of arms and legs and headphone cord. That was just what I needed to break the tension I had built up in my head.

I laugh. "Wish. Granted. That was exactly what I *glimpsed*. You did it!"

Noah holds out his hand with a grin. "Put 'er there, partner."

Yeah. Still tension. I shake his hand, trying to ignore the tractor beam pulling me toward him.

"I guess I'm officially a fairy godmother now," he says.

I can't stop smiling. He's looking at *me* today—not just plotting points on an invisible "paranormal activity" graph. My voice sounds a little breathy when I quip, "I'll make you a membership card."

He glances at our still-linked hands. "It should probably say 'hapless human male.'"

Oh no.

It always ends very badly for the hapless human.

All the fairy research I did slams into me like a wrecking ball. How many stories did I read of fairies getting infatuated with some dude, luring him away from the woman he truly loves, and destroying his life? So many.

How many men has my own family chewed up and spit out?

My grandpa.

My dad.

Kiet.

The smile slides off my face. I snatch my hand back. "I've gotta go."

"You— Huh? Can we . . . talk . . . first?"

I'm already halfway out the door. "I really can't be late for class."

"Later then?"

"Yeah, I don't know. Maybe."

No matter how fast I walk, he stays right next to me. He makes it so hard to do the right thing.

"How about we go somewhere tonight?"

"I have the football game."

"Then after that."

"It'll be late—"

The bell rings, and people flood the hallway. I slow my pace and control my breathing. The show must go on. I grit, "Arm."

He wraps his arm around my shoulders with an audible sigh. To keep my heart from bursting and my thoughts in check, I say, "Just one more week until our contract is up. You and Holly are going to be a total power couple. I'm pretty sure she was giving me a jealous look yesterday. So—"

"Does your cloaking device have an off switch?"

By now I've watched enough *Star Trek* to know he's calling me out. He knows I'm hiding. Actually, he might be calling me sneaky and belligerent, because Romulans were the ones who used cloaking devices, and they could be real a-holes.

How did I get myself this tangled up inside? I'm a science project to him. A very Romulany test subject. And he's Holly's Prince Charming—they belong together. I know all this. Unfortunately, my heart doesn't give a rip about facts.

Maybe this was Morgan le Fay's problem too. Maybe her heart just took over and made her do evil things like seducing men and sabotaging their lives even when she had every intention of leaving them alone.

I glance at Noah, my rebellious heart trying to squeeze the fight out of me. His head is tilted toward me and his gaze is locked on, waiting for a response.

"Hi, Charity! Hi, Noah!" Gwen calls as we pass. She scrunches her nose like, *You guys are so cute.*

We both say, "Hey."

We stop outside my classroom, and I slide out from under Noah's arm. "See ya."

He captures my wrist. "Will you . . . ? I just . . ." He bites his lip and clenches his free hand. "Seven days, right?"

"Right." Perky, perky, perky.

"Okay." He releases me. "I'll talk to you later."

I don't *glimpse* anyone's destiny at the football game, even though I try everything from meditation to visualization to chanting to telepathy. Afterward I force myself to go out for pizza with the squad, and I make a big show of sitting by Carmen.

Saturday morning, I wake up to a text from Noah: Buenos dias ☺

I snuggle under my comforter and text back a good morning.

Noah: Any glimpses?

I groan into my pillow and text back: Nope.

Noah: Want to do something? Since we're dating, we should go on a date. Be seen. Right?

I already made sure I wouldn't be tempted to spend time with Noah today by packing my schedule. Sorry. I promised Sean I'd watch his rehearsal, and later I'm going to help Memom make some table centerpieces.

Noah: Memom?

Me: My grandma 😵

Noah: How about tonight? Next Generation marathon at my house?

Me: How does that count as being seen?

Noah: We can post a selfie.

I try not to smile and fail. I should say no. Keeping my distance is the right thing to do. But my thumbs betray me and type: maybe.

26

It Would Be Okay If I Never Hear the Word "Data" Again

Sean and I have lunch at a gourmet grilled-cheese food truck after his ballet rehearsal. Between mouthfuls, I say, "I had no idea it was possible to jump that high."

"It's called leaping, hon. By the way, I've been meaning to tell you, I got accepted into the BFA program at SMU."

"What?!" I throw my sandwich down. "Should we hug?!" He nod-laughs, and I run around the picnic table for a hug-and-squeal.

When we sit back down, he says, "You know, if it weren't for you, it never would have happened."

"No, it was all you. You work so hard."

He steals my pickle. "Yeah, but you're, like, the wind beneath my wings."

"Har, har, har."

For a couple of minutes there's no more talking, just crunching. Then I circle back around. "The thing is, so many wishes have gone completely off the rails. How come yours turned out so good?"

He wipes his hands on a brown paper napkin. "I've been thinking about the Vindhya nightmare. The thing is, I knew how to make someone homecoming queen, and I just went for it. But I didn't know *her.*"

"Yeah. Same."

"With you and me, it was the opposite, right? You didn't necessarily know anything about ballet, but we just hung out and talked and eventually got there."

"You're so right," I say. Sean and I share the same look Hope and I gave each other when I was six and we broke our mom's iPhone. Clearly, neither of us knows how to fix this right now. I ball my paper up. "All right, as much as I enjoy all this soul-searching, we've gotta go. I promised Memom we'd be there by two."

He grimaces. "How did you rope me into making wedding centerpieces?"

When I get home—more than a little covered in glitter—there's a notification on my tablet that I have a Facebook PM. I drop my backpack and stare at the notification for several seconds, suddenly nervous. It has to be from Kelly Bodworth because I don't know anyone else who would try to contact me through Facebook. Part of me is relieved to, hopefully, close the final chapter on the Cindies, for better or worse. But given the likelihood that I messed up her life, an equally vocal part of me doesn't want any more reasons for self-deprecation. I stand in the middle of my room, indecisive, for almost a full minute. Eventually my curiosity, combined with my desire for closure, wins out. I drop into my desk chair and navigate to Messenger.

The message from Kelly says:

> Dear Charity, Wow, it's been so long! Of course I remember you! How could I forget? ☺ How are you? So, you asked about Juggernaut. The first year I had him, he chewed everything in sight. My entire family pretty much hated him. Eventually he started to grow out of it, though. Then, a few years ago, I started talking to this guy on Snapchat a lot. I didn't know him, but he seemed really nice and cool. After a while we set up a time to meet. Horrible decision, I know! I rode my bike to the meetup, and— long story short—it got creepy fast. Just when I started to panic, Juggernaut showed up and got right in between us, barking and snarling. He had managed to somehow break out of the yard and follow me! Ever since that happened, my parents will barely let me use social media at all. The whole thing freaked us all out. But, anyway, you asked if I'm still glad I got him—

YES, YES, YES! He's the best, best dog. He
saved me! He's my hero! I don't even know
what would have happened to me without him
that day. Stay sweet, K.B.

I reread the message a couple of times, letting it sink in.

It's a bona fide Happily Ever After. That makes two.

Nothing is random. That's what Noah would say. *Look for the patterns.* So I pull out a piece of paper and start writing what Sean and Kelly have in common:

No headache.

Time. They both took months.

I pause, my pen hovering. Because that's not a real pattern. Carmen and Sara both took a long time too, and neither of them gave me a headache. And both of their HEAs are definitely iffy.

Still, even though it's not an answer, it feels like a lead, a thread to follow. I flip the paper over and make a chart with all my Cindies along the side and characteristics of their transformations at the top. It's pretty easy to see that the biggest fails were all on the low end of time, and they all gave me a headache. But more time doesn't necessarily guarantee success either.

I go back to the iPad and write a note to Kelly:

Glad Juggernaut was there when you needed
him. I've been kind of off my game, but your
note helped. Thanks for writing back.

It's still only seven. I fold up the chart, stick it in my back pocket, and—because I'm a moth and he's my own personal bug zapper—I head to Noah's.

———

Noah probably could have mentioned that it was going to be a *family* movie night. When I arrive, the whole TrekkieFam is already deep in it. As Noah leads me into the living room, they all look up, and Dad pauses the show.

Nat looks surprised. His dad looks confused. His mom looks skeptical. It's not exactly a warm welcome. Not that I deserve one. My stomach knots, once again waiting for them to tear into me about the Deanna Troi dress.

"Hi." I force a smile.

They offer a jumble of "Hey there," "Oh, Charity, hi," and "Welcome in."

Noah's standing next to me, unhelpfully saying nothing. I'm tempted to dive behind him rather than face his family. Instead I clear my throat and confess, "I want to say I'm sorry. About the Deanna Troi dress."

Lisa's up off the couch in an instant. "What happened to the dress?!"

Wait. What?! He still never told them?

Noah goes, "Nothing! The dress is totally fine, Mom."

She looks at us, confused. Waiting for an explanation.

"I, um, knew someone else who needed a costume, so I loaned it to her without permission. I'm . . . sorry."

Lisa exhales, with her hand on her heart. "Why didn't you just ask?"

"I didn't think you'd say yes."

She gives me a forced smile. "Okay. Well, that was not the best judgment, but your heart was in the right place, wanting to help a friend. And I'm glad you told us."

Dad chimes in, "Yeah, no harm done. Come on in and join us."

Natalie scoots a few inches closer to Dad. "There's room right here."

It shouldn't matter that Noah's family is inviting me in. But it does. And I never want to break their trust again. I squeeze in next to Natalie, and she offers me a big metallic smile and a bowl of popcorn.

Noah sits on the floor next to us, so I guess I got his seat. I spend the next three hours consuming *Star Trek*-themed snacks—like Romulan ale (which I'm pretty sure is blue cream soda) and the "Klingon delicacy Gladst" (kale chips)—while getting an intense introduction to *Star Trek: The Next Generation*. Pretty much every definable thing is better than the original series—the special effects, the plotlines, the props, the lack of blatant sexism. But I miss Spock.

Half of my brain pays attention to the show, while the other half plays Disclosure Pong. Do I tell Noah about Sean's and Kelly's happy endings and ask for his help . . . or not? On one hand, I don't want to, because I want him to realize I'm a real girl—not a lab rat. But he *is* the guy who could track down a fairy godmother just by analyzing the data sets of a few Cindies. If I'm going to get help from anyone, it's him. And besides, I'm not supposed to want him to want me. Better to be a science project than nothing at all.

After the fourth episode, I announce that I need to get going. His parents invite me to come again next weekend for *DS9* (which I remind myself to look up later), and Noah walks me out. The door clicks behind us, leaving us standing in the soft porch light. Noah shifts from foot to foot, not quite looking at my face. "I'm really . . . glad you . . . came."

"Me too."

He looks like he doesn't know what to do next. If it were anyone else but me standing here, I'd say it's time for some kissing. But the kisses belong to the Cinderellas, not the fairy godmothers. Speaking of Cinderellas . . . I pull the paper out of my pocket and begin unfolding it, grateful to have something to do with my hands. "So, hey. I've been comparing my Cindies, trying to figure out if there's a pattern to which happy endings went wrong, and I thought . . . maybe you'd like to take a look."

"Oh. Kay." He takes the paper and studies it for a moment. "Bryce? Kelly?"

"Surprise."

He shoots me a disappointed look. And I give him a sheepish smile. He shakes his head, pushes his glasses up, and says, "Hang on, okay?"

He goes back in the house and returns half a minute later with a tablet. "I need more information."

He proceeds to spend an hour asking me details about every *glimpse*, every wish-granting period, my relationship with each Cindy, and the results. I almost give myself whiplash seesawing between loving sitting in the dark receiving 100 percent of Noah's attention and hating that I'm under scientific observation.

At one point his mom sticks her head out the door, sees us sitting on the steps with a tablet between us, and goes back in without a word.

Without even looking up, Noah grumbles, "Nice, Mom. Subtle."

This form of mom behavior is incomprehensible to me. "What was that?"

"She wants me to know that she's watching."

"Why?"

"Because she wants me to be a virgin until I die." He looks up. "Doesn't your mom— Never mind."

This feels like a seriously personal conversation to be having on the front porch. But I still find myself admitting, "My mom's too worried about blue whales *not* procreating to worry about whether I am."

"Why aren't the whales procreating?"

"It's a great big ocean. Hard to find that special someone."

Noah laughs.

"What? That's really why."

He shakes his head, still chuckling, and goes back to the spreadsheet he's making. "So, what are the criteria you're using for whether someone's wish has a positive outcome?"

We stick to analysis and algorithms until long after midnight.

I sleep until after noon the next day. It's glorious. Except that when I finally make my way out to the kitchen, I find a note that says: *Hey there, sleepyhead. I've got a quick trip to Portland. Be good* ☺ *I'll see you Tuesday. Love, Mom*

I listen to the mantel clock tick for a while.

Then I dye my hair acid green, like toxic waste, and go back to bed.

Four hours later the doorbell rings. I shuffle out to see if there's a package and find Noah, looking anxious. Swinging the door open, I grouse, "Did you forget how to use a phone again?"

"No. Did *you*? I texted you about eighteen times."

Oops. I guess I never checked my phone today. I hit him with a little sarcastic "Shocking. That's so unlike you."

Unfazed, he says, "What did you do to your hair?"

I had forgotten about the acid green until this moment. I shrug. "I got mad."

"At your hair?"

I roll my eyes.

He gestures at my athleisure wear. "Are you okay? Did you have a *glimpse*?"

"No *glimpse*. I'm fine. Just lazy."

He looks past me into the house. "Is your mom home?"

"Nope. She's in Portland." That came out a little snippy. It's like I hate the ocean. Sigh.

Noah has that scientific-researcher look on his face. Damn it. He's adding everything I say to his mental database of fairy godmother facts. I just know it. "So this—" He gestures at my hair. "This is because your mom's gone again."

It's not a question. "Did you need something?"

"Can I come in?"

I take a step back and wave him in. He sits on the couch with his tablet, so I close the door and join him.

He wakes up the screen with a double tap. "So I've been looking at our data set here."

Data set. Bluch.

"Do you think the headaches you had with Holly and Olivia and Vindhya are connected to the migraines you got with Greg and Kade?"

"No. They were totally different. Not even really painful. Just annoying."

"But what if the *glimpse* shows the desired end state, and your headache is a warning that the trajectory doesn't align with that end state? So, a little off, a little headache. Way off, big headache."

"How does this help me?"

"Well, if I'm right, we can estimate how much of a trajectory correction you'll need to make for each Cindy. Of course the longer something has been going on the wrong trajectory, the farther it will be from its intended destination. So the best thing would be to use the headaches to guide you as you go."

"Sounds like we're back to magical enslavement. I'll be even more of a puppet than I was before."

"Not if you can control the *glimpses*."

"Which I can't. And I've been trying." I smash a throw pillow over my face to cover my frustration.

"Can't *yet*."

"Whatever." The throw pillow makes a hard landing next to me.

"There's more."

"Okay."

"I think you were on to something with the time correlation."

"Yeah?"

"But the variable is relationship."

"So, what I said."

"Not really. Relationship is hugely complex. We could partially summarize it as time plus knowledge or understanding plus trust plus affection . . . The way you described Kelly, you were already friends before the *glimpse*. And with Sean, that friendship developed."

I pull my knees up and hug them with a little whimper.

Relationships are the linchpin? The one thing I suck at most? My own mother left town without saying goodbye, for crying out loud.

So, thanks for that, Universe.

I stand up and get a little distance from Noah and his *data set.* "You're wrong. Kade's wish turned out fine, and that took the least amount of time. And zero relationship. I never spoke to him, and you literally can't stand him."

"Yeah, but—" He scrolls around his massive spreadsheet. "It seems like the depth of relationship needed for success roughly correlates to the amount of change required from the Cindy. Kade didn't need to become a Rhodes Scholar. He just needed a few percentage points on one paper."

I flop into an armchair that Mom strategically placed at the perfect angle to facilitate conversations that never happen. For a minute or so I digest Noah's latest assertion while massaging the spot between my eyebrows. Big change needs a deep relationship. And the farther off course I am on the destiny front, the more my head pounds. It doesn't feel *not* true.

Finally I say, "So, for instance, you'd say that because Vindhya needed to become really popular to win homecoming queen, that was a big change. So we needed more of a relationship. And the headache . . . ?"

Noah shakes his head. "Vindhya was already popular."

I am so confused right now. "Are we talking about the same person? No one even knew who she was."

Noah makes a noise like that was ignorant. "Charity, I love . . . that you want to help people. But you have a very narrow perception of whose opinion matters."

Ouch. I cross my arms defensively. But I'm still listening.

He switches to a different spreadsheet and gestures to it like that will convince me. "The top twenty percent of JLHS students are invited to the honors program, including Vindhya. Of the STEM extracurriculars offered on campus, fifty percent of participants are honors kids, so the other fifty percent *aren't*—so that's . . . another . . . let's say eight percent of the student body likely to know her. Vindhya is also in orchestra."

I do a double take. This is brand-new information.

Noah's still going. "There are eighty students there and another two hundred plus in band and choir. Assuming Vindhya was generally well liked in her circle of influence—which she was—she already had about thirty-five percent of potential votes. Considering that the other three candidates had to split all other ballots between them, Vindhya could have won the popular vote on her own."

The only appropriate response is an openmouthed stare. Right? So I do that for a while. Then I muster enough living brain cells to say, "So you're telling me she never needed me?"

"I'm telling you that whatever change she needed to make, it had nothing to do with popularity."

I gulp air and hold it, squeezing my eyes closed, shutting out

Noah and his maniacal data analysis. Since the day I met him, every piece of myself has toppled like dominoes. And this last one feels like it's crushing me.

Everything about me is wrong. My own *glimpses* are lying to me.

My methods are broken. My motives are suspect.

I can't control my magic.

My family abandoned me.

My Cindies don't need me.

My head swims and my lungs burn from lack of oxygen. I cover my face with my hands to muffle a moan.

"Breathe, Charity. Okay? Breathe." His fingers brush my wrist.

I pop out of my chair. "You know what? Thank you for working on that, but . . . could you please go? I need . . . I just need . . . to think."

He hangs his head, and his shoulders rise and fall a couple of times. Then he stands and walks past me. At the door, he pauses. "I didn't mean to hurt your feelings. I—"

"Just go."

27
Eating Your Feelings Is Underrated

I ride to school by myself on Monday and, after avoiding Noah all day, I hit the locker room way early for Poms. If he happens to be looking for me, which he probably isn't, I'll be safe in here.

Gwen beat me here, though. She's perched on a corner bench, clearly hiding so she can stare at her phone in peace. A glance at my own phone tells me we have eleven minutes before warm-up. I ease myself silently onto a bench and study her profile. Every twenty or thirty seconds, she touches her screen.

I think about what Noah said about relationships—time plus trust plus blah, blah, blah . . . It's sad, really—I *should* be friends with Gwen. We've had all the time in the world. I've been her teammate since freshman year. But the only things I know about her are that she's boy crazy and phone addicted. I've never tried to go deeper. Not with Gwen. Not with anyone.

I desperately want to know that there is more to Gwen. I focus on her so hard my hands start buzzing, as I silently, urgently ask, *What could you be?*

The world suddenly tilts like a carnival ride, and I grip the bench to steady myself. The locker room shivers but doesn't disappear. A new image overlays it, staticky and glitching:

A middle-aged Gwen sits staring at a laptop screen. She's crying.

I'm so shocked that I lose focus, and the image vaporizes. I sit stunned for a second, still gripping the bench like my life depends on it. I did it! I flipped the switch! But . . . she's going to be pathetic and alone and still screen addicted when she's forty. That legitimately sucks. Maybe that's why the Universe only shows me a select few destinies—because the ones I don't see are hopeless.

IRL Gwen touches her phone screen placidly. And a determination to see something better for her wells up in me. I use it to call the *glimpse* back. It's more opaque this time. More steady.

Middle-aged Gwen stares at her laptop screen and cries. She wipes under her eyes, blows her nose, and then adds the used tissue to a pile on her desk. She starts typing, and a satisfied smile spreads across her face.

I'm so confused right now. In frustration I try to search for clues to the *glimpse*'s meaning. To my surprise, I'm able to shift my focus around the perimeter of the scene.

Above future Gwen's desk is a whole shelf of books that say, "Gwenеth Strope," on the spine. And there's a little pink-gold trophy that says "Romance Writers Association—best debut of the year."

I let the *glimpse* go and pry my cramped fingers off the bench. My heart is pounding. I fumble out my phone and text Noah: Are you there? I have something important to tell you.

I watch the screen anxiously for almost a minute, but it remains still and silent, a dead thing in my hand.

I hear Coach's muffled voice through the door, yelling, "Two minutes, ladies! Line it up."

Gwen stashes her phone and starts for the gym. She notices me and says, "Hey, Charity. You coming?"

"In a minute." My heart is still racing.

As soon as she's gone, I try calling Memom. She needs to know it's possible to control the *glimpses*. This is huge. It's a game changer. The call rings and rings, and finally connects to an old-school voice message. The "Wedding March" plays too loudly, and Memom practically yells over it, "I'm busy planning a wedding! Leave a message! Who knows? Maybe you'll get lucky, and I'll figure out how to listen to it."

My heart sinks. Having huge news and no one to share it with is horrible. When the message thing beeps, I say, "Hi, Memom. It's Charity. Don't say 'get lucky.'"

Once again I'm on my own. With a sigh I put the phone away, pinch an imaginary pencil between my shoulder blades, and march to the gym just in time to avoid penalty sprints.

⌒

I have all of Poms practice to think about the *glimpse* switch. By the time Coach dismisses us, I feel like I'm going to burst if I don't talk to someone. On my way to my car, I pull out my phone to call Sean, even though I know he's at the ballet. But there's a message from Noah: **Sorry, I had a line at the AM. What do you have to tell me?!?!**

That's the thing about Noah—if something's important to me, then it's important to him. Even if I've been avoiding him all day and the last thing I said to him was basically "Leave me alone."

So I drive to Arctic Marble. When I walk in, the little bell above the door jingles. Noah looks over and gives me a smile like he's been waiting for me—like every time that bell jingles, he hopes it'll be me.

It makes it so hard to convince myself that none of it's real.

I wait in line behind a man holding a little girl wearing a ladybug costume. And when it's my turn, I step up to the counter.

I thought I was protecting myself by avoiding him all day. But now—with only three feet of countertop between us and locked in place by his eyes—I feel like I'm waking up after being half-comatose for the past twenty-four hours. The closer I get to him, the closer I want to be. If the crappy counter wasn't in the way, I'd . . .

I'd do something impulsive that would make our impending breakup even harder. Something like wrap myself around him and tell him Holly can't have him after all. I pat the counter with bitter gratitude.

Noah studies me. "You're here."

I manage a throwback snark. "Actually, I'm down at the Tastee Freez."

"What's up? I missed . . . seeing you."

I lean in—only to make sure that no one else hears me, not at all because I'm pulling a Morgan—and whisper, "I found the switch."

He throws both hands in the air and cheers like I just kicked a winning field goal. The ladybug girl startles and stares. With a wink, I *nudge* her interest to a giant ice-cream-cake poster on the wall.

Quieter, Noah says, "So?"

"So I *glimpsed* Gwen. And I could turn it off and on and everything. She's going to be a writer."

"How's your head?"

"Fine."

"She must be on course." So cocky.

"Yeah, yeah, you're very smart."

"I want to hear all about it." The doorbell jingles, and a whole boys' basketball team piles in. Noah deflates a little, but changes gears seamlessly. "Can I interest you in a mixer?"

"Sure." The basketball team is so loud behind me that I practically shout it.

He sweeps his arm broadly over the selection of mix-ins. "And what does the lady desire?"

"Hmm. Surprise me."

"Bold move."

"Tell me about it. I'm still on insulin from the last time I was here."

I get jostled from behind. The basketball players are getting restless.

"Right, then." He rubs his hands together. "You look like a peppermint patty girl to me." He ladles some candy onto the marble mixing counter. "A little sweet. A little bite. Super refreshing. Kinda mysterious. I mean, seriously, what's that white stuff made out of?"

I can't help but smile. Honestly, after yesterday I didn't know how that would ever happen again. But that's the Noah magic.

He adds some vanilla ice cream and cuts it together. Then he scoops it into a paper cup, adding a pink spoon and a mint leaf with his signature dorky flourish. Melts me every time.

He slides the cup toward me. "My lady."

"Thanks. How much?"

"I've got you." He takes a five out of the tip jar and puts it in the drawer.

"Thanks . . . again." My lips try to form a moony smile, but I force my face into something I hope conveys only politeness. Keep. It. Professional.

There's a flash of something like sadness in Noah's eyes before he turns his attention to the next person in line. But then he greets them so cheerfully, I must have imagined it.

Since Noah is obviously going to be busy for a long, long time, I slip out the door with my mixer. When I get in the car, I realize I have a voicemail from my mom—she called while I was at school. I tap "play."

"Hi, sweetie. Listen, Representative Hannon has invited me to speak at an ocean-life-awareness dinner she's throwing. So I need to extend my trip a few days. Miss you so much. Love you."

I delete the message and decide to eat the mixer instead of dinner. It's delicious.

28

That Feeling When You Miss It By *That* Much

*H*olly and Kade enter the hotel ballroom arm in arm. He's
wearing a black tux, and she has on a hot red mid calf cocktail
dress. A few people close to the door nudge each other and point. Then
more and more people turn to see the couple. Holly looks nervous, but
Kade works the crowd like a pro, greeting everyone with fist bumps,
hand slaps, and celebrity smiles. Some of that confidence seems to rub off
on Holly as she navigates the room on his arm. The girls—even the ones
that are clearly with other guys—look like somebody took their candy.

I blink the *glimpse* away, massaging the spot between my
eyebrows. The Holly headache is like a metronome cranked to
max this morning. IRL Holly is watching early-morning football
practice as usual. And I'm watching Holly from a distance.

When I conjured the *glimpse*, I thought I'd see something in
Holly's future. But the Universe is still showing me exactly the same
moment that it did last time. It makes me think it was a turning

point. . . . Something was supposed to happen at prom that I missed.

I'm here because—and I've given this a lot of thought—I still want to clean up my messes. Maybe none of the Cindies needed me in the first place. But then, what are the *glimpses* for? And why would I get the "red alert, incorrect trajectory" migraine? Noah would say we need more data. So that's what I'm here to get.

I focus on Holly again. Her head is tilted to one side, and she looks a little glazed. *There's something better for you,* I silently declare. *You're more than this.* With sheer determination, I demand to see what Holly could be. I call the *glimpse* back to me. The world tilts and prom shimmers like a sheer curtain over the football stadium.

Holly and Kade enter the hotel ballroom arm in arm. What am I missing? I turn the image to pan the room. Weirdly, I see myself pretending to listen to Scarlett while surreptitiously watching the HEA moment unfold. I sweep past myself, looking for clues to where I went wrong. I get all the way back around to Holly and Kade as they move forward through the crowd.

Holly looks nervous, but Kade struts through the crowd. . . . I take a closer look at Holly's face. Nerves. Stage fright. That's all I see.

I look again at Kade. He's saying things I can't hear because of the music and the crowd noise. I'm not a great lip-reader, but these are pretty standard: *Hey, man. What's up?* He listens for a moment, and then, I think, he says: *Yeah, check it out.*

Come on. Come on. What am I supposed to see? I shift to the faces of the people around Kade and Holly. They're talking, laughing, looking self-conscious . . . standard prom stuff. Wait. Why are so many people looking down? I shift my angle. *Kade's tie is a little crooked. His jacket is unbuttoned. His tux pants are creased down the front. His shoes . . . his shoes are unexpected. He's wearing white Chucks that are covered in hand-tinted comics.* I freeze the *glimpse* and study the drawings more closely.

I blink the *glimpse* away with a sinking certainty that Holly was supposed to make Kade custom shoes for prom. And it's *Kade.* He's an influencer, a trendsetter.

She was meant to be an artist with her work on display that night. Everyone was supposed to see her talent. Instead I perfectly orchestrated everything so that they would never see her as anything but somebody's girlfriend.

I flee to my car. I want to have yet another breakdown, but I can't afford the damage that would do to my face. So I crank some electro house, lean back, close my eyes, and let the deafening repetition blast every thought out of my head.

The knocking on the window next to me is barely discernible over the electronic rhythm. I consider pretending I didn't hear it. But instead I open one eye to see Carmen, Gwen, Scarlett, and three other Poms girls crowded around my car. I secure my game face, turn the music off, and roll down the window.

"Hey, Charity." Scarlett peers into the car like she's looking for something. "Are you okay? You looked kind of upset."

"Yeah. No. I'm totally fine."

"It's Noah, isn't it?"

"No. We're fine."

"Oh, because Jameela said she heard that you guys are breaking up. And Surya said Noah ate lunch with some guys yesterday."

"Well, don't believe everything you hear. Noah and I are doing super fantastic." I gather my stuff and climb out of the car. "I was just doing a little light meditation before school."

As we walk toward the school, Carmen says, "No offense, but I liked your hair better the way it was before."

Gwen says, "Same."

"Okay, thanks, guys. I'll take that under advisement." From over Gwen's shoulder, I see Noah pull up in his mom's white minivan, and I jump at the excuse to get away from my teammates. "Oh, Noah's here. See you guys later."

I jog to his van and am inside by the time the engine goes silent.

"Hi there." He sounds somewhere between surprised and delighted. "Missed me?"

"Listen, we've got a problem."

"I'm great. Good morning to you, too."

I lean over the console, like I'm telling him a secret, even though there's no one else in here. "This is serious. There's a rumor going around that we're cooling off. Scarlett's about to investigate like she's going for a Pulitzer. We *can't* peter out—not if you're going to get Holly to ditch her football-star homecoming-king boyfriend. Which she *needs* to do, because her HEA is a disaster.

She was supposed to put her art on him, not *date him*. She needs to be rescued by you, so we have to go down in a blaze of glory."

"Rescued. Wow." He pretends to flex his biceps.

"This is serious!"

He makes a face so serious that he's obviously not serious at all. "What do you suggest?"

"We need to be seen together more."

"You mean like I suggested on Saturday?"

"No more ditching each other at lunch or between classes."

"Okay. You are hearing yourself, right?"

I am. And I'm trying not to lose my nerve. "We need to look like we're a couple."

He leans to center, way into my personal space. "Remind me again. What would help with that?"

I feel like he's teasing me. But I'm finding it extremely difficult to concentrate—as always—when he's this close. I sway involuntarily toward him another inch. "We . . . ah . . . just need to . . ."

Noah closes the gap between us very, very slowly—like I'm a creature that startles easily. But I can't seem to cut and run at the moment. I close my eyes and feel his breath like a warm ocean breeze across my lips.

"LEVEL UP, PLAYA ONE!" The Mouth pounds on the hood of the car. The atmosphere inside the car is instantly drained of its magic.

Without pulling back, Noah says, "Can you wait right here while I, just real quick, murder that guy?"

A dude in an EAT. TROMBONE. SLEEP. REPEAT. T-shirt presses his phone to the windshield and snaps a picture. Noah grits his teeth. "And that guy."

I sit back, partially devastated, but partially relieved. I mean, what happens after the kiss? Awkward truths. Broken hearts. Sad Ever Afters. I really, *really* need to keep my lips to myself. I decide to play the whole thing off like it was part of the grand plan. "It's good PR. Just what we needed."

Noah laugh-sigh-moans. "PR."

"Yeah. We need to maximize our social media presence. Start some favorable rumors. That sort of thing."

Noah doesn't say anything. He looks like he's trying to remember pi to a hundred places or something.

I say, "Time to go in, I guess."

"Wait." Noah stops me with a hand on my arm. He swallows. "You were about to say something. We just need to . . . ?"

"Oh. Um . . . We just need to do a better job of . . . pretending . . . we are . . . really into each other."

"Are you really just pretending?" His voice is soft, but the question is like a bludger.

"Of course," I lie, trying not to panic. *Does he know? Am I being that obvious?* "It's what I do. I'm practically a professional pretender."

"I noticed." Noah drops his hand with a sigh and opens his door. "I just wish . . ." He hesitates, and my heart throbs. "I wish you weren't."

29
Dostoyevsky for the Win

*H*oping to work on the Vindhya situation, I finagle a hall pass during second-period study hall. Not to brag, but these are the moments when it's really handy to have *nudge* powers.

I remember from our wish-granting phase that she has AP Chemistry this period, so I stand outside the door of that class and try to peek in without being obvious. There she is, sitting in the back row with an empty seat next to her. The wall she's built around herself is almost a physical thing.

Show me what you could be.

I grip my oversized hall pass tight as the school momentarily turns into a carnival ride. Then I'm back at the homecoming football game.

Vindhya is rocking a deep-red sari, standing in line with three other girls in formal dresses on the track that rims the JLIIS football field. Vice Principal Martinez says, "Vindhya Chandramouli," into a microphone before placing a silver-and-rhinestone tiara on her silky black hair. The crowd in the bleachers goes wild—cheering, pounding feet, banging cymbals. . . . Vindhya perches carefully in the back of the VW Bug convertible and waves regally as the car makes a lazy path along the track.

I blink it away and walk nonchalantly toward the bathroom just to make it look like I've got somewhere to be. What am I missing in the *glimpse*? What on earth did she need me for? What went wrong?

I make a U-turn and stop outside the door of AP Chemistry again. I call the *glimpse* back.

And it's exactly the same as before.

I compare every person around Vindhya to my memory of IRL homecoming. After all, that was how I found the problem with Holly's HEA—the shoes were different from what really happened.

But everyone looks just how I remember them. The STEMers are sitting in a big group behind the pep band, looking deceptively innocent. The homecoming court is the same. The vice principal even has the same outfit on.

This is like the hardest "find the differences" picture in the history of everything.

I pause the scene and study Vindhya. Her sari, her hair, her shoes . . . they're all exactly the way I remember them. But there is something a little different. Her eyes are just her eyes—deep brown with lashes so thick that they make the rest of us itch to stick on falsies.

She's not wearing eyeliner.

———

Noah and I make an appearance at lunch. I know we need to do something impressive to dispel the rumors that we're cooling off. So I bust out a tube of lipstick called Burning Down the House, coat my lips with it, and say, "Okay, hold still."

"What are you—" He looks genuinely worried.

"Sshh." Careful not to pucker, I press my lips to his cheek. It's a little bit scratchy. But also soft. Warm.

My heart thuds, and I linger a moment longer than strictly necessary before pulling away to check my work. A perfect red lip print just below his cheekbone.

Noah's eyes are closed and his lips are parted. If this were real, I'd kiss him right there at the corner of his mouth. It's physically painful to resist.

To distract myself, I say, "Vindhya wasn't supposed to wear eyeliner at homecoming." I stamp another lip print a little above and behind the first one. "What do you"—another one, on his jaw—"think that means?"

He stammers, "Uh . . . I don't . . . I don't know."

I press one last kiss on his now feverishly hot cheekbone. I like that I can make him flustered. His heart may belong to Holly, but there are a few blood vessels in his cheeks that dilate just for me. It's like I have a little piece of him for myself.

He turns to me, looking dazed. I bite my lip, mid smile.

Oh, my godmothers. Is this how Morgan le Fay sucked in her victims too? I mentally smack myself to stick to business.

I snap a picture of him and post it.

It's all over the feeds by the time I take my seat in lit class. Holly even comments on Scarlett's repost of it: *Can hardly believe that's the same kid I used to have frosting fights with! They grow up so fast.* ☺

I definitely detect some wistfulness there. Just like we planned.

It sucks.

"Okay, phones dark and out of sight." The lit teacher calls the class to order. "Get out your Dostoyevsky. Today we're talking about self-loathing in *Crime and Punishment*."

It's like she hit me over the head with a big-ass light bulb.

Self-loathing. The Vindhya puzzle clicks into place. The eyeliner. The makeover. The memory of Vindhya at Angelic Hair and Nails saying something like "Can you just make me a different person?"

I almost jump out of my seat. The teacher sees me come to attention and says, "Did you have something to add, Charity?"

"Can I use the restroom?"

"You should have—"

I give her a *nudge.*

"Sure. Take your time."

Sixty-three seconds later I skid to a stop in the math-and-science

303

hall. Panting, I knock on the door of Vindhya's calculus class. The teacher opens the door, giving me a view of the whole room—including Noah. His eyebrows go up. The teacher says, "Yes?"

"I need Vindhya, please. It's an emergency." I don't even bother *nudging* him. It's a well-known fact that teachers adore honors kids, always assume they have pure motives, and let them do pretty much whatever they want. This plays out in my favor now, as the teacher calls out Vindhya without asking any questions.

She doesn't say a word as she steps out of the classroom. The door closes softly behind her, and she stands in front of me with her arms crossed and a defensive look in her eyes.

"Here's the thing." I lick my Burning Down the House–stained lips. "You never needed eyeliner. Or a haircut. Or 'popular' friends. Or a fairy godmother."

She gives no hint that she can even hear me.

"You were already everything you needed. You could have won without me—just ask Noah. It's simple percentages. The only thing keeping you from being homecoming queen was that you couldn't see yourself very well. Trust me, I get that. I should have told you how powerful you are. I should have kept telling you until you believed it."

She still doesn't move, but a single tear makes a slow trail down her cheek. She looks past me and whispers, "Great speech. And thank you. But it doesn't matter. No one I thought was my friend likes me anymore."

"They would if you'd just—"

She shakes her head. "No. It would take a miracle."

For the first time all week I feel hope expanding in my chest. Because miracles—especially the bringing-people-together kind—happen to be my specialty. Seems like maybe Vindhya needs a fairy godmother after all.

30
Hope Drops a Truth Bomb

I feel like you're doing it again." Noah changes lanes. He uses his turn signal and everything.

"Define 'it.'" We're on our way to school, and I'm feeling good today. Strong. Hopeful. My hair is a bright raspberry to match my mood.

His eyes shift toward me and then back to the road. "Listen." He pauses and then, like the words could be dangerous, he approaches them cautiously. "It seems like you're concocting some elaborate scheme to manip . . . maneuver people into doing something. But all the data shows that only relationships create transformations. Don't freak out."

"I'm not freaking out."

"Okay, but, generally speaking, any sort of honest conversation ends in you freaking out."

"That's because you tend to find pressure points and then poke them."

"Touché."

We lapse into silence. After a few minutes I restart the conversation. "This is different. It's not based on a random *glimpse*. I *did* talk to Vindhya—"

"One conversation is not a relationship."

"And I don't have a headache."

"Charity, you can't turn people into your pet projects—"

"*I* can't?! Nice double standard."

"Excuse me?"

"Ever since I told you about my magic, you've been studying me. You treat me like a research project."

"That's not true." He looks appalled.

"Seriously? You're constantly 'testing a hypothesis.'"

"That's just what I do."

"Every time you get a new tidbit of data about me, you get that mad-scientist look in your eye and say, 'Fascinating.'"

"It . . . it is," he stammers. "You are. I can't help—"

"You made a massive spreadsheet about me."

"You *asked* for my help. You aren't allowed to be mad at me for giving it."

I cross my arms, because even if he's not wrong, I still feel the way I feel.

He is quiet again, as if turning into the school parking lot requires all his massive brainpower.

But we're running out of time, and this whole *honesty* thing has derailed the conversation I was trying to have. I circle back around with "So are you going to help me or not?"

He groans in protest.

"Please?" We pull into a parking spot right in the front. "I'll forgive you if you help me."

He turns to me with a look that says *cheater*, and I take the opportunity to bat my eyelashes. "Pleeeeease?"

"Fine. I'll help you." He takes a "serenity now" breath, rolls his window down, and yells, "TREVON!"

A guy walking past stops and turns to see who yelled his name. Noah calls grumpily, "Trevon, get in the van."

Trevon spreads his arms. "Dude, that's the creepiest thing anyone has ever said to me."

Noah huffs, *"Please."*

With a shrug, Trevon heads toward us. I ventriloquist whisper, "Who's that?"

Noah is still seriously unamused. "Robotics Club president. You're welcome."

Trevon climbs into the back seat with a warning look. "Just for the record, at least three people saw me get in here."

Well, so far this meeting is going not great. I turn around with a winning smile and hold out my hand. "Hi, I'm Charity."

He hesitates a moment, then shakes my hand. "Trevon."

"You're president of the Robotics Club, right?"

Trevon crosses his arms and leans back. Shields up. "Why?"

"I heard you guys are having a little trouble with your project for the regional meet."

"So?"

"So, I think I can help you."

He goes, *"Pfft."*

"Okay. Not *me* exactly. You need your star coder."

"If this involves groveling to Vindhya Chandramouli, you can take your 'help' and stick it up your—"

"Hey now," Noah interrupts.

I rip off the Band-Aid. "It's time to make up with Vindhya."

"Not gonna happen. She made it pretty clear how cold hell will be when she forgives us for the homecoming stunt."

"If you just say sorry—"

"No way. She's been a narcissistic skeeze gremlin ever since she turned high fashion."

I counter, "That's kind of harsh. I mean, just for the record, glamour and genius are not mutually exclusive. Why can't Vindhya be both if she wants? Besides, you humiliated her in front of the entire school."

Trevon is stalwart. "She deserved it."

I'm itching to *nudge* this in Vindhya's favor, but, you know, long-term decisions, wicked witches . . . yada, yada. I grit my teeth behind my smile. "You need her to win, so you need to get over it. It's pretty simple logic. You're supposed to be the smart kids. You're acting like total assclowns."

"And who made you the jury? Screw you."

"Come on, guys. Keep it civil," Noah protests.

I take a centering breath and *nudge* him after all, just to de-escalate things. I feel his defenses drop a little and use the window to offer "I'm trying to help."

"Why?"

"Because Vindhya's my friend. And she *needs* to code. And she misses you guys." Trevon visibly softens, so I go to phase two. "Isn't there an academic awards assembly tomorrow afternoon?"

Noah says, "Yeah."

Trevon looks like the dots aren't connecting. "So?"

I hit him with my most disarming fairy godmother smile. "Trevon, have you ever heard of a Grand Gesture?"

⌣

Did I say I needed Noah's help? He's actually crucial to every part of my Grand Gesture plan, which goes like this:

Trevon and Noah use their study halls to program a robot.

Noah enlists Carlos and the Mouth—AV Club members with access to the auditorium tech control room—to assist in hijacking the assembly.

Trevon and Noah convince the Robotics Club to participate.

Grand Gesture.

Happy ending.

Which brings us to last period Thursday and the academic awards assembly. As the humiliation happened in front of the whole school, the Grand Gesture has to be equally public. Even though I peel out of my last class and book it to the auditorium tech control room, Noah, Trevon, Carlos, and the Mouth are already waiting for me.

Which means they must have been released from their sixth-period classes early. I'm telling you, these honors kids get so many perks.

I give Carlos and the Mouth a nod. "Hey, guys. Thanks for helping us out. Did Noah already explain the plan?"

Carlos grins and gives me the thumbs-up. "It's cool. We got it. No problem."

The Mouth says, "Martinez is gonna have our butts in detention for this stunt." He shrugs. "But, you know, anything for our Most Valuable Playaaaaa!" He holds his fist out toward Noah.

Noah bumps his fist, blushing.

I swallow. "Well, I, uh . . . owe you one."

Trevon says, "This is real touching. But are we doing this or what? I got a robot in excessive downtime here."

Ah yes. The robot. Picture a puppy made out of an Erector Set, with a circuit board strapped to its back, a coiled wire for a tail, wheels instead of feet, and a couple of extra limbs. Okay, so that sounds more like a giant insect, but trust me, it's a puppy. There's also an MP3 player clamped on to the top of its head.

Trevon holds out his ThinkPad and walks me through how to initiate RoboPuppy's new program. Then he makes me repeat the steps back to him, like there's a good chance I'm not capable of even the simplest technological task. He's about to have me recite it all a second time, but I'm saved by the band striking up the school fight song to kick off the assembly. Trevon says, "We gotta get in there. Now that you've roped me into this, don't screw it up."

"I won't. I can handle it."

Noah holds an invisible communicator to his mouth. "Stardate 76180.4: Under the command of Captain C. Keller, we are embarking on a mission to alter the course of destiny."

"Would you just go?" I give him a shove out the door.

Trevon and Noah both head into the auditorium. They have to sit onstage since they're both in National Honor Society and have perfect 4.0 GPAs. Which is why it's my job to operate the robot that is—if all goes according to plan—going to execute the Grand Gesture that will melt Vindhya's heart and undo all the wish damage.

I glance up at Carlos. "This is going to play through the sound system, right?"

He gives me yet another thumbs-up. "It's all set up on the wireless."

"Awesome."

Through the monitors, I can hear Vice Principal Martinez saying, "Please hold your applause until *all* the names have been called."

Gotta do this. I slip RoboPuppy out of the booth and into the auditorium. "Be a good boy," I whisper as I set him in the aisle. Then I slip into a seat in the back row and use Trevon's ThinkPad to initiate the program (which is actually easy, so there, Trevon). RoboPuppy's not radio-controlled like an RC car. He will run through a series of preprogrammed commands. So all I can really do now is hope that everything goes as planned. I watch, holding my breath, as RoboPuppy makes his way down the aisle. A few kids on the ends of rows notice him and point him out to the people around them.

RoboPuppy makes a series of ninety-degree turns and forward advances that eventually get him onto the stage with Ms. Martinez and the honors kids. He stops a few feet from the podium. By now the robot has everyone's attention. Ms. Martinez stops talking and looks around hesitantly. Vindhya, sitting in the front row onstage, cocks an eyebrow.

RoboPuppy slowly raises one of his appendages in an arc until it touches the button on the iPod. Music reverberates through the auditorium:

Baby come back! Any kind of fool could see,
There was something in everything about you.

The crowd seems to hold its breath, wondering what's happening. Ms. Martinez looks peeved that her boring speech has been interrupted. Vindhya watches RoboPuppy with her lips pressed tightly together. Then every member of Robotics Club stands up and sings along. "Vindhya come back! You can blame it all on me. I was wrong, and I just can't live without you!"

Vindhya's stern expression morphs into a tight, closed-mouth smile. She looks down.

Ms. Martinez stomps over to RoboPuppy, flutters her hands around him for a moment, and then presses pause on the iPod. With the music stopped but the room still buzzing, she returns to the podium and says into the mic, "All right, *all right*. That's enough. Everyone, please take your seats, and I will announce our National Merit Scholars."

The assembly proceeds as normal, except for two things: RoboPuppy sits onstage as a constant reminder of the Grand Gesture, since nobody programmed him to leave. And when Vindhya's name is called for National Merit, the STEMers go absolutely wild, chanting Vindhya's name.

Her armor cracks, with a smile that says, *I can't stay mad at you.* In their seats on the stage, Noah and Trevon do a subtle fist bump. The familiar, heady rush of a happy ending courses through me. There's really nothing better than this.

When the assembly lets out, I watch Vindhya's reunion with the STEMers, complete with lots of hugs and high fives. I don't look away until Noah jogs down the aisle and catches me in a feet-off-the-ground hug. He says gleefully, "Man, I can't believe we pulled it off."

I can't help but snark a little. "Oh, so you like my *maneuvering* now?"

He sets me down, still smiling. "Yeah, maybe the Grand Gestures aren't so bad. I concede the win." He bows to me. Which is bananas, because this moment should be all about him.

"Hey! You!" I grab him by the shoulder and hoist him back up. "You got a National Merit Scholarship. That's amazing."

"Thanks." His cheeks pink up.

Somebody walking past claps him on the back. "Good job, dude!"

He says, "Thanks, man." Then he turns back to me. "You have Poms now?"

"Yeah." We join the stream of people pushing through the double doors.

"Want to have dinner together after? I'm already starving."

"Yes. And I'm buying. It can be your 'congratulations on being a flipping genius' dinner."

He puts his arm around me like it's normal now, and we navigate the crowd in the hallway. He says, "I know a great little Spanish restaurant where we're sure to be seen by our voting public."

"Sounds *fabuloso*."

He's waiting for me outside the gym when Poms lets out. I'm wiped from dancing and still high on helping get Vindhya on the right trajectory, but seeing him leaning on the wall and knowing he's there for *me*—it's an emotional flash bomb. It makes me feel special and cared for and connected . . . and painfully aware that I'm handing all of this over to Holly tomorrow night. This is her Prince Charming, and all the sweet moments with him rightfully belong to her.

But I hug him anyway. Every girl on the squad gets an eyeful as they file out of the gym. Gotta make these last twenty-four hours count, right? I pretend that's the reason I hold on so long.

Ten minutes later we pull up to Taco Bell. I give Noah a scathing glare. *"Spanish restaurant?"*

He fakes an earnest "What?"

I punch him in the arm. "I believed you! I spent the past hour dreaming about tapas."

He opens his door. "Come on. All-you-can-eat hot-sauce packets. My treat."

We eat our way through a pile of paper-wrapped imitation Mexican food, rehashing the Grand Gesture and generally pretending that tomorrow isn't our last day as a couple. I can tell Noah's trying not to sound like he's doing research, but he can't help asking about my re-*glimpse* of Vindhya. And it's okay. It's actually nice to have someone to talk to about it. I answer his questions in between mouthfuls of cheap, greasy taco.

"But 'destiny' implies future, and the *glimpses* are showing you the past now?"

"Sometimes."

"So what would you say you're seeing?"

"It seems like a turning point, maybe? With Gwen it was potential—seeing her not for what she is right now but for the best version of herself."

"Fascinating," he says. And he sounds just like Spock. He squeezes hot sauce onto his last taco. "That's a pretty cool superpower, Captain Janeway."

I'm not sure who that is. I decide to look it up later.

I lick my lips. "Now that I can control it, I could *glimpse* you."

He freezes with the taco halfway to his mouth. There's a beat. And then he shakes his head.

"We could find out what's going to happen with Holly, or if you're going to win a Nobel Prize someday." I try to make it sound like I don't care about that first thing at all.

"No thanks."

"Why not?"

"Because I'd rather figure it out as I go along. I don't need a fairy godmother after all." He crunches into his taco, and I take a pensive pull of my drink. Just as I'm starting to sink into "he doesn't need me" syndrome, he nudges my side. "Besides, you're already enough of a know-it-all."

I elbow him harder. "Takes one to know one."

He smiles his dorky smile. The one so adorable he should probably save it just for Holly. I dump some ice chips into my mouth and crunch them loudly. Around the ice I mumble, "I gotta get going. I've got a test in almost every class tomorrow."

"Let's study together."

My heart jumps around like he just proposed. No one has ever said those words to me before. I should definitely make an excuse to not do that. But my mind is suddenly a blank. So I go with "Um. Sure."

Which is how we end up back at my house. As I unlock the front door, Noah texts his mom his whereabouts. We walk in, and he glances around the barely lived-in room. "Where do you usually study?"

I point toward my room and then lead the way. Even though Noah has been in my room before, this feels different. Last time I was too sick to care. Now I overthink everything. I really half-assed making my bed this morning—didn't bother to smooth the duvet or position the pillows decoratively. And my pajamas and towel are in a pile by the bathroom door. Is that a dead spider in the corner?

I tell myself to chill out. I should do what I would normally do if Noah weren't standing right behind me. I cross to the bed, drop my backpack on it, toe off my shoes, and settle in, tucking my feet under me. Noah stands a few feet from the bed looking indecisive, so I pat the spot next to me. "It's okay."

He hesitates and then sits. His backpack goes next to mine. His shoes come off. While I'm taking up the smallest possible amount of space, his long legs seem to cover the whole bed. We unload our books and papers in silence. He opens a physics book and starts reading. I need to tackle trig.

Mostly we don't interact. He does his work, and I do mine. But he's *there* in every inch of my consciousness.

Okay, Charity. Concentrate. I stare at the first problem:

Find the length of side AC of a triangle, given that side BC is 12 cm and angle Aθ = 0.6

I write, *sine θ = opposite/hypotenuse*

.6 = Noah's arm brushes against mine for 0.6 seconds as he turns a page.

I crumple my bedspread in my left hand and write $= 12/AB$

$AB = .6/12$

So $AB = .05$

0.05 inches separate Noah's hair from my cheek. It smells like Curl Commando and Old Spice. Like looking for the *glimpse* switch but getting lost in him instead. Like a new friend and fake dating, deep car talks and sitting on the porch at midnight. He smells like a dozen sweet hugs that never really belonged to me.

Side x = me leaning in a little.

He turns his face slightly toward me. Not touching him feels like resisting the pull of a thousand fat rubber bands. I clench my jaw and stare at my notebook.

Apply Pythagora's theorem: $x = \sqrt{.05^2 - 12^2}$

$12^2 = 144$. He shifts, and my knee is touching his thigh. I have 144 goose bumps.

I think I did something wrong. $\sqrt{-143.9975}$ is an imaginary number. Am I imagining all the tension in the space between us?

I start over. If $0.6 = AB/12$, then why is Noah here? Does he like me a little, not for science or to win back Holly? I start to write, "AB =" but I press too hard, and the tip of my pencil breaks off. That tiny sound snaps all the rubber bands at once.

And then we're kissing. We're kissing like all the *almosts* and *not-reals* we've been stacking up are exploding in a chain reaction. My books clatter to the floor. Eyes closed, I devour every sensation. His lips are soft, but his chin is scratchy. His hands are in my hair, fingers pressing into my scalp. I'm sinking and flying at the same time.

Making out with Noah is the new thing I want to do every minute of every day. But this annoyingly coherent thought breaks through the haze of pure sensation—*Is he pretending I'm Holly?*

I try to throw it away, to cram it down, to smash it. But it keeps coming back with greater clarity.

I pull back a few inches. We study each other, panting for air. But does he see *me*? Part of me doesn't really want to know the answer. I just want to keep making out and pretend that it doesn't matter. I search for what to say, while his eyes ask me questions.

The tablet on my desk chimes. It's disorienting for a second—a sound from outside the make-out bubble. Then I scramble toward it, half falling off the bed, babbling, "It's my sister! It's Thursday. I forgot to call her."

I get to the tablet and tap the green circle to answer the call. "Hope!" I blurt her name with too much volume and not enough air. My face—complete with red cheeks and swollen lips—pants at me from the upper-right corner of the screen.

"Hey, don't we have a date?"

I hastily finger comb my hair, still trying to catch my breath. In the selfie box, I can see Noah gathering books and papers behind me. "Yes! Hi!"

"Who's the boy?"

"He's, um . . ."

He crouches next to me and waves at the tablet. "I'm Noah. Nice meeting you."

Hope says, "Hi."

I add, "Can you hold on one sec?" I cover the camera with my palm and whisper, "I need to take this call."

"But we're going to talk about this later. Right?" He looks too cute to be real, with his disheveled hair, flushed cheeks, and earnest, searching eyes.

"Right."

He retrieves his stuff, says, "Bye," and taps the doorframe on his way out. I resist the urge to hang up on my sister and call him back.

Hope comments, "So he's cute, in kind of a dorky way. Is he a good kisser?"

"Yeah-e-e-s." I bite my lip.

Now my big sister will ask for all the juicy details. She'll need to make sure the guy is good enough for her baby sis. Then she'll dissect every element of the emotional and relational landscape, so that she can draw her little sister a detailed map of how to proceed.

Hope doesn't. Instead she says, "End it now. Before someone gets hurt."

I should probably say something like, *That's the plan.* But my head is still spinning from Noah's kisses, and I feel like I just slammed into a Hope-shaped brick wall.

Hope declares, "It's not going to work."

And suddenly I'm mad. Because she didn't ask me one single thing about him. I'm mad that my own sister doesn't want to hear how I feel. I'm mad that she's in Thailand instead of right here next to me. So why should she get to tell me what to do? I spit, "You know what? I'm doing absolutely fine making my own decisions. It's none of your business anyway."

Hope doesn't immediately respond. Just when I'm starting to think the screen has frozen and I've been picking a fight with dead air, Hope says, "Chay, I see the *glimpses* too."

I'm not sure what blindsides me the hardest—the complete and sudden change of subject, the revelation that Hope shares my abilities, or finding out after seventeen years that I don't know my sister at all. Never mind, I *am* sure. It's totally that last one. I eke out, "What. The. Fffff—"

"I should have told you on Tuesday."

Tuesday? She should have told me six years ago. Or any one of the two thousand or so days in between. I splutter, "What. What the . . . How? You're a fairy godmother?"

Her nostrils flare. "*No.* I see *glimpses.* I don't grant wishes."

"Ever?"

She shakes her head adamantly.

"Why not?" Even though I have sworn off the wish-granting myself, I have no idea if Hope's reasons are the same as mine, if that's a recent thing, a permanent thing . . . or really anything about her, it turns out.

She looks fierce. "Because people are greedy, selfish, ungrateful jerks. That's why. They don't deserve our help."

"Wow." I press my finger between my eyebrows, recalling a

whole lot of recent pain. "But what about the aftermath . . . ? Don't you get sick from ignoring the *glimpses*?"

"Why do you think I'm in the middle of nowhere? I was tired of feeling hungover all the time. I probably see three people in a week here. It's hard to *glimpse* anything when there's no one around." She sounds triumphant, like she's beaten the system. "Besides, elephants are a whole lot more trustworthy than people."

I mumble, "I like people."

"Fine. It's your life. Do what you want. Grant wishes for everybody and their brother if you want to. But you can't get involved with anyone. Remember what we talked about? Fix and release."

She's telling me something I already know—that I've always known. But she's giving the thing words and substance and making me look it in the face. I sit like a sad mime while she plows forward. "The fairy godmother doesn't get her own story. She just pops into other people's stories once in a while. We're the Universe's designated side characters."

I consider putting my hands over my ears and singing the ABC song.

"Think about it. Have you ever heard of anyone in our family transmitting a *glimpse*? Do *nudges* work on us? We're outside the system. You know I'm right."

I whisper, "I found the switch. I can control my *glimpses* now. And I know the secret to happy endings—"

"None of that matters. Controlling our magic doesn't make

any difference. Being alone is part of who we are. It minimizes the damage we cause. Trust me. Damage control is all I do twenty-four/seven."

No. I don't accept this. Like a cornered cat, I claw at her. "Just because you couldn't make it work with Kiet doesn't mean I can't—"

"This isn't about only me." Hope has tears in her eyes, but her voice doesn't waver. "Chay, look at our family. Do Memom and Mom so much as speak to each other? Do we even know who Mom's dad is? And how about our parents—they couldn't even stay within three thousand miles of each other. They can't even be around for *us*. You know I'm right. We're all fixers. It's always about somebody or something else. How can we ever prioritize our own happiness, our own needs? Anyone we try to hold on to is going to get burned."

It sucks. And I do not forgive Hope for saying it. But I know she's right. I feel it in my core. I know it from my own fairy research. Even when I was kissing Noah, I knew it wasn't real.

I bite the inside of my cheek until I can taste blood. But I nod. "Okay. I get it."

Hope sighs. "I'm really sorry, Chay. But that's how it is for us."

A feeble voice of selfish optimism whispers, *Rebel . . . hold on to him . . . you could be happy.* But the voice of reason is much, much louder. I can either take Hope's advice, or I can be selfish and destructive. It's as simple as that.

31

This Is How Noah Goes to War

*N*oah is waiting for me on the first bench in front of the school. I sit in my car and watch him flip his communicator open, closed, open, closed. . . . Sooner or later I'm going to have to get out of my car and face this day, but I might as well wait until the last possible second.

We didn't ride together because he has to go to work right after school. It's a win, because it saved me the trouble of coming up with an excuse to drive myself. See, my plan is:

Minimize contact.

Make it through this day.

Control the fallout.

When there are five minutes until first period and only a handful of stragglers are left outside, I haul myself out of my car. I really want to trudge, or possibly slog, toward Noah. But I force a calculated bounce into my steps.

If I act pathetic or standoffish today, this will all have been for nothing. Everyone has to believe that I'm completely into Noah so that he can thoroughly dump me tonight, save Holly from an otherwise horrible fate, ride off into the sunset, and live happily ever after. Or at least have a happy couple of minutes or whatever.

He sees me coming, pockets the communicator, and jogs to meet me. Sixty percent of my brain is screaming, *I can't do this.* With a finger on my neurological panic button, I compose a flirty smile.

He doesn't hesitate—just collides with me, takes my face in both hands, and kisses me like we're picking up where we left off last night. I can't pull away without making it obvious to everyone within twenty yards that something's not right. So I let him kiss me. And it's sweet and tender and pure and eager.

Torture.

Treasonous longing claws up my throat, scalding and bitter.

He draws back, his eyebrows pinched together. "What's wrong?"

"Nothing." It's bright. Chipper, really.

"Liar." He rubs his thumb across my cheek, the way you would catch a teardrop. Only I'm not crying.

He looks like he's about to say something honest, so I jump in with "We're going to be late."

I sidestep him and take off, as close to a run as you can get with a peppy walk. Noah jogs to keep up with me. "Are you freaking out because of last night?"

I don't slow my pace or look at him. "We only have four minutes to get to class."

"I know it changes things, but I—"

"It doesn't change anything." We stop at my locker, and I race through my combination.

"You can't seriously *still* think I want you to set me up with another girl. I've tried to tell you so many—" He breaks off, his eyes searching my face. When he speaks again, his voice is somehow both soft and determined. "Charity, I want to be with you."

He may as well have bodychecked me into the locker. I feel the pain in every neuron, in the tightness of my chest and how hard it is to inhale. The sweeter his words, the more painful it is when they slam me against the brick wall of incontrovertible truth: the fairy godmother doesn't get the happy ending. Anyone I try to hold on to will get burned. I either hurt him a little now or utterly break him later.

I close my eyes for a second to gather strength to break my own heart and then stab Noah with the shards. Then I turn to him and laugh in his face—a tinkling giggle, like what he said is so, so silly. "Oh my gosh. You remember all this is only pretend, right?"

Noah looks ill. What's left of my heart calls me names I can't repeat. I dive into my locker so I don't have to keep looking at him.

After a few seconds of tense silence, he says, clipped and quiet, "There was no one around last night. That wasn't for show."

I come up, clutching my books like a body shield. "Well, of

course we couldn't have our first kiss in front of everyone. That would be *so* awkward. We had to practice."

I shut my locker, wheel around, and head to class. This is my getaway. Just have to keep it together for a few more seconds. And then an hour, and then the rest of the day. I can do this.

He strides beside me, his initial hurt sounding more like anger by the second. "So you want me to believe that you felt nothing last night. It was all a rehearsal for . . . for this . . . *play* we're putting on for Holly."

"Right," I chirp. His anger helps. It's easier to be horrible to someone who's pissed. Although my heart still feels like it's being repeatedly WWE body slammed. Thankfully—for both my brave face and my attendance record—we arrive at the classroom for my first-period class. I practically dive through the door, only to find that Noah has a grip on my upper arm. My momentum pivots me toward him, and his other arm locks me in place right up against him. It's so hard to pretend like I hate it.

"Fine. We'd better make it count, then." His eyes glint, like, *Game on.* He kisses me on the mouth. It's an angry kiss full of challenges and accusations. I try to kiss him back with incontrovertible evidence of my indifference. But in two heartbeats we're melting into each other like butter in the sun.

From within the classroom comes a chorus of cheering and whoops. There's the familiar click and swoop of a photo uploading to the collective consciousness. The bell rings. Mrs. Karakus calls in her "we are not amused" voice, "That will be enough of that. Charity, take your seat."

Noah slowly releases me, with a look like he's holding a straight flush and he knows all I've got is a pair of sevens. I meet his eyes, poker-faced, admitting no such thing. Then I enter the classroom amid catcalls and a rousing chorus of "Noah and Charity sitting in a tree."

I hear Mrs. Karakus behind me say, "This isn't like you, Noah. Get to class before I'm forced to write you up."

Since it's the last day before fall break, Mrs. Karakus puts on a documentary, and I have time to pull myself together. I've barely gotten my heart rate under control when Holly walks in and hands the teacher a note. My head immediately breaks into a tap dance. I press a finger to the spot between my brows, wondering defeatedly what the problem is. I'm doing everything I can to undo the Unhappily Ever After I created. So *why* does Holly still give me a headache?

⸻

Holly happens to be two people ahead of me in the lunch line, and I have a proximity headache that will not quit.

Kade walks up and she welcomes him into line with a kiss that makes *me* blush. *NO!* I mentally shout. She's supposed to be pulling away from him now, losing interest. Otherwise, how is she going to let Noah rescue her from this soul-numbing un-HEA I accidentally locked her into? In desperation, I conjure a *nudge*—a grenade of pure indifference—and launch it at her.

The weird thing is, even though I'm sure I hit the mark, she keeps kissing him for a few more seconds. Finally, she pulls out of the kiss and turns her attention to her tray. Delayed reaction?

I see Noah approaching in my peripherals and subtly brace myself against the food counter. If he kisses me, I don't think I'll be able to hold it together. So—despite the fact that I promised Noah I wouldn't *nudge* him anymore—I seriously consider buying myself a couple minutes fairy-godmother style. But just as Noah gets close enough to reach for me, Sean steps between us with a "Walk with me, Charity."

I take Sean's arm with maybe too much visible relief and a rush of pure affection.

As we pivot, I catch a look from Noah like he knows I just got a major out. I wiggle my fingers at him, mostly for the benefit of our audience. Holly watches dispassionately. My head pounds.

Sean expertly maneuvers us into the courtyard and out of earshot of our classmates. "Charity." He draws my name out into a whole sentence that means, *Young lady, I am very disappointed in your choices.*

"Please don't, Sean. Not today. Whatever sins I've committed, I'm already paying for ten times over. I'm getting my ass kicked out there."

He puts his free hand on top of mine. "Would it help if I said I told you so?"

"Not really."

"Anything I can do, though? For real?"

"I'm going to need a ride home from Surya's party tonight."

"You've got one."

After we say hi to the drama club and some drumline guys, we meander past Kade and Holly. She's clinging to his arm and pleading, "Don't be mad, K. I didn't mean to zone out. I don't know what came over me. . . ."

My head bursts into a bludgeoning rhythm.

I hazard, "Sean? Do you think that Holly and Kade are good together?"

Sean tsks. "That depends on what you mean by 'together.' I don't think they have an actual relationship."

"They've been dating for months."

"There's more to a relationship than time. You know, things like honest conversations, knowing things about each other . . ."

I huff. "Exactly! How do I make her realize he's not good for her?"

"You don't." He stops walking and turns me to face him. "Charity. Stay in your lane."

He holds me in place while that sinks in. And suddenly I'm hearing Memom telling her version of the Rapunzel story. *She was determined to run away with this loser she thought was a prince. Our great-auntie could see what a phony he was, but the girl . . .*

It's suddenly so obvious. She doesn't need to be rescued. I've just got to set her free.

I give Sean's arm a hard squeeze. "Thank you. Um . . . There's something I've got to do. I'll see ya later."

I intercept Holly as she gets up from Kade's table and drag her into the bathroom with me.

"Charity! What the hell?"

"Holly, I need to tell you something." I check in with my head. It's clear. I must be on the right track—no more maneuvering, just brutal honesty. Mostly brutal for me, actually. "I saw some of your art, and you're really talented."

"Thanks?"

"Noah told me how great you were, but I didn't really get it until I saw some of your drawings for myself." She looks longingly at the door, so I talk faster, before she can escape. "I was so focused on getting you together with Kade last year that I didn't take the time to get to know you . . . to find out all the things about you that Kade ought to love . . . that Noah already loved."

"Loved?!" She takes a step back. "Why are you telling me this? Why now?"

"Because I'm sad when I see you with Kade. It seems like you decided your real self—that girl who loves ice cream and makes comics, bakes cookies and hates running—she's not enough, so you made up this other girl for him. You wouldn't have to do that for anybody who's worthy to have you. Somebody like Noah."

She scrunches her face. "Are you seriously trying to set me up with *your* boyfriend right now?"

I try to say yes, but I can't force the word out of my mouth. It comes out "Yuh . . . Ugh . . . I can't even—I just want you to be free. To be yourself."

Holly's eyes shift left. Her teeth dig into her lip.

The bell rings, making us late for class. I startle. "Oh crap! I've got a test. I gotta go." As I throw open the bathroom door, I call back, "Please, just . . . be you! Think about it!"

⌒

By the time the last bell rings, I can barely drag my half-dead carcass to my locker. Between baring my soul to Holly and enduring Noah's emotional waterboarding . . . I am done. Carmen, Scarlett, and Gwen—completely oblivious to my plight—escort me down the hall, chattering about what they're going to wear to Surya's party. In the midst of feeling sorry for myself, I take a moment to appreciate that Carmen isn't left out anymore. I even find myself smiling a little. Then I spot Noah.

He stands between me and the front door, arms wide. "Come give me some sugar before I go to work, my little tribble."

Smile gone.

Scarlett says, "What's a tribble?"

Carmen says, "OMG, you guys are so adorbs."

I hesitate, desperately searching for an excuse to avoid my fate. Carmen says, "Go on."

There is no mercy in the Universe. I'm one of the "red shirts" volunteering to explore a new planet. It's going to kill me, but it's what I signed up for. When I'm in range, Noah pulls me into the circle of his arms.

I wrap my arms around his neck, snuggle in, and whisper in his ear, "If these people weren't here, I would punch you in the throat so hard."

He calls out, "Be gentle."

I pull back just until our noses brush. "You suck."

He seems to be having trouble breathing. "All . . . your idea."

I thought maybe I could be this close to him and resist pressing my lips to his. But my willpower crumbles one sense at a time. I breathe him in. Close my eyes. One tiny shift—a feather-soft brush of my lips against his—draws a soft whimper out of him. With that sound, my shields are down and I'm at full impulse power. I pull him toward me with both hands and kiss him recklessly. A kiss that tastes like longing and self-destruction and cherry Coke. *I hate this,* I think. *I hate this . . . I love this . . . I hate this.*

The girls go, "Aaaaaaaaaaw," and Noah pulls up, looking like his number just got picked in Powerball. He kisses me one last time—a gentle brand on my forehead. "See you at seven."

32
This Is a *Little* Illegal.
And Totally Self-Destructive.

I head straight home to get ready for the party. I have four hours, but lots to do. Hopeful raspberry seems wrong tonight, so I survey my closet looking for a better choice of hair color. Jet black is almost dark enough for my mood. I take the box into the bathroom. But for some reason I can't make myself completely erase the raspberry. I end up with a black top layer, with raspberry hiding underneath. No one but me needs to know it's there.

I paint my nails. I shave my legs. I'm extra careful with my makeup. I don't want to look goth. And I don't want my face to melt if I cry. When I cry. It's tricky, as a makeup problem. I go with a retro look—heavy winged eyeliner on top, an obscene amount of waterproof mascara, red lips.

I spend forty-five minutes staring at my closet before I get dressed, eventually picking a short dress with hidden pockets. I'm strapping on sandals when I hear the garage door open. Even though it's almost 7 p.m. on a Friday, it feels weird that my mother is home. I secure my shoe and head out to investigate.

"Mom?"

She kicks off her heels and drops her purse on a stool with a weary sigh. "Hi, sweetie."

"What are you doing home?"

She finds a tumbler in the cupboard and fills it with ice from the dispenser in the refrigerator door. "I live here." She yawns. "Oh gosh. It's a gin-and-tonic kind of night." She finally looks at me. "What are you dressed up for?"

"Party."

"Whose party?"

"A guy from school." I'm not trying to hide anything, but it's not like she'd know who Surya is if I said his name.

"There won't be any alcohol at this party, will there?"

I cop attitude. I mean, she doesn't get to traipse in here, after leaving me to my own devices for *years*, and act like she cares about things like who my friends are and what I do in my spare time. So I snap, "Don't worry about it. I can handle myself."

"Don't tell me what to worry about. I'm your mother." She pours gin into her tumbler, which seems super ironic while she's lecturing me about hypothetical alcohol.

I'm spring-loaded to tell her off, but the doorbell rings. I march to the front door, Mom trailing behind, and throw it open. Noah stands there with a handful of daisies. His shirt says WE ARE

IN UNSURVEYED TERRITORY. His hair is messed up like he's been running his hands through it. My heart flutters at the sight of him.

He breathes, "Wow." Then proceeds to stammer, "You . . . uh . . . you changed your hair."

"Yeah," I mumble. "Are those for me?"

"Oh, yeah." He shoves them toward me. "My dad always says flowers are the magic carpet that apologies ride on."

I take the flowers, which is a first for me. I don't even know what to do with them. "Apologies?"

"Charity," Mom says from behind me, "who's your friend?"

Seriously, Mom? Tonight you're going maternal? With an audible sigh, I back up to allow Noah in. "Mom, this is Noah. Noah, Kate—my mom."

He reaches out to shake her hand. "Nice meeting you. I was starting to wonder if you were imaginary."

Mom looks like he poked her in the eye, but she composes herself quickly. "How do you two know each other?"

"We're, um—"

"School. We go to school together." I set the flowers on the coffee table, pick up my purse, and edge toward the door. "We're heading out."

Mom has a funny look on her face. Suspicion? Confusion? She's gripping the back of the armchair with one hand, like the shock of meeting Noah might knock her over. Is it really that mind-boggling that I have a friend? Gee, Mom, thanks for the vote of confidence.

She composes herself with a quick inhale. "Really good to meet you, Noah."

As soon as the door clicks behind us, Noah says, "I was out of line today. I'm sorry."

"NBD." I walk toward the van without pausing for this conversation.

"Are we going to talk about this?"

I open my door before he can do his chivalry thing and slide into the car. "There's nothing to talk about." I slam the door without waiting for a response.

He gets in on the driver's side and drags his hand through his hair, demonstrating how it got to its present state. Then, without a word, he starts the car and backs out of the driveway.

Surya's house is only a few minutes from mine. Part of me wishes he lived in Utah. I want to stretch out this last car ride for days—my last minutes of being with Noah. But part of me also just wants to get it over with, to trade in the tension and dread for the finality of ending it.

Noah's fingers drum a frenetic rhythm against the steering wheel. He turns into Surya's neighborhood, following the robotic instructions from his phone. Cars line Surya's street. We have to park a block away.

I reach for the door handle.

"Do you want to hear my idea?" Noah's voice pierces the loaded silence.

I don't say yes, but I also don't make a break for it.

He says, "We scrap the plan. We don't break up tonight. We just give this time and see where it goes."

What wouldn't I pay to give in to that wonderful, beautiful, doomed idea? If I even look at him, my willpower might crumble again. I fix my eyes on the dashboard. "It doesn't go anywhere. We made *this* up to get you Holly, remember?" Then I'm out of the car and striding toward Surya's house as fast as strappy sandals will carry me.

Noah grabs my hand, forcing me to stop and face him. "The only reason I went along with this ludicrous plan was to spend more time with *you*. I've spent every minute of the past ten days trying to show you that we should be together."

"Holly is your true love."

"I don't want Holly anymore!"

I jerk my hand away and say flatly, "And I don't want to be the consolation prize." I walk.

He keeps pace with me. "What the heck is that supposed to mean?"

My fairy godmother voice doesn't fail me—kind and patient and condescending. "Cold feet are normal at this stage. But you went to great lengths for her, Noah. When you love someone like that, it doesn't just vanish overnight. The past few days, it maybe felt a little too real. You got confused. You're letting me stand in for her."

I hate how logical and reasonable that sounded. How clearly true.

"You're wrong."

I look pointedly straight ahead. Only a few more houses, and we'll be there. "I'm sure you don't think it consciously, but—"

Noah's voice is strained. "So, basically, you're calling me a desperate, confused, deluded player."

"You're taking this too personally."

"What is it besides *personal*?" He stops me again, so I'm forced to look into his eyes. "Stop trying to convince me that I don't like you. I love you, Charity."

It's all I can do to inhale. His blue-green-gingerbread eyes are like wishing wells. It would be so easy to fall in and drown in all my wishes. I manage, "Don't be silly."

"That's it? I love you. And that's all you can say?"

It really, really is. I swallow, but the lump in my throat won't go down.

"If you want me to leave you alone, all you have to say is 'Noah, I don't like you. I never did, and I never will.' Just say it."

The look of desperation on his face causes me physical pain. I close my eyes for a second, trying to find the strength to either tell the biggest lie of my life or be more honest than I've ever been.

"Fairy godmothers don't get the Happily Ever After." My voice sounds far away in my own ears. "We're fix-and-release people. I tried to tell you—relationships don't work for me. But it's the hapless human who really gets burned. I wouldn't mean to destroy you, Noah. It would be an accident. But that is what would happen."

"You're talking about *fairy tales*—" He draws an invisible line between my heart and his. "This is real."

I finally break away from his gaze and find the strength to keep walking. "I'm sorry, Noah. But it's simple math. There are zero reasons left for us to be together. We're sticking to the plan."

I climb the steps to the front porch, Noah following. The house cannot contain the sounds of the party—the happy chaos seems to call to us from within. Noah raises his voice above the din. "You know what, Charity? I might be confused, but you're a hypocrite. You try to get everyone else to 'embrace their potential' and believe in 'magic.' But you don't do it yourself. Because you're scared. You're a scared little liar."

Now I'm mad. How dare he call me exactly what I am? I resist the impulse to shove him off the porch and into the bushes. Instead I hit him with a *Star Trek* quote. "Insults are effective only where emotion is present." I raise my hand, palm out, and spread my fingers in a Vulcan salute. "Spock out."

He looks like I blasted him with a neural disruptor. Surya opens the door, the cacophony of loud music, talking, and laughter flooding into the heavy silence between us. Surya, oblivious, says, "Hey, guys! Come on in! Join the party!"

I step over the threshold, where the noise is even louder.

Noah yells after me, "You're not Spock! *I'm* Spock."

I march down the hall, pretending I can't hear him. One of the cheer girls approaches with a tray of rainbow-colored plastic shot glasses. She does a big-eyed, open-mouth *I'm too happy for a regular smile* face, not noticing the tension zinging between Noah and me. "Hey! Want a Jell-O shot? Tastes like Jell-O, gets you messed up like vodka!"

Typically, I abstain from this sort of thing. The fairy godmother must stay in control at all times. But between Noah's accusations, the deeply depressing thing I am about to do, and my mother's specific line of questioning about alcohol at the party, I'm the easiest sell ever. "Absolutely I would!" I grab a Jell-O shot and dump it into my mouth. Hmmm. Fruity, with an invigorating afterburn.

Noah says, "Your liver can only filter 1.5 ounces of alcohol per hour."

I shoot him a visual *bite me* and pointedly take another shot from the tray.

Cheer girl yells, "Guys! Charity's doing Jell-O shots!" And the hallway is suddenly crammed with people clambering for their own edible booze. They empty the tray. I hold up my electric-blue Jell-O in salute, and we all do bottoms-up.

Noah yells in my ear, "You know, alcohol-related accidents are the leading cause of death among teens."

I look at him with shock and betrayal, like he said something more like, *I don't know what I ever saw in you.* I can feel the eyes of the crowd on us. "How could you?" There is a sob in my voice, and a natural raspiness because my throat is really burning from the vodka. I storm away, pushing through the crowd.

By the time I get to the back patio, female voices around me are saying things like "What's going on?" and "Is Charity okay?"

Scarlett muscles her way in next to me. "Charity, what happened with Noah?" She sounds too much like a journalist with an exclusive to really be comforting.

I let the tears come. "Why doesn't he love me, Scarlett?"

She looks confused. "He does. Right?"

I shake my head. "No. He loves Holly. He always loved Holly."

She's shocked now. The girls around lean in for more. "What?! What a two-timer!"

I cry harder, the truth and the show blending seamlessly so that even I can't quite find the dividing line. Someone hands me a tissue, and I wipe my face with it. "No he's not. He told me . . . before . . . but I just thought maybe I could make him love me instead."

Carmen swims into my line of vision. "That is *so tragic.*" She hugs me, and I'm not sure who's comforting who. I pat her on the back.

Scarlett says, "Kade is going to freak when he finds out. Is that why Holly dumped him this afternoon?"

She did?! Of course she did. Didn't I know that's what would happen after our heart-to-heart in the bathroom?

Gwen's voice comes from the crowd on my left. "Scarlett, jeez. Insensitive much?"

One of the other girls says, "Wait, so did you guys break up?"

I nod feebly. "He said he just can't do it anymore."

I wipe my face again, registering a shuffling and murmuring among my ladies-in-waiting. A moment later Noah stands in front of me. I know it's him without lifting my head past his knees. He's wearing The Jeans. He reaches for me. "Charity, stop this." I shake off his hand. He reaches for me again. "Can we please go somewhere else and talk?"

"No. No. You were right. It's better this way. I'll be okay." I offer him a shaky, tearful smile, but my eyes say, *Your wish is granted.*

"Charity—" He has that pleading look again. The one my heart has no defense against. But I've already given him everything.

Everything.

Sean appears. The crowd parts for him like for no one else. He shoulders past Noah to help me up. "I'll take it from here."

Noah states flatly, "She came with me. I'll take her home."

Sean puts his arm around me protectively, and I sag against him. My real friend. He faces off with Noah. "You've done enough. Go home, before Kade goes Neanderthal about the whole stealing-his-girlfriend thing."

With that, Sean escorts me back through the house. But not before I see Noah's expression—it's more like *There's a knife in my*

"Charity had a boyfriend?"

"Not in the conventional sense."

Sean's telling it wrong. I blurt, "I messed up, Memom. I feeled in love for Cindy."

Memom says, clearly horrified, "I'll make some tea."

My eyes are too heavy to see with. Every time I blink, they open like a creaky gate. Screw it. It's too much trouble to open them anymore.

⟜——

"She's my daughter. Of course I came."

I lift my eyelids a millimeter and see mauve. Memom's couch. Whatever. I fall back asleep.

⟜——

I wake up to bright daylight and instinctively throw my arm across my eyes to block it out.

"Oh good. You're up." Memom's chair creaks as she pulls herself out of it. "I'll get you some tea."

She clangs around in the kitchen. My head is pounding, and I feel like I swallowed a piece of sandpaper. But, let me tell you, it sucks 50 percent less than ignoring a *glimpse*. A few minutes later she returns, pushing her fully loaded tea cart. I force myself to a sitting position with my eyes kind of open.

"Drink up. It will help." She pours two cups, then settles back into her chair. "Your mother was here. She went to get some breakfast."

"Am I in trouble?"

Memom shrugs. "Not with me." Her eyes twinkle. "I had a vodka incident in 1978 that—"

"Incident? How does something reach the level of an *incident*?"

She takes a dainty sip of tea. "It's midway between a mistake and a twelve-step program."

I lay my head back and groan. "That's probably all I need to know."

She chuckles again about something that undoubtedly happened in 1978. "So, tell me what's going on."

I can't. Not at first. Where do I even begin? How do I put any of it into words? Eventually I say, "Well, there's this boy. Actually, I got a *glimpse* last year—"

I abruptly abandon the story and blurt, "Memom, I can control the *glimpses*. I can turn them on and off!"

Memom's deeply wrinkled face manages to look incredibly childlike. She reminds me of a toddler who ate all the cookies and knows she's busted.

Realization filters through my hangover. "You knew."

Proverbial cookie crumbs are freaking everywhere. She hedges. "Well . . ."

I launch myself off the couch. "YOU KNEW IT WAS POSSIBLE! Why would you hide that from me? *How could you?*"

"I was afraid . . . if you knew how to control them, you'd decide not to have them at all." She looks so sheepish that I almost can't stay mad at her. *Almost.* Her lip trembles. "Like Hope, and like—"

"Memom, you were the one person I thought I could rely on! I wanted to be a fairy godmother because of you. And you purposely kept me in the dark about my own magic! I can never trust you again."

She's full-on crying now. If you've never made your own grandmother cry, let me suggest you *don't.* It is soul killing. I'm immediately filled with remorse. With a sigh, I sit back down.

She sniffles. "I'm sorry. I'm so sorry. I just didn't want to lose you, like I lost my Katie."

"You didn't lose me. I'm right here." Mom stands in the doorway with a café paper bag and a cardboard tray of coffee cups. She still doesn't freaking know I don't drink coffee.

Memom and I both straighten up and wipe our noses, like kids facing the principal after a fight.

"Charity." The way she says it, it means, *What do you have to say for yourself?* She holds out a paper cup to me. I look at it stoically. Eventually she gives up and sets it on the coffee table. She sits with a heavy exhale and begins rifling through the bag, pulling out pastries and bagel sandwiches. She holds a sandwich out to me. "What happened last night with Noah?"

I take the bagel from Mom and unwrap it to buy time. My stomach is roiling in Hangover Land, but I've heard that eating can help, so I take a nibble.

Mom loses patience. "Well?"

"Nothing. We were kind of a thing and then we broke up. I drank too much, mostly because you didn't want me to. The end."

She purses her lips. "Let's put the rebellion drinking in the parking lot for right now and focus on the breakup. What happened?"

I seriously do not get why we're having an inquisition about this. The woman barely looks at me for weeks at a time. I have such a headache, and I'm so not in the mood. I drop my bagel onto its wrapper. "Why are we talking about this? Why are you even *here*?"

She looks at me like we're in a board meeting and I'm blocking her budget override. "You're my daughter. When Memom called—"

"Thanks a lot," I mutter, shooting Memom the stink eye. She pretends not to notice and starts flipping through a *Contemporary Bride* magazine.

Mom presses on. "Noah seems like a nice guy. You should think about—"

And that is absolutely the last straw. The headache, the heartbreak, the crappy coffee, Memom's betrayal, and seventeen years of mommy-abandonment issues . . . it's all I can take. I get to my feet, and I let her have it—the truth. "Mom, for as long as I can remember, you've been working late, leaving early, glued to your phone, flying off to Belize or God knows where. I get *whatever* scraps of your attention are left over, if I'm lucky. Now all the sudden you're going to reappear and give me advice about relationships? It doesn't work like that! Give me one good reason why I should listen to you."

She stands so we're eye to eye. "Because I *previewed* it."

"*Previewed it?*"

Memom interjects, "He *flashed* her."

Okay, we really need to agree on our terms here. And also: "WHAT THE EFFING CRAP?!"

All this time, my mom has been getting *glimpses* or *flashes* or *whatever*, and she never *freaking* mentioned it? I grit out, "The magic didn't skip you."

"It doesn't skip any of us."

I level my anger at Memom. "You were hiding this too."

She gives me a pathetic sad-puppy look.

I throw my hands up. "Why didn't you tell me?"

Memom looks around the apartment. "She swore me to secrecy. What could I do? I'm held hostage here."

Mom snaps, "I pay for this swanky retirement home, and somehow you make it sound like an act of terrorism. Thank you, Mother."

I stomp my foot like a toddler. "Stop arguing, you guys! This is about ME."

Mom and Memom look at each other like they're having a silent spat.

"WHAT?" I demand. "I want to know. Why can't two grown women figure their stuff out and get along? Why did Hope and I have to split our loyalties and keep your secrets and deliver your messages all these years? WHY?"

Mom presses her lips together and studies her shoes before answering. "Memom wanted you girls to grow up as fairy godmothers. I didn't. It's as simple as that."

Memom gets to her feet, decrepit but ready for battle. "You can't change who you are by ignoring it, Katie. And you certainly can't put these girls in a mold that you—"

"I seriously do not need to have this conversation *again*, Mother. We've been circling the same ground since Hope was twelve years old."

"Well," I point out, "we're all grown-up now and it's not really up to either one of you anymore. So maybe, *maybe*, you could just, like, CUT IT OUT!"

We go silent, facing one another in a three-way standoff.

Mom sighs. "Can I have a few minutes alone with my daughter, please?"

Memom nods primly and takes a *Contemporary Bride* magazine off the table. As she passes me, she puts her hand on my arm and whispers, "Mothers are just people with their own set of problems. Please know that."

As soon as Memom's out of sight, Mom says, "Charity, I—"

"All these years, you never told me?" Tears spring to my eyes. "I needed you."

She looks at her hands. "I couldn't help you, not with this."

My hands clench into fists at my sides. "Whatever you have to tell yourself."

"Charity, please try to understand." She drops into the armchair with a heavy exhale. "My mother never had a healthy relationship—not with me, certainly not with a man. I never knew who my own father was. She couldn't hold a job—just wandered wherever the *previews* led her, living for other people's Happily Ever Afters. I never got to put down roots or make friends. Half the time we didn't know where our next meal was coming from. I never felt as important to her as her Cindies. I vowed that I would never grant a wish. I wanted a better life for you and Hope. For all of us."

"So instead of granting wishes, you became a workaholic. That's better?"

"I'm a fairy godmother! I'm hardwired to fix things. Work is my outlet. At least I've given you stability."

"You know what I needed more than stability?" I glare at her. "A *mom*."

She turns her palms up. "I'm doing my best."

I hold her gaze while my head pounds and my stomach roils. I'm seriously never drinking alcohol again. I break the stare-off and sink into the couch, pressing my palm to my forehead.

She pushes the coffee cup toward me for the umpteenth time. "Drink. It will help."

I look at it resentfully. Coffee. The evidence of my mother's indifference toward me. "Hope was right. We're cursed. Whether or not we grant wishes, we are doomed to push everyone away from us."

"No we're not, Charity. You're not."

"What makes you so sure?"

"Because there's no such thing as curses. We each make our own choices and create the best life we can. Besides, I told you. I *previewed* it."

I shake my head, refusing to believe, then regret the movement. "So you met a guy for two minutes, got some download from his adolescent brain, and decided to play God with *my* life?"

Sweet Romulan ale. I've turned into Noah.

Memom clucks in the kitchen.

Mom crosses her arms like a CEO. "First of all, I'm not playing anything. I'm trying to help. And secondly, I didn't get a *preview* from Noah. I got one from you."

"Me?" My head is spinning, trying to make sense of that word. "You couldn't."

"I did."

"No. No. We're immune to the *nudges*, and we don't transmit *glimpses*."

"Well, I'm telling you it happened." She's using her *because I said so* tone.

"But fairy godmothers don't go to the ball."

"Where do you come up with this stuff? Who makes these

rules?" She smiles wryly. "Look, I just don't want you to limit yourself."

Memom blats, "HA!" Apparently the magazine is really entertaining.

I pick at my bagel morosely. "Why do you care?"

"Because you're my daughter."

"I didn't know you remembered."

She looks like I stabbed her. Good.

I rub my temples, feeling bereft. I've lost everyone—Hope abandoned me, Memom has been keeping unforgivable secrets, turns out I never knew my mother, and I gave up Noah to the Other Girl. I am alone and adrift.

Mom picks up the freaking coffee cup again. "Honey, try to drink a little. Please. You'll feel better."

"Ugh!" Just to get her off my back, I snatch the cup out of her hand, brace myself for the bitter taste of coffee, and tip it into my mouth.

It's orange juice.

I look at the cup like I've never seen one before. She knew what to get me. My mom knows I like orange juice.

Blinking back tears, I lift my face toward her. She hesitates for a moment, and then, with jerky movements, she comes to my side and puts her arms around me. She murmurs, "I hoped I could protect you from the *previews*—from that life—but it turns out ignoring something doesn't make it go away."

I sit stubbornly rigid in her embrace. "That seems like Business 101."

She chuckle-sniffs. "Yeah, but parenting is much harder than running a company and saving the ocean." Her arms tighten a little. "I'm sorry I'm so far from the mom you need me to be." She chokes at the end. I give in to the hug and wrap my arms around her. I know she probably won't change, but, after all, she knows I like orange juice. This is a happy moment, and that is enough. She holds me, rubbing my back.

After a few minutes I pull back a little. "I researched this, though. Fairies can't love. We destroy anyone who loves us."

"What did I tell you about believing what you read on the internet?"

"Not to."

"Fairies *can* love with our whole hearts."

"How can you be so sure?"

"Because I love you."

My heart feels like it's swelling up like a balloon. "What did you *glimpse*?"

Mom's eyes twinkle—anguished tears mixed with secret hopes. "Some things are better to discover along the way."

"Okay? And?"

"And will it make you happy if you and Noah go your separate ways?"

Even hearing those words spoken out loud reopens a hundred

fresh wounds on my heart. Of course I'm not happy. But I know now that fulfilling *glimpses* is no panacea leading to ultimate happiness. I straighten up and go into teacher mode. "Mom, you wouldn't know this, because you don't grant wishes, but the *glimpses* don't tell the whole story. All they are is happy snapshots. So, I know that you think you're helping me. But the fact is, despite whatever *preview* you saw, I'm still most likely going to end up heartbroken—and hurt someone I care about in the process. What's the point? I *really* don't need to go through it twice."

She puts her hands on my shoulders and looks at me like she's using X-ray vision. "Charity, life has heartbreak in it. I can't promise you it doesn't. And love is messy, and it's hard work. I'm not telling you you'll be happy every minute forever. But—" She hesitates a moment with her mouth open, like she's not sure if she should tell me the next thing. Then she takes a deep breath and says, "If you spend your life trying to protect yourself from getting hurt, you'll end up missing the best parts. Some people are worth breaking your heart over."

For a moment I look at her in stunned silence. Then I take a drink of orange juice.

"Charity, whatever you decide to do, I'll support you. It's not about whether or not you choose to be with Noah. I just want you to know that you are lovable and capable of great love."

A tiny electron of hope sparks in my soul and zaps my brain with possibilities. No curse. No more staying above it all. No more being the Ice Princess. Noah could wrap me up and thaw me out with his hypotheses and his sharp insights and his relentless fandom. I could be part of TrekkieFam instead of hovering on the fringes. I could mess up, break down, or totally fail, knowing that Noah has seen me at my worst and still believes the best about me. Life could be all full of laughter and soup when I'm sick and probably Comic-Cons. A smile trembles on my lips.

And then my emotional pendulum swings all the way in the other direction. Despair takes over. There is no way Noah will want me after the things I said, after what I did.

My aching head drops into my hands. "I screwed it up, Mom. Publicly, irrevocably. You have no idea how bad I burned him. If you had only told me all this *before* the party . . ."

There's no response.

"What do I do?" I plead.

She sighs heavily, defeated. "I don't know, honey. I've wrecked my share of relationships too, remember?"

Memom's head pops out of the kitchen. "What's with the negativity? *We're fairy godmothers!*"

Memom shuffle-skips to the front door and takes her oversized purse from the hat stand. "What are we waiting for? Let's go get your young man back!"

Mom and I glance at each other dubiously. Then she stands like a soldier and holds her hand out to help me up. So this is it. I can either accept Hope's version of reality and my own brokenness, or I can do everything possible to chase down what I want—even though I don't know my destiny or if Noah could ever forgive me. I can self-protect and keep my distance from a mother who is sure to continue disappointing me, or I can forgive her and let her in again even if it comes with a side of heartbreak.

I feel the corners of my mouth turn up as I reach out.

As soon as I take Mom's hand, the throbbing in my head fades away. I scoop up my orange juice, and we join Memom at the door. She leads us out into the sunlight with a gleeful "He-he! Destiny, here we come!"

———

As Mom navigates the Saturday traffic, Memom says, "Charity, you'd better fill us in on this Noah fellow, so we know what we're dealing with here."

I tell them about Noah figuring me out because he's a legit genius, and that he works at an ice cream shop and loves sci-fi. Memom laughs until she cries over the pepper-spray incident and the Frankenfrosty. I tell them about Nat and Lisa and Paul and Dr. McCoy, and about the closet full of cosplay costumes. They both gasp and groan over the fake-dating situation. We're fifteen minutes from home when I finish with what happened at the party last night.

When it's clear I'm done talking, Memom complains, "You're a terrible storyteller. You left out all the kissing parts."

Mom says, "Mother!" She glances at me in the rearview mirror, gasps, and says, "Charity, your face."

I stretch my neck to look at myself in the mirror. Flaking mascara, smudged eyeliner, blotchy cried-off makeup, after-party hair. I'm a hot mess.

She moans, "You can't go into battle like that. We'll have to go home to clean you up first."

Memom counters, "He could be with that Holly girl right now!"

Mom CEOs it. "I understand the problem. What I want is a solution."

Memom says, "I have wet wipes!" She digs a package out of her purse and hands them to me.

I scrub my face clean and glance in the rearview mirror again. Hangover hair. It's gross. "Anybody have a hair band?"

Memom produces one like magic.

As I whip my hair into a black-and-raspberry messy bun, I ask, "How *do* you ignore the *glimpses*, Mom? I ignored a couple, and I thought I might literally die."

She laughs, one *Ha*. "When I feel one coming on, I shut it off. If one slips partway through, the aftermath is just a dull headache for a few hours. Nothing a few Motrin can't take care of."

So *that's* the deal with the headaches. So many things make sense now. I toss out, "You know those things are destroying your liver."

Mom shoots me a look in the rearview mirror. "I don't need a lecture about liver health from a teenage girl with a hangover."

I shrug and lapse into silence. But it doesn't last. Too many questions are bubbling right at the surface. "Do you think you'll start granting more wishes now, since this one?"

She shakes her head. "Definitely not. Nothing less than love for my daughters will tempt me."

"What about Hope? Do you think she'll ever stop hiding in Thailand?"

Mom's eyebrows pinch together. She presses her finger against the spot between them. "Hope has to find her own way. But maybe now that we're all telling the truth . . . Maybe if she knew she could control the *previews* instead of isolating herself . . ." She pauses. "What about *you*?"

I consider my answer carefully. A few days ago I would have said *never again.* But then Vindhya made up with the Robotics Club, and I *glimpsed* Gwen of my own free will. And there's Kelly and Juggernaut. What if I hadn't brought them together? I've learned so much about what the *glimpses* are trying to tell me, about what people are capable of when they know what's possible, and about unfinished stories and how messy life is. On one hand, there's Memom, recklessly wish-granting, never stopping to question any of it. But there's also Mom and Hope denying the *glimpses* completely, and that hasn't made them happy or whole. Plus, do I really want to live the rest of my life with my frontal lobe throbbing?

And there are those moments when my Cindies shine with all the power and beauty inside them, when I know what my purpose on this earth is. I hope for people. I see in them what they can't even see in themselves. I hold their hands while they do hard things. Sure, I've made a huge mess of it. I've pushed too hard and been insensitive. I've cared about the agenda more than the people. And yeah, I haven't looked deep enough to always see the things that really matter. But this fairy godmother thing didn't come with a helpchat, you know?

Didn't someone say *Failure is the best teacher?* Forget it. It's probably from a Marvel movie. Anyway, it's really true.

I answer slowly, choosing each word. "I'm going to keep learning how to control it. I'm going to be . . . more careful. And I'm still going to help people."

Memom whoops with joy. Mom nods her acceptance of my path.

We pull off the freeway. I venture, "Memom, you don't have any deodorant in that bag of tricks, do you?"

She pulls out deodorant, body mist, and a travel toothbrush. "I'm the maid of honor at Lonnie's wedding next weekend, you know. According to *Contemporary Bride* magazine, these are essentials."

As I scrub deodorant in my pits, I snark, "What happened to 'take your time and don't rush things'?"

"When you're eighteen, all you've got is time and a whole lot to learn. When you're eighty-six, it's now or never."

I sigh. "You know, I'm still mad at you for not teaching me

how to control the *glimpses* and for never telling me about Mom and Hope."

"I'm an old lady. It's not safe to hold grudges. I could die any second and then you'd feel terrible."

I have to laugh, because she loves playing the old-lady card so much. "You're such a brat. And you can't die. Not ever."

"So you *do* forgive me."

"Fine. Whatever." I stick the travel toothbrush in my mouth and scrub the sweaters off my teeth.

So, thanks to Memom and *Contemporary Bride*, I am cleanish, deodorized, and minty fresh by the time we pull up at Noah's house.

34
Happily Ever After? I Got Nothin'.

"Noah's not here." Natalie looks genuinely broken up about this information. "He was gone until late, and then he left early this morning. Did you try his phone?"

I can't just text him a "sorry." This situation *obviously* requires a Grand Gesture. An in-person, grovel-on-your-knees, epic-apology, boom-box-over-the-head Grand Gesture. I bite my lip. "I really need to see him."

Natalie's face lights up. "I know! My mom and dad can track him on their phones!" She shoots me a tween-attitude face. "They're total helicopter parents."

From inside the house, Noah's mom calls, "I heard that!" A few seconds later, she appears behind Natalie. She looks at me with deep suspicion and says, "What's up?" But it sounds like, *Get off my property.*

I mumble, "I'm just trying to find Noah."

She purses her lips and accuses, "He said you two had a complete warp core breach." She shakes her head. "It's a Kobayashi Maru situation."

Aha! I know this one. It's from *Wrath of Khan*. She's saying this is hopeless. I look Lisa in the eye and, repenting as best I can, quote, "I changed the parameters of the test. I don't believe in no-win scenarios."

That must be the right answer. Her eyes light up, and her mama-grizzly countenance morphs into determination. "I'll get my phone."

Natalie yips, "I'm coming too!"

"Wait." I gulp. Knowing *Star Trek* opens doors has given me an idea. "There's one more thing I need, if it's okay. Can I run up to Noah's room for a second?"

Lisa waves me inside.

Ninety seconds later, the three of us are crammed into the back seat of my mom's car, making hasty introductions. After a formal handshake with my mom and Memom, Lisa checks her phone and says, "Noah's a few blocks away. Go to the stop sign and turn right. Hmmm . . . This address seems familiar."

Natalie leans into her mom, concentrating on the map. "Oh! That's Holly's house!"

My stomach plummets. He's in the clutches of the temptress, probably breaking out of the friend zone at this very moment.

This needs to be a helluva Grand Gesture. I start pulling on the Gorn costume, trying not to elbow Natalie in the face while I wiggle into the revolting, rubbery green monster suit. This is possibly the worst idea I've ever had.

"Left up here," Lisa directs, as if me car-changing into a Gorn suit is too normal to notice.

Mom turns.

Natalie zips me up and helps me jam my hands into the monster mittens.

Memom says, "Here's the plan: Don't say a word. Just suck his lips off. Boys go in for that cave-girl stuff."

Mom glares at her. Lisa looks offended. Natalie's face is frozen in disbelief. I cram the Gorn mask over my head. It smells like old balloons and stale Cheetos. I can only kind of see through the sparkly silver mesh eyes.

Natalie's muffled voice comes from my right. "Quote *Star Trek*. Tell him you're a doctor, not a miner."

Lisa says, "No. Tell him, 'I am and always shall be your friend.'" She sighs, then snaps to attention. "Oh, there we go—the blue house right there."

My phone chirps on the seat beside me. I glance at it—a text from Scarlett: **OMG! Have you checked your feed today?** I decide I don't have time for Scarlett's amateur reporting right now. Plus it's not going to be possible to use my phone with rubber Gorn claws, and I just got the damn things on.

Mom pulls up at the curb, and we all pile out in a spot-on

impression of a clown car. The Gorn suit is too big. It droops between my legs and bunches at the knees and ankles. This is officially the most humiliation I could heap upon myself. But if it shows Noah how far I'd go to get him back, it's worth it.

I turn to the group. "You guys wait here. Okay?"

This suggestion is met with a chorus of objections:

"Like fun I will!"

"No fair! I always get left out."

"I am the *mother*," from Lisa and Mom simultaneously.

So, I am forced to do the ultimate walk of shame to Holly's front door with two middle-aged helicopter moms, an old lady with no filter, and a time bomb of tween angst. And, oh yeah, I'm Gorn. I feel sweat beading on my forehead.

To stall, I yank off one glove and swipe my phone awake. I have thirty-seven notifications, which seems like a lot. It can only mean one thing: everyone on earth is posting memes of me having a pathetic, drunken pity-party last night. I don't have to look to know.

Can't handle that now. Must go ring Holly's doorbell and ask if I can have back the guy I gift-wrapped for her last night. I tuck the phone up my sleeve and put the glove back on.

Natalie edges up next to me and whispers, "You look really weird."

"Thanks?"

"Are you going to fist fight Holly?"

"I sincerely hope not."

"It's kind of gross to think about you making out with my brother."

"You don't actually have to think about it."

"Are you going to, though?"

"If at all possible."

She makes a barfing noise. Lisa shushes her.

I ring the bell. We all stare at the door, waiting. Mom leans in and whispers, "Breathe."

I release the breath I've been holding.

Natalie's phone chimes. She pulls it out and looks at it.

Holly's dad answers the door, registering the group of us with approximately the look you would have if aliens landed and then came to your door selling cookies. Like, *These aliens are very unnerving, but let's withhold judgment until we taste their cookies.*

I say, "Hi. We're looking for Noah?" It comes out as a question.

He looks even more befuddled but says, "Oh, yeah, they're out back." He turns and waves us in. "This way."

As we walk, Natalie says, "Charity, you should look at your feed."

I say, "Okay." But I really mean, *Later.* Because I see my destiny teetering on a cliff's edge through the glass of the back door.

Noah and Holly are standing too close, looking too sincere, saying too many words. I remind myself that it's my own fault. They look up when I open the patio door, and both their mouths fall open.

Noah locks eyes with, well . . . Gorn. He presses his lips together.

I step forward, and my entourage follows me out.

This is the moment when I either claim my destiny or muck it up for all time. Noah waits silently for me to say something. I stand, stiff and indecisive, until Memom whisper-yells, "Give 'em the magic!" and shoves me forward. It takes a couple of fumbling steps to recover my balance. Now I've got a little space cushion from the Pushy Women Club behind me, and I'm close enough to read Noah's T-shirt. It says I SUGGEST YOU AVOID EMOTIONALISM, AND SIMPLY KEEP YOUR INSTRUMENTS CORRECT. SPOCK. OUT.

I take my green rubber head off and clutch it with both clawed hands. *Deep breath,* I tell myself. *Spit it out.* "Remember how I said that I wanted you to be with Holly?"

"Yeah?"

"I lied."

I can't read Noah's face at all. Holly looks a tad affronted.

Natalie whines, "Charity, you really gotta check your phone."

I ignore her and soldier on. "And I lied about not wanting to be your friend anymore. And about everything between us being pretend. And about not needing you. I'm a scared little liar, just like you said. I'm like Gorn. . . . I'm just a big fake."

Noah stares at me with a bemused expression, like he's trying to figure out what to say or why I'm wearing a Gorn costume or possibly why all these people are here.

"Say *something*, son," Lisa prods from behind me.

That snaps Noah out of it. He looks around, nods like he's come to a conclusion, and says, "Okay. Right. Holly, we're good?"

She smiles and says something only he can hear. They hug.

That's his reaction to me baring my soul? Embracing the Other Girl? If I had a phaser right now, I'd blast Holly with it. And she would be momentarily suspended in a burst of glowing-red bad special effects before she collapsed like an empty puppet.

The hug is quick though. Noah pulls away from her and walks forward. He takes my Gorn arm and propels us through the crowd, greeting everyone and shaking hands like it's some kind of reception line. "Kate, good to see you again. Mom. Nat. Thanks for coming. You must be Memom. Good. Good. Mr. Butterman, thanks for hosting. The lawn's looking great, by the way."

With that, he steers me through the patio door. Undeterred, Natalie follows us, clutching at Gorn's rubbery folds, jabbering, "No way are you leaving me out, plus, Charity, I keep trying to tell you to check your phone and you really need to because—" Noah unceremoniously shuts the patio door, cutting off her voice but not her emphatic gesturing. She presses her phone against the glass. It's playing a video of Holly and Noah standing pretty much exactly where they were standing ninety seconds ago. Holly's lips are moving, but I can't hear the sound.

The vertical blinds close with a clatter.

I drop the Gorn head on the floor, tear off the rubber hands, and fumble my phone out of the sleeve. I swipe it awake—162 notifications. I scroll through my feed. It's video after video with the same hashtag: *#whycharityandnoah*.

I start with the Holly and Noah video that Nat was trying to show me:

Holly says, "Because I don't need a boyfriend. I'm busy getting to know me." She holds up a half-finished panel of comics with a wink and a smile.

Noah offers her his hand. "Just friends?"

Holly shakes his hand. "Friends."

I scroll to the next one: *#whycharityandnoah*.

Scarlett says, "Because I already trademarked 'Nority' as their couple name."

And the next:

Surya says, "Noah's a cool dude."

And the swim team goes, "Hoo-ah!"

And the next:

Carmen coos, "You can tell they're in love."

A new alert dings and a post from Natalie pops up:

"GROSS, you guys. Noah has death breath. Do NOT kiss him!"

I keep scrolling:

Trevon says, "A smart girl one time told me not to act like an assclown. She should probably take her own advice."

"Yeah," Vindhya says. "Because she deserves to be happy."

RoboPuppy nods his Erector Set head up and down, and she pats him lovingly.

Carlos and the Mouth shout in unison, "'Cuz they go together like Classic Rock and a Record PLAYAAAA." They double high-five.

Gwen waggles her head. "Because dorky is the new sexy, right?"

Kade shrugs with his signature cocky jock grin. "Noah's a good guy."

Behind him, the football team hoots and hollers and makes it rain ten-dollar bills.

Greg the Waiter pushes his paper hat back. "Man, it gives the rest of us hope!"

Sean declares, "Because no one else is good enough for my best friend."

Noah looks through the screen at me with those wish-filled, every-color eyes. "Because fighting with her is warp-ten better than getting along with everyone else."

I look from video Noah to real Noah. "Wha—"

He gives me his adorable smile. "You wore Gorn for me."

I glance down at my hideousness and shrug my big, green, rubbery shoulders. "It's my Grand Gesture." Suddenly I'm indignant. "Hey! You *totally* sniped my Grand Gesture!"

His eyebrow quirks down. "Well—"

I lecture, "Didn't I teach you anything? The party who screws up is the one to execute the Grand Gesture, in direct proportion to the magnitude of the offense. That's obviously me."

He folds his hands behind his back and paces like a lawyer in a movie. "Unless the party of the first part—that's you—is so dang stubborn that the party of the second part—that's me—figures he could die of old age before she'd admit she needed him."

"That is exactly the kind of cynical—"

He puts two fingers on my lips to shush me, and the gentle pressure makes it utterly impossible to speak or move or look away from him. His voice gets less lawyery and more husky. "And if the party of the second part cannot imagine a life without you in it, then he, I, would do absolutely anything to be with you, including track down every single person in California and *beg* for their help." He moves a little closer. "Look, you said there are no more reasons for us to be together, and I've already posted twenty-three. So, I guess the question is, how much more data do you need?"

Even though my eyes seem to be having some kind of onion reaction, I manage to quip, "Well, at least two more. I mean, twenty-three is such a random number."

He holds up his phone. "Okay. Reason number twenty-four. Charity needs to let her inner Trekkie out."

Click.

Too late, I realize what he's doing. "Do not post"—the phone swishes. *Dang it*—"that. You suck."

He slides his phone into his pocket and gives me a look filled with sweet wishes. That look I can never resist. So I offer, "I guess reason twenty-five could be, um, that I'm totally in love with you."

With a relieved laugh, he closes the gap between us, picking me up in a tight hug, which feels kind of gelatinous in the Gorn costume. But still great. I kiss him, and it's salty and shaky and wonderful.

The room wobbles, and I close my eyes against a wave of dizziness. It feels like a *glimpse*, but instead of a new scene replacing this one, the moment we're in right now shimmers and shifts so I'm watching the two of us hugging and kissing and giggling and crying. This is it, I realize. Our destiny moment. Our very own Awkwardly Messily Happily Ever After.

Acknowledgments

It takes all kinds of magic to bring a book to life. From that first glimmer of an idea to finding it on a library shelf, there are glimpses and nudges all along the way. And I've had so many fairy godmothers in the process.

Kim Lionetti at BookEnds, thank you for snatching me out of the slush pile and nudging this story out into the world. Jessica Smith at Simon & Schuster, you were able to glimpse both the potential and the problems; this book needed your fairy dust. And to the design and marketing teams at Simon & Schuster: you're magic.

To the Charglings—Mary, Laura, Keith, and Karen: none of this would have happened without your spot-on critique and insights. How did I get so lucky?! Mary, I always eventually take your advice, starting with that time you said, "Maybe you should write a novel."

AZ YA Writers, thank you for embracing me and treating me like a legit author until I started to believe it myself. I want to be just like all of you when I grow up. To the godmothers of Sun vs. Snow—Amy Trueblood and Michelle Hauck, and my mentor Kelly DeVos: thank you for helping me polish those first pages and the dreaded query letter.

Kerry, you loved this book from the start, and you've always loved me more than I deserve. Christi, you are the beta reader of my dreams—every time you text me fiction commentary, my heart grows three sizes. Monica, thanks for being the keeper of the journal and for flying out to be with me all those times. You are all Amazons.

Sasha and Mama Leslie, you literally prayed this up. And you fed me, body and soul—with muffins and tea and laughter and tears. Anna Ho, thank you for reading and encouraging and being the best boss ever. You're stuck with me.

Dad, you knew decades before I did that I was a writer. Thanks for keeping every newspaper clipping and silly story. Mom, thanks for the thousands of hours you read to me and let me read to you. (Remember the summer of Austen in the kitchen? It happened.) Gretchen, every sister I write, they're all a little bit you. And thanks for all the vocab words.

Elsa, I wrote this story hoping you'd love it. I hope we can always be book crazy together. Annika, who gave this book its first fan art, thanks for agreeing to stay eight forever. I'm sorry about the kissing parts. Emory, thank you for all the surprise hugs. Don't repeat the swears, okay?

Matt, I love our life. Because of you, I believe in happily ever after, Prince Charming, magic, and true love. You're also the most wildly biased beta reader I can imagine. Thank you for thinking everything I write is better than it is.

Okay, now on to the next book . . . Everybody dust off your magic wands, and let's go!

About the Author

G. F. Miller absolutely insists on a happy ending. Everything else is negotiable. Her wish is to go everywhere—and when a plane ticket isn't available, books fill the gaps. She cries at all the wrong times. She makes faces at herself in the mirror. She believes in the Oxford comma. And she's always here for a dance party.